THE VAMPIRE'S LADY

THE VAMPIRE'S LADY

D. J. Marteeny

iUniverse, Inc.
New York   Bloomington

The Vampire's Lady

This is a work of fiction. All of the characters, names, incidents,
organizations, and dialogue in this novel are either the products
of the author's imagination or are used fictitiously.

iUniverse books may be ordered through booksellers or by contacting:

iUniverse
1663 Liberty Drive
Bloomington, IN 47403
www.iuniverse.com
1-800-Authors (1-800-288-4677)

ISBN: 978-0-595-52194-4 (pbk)
ISBN: 978-0-595-62257-3 (ebk)
ISBN: 978-0-595-50933-1 (cloth)

Printed in the United States of America

To my husband, children,
and my entire family.
Your encouragement and support
have made this book possible.

Prologue

He was running wildly, his breath coming in painful gasps. He was surrounded by a thick, dark mist. Nothing was clear to him … nothing but the sense of evil. The smell of it permeated the air. Was this a dream, or some terrifying reality? He couldn't be sure, but he knew he must keep going. There was some place he needed to be … something he needed to do, and quickly. He tried to hurry. The sense of desperation was almost smothering, but his feet felt like lead weights. Then, he heard it … the sound that shattered his soul!

"Julian!" The agonized scream pierced his heart like the fine point of a steel blade. He continued up the rocky slope, his fury and terror giving him renewed energy. The jagged rocks tore at his bloody and battered body. He had failed her, failed to keep them both safe. He had underestimated their enemy, and now that son of a bitch had her, and he would revel in her pain … and Julian's. Terror seized him, for he knew she would pay a heavy price if he did not reach her in time.

They had been badly outnumbered. Even with his superior strength, he couldn't fight all the hordes of hell. They served that demon bastard they called "master." He had fought them until he could barely stand, but he was alone. His men had not reached them in time. He should have waited for reinforcements, but there was no time … no time. "I tried … God knows I tried," he thought as he stared at the wooden stake in his hand, blood streaming down the sides. But the beast had taken her anyway, had ripped her right out of his arms. He tried to close his mind to the terror he knew she must have been feeling.

"Julian!"

The cry was a little weaker this time. He must push on. He must keep going if there was even the slightest chance he could save her. With his last ounce of strength, he surged forward, his desperate climb finally coming to an end as he reached the summit of the small mountain. He hid behind a large boulder as he paused for breath, hoping to regain the strength he needed. But would it be enough? Would this curse that had been forced upon him give him the power to save her? There was only one way to find out.

Stepping from behind his stone sanctuary, he prepared for battle yet again, but the scene that met his horrified eyes stopped him dead in his tracks. A dark figure loomed in the distance, standing dangerously close to the edge of the treacherous cliff. Its grotesque head was bent over a small form, lying limp and motionless in its arms. Fear seized Julian, for he couldn't sense any sign of life coming from the tiny, broken body—but his fear was soon replaced by a fury so great he forgot all danger to himself as he charged the creature.

"Damn you to hell!" he screamed, his burning rage urging him on as he ran with the bloody stake held high. It was so far … would he reach her in time? He had to, there was no other choice.

The head of the creature rose, and Julian's blood froze in his veins. Saliva, tinged with red, dripped from sharp, jagged fangs as the creature hissed its hatred at Julian.

"My damnation is already assured, vampire, and your chance for a mortal life is quickly slipping away!" the creature spat as it stared down at its limp captive, a clawed finger caressing her pale face. "She is moments from death, but you can still save her. Only you have the power. Only you, Julian."

The words were but a faint whisper on the gentle wind, but as the creature continued its rambling, the voice grew louder, the message clear. "The choice is up to you. You know what I want. Say you will join me, lead my armies, and I will give her the gift of immortality. She will be yours forever, and together we will be unstoppable!" The dark figure watched the conflict behind Julian's tormented eyes.

"Hurry, my friend," it taunted as Julian drew closer. "Time grows short."

Despair overwhelmed Julian as he slowed, stopping a few feet from the figures teetering on the cliff's edge. Looking at the small figure so bloody and pale, Julian knew it was already too late. He screamed in frustration, his hatred overwhelming him.

"I will kill her myself before I let her become the monster you would make her!" he shouted, raising the stake high to strike a killing blow as he lunged at the dark figure.

Hesitating only an instant the creature hissed back at him, "Are we so different, my friend?" A slow smile formed on the hideous face, and triumph flashed in the red eyes before it struck quickly and precisely, before Julian had any hope of reaching it. With lightning speed, the clawed hand shot forward, slicing into the chest of the figure it held in its arms. With a jerk, it pulled an object free … a tiny heart, still beating slowly in his bloody palm. With a last look at Julian, the creature leaned over the cliff tossing the lifeless body into the wide abyss.

"*No!*" Julian screamed in anguish as the stake came down, severing membrane and bone and gashing a large hole in a huge black wing.

"*No!*"

Chapter 1

"*No!*"

Julian awoke with a shout, his body covered in sweat as he again lived the anguish and terror of that awful night. Sitting alone in the stillness, his face buried in his hands, Julian took a few seconds to calm himself, inhaling deeply until the blood racing in his veins slowed.

"It's just a dream," he said aloud, as if he needed to hear the words spoken. "It was just a bad dream."

Except he had never actually dreamt during the many centuries of his long existence, didn't know he could. "God, what's wrong with me?" he wondered as he fell back against the pillows, his forearm thrown across tired eyes in an attempt to block the images invading his mind. But God had nothing to do with it. God had forgotten about him a long time ago.

He lay for a moment longer, and then, knowing that any chance of further rest was futile, tossed the black satin sheets aside ,throwing his long legs over the side of the large wood bed frame. Leaning forward, elbows on his knees, hands cupped, he stared into the blackness, waiting for his eyes to grow accustomed to the dark. Coldness seeped into his bones as a chill crept along his spine , the memory of the dream lingering —a memory that still had the power to torment him.

He thought he had succeeded in blocking her death from his mind. He didn't want to forget her—her beauty, her sweetness—but the good memories had been all but wiped out by the horror of that night. Her broken body was all he could see when he thought of her, even years later, so he'd pushed the memories to the back of his mind. The pain and guilt were more than he could bear. He had been a fool to think he'd succeeded in forgetting the worst moment of his entire existence, even for a little while. It was part of who he was.

And whether he liked to admit it or not, it had made him stronger. It had been the driving force in his decision to fight the evil ones through the centuries. He could not save her, but he could avenge her and prevent others from suffering her awful fate.

From the monitor on the ancient wall, a familiar voice reached his ears: "Nightmare?"

"Yes," he replied.

"I'll be right down." The voice belonged to a young man.

"There's no need. I'm fine. I just need a hot shower. I will be there soon."

"Right."

As he listened to the voice through the intercom, a fleeting smile stole across his handsome face—a face almost to perfect to be, well, human. Thomas Thibideau was the only human Julian could trust to keep things secure during his daylight hours of seclusion. Yes, this particular human had indeed been a fortunate find. The fire was always lit in the great stone fireplace when he awoke from his slumber every evening, the flames spreading the only light and warmth the cold, dark room possessed. "Thomas certainly takes good care of me," he thought, his mind drifting back to the day the two had met—actually, collided was a more appropriate word.

It happened nearly ten years ago in the great city of New Orleans. It was a city where strange happenings were normal, and one never knew who or what they might come across in the twilight hours. During that time, Thomas had worked as an orderly at the local blood bank, a frequent haunt of Julian's, for these were civilized times and the days of killing for his survival were over. The young man had discovered Julian stealing a few pints of whole blood from a freezer unit. Their first meeting was, to put it mildly, violent and almost certainly lethal for the young man.

Thomas had attacked the would-be thief, thinking him some unfortunate street person stealing blood for profit. He should have known something was not quite right the minute the beam from his flashlight fell across the tall, muscular form. No street person wore silk and Italian leather! And there was definitely no mistaking the strength and agility of the thief as he fought back with a skill and ferocity Thomas had no hope of matching.

Julian had grabbed Thomas's neck in a vice-like grip and stared into his terrified eyes. The much smaller Thomas had thrown everything he had at the stranger in an attempt to escape, and ultimately the young man's will to survive made Julian think, "He may be useful."

Rather than kill him, Julian simply placed a hand over the young man's nose and mouth, suffocating him until he passed out. He left that evening with Thomas slung over a shoulder and twenty-four pints of blood tucked securely under his arm. Thomas had agreed to stay and work for Julian after a little friendly persuasion helped him believe the unbelievable and accept the reality of what Julian was. They had been together ever since, and Thomas was one of the few people Julian trusted with his very life. Yes, he had proven to be quite a find indeed.

Julian rose from the bed with a grace and agility that belied a man of his size and stature, staring around the room that had become his daytime refuge and prison. Pieces of the past he actually wanted to remember lay scattered before him, bought by wealth accumulated over centuries of living. His skill and cunning had allowed him to amass a fortune in rare and ancient artifacts—among other things—as he traveled the world.

It also allowed him to bring, stone by stone, portions of his ancestral home from deep within the Carpathian Mountains to this isolated spot in the New England countryside. He had been a mere boy when he had left his home and loving family to find himself. What he found was more than he bargained for—much more—and there was nothing he could do that would ever change that. Not now, not with her gone. The few family heirlooms he had managed to recover gave him some solace, some link to a happier time.

Along the far wall was a large fireplace, exquisitely carved from solid marble, its beauty forever timeless. An elegant Queen Anne's chair in rich burgundy velvet was perched beside the hearth. A carpet of the finest silk spilled burgundy, gold, and green across the floor, coming to a stop before a tall, antique armoire, the dark wood perfectly matching the king-sized bed. They were all luxuries from centuries past with no one to admire them … no one but him.

A realization came to him. The dream … it was trying to tell him something … send him some sort of message. To be sure, it was a painful reminder of how much he had loved and lost, how close he had come to actual happiness … a normal life with someone who actually cared for him despite what he was. But there was an underlying meaning, a reason the dream had come back to haunt him now—at this particular time and place—and the tension he felt building inside warned him that he must figure out this riddle … and soon!

Usually, this room held peace and comfort for him, but not tonight. He could feel the change in the air … someone was near, newly arrived, with a connection to him, awakening memories and feelings buried long ago. He thought all emotion had died with her. But this new presence had caused them to stir inside of him. "Why, or more importantly, who was out there? Am I to be given another chance, or is this just the imaginings of an overtired mind?" He wasn't sure, but for the first time in a long time, he felt a sense of hope.

Turning, he reached for a pair of black slacks thrown carelessly across the chair and, in one quick movement, slid his long legs into them. Walking to the fireplace, he stood before the flames, his chilled body slowly coming back to life. A goblet of the finest crystal sat atop the mantle. It was filled with life-giving liquid, the ruby red color looking almost black in the darkness. "Thomas, again," he thought, tilting his head back to empty the glass of its precious contents , feeling the strength and power returning to his limbs. It was just a taste. His power wouldn't reach its full potential until he had hunted, but it started the process.

He could feel his blood warming as he moved around the room, his beautiful grey-blue eyes seeing perfectly in the darkness. Pulling out a heavy, black robe from deep within the armoire, he wrapped it around a body as hard and perfectly formed as the marble mantle above the fireplace. Even the long centuries had not left their mark on its perfection, and his lean, muscular frame glistened in the firelight. His flowing tresses of shoulder-length hair shimmered with red gold highlights as he ran his hand through the tangled mass of color, making it hard to tell if it was dark brown, auburn, or a bit of both.

His thoughts turned to the hot shower he knew Thomas would have waiting upstairs. He made his way toward the door of the cavernous room his sensual movements as graceful as the Black Panther whose shape he sometimes assumed. He moved through a short hallway and climbed the stone steps leading from his underground chamber to one of four tower rooms on the second floor of the ancient mansion where he had made his home.

Small candles, which his keen eyes really didn't need, flickered from stone sconces on the wall as he climbed to the top of the staircase and stood before a heavy oak door. He pulled on the nearest sconce, causing the door to swing inward. He entered a room that was decorated almost identically to the one he actually slept in, deep in the bowels of the mansion, hidden from prying eyes. The only difference between the two rooms was a long, narrow window alongside the fireplace through which the early morning sun would bathe a viewer in its warmth—or so he was told. It also boasted a luxurious master bath with all the modern conveniences.

Walking over to the window, he pulled aside the heavy gold curtains and stared out into the ever-approaching night. It was twilight … the only time during his life of eternal darkness when he could actually gaze upon what was left of the setting sun. It was a time of conflicting emotions, a combination of pleasure and pain as he watched the golden orb sinking lower into the night sky, darkness close on its heels. A deep sigh escaped him.

The house was perched atop a steep cliff that, even at night, had a breathtaking view. At dusk, a soft, swirling mist skimmed the tops of giant fir trees hundreds of feet below him. What he wouldn't give to see this sight at sunrise, to feel the warmth of the sun's rays falling across his face! As he continued to stare out the window, a deep melancholy gripped him.

"So long ago," he thought, "everything was taken from me in an instant of pain." He remembered the sharp fangs piercing his throat , changing his life forever.

"And forever is a very long time" he spoke aloud, shaking his head to bring himself back to the present. He continued to stare into the blackness, where he could just make out the outline of a stone bridge in the distance. The bridge provided the only access to the dusty gravel road that connected Julian's sanctuary to the rest of the world.

Reaching for the brass window latch, he turned the metal knob slowly, causing the window to open outwards. Leaning into the evening air, he inhaled deeply. Then it hit him like a splash of cold water on his tired face … a familiar scent of memories long past, emotions long dead. His sharp eyes searched the night, scanning his domain for any sign of movement. It was near, the presence that had caused the dream to start … reaching out to him. He could feel it in the night air. Were they as aware of him as he was of them, or were they oblivious, ignorant of the connection?

His attention was drawn to the tiny, shimmering lights of a small cottage nestled at the base of the hill, just inside the gates to the estate. Once part of the original property and connected to the stone manor house, his lawyers had convinced him it would be a good idea to sell the cottage, which he had recently done. A slight frown creased his handsome brow. "The new owner must have arrived," he thought, as an almost overwhelming urge seemed to draw his gaze toward the house. There it was again … a memory reaching out to him, searching, like a hand taking hold … drawing him in.

"The cottage … it's coming from the cottage," he said, not even realizing he had spoken the words aloud. Just as he allowed himself to hope, a voice penetrated his mind like a physical pain he could not shake. It took control, wiping out all rational thought. Pure evil surrounded him, filling him with the coldness of an approaching dawn, as he heard the horrible words: *"I know she is near … I will find her … you cannot save her!"*

His hands sprang to his head, covering his ears as if flesh and bone could prevent the unseen force from entering there. When nothing further happened, he spun around, his hands dropping to his sides as his eyes searched every shadow, every darkened corner of the room, looking for something he knew in his heart was not there. But he had to be certain. Gliding around the room, he searched every inch, every hidden recess. Finding nothing, he willed himself to relax. "It's the dream. It's playing with my mind … the memories taunting … haunting me. Someone or something wants me to remember the things I would prefer to forget. But why?" Unable to shake the feeling of unease, he walked into the bathroom.

A long, hot shower was what he wanted to clear his head. He turned the crystal knobs of the shower, sending steaming water spilling forth to soothe and relax. But he knew even before he stepped under the scalding liquid that no amount of hot water could rid him of the chill that had entered his body when those words invaded his mind. He recognized that voice … he had hoped he would never hear it again in his lifetime. He also knew they were all connected: the dream, the strange presence at the cottage, the message. The chill seeped deeper into his heart as the jets of water pounded his body. If he was right, unimaginable horror was about to descend upon them all. Would he be ready this time to prevent the devastation that was sure to come with it?

Turning off the water, he stepped from the shower and threw the robe over his wet skin. The shimmering light of the hovering moon called him back to the window. Had he imagined the strange presence, or was it real? "I have to know," he thought, as he dressed in a fresh pair of pants. "*I know she is near!*" the message had screamed in his mind. Could it be possible there was another, blissfully unaware they possessed the means for his salvation and redemption? Was he to be given one more chance at happiness and a normal life? If this were indeed true, he had to find whoever it was, and soon, for danger was coming—and it was hunting them both.

He stood in front of the window, eyes closed to clear his mind as the transformation came upon him. Bones twisted and muscles contorted as flesh and blood transformed. He fell through the opening in a flurry of wings. Disappearing into the night, he circled the blackness, catching the wind just right, swooping upward, ever upward, high above the clouds.

He wondered what the human population would think if they could actually watch a vampire transform, forgetting the myths and legends, controlling their fear long enough to witness a true miracle of nature. Their only concept was what they had seen in horror movies—a vampire bat, blood dripping from razor sharp fangs—and he knew a lot of fellow vamps that fit that description or worse. But he was different.

Many of the older vampires had an animal to call, to use as necessary or transform into, depending on the situation. It was one of the many ways they protected themselves from those who did not understand them … or were afraid to. The proud eagle suited Julian, as did the black panther with its stealth and grace. Yes, humankind would truly be surprised to learn that the large bird now flying high above the ground, its outspread wings reflected in the moonlight, was really a vampire. And they would be even more surprised to learn this particular vampire was there to protect them.

As a young man, Julian had once researched the Rig Veda, an ancient Indian collection of sacred hymns to the gods. The book told the tale of the god Indra who stole soma, the drink of immortality, while riding on the back of the majestic eagle. The hymns further told of how Indra then gave the miraculous elixir to the ancestor of mankind, Manu. "What better form for an immortal being than that of this magnificent bird?" Julian had thought. Thus his choice was made when this new life was forced upon him.

The giant bird began its descent, circling until it gracefully touched down near the edge of the woods. Here he could remain hidden among the giant trees while he studied the tiny house before him, as the feathers covering his body fell away to reveal the muscular form beneath.

His view included the back of the small cottage and a long, wraparound porch extending its full length. As he approached an ancient oak tree, large enough to hide him completely, he felt the first stirring of recognition. Though he had yet to see anyone, he knew someone was there, a somehow familiar stranger sitting only a few feet from him enjoying the night as he only wished he could do.

Feelings he thought long dead—longing, love, lust—came flooding back, his blood rising to a fever pitch as he fought to control the hunger. He should have fed first, but he had been in a hurry to find answers to the strange feelings assailing his senses. He had forgotten the cardinal rule. He needed blood to be at full strength, and full strength meant power and safety for himself and those he was responsible for. He had been careless in not feeding first, and carelessness was dangerous. Yes, he must feed soon, but first …

His gaze was drawn back to the porch where he sensed movement. Someone was there … a woman, and the pull was strong. "It can't be, there could not be another …" his thoughts were chaotic. He had felt this same connection a long time ago, when he had first encountered her. He had thought then that she was one of a kind. He still did, but was he mistaken? As his keen eyes scanned the porch, the voice once again invaded his mind, the message clear: *"I know she is here."* Fear, mingled with hope, filled him as he focused on the small figure sitting quietly on the porch, blissfully unaware that a stranger's eyes watched her so intently.

*****

Sliding down into the comfortable cushions of the old rocker, a glass of wine balanced loosely in her hand, Adrianna Avanie—Addie to her friends—reveled in the peaceful serenity of her surroundings. Just moments ago, the setting sun had splashed red, gray, and blue against the darkening sky as it sank lower and lower into the woods. It was soon replaced by the silvery light of the rising moon, its glowing brightness casting shadows across the lawn.

"Kate doesn't know what she's missing," Addie said aloud, thinking of her roommate, Kate St. John, who was already fast asleep. Adrianna knew she should probably do the same, but she was having trouble relaxing … again. As a matter of fact, her strange restlessness was becoming the norm since they had finally settled into their new home. Deciding the warm night air and beautiful sunset were just what she needed to unwind a little, she had poured a glass of her favorite red wine and strolled along the back porch in search of her favorite chair. It was so quiet here, so peaceful. It was as if there was not another living soul for miles around.

One of the things that had attracted her to the house in the first place was its isolation. Her mind drifted back to the day she had first come across the tiny cottage while driving home from a buying trip with Kate. In a hurry to reach their apartment before nightfall, after a weekend in the city, they had taken a wrong turn and ended up in the driveway of what seemed to be an abandoned house. The building, with its peaked roof, quaint gingerbread trim, and beds of colorful wildflowers along cobblestone walkways, seemed like something out of another time and place. It beckoned to her.

When they found no one home to help them with directions, they left, eventually finding their way. But she couldn't get the house out of her mind. Winwood, the small New England town in which she and Kate had grown up, was full of similar houses, but this one was somehow different. It had a certain presence, an atmosphere that struck a chord deep within her and drew her to its serene beauty.

Weeks later, as the noise of the bustling town and the pressures of running an upscale boutique began to overwhelm her,the cottage was often in her thoughts. Normally, she loved the dress shop she and Kate had opened soon after graduating from college. She thrived on the excitement and energy of running a successful business. The frequent buying trips to New York, the holiday sales, haggling with customers over prices, and watching their profits increase with each passing year was something she had always enjoyed, but in the past few weeks, she had sensed a change in herself.

The dynamics of such a busy life were beginning to make her edgy and nervous. She found herself losing patience with long-standing customers whose quirks never used to bother her. She longed for the peaceful serenity and isolation of the quiet countryside. One day, she actually found herself discussing with Kate the idea of buying a small home away from the chaos of the business district where they spent so much of their time. Both girls agreed they had outgrown the small, two-bedroom apartment they shared above the boutique. On more than one occasion, usually when the town's college students were home around the holidays and the noise level of the town rose, they joked of moving away from it all.

For Addie at least, that need seemed almost urgent. She frequently found herself thinking of the cottage nestled at the base of a hill surrounded by, well, nothing. Its beauty and solitude were exactly what she was looking for. One day, she broached the subject of the cottage to Kate, and to her relief and excitement, she found that her friend agreed with her. The two of them soon set out to gather what information they could about the property.

After weeks with no progress, they had, quite by chance, stumbled upon the attorney in charge of the upkeep of the tiny house. They were informed that, although empty, the place was not for sale. A wealthy businessman owned the cottage, as well as all the surrounding acreage and the great stone mansion on top of the hill. The gentleman was somewhat reclusive.

Not being one to give up easily, Addie badgered the attorney to keep trying. She explained that since they spent most of their time in town, his reclusive client wouldn't even know the two women were living there. Something in her reasoning must have struck a chord with the owner because, a few weeks after their initial meeting with the attorney, the women were informed that their offer had been accepted. It had taken only a few months to settle the legalities, and as the warm summer days began, Addie and Kate found themselves moving from their tiny apartment to the lovely cottage in the quiet countryside. They never looked back.

For a while, their weekends were busier than their work weeks, consumed by the hard work of restoring the wildflower beds to their former glory and scrubbing, cleaning, and painting the little cottage. But after just one month of backbreaking manual labor, the house had truly become their home. They had gone to a few antique shops and found the perfect furnishings.

There were antique end tables with tiny clawed feet to match the blue velvet couch that had once belonged to Addie's grandmother. Two large hurricane lamps of milk glass with tiny silver-blue and mauve flowers completed the room, along with various knick-knacks. Kate had contributed a lovely walnut dining room table, chairs, and hutch she had found in an out-of-the-way shop in New York, leaving only the bedrooms. It had been a lot of hard work, but it was well worth the time spent, for Addie really believed this was where she belonged.

She took another sip of wine, and a small frown creased her forehead. The only disappointment over the past few months was the absence of the previous owner. She hadn't really believed he was a recluse, but out of respect for his wishes, the women had never imposed on their only neighbor's privacy. But Addie had hoped, over time, his curiosity would get the best of him and he would take the first step toward making their acquaintance. That hadn't happened yet. All of the legalities had been handled by his lawyers, and not once had they met their elusive mystery man.

As she gazed across the freshly mowed lawn, her eyes traveled to the old stone bridge in the back yard and up the hillside to the magnificent Victorian mansion perched on the cliff's edge. "Who are you?" she wondered, and why did she even care? She wasn't sure, but she couldn't let it go. For some reason, she felt it was very important to meet this particular man. As a matter of fact, the feeling had been so strong that, about a week after settling in, she found herself walking across the bridge, up the hill to the main house, hoping to come across someone, anyone, to prove she and Kate were not the only people living in the area. There had been no one home on that day, and she had left frustrated. Maybe she should try again the next weekend. She made up her mind to do some sleuthing on her own and find out what she could about the big house and its strange inhabitant.

Eyes closed, rocking rhythmically, the calm around her was suddenly shattered as she experienced a strong sensation of being watched. Hair prickling on the back of her neck, she sat upright, tense and alert. Glancing from side to side, she assured herself that she was alone on the porch. Eyes straining, she scanned the back yard, trying to get a clear view of the woods near the edge of the property. Her eyes were drawn to a large oak just inside the entrance to the woods, its base camouflaged by the surrounding undergrowth.

"Is someone there?" she wondered, trying not to give in to the feelings of alarm rising in her. Getting up from the rocker, she leaned as far forward across the banister as she could to get a better look, but the distance was just too far. It was impossible to see clearly. Only the blackness of the night woods stared back at her. But something was out there—she could *feel* it—yet for some reason, the alarm she had felt a moment ago was gone. Whatever was there, she somehow knew, meant her no harm. Shaking her head slightly, she scolded herself, "You're letting your imagination run away with you. There's nothing out there. You're just not used to the quiet countryside. It's probably some poor woodland creature, more afraid of you than you are of it. Remember, this is what you wanted ... the quiet ... the solitude. If it's a little creepy, you have no one to blame but yourself!" Laughing a little nervously, she decided to call it a night.

"I just need to get some sleep," she said aloud as she stepped into the cozy living room and locked the French doors behind her. Fluffing the lace curtains a little, she gave one last look at the old oak, but seeing only darkness, she let the curtains flutter sideways as she made her way through the cozy but cluttered room. Entering the hallway, she continued up the staircase, passing the first bedroom door on her left and smiling slightly as she heard Kate's light snoring.

"Yes, that's definitely what I need." She chuckled and hoped she, too, would soon be sound asleep. Having already taken a hot shower, she went straight to her own room. Dropping her robe on a nearby chair, she paused at the window, staring out at the many stars sparkling in the night sky. She felt a strange anticipation as she stared into the darkness, but she could find no reason for it. "Go to sleep, Addie," she told herself, climbing into bed and sinking deep into the soft mattress. Within minutes, the wine and the night air had worked their magic as she drifted off into a deep sleep.

Outside in the warm night air, Julian stepped from behind the aging tree and walked the short distance to the wood's edge. His keen eyesight had allowed him to watch her from a distance as she sat enjoying the evening air, but when he saw her rise suddenly, he could feel her tension as she scanned the night, searching for him! Quickly, he stepped back into the shadows and the darkness hid him once more.

"Had she seen me?" he wondered. "No, that was not possible. It was too great a distance." But he was sure she had sensed his presence and known he was there.

"How was that possible?" he asked himself, for he had not made the slightest sound. "Who is she? And why should it matter so much to me?" Both were very good questions that he had every intention of answering.

"And the sooner, the better," he said to the darkness.

But now he must hunt. The craving, the thirst was calling to him. His need was overpowering. As the change came upon him, he was preparing to leap into the night sky when he stopped, his muscles tense.

Someone, or something, was nearby, watching and listening—and this visitor was decidedly unfriendly. He could smell the evil. He took to the night sky, his eagle eyes scanning every inch of ground where he had recently stood. There! A dark shadow was hidden behind a large boulder, only a few feet from the old oak tree. How had this intruder gone unnoticed by him? The evil emanating from the dark figure was unmistakable. There was no way he would not have picked up on such a foul stench. Had this strange visitor only just arrived, or was he so wrapped up with thoughts of the woman that he had blocked out everything else? This was not good; he was getting careless. He climbed higher, and then turning quickly, the great bird dove toward the hidden shadow. Sensing the eagle's approach, the dark figure spun to face its attacker, red eyes glowing as the enormous bird swooped ever closer. Just as the eagle was about to strike, the shadow began to run with inhuman speed.

Deciding ground pursuit would serve him best, the great bird set down in a nearby clearing. Within seconds, the feathers fell away to be replaced by coarse, black fur as the panther took shape. With a burst of speed, the animal took off in the direction of the mysterious intruder, but try as he might, he could not find the creature. In the short time it had taken him to change, the strange figure had disappeared among the trees and foliage.

He backtracked to the spot where he had last caught sight of it, but found nothing, not a trace. Whatever it had been, it was gone. The only thing left behind was a feeling, a coldness, a scent of evil that the great cat sniffed in the evening air. That troubled him more than anything else he had experienced the entire night. "I must find Christoff!" With that thought, he shifted again, taking to the skies and heading back to the shelter of the mansion.

*****

Some distance away, hidden by tall trees and knee-deep foliage, the tall, muscular form of a man appeared. He gloried in his nakedness as a twisted smile formed on the handsome face, the perfection disguising the evil that filled his black heart. He preferred this human form, with its flawless olive complexion and ebony curls flowing nearly to his waist, for its beauty allowed him to indulge in all the forms of pleasure and decadence his kind craved. The weaker human race begged for his attention.

He was deep in thought as he caught sight of the bird, now but a speck in the night sky. That had been a close call. He should have been more careful, should have known Julian would be aware of his presence. Oh well, all was not lost. He had not failed to notice how much the vampire had been drawn to the woman in the cottage. He had no doubt she was the one his father was seeking, but still, he must be sure, for he had seen his father's wrath on too many occasions. He went to great lengths not to be on the receiving end of that anger, so he must be certain his information was correct.

"Great will be my reward when I bring him news of what I have seen." He wondered how his half brother was faring with his assigned task. The tall, muscular body began to reform … changing … disappearing … until something altogether different stood in its place. The shape of the giant beast made travel easier, so as the change became complete, he hurried to bring his news to the one who waited.

Chapter 2

The few candles attempting to pierce the smothering gloom in the dark, cavernous room cast dancing shadows along bare walls. In the center he waited, perched on a throne of granite, a black shadow, large and brooding. *"She is here. I can feel her. She must not reach him."* The red eyes blazed with anger as the massive head turned slowly toward the large wooden door. A slight creak alerted his pointed ears to an arrival. The stench of something dead entered the room long before the actual figure. The skeletal creature, all claws and sharp teeth, entered cautiously, terror evident on its skull-like face.

"Did you find her?" the deep voice spat out the dreaded question.

"No, my lord ... I ... I'm sorry. I searched where you told me, but the wench was nowhere—"

"And it didn't occur to you to seek elsewhere!" the dark figure roared in anger as it rose to its full height, wings outspread, towering above the trembling figure now on its knees with head bowed.

"My lord ... forgive me ... I tried ... ahhh!" The piteous cry was cut short as talons dug into the trembling creature's throat, snapping it in two. Red eyes burned into the lifeless eyes, and then, with a sound of disgust, the towering monster tore the head from the mutilated body and dropped the remains to the floor, where they burst into flames leaving only a pile of ash.

"Fail me and pay the consequences," the voice hissed in anger as it lowered its large bulk back into the waiting chair. "Is there no one competent enough to do my bidding?" The question was asked although no reply was expected.

"But all was not lost," it reasoned. He had sent them out to join the hunt—blood of his blood, his own sons. They would surely not fail him. He should have sent them in the first place. His minions were followers, not leaders. But he rarely let his offspring out of his sight. Julian had grown strong over the centuries and he would savor his revenge. He hesitated to put his sons at risk, but incompetence had forced his hand. He knew there was no real cause for worry, for his offspring, too, had grown in strength and power. They were, after all, a part of him.

His evil mind drifted back as he focused on the image of his eldest son, Enoch. He was so much like his mother. An exquisite, dark beauty, she was a woman to behold. She was the Countess Elizabeth Bathory, known to many as the Blood Countess or Countess Dracula. The red eyes blazed with anger at the thought of the last title for the woman who bore his firstborn son.

"Dracula! Psssst!" He spat out the name. "As if that pretender to my throne could ever hope to claim a woman like Elizabeth."

The legend told the tale of her bathing in the blood of virgins to retain eternal youth. "Legends … bahhh!" His twisted mind continued its rant. "Her beauty was flawless, timeless. She needed no magic, no ritual, to retain what came to her naturally." An evil grin spread across the horrid face. Sometimes, though, she did have a flare for the dramatic, a talent for causing pain, as her countless victims would bear witness to—if they could. She understood what the blood meant, the power it held, the life it sustained. It was a gift, and one she used well.

Those were good times, the hours spent in her company. But all good things must, eventually, come to an end. They had come for her while he was away, training his son to follow in his footsteps. They would not have dared to approach her had he been there to fight alongside her. Her demise came after she was imprisoned behind brick walls in a room in the Cachtice Castle around 1614. That was a sad day indeed, but there would always be a part of her with him in his son, Enoch. No one could ever take that away from him.

His son would find the woman he sought, the woman of his enemy, Julian. The vampire must not be allowed to make contact with her, his sons must find her, even if a hundred more had to die before their search was through, or they, too, would suffer his wrath.

While the brooding figure sat waiting in his stone fortress, another searched a city miles away under bright lights while people from all walks of life tried to forget the monotony of their daily existence in drink and companionship. In the line of people gathering to enter the newest entertainment complex in the area, one figure in particular stood out among the rest. He was tall with long, dark hair appearing almost black against skin so pale it looked almost translucent. His movements were slow and sensual as he made his way through the throngs of people. A slight smile played across his handsome face as he noticed the many female eyes following his every move.

But he ignored the inviting looks cast his way, for none of them was the one he sought. Too blonde … too tall … too buxom—not that he minded.

He made a mental note to revisit one particularly pretty, blue-eyed blonde gazing at him from across the room. He could read her thoughts … smell her desire. She would serve his needs well, but that must come later, after his task was accomplished. His father had given him a job and trusted him to fulfill a mission. He knew better than to fail his lord and master.

If the one he sought was here tonight then he, Enoch, would find her. His large black eyes searched through the crowded room, peering deep into secluded booths and darkened corners until, with a feeling of triumph, he was sure he'd found what he was looking for. A petite brunette with large brown eyes was standing near the exit, waiting. "Let's not keep her waiting any longer," he thought as he moved slowly toward her. "Is this the one father has us searching for? She fits the description perfectly." He mentally caressed her long, dark hair.

But something wasn't quite right. His sharp eyes scanned the crowd of people around her. She was alone; she had no protection. Surely, if their enemy had marked her as his own, she would be well guarded. "Julian!" he thought in disgust. He could think of nothing that would give him greater pleasure than to cause Julian unendurable pain. And there was no better way to do that than to destroy his woman.

He continued to move through the ever-thickening crowd until he was mere inches away from his quarry. But the closer he came to the woman, the more he was convinced that she was not the one his father sought. Even better, for then she was his to do with as he pleased, and the smile on his face grew even larger as he thought of the carnal pleasures awaiting him. Yes, he could use a little snack before he continued the search. Surely his father would not begrudge him that if he ultimately accomplished his task.

He walked directly up to the waiting woman, black eyes capturing brown, sending a silent message … mesmerizing. Within seconds, the pretty brunette was following him through the exit, leaving the noise of the nightclub for the quiet seclusion of the wooded park across the street. "Like leading a lamb to the slaughter," he thought as he took her hand, leading her deep into the shadows cast by an enormous elm tree. Leaning back against the cold bark, he pulled her close in a smothering embrace as she gazed up at him with adoring eyes. His large hand slowly tilted her head to one side, smoothing the dark locks away from the silken neck. He bent his head and marked a trail of quick, sharp bites down her petal-soft skin.

"I will show you pleasures you can only dream about," he whispered as he watched the pulse in her neck beat rhythmically, eyes blazing red as the hunger rose within him.

"Hey, motherfucker! What the hell do you think you're doing with my girl!" screamed a half-crazed figure charging toward them from the parking lot. Anger burned in the young man's eyes as he reached the couple ,grabbing the girl by the arm,

"You little bitch!" he said, shaking her roughly as he pulled her away. "I leave you for one second, and you're off whoring around with someone else." Raising a hand to strike her, he found himself caught in a grip of iron, his hand squeezed so tightly he could hear the bones crunching even as he screamed in pain.

The girl, shaking her head as if waking from a dream, gazed questioningly at the boy standing beside her. Then, turning slowly, her eyes traveled upward to stare into the face of the stranger. Once so beautiful it was almost feminine, she watched in horror as the perfect features began to transform before her very eyes.

Skin bubbled and cracked as something out of a nightmare began to emerge. The skin literally melted away, leaving moist tendons clinging to the skull, while eyes like liquid fire filled the sunken sockets , saliva—tinged with her own blood—dripped from a mouth full of razor-sharp teeth. The terrified couple was frozen to the spot. Before she could react, the creature grabbed the horrified girl with its free hand, pulling them both hard against its chest.

"Just when I was about to have a little entertainment before dinner, you had to go and ruin it," the drooling monster spat out, turning slowly to stare at the boy. "Now I guess I'll just have to eat and run."

With lightning speed, the sharp teeth tore into the soft tissue of the boy's neck, ripping out a huge chunk. Blood flowed freely from the gaping wound before the hideous mouth clamped down on it. With a sucking sound, the creature completely drained the body of any remaining blood. When it had finished, it tossed the lifeless form aside as if it weighed nothing at all. The broken body slammed into a nearby tree and slid slowly to the ground, where it lay motionless.

Turning to the hysterical figure in its other hand, the creature decided to go more slowly this time, and its sharp teeth sank into the supple flesh, silencing the girl's terrified screams. The dark figure rocked and moaned, consumed by the hunger as it drank deeply. The tiny figure gradually fell limp in the arms wrapped tightly around it. Finally, hunger sated, the monster dropped another lifeless body to the ground, where it looked like a sleeping child. As it stared at the crumpled figure lying motionless at its feet, a trickle of doubt filled the evil mind.

"When you find her, bring her directly to me!" His father's words ran through his mind as panic seized him.

"If she was with this boy, she could not be the one my father has been obsessed with for as long as I can remember," he told himself. The panic began to subside. If she was the one, she would have been more closely guarded. He would not have gotten anywhere near her. No, he felt perfectly justified in destroying this little beauty, as well as the boy. After all, his father would want no trail leading back to him. How did the saying go? Dead men tell no tales. Well, these two would not be telling stories to anyone! He had seen to that, but he was a little concerned. If this was not the right woman, his father would expect him to continue the search. He had to bring some news back to his lord and master, or else.

"There, in the park! By the big tree!"

Shouts were coming from the direction of the nightclub. Turning slowly, the red eyes focused on a tall man, waves of long, blond hair billowing out behind him as he ran with inhuman speed ahead of the approaching crowd. Hatred filled the creature's evil heart as it hissed at the figure now only a few feet away,

"You're too late to save them yet again, vampire, and I, sadly, must leave you. But you can be certain we will meet again."

Huge black wings burst forth from the creature's back, lifting the dark form high off the ground just out of reach of the blond vampire. Before the newcomer could react, the wind began to rise as the leathery membranes beat back and forth, forcing the oncoming crowd to back away. Swooping inward, the wings completely encased the hovering figure. The black cocoon began to spin faster and faster, like a top on its pointed spindle. The swirling air propelled bits of grass and dirt outward as the onlookers watched in frustration. Then, as quickly as the whirlwind began, it ended. When the dust settled and the wind quieted, the dark form at the center of it all had vanished!

"Damn!" The blond vampire's eyes blazed liquid fire as he fought to control his anger. "He was within my grasp, and I let him escape. Damn it all to hell!"

"There was nothing you, or any of us, could do, Simon," said a young man with black hair sticking out in all directions, his spiked mohawk tipped with blood red highlights. "He was too powerful. I've never seen anything like that. The force of the wind was so strong, we could barely move!"

"You are but a human, David. I am vampire. Nothing should have held me back. I should have that black-hearted soul in my hands as we speak!"

"Simon—"

"I know, I know. Ranting about it doesn't change a thing. Come, we have more pressing problems."

Reaching the spot where the creature had disappeared, the vampire knelt to examine the lifeless body of the young woman lying there, turning her head slightly to stare at the two puncture wounds on the side of her bruised and bloody neck. The young man knelt beside him, sorrow etched on his face.

"Any chance one of them is still alive, Simon?"

"No, the creature was very thorough." Lifting himself with a grace unnatural for someone so large, Simon began giving orders. "Adam, anything?" he said to the figure kneeling alongside the body of the dead boy. He already knew the answer.

"Sorry, Simon, this one's gone, too."

"Shit!" With sheer force of will, Simon fought against the frustration ready to consume him.

"Then take David here and a few other helpers and dispose of … who called the police!" he shouted, turning quickly in the direction of a siren's shrill call that shattered the stillness of the night.

"We had some frightened people inside," David said. "When the screams started, every cell phone in the place lit up. Someone must have felt it was their civic duty to call the squad. Sorry, Simon, we couldn't convince all of them to be silent."

Simon's blue eyes bled crimson as a black-and-white screeched to a halt nearby. "Great!" he said. "There's no time to make things right now. We must notify Julian immediately." He cast David a knowing look and continued, "Answer their questions without giving too much information. Do the best you can."

"Got it covered," the boy replied.

"Adam, you come with me."

Adam nodded and stood alongside the taller vampire. Blending with the night shadows, the two figures disappeared, only to reappear moments later inside a luxurious, mahogany-paneled office in the back of the club.

"We have a problem," Simon's deep voice broke the silence in the room.

The woman seated behind the ornate wooden desk lifted her head slowly, locks of red-gold hair falling around her shoulders.

"One that is easily taken care of, I hope," she said, her ebony eyes sweeping over the two vampires.

"That depends on how creative David is when answering the questions put to him by our local law enforcement," Simon said.

"Why are the police here?"

"We've had another incident. Two more young people have been attacked. They are dead."

"And the one responsible?"

"The bastard is gone," Simon said with tightly controlled anger. "I'm on my way to inform Julian now. That's why I left David to handle the police."

"He has been reliable in the past, for a human. Still ..." She sat deep in thought. "Perhaps I should join them, see if a little friendly persuasion is needed."

"My thoughts, exactly," Simon agreed. "Adam will come with me. We shall return shortly."

Nodding in agreement, the woman rose gracefully and walked around the desk to join them.

"Walk with me," she said. "Tell me everything." She linked her arm through Simon's. They made their way through the club, deep in conversation, and then went their separate ways at the front exit.

"I will wait in my office for your return when I finish out here," she said.

Simon nodded in agreement, watching for a moment as she walked away. She moved with purpose toward the flashing red lights while the two vampires took to the night sky, heading to the old stone mansion perched atop a distant cliff and the vampire who waited there.

*****

Julian burst through the window in a flurry of wings, his mind filled with questions about the woman at the cottage. Regaining human form, he found Thomas leaning casually against the fireplace, another goblet of ruby liquid waiting in his outstretched hand. As Julian reached for the cup, Thomas asked casually, "In a hurry were we, Jules?" A mischievous smile flashed across his handsome face. Julian scowled at him, more for the use of the pet name than any other reason. Only Thomas would even dare to think he could get away with such familiarity. Downing the precious liquid, Julian felt some control returning, but he needed to feed—really feed—soon.

"What are you talking about? And I've asked you repeatedly not to call me that."

Gesturing with his finger toward a drop of blood on Julian's chin, Thomas chose to ignore the scolding. "You've got a spot just there. And the reason for my comment ... you usually find time to dress in more than a pair of pants before you become the bird of prey. Something must have lit a fire under your tail-feathers when you didn't even take time for your second blood cocktail. You should have fed while you were out. It's not smart to wait too long, as you well know."

Julian glowered at Thomas and paced restlessly.

"I had every intention of doing just that, but I was interrupted," he said. Julian was purposefully vague about what had happened while he was gone. Now was not the time to get into a discussion about strange premonitions and haunting memories. "And when did you become my keeper?" He was unable to hide the irritation in his voice, but as soon as the words were spoken, Julian knew he was being unfair to the man who had stood watch over him for these past ten years.

"When you snatched me from my home and everything I loved, or have you forgotten?" Thomas said. "It wasn't my choice to come here and baby-sit the night breed during all those beautiful, sunny days so no harm would come to you in your weakened state. Believe me, I'd much rather be at the beach!"

"I'm sorry, Thomas. I didn't mean—"

"Yes, you did ..." But then he realized the vampire was truly sorry. "It's okay. I'm used to all sorts of abuse from your kind," he said, his mischievous smile returning again. Then he turned serious and continued, "I'm just concerned, Jules, that's all. You're acting a little strange. It's not like you." Taking a closer look at his friend, Thomas became even more concerned. "You look a little tired, Jules, even for a vampire. Do you need someone sent up to you since you didn't have time to hunt? There are three or four of our feeders still here, I think."

"Yes, that might be best. Believe it or not, I'm not in the mood to track down my supper right now."

"I wish you'd tell me what's bothering you. I can tell when something is not right. You've been acting weird ever since you awoke this morning. Does it have anything to do with that nightmare you had?" Thomas knew he had hit the nail on the head by the look that flashed across the vampire's face. "You know I only ask because—"

"I know, I know, you're concerned. Look, Thomas, I had something to attend to this evening, that's all. It's nothing to worry about."

"But maybe I can help," Thomas pointed out.

"There's nothing you can do, at least not yet," Julian said, not wanting his friend to feel unappreciated, yet hesitating to say any more. Thomas was still ignorant of a large part of Julian's past. There never seemed to be a right time to talk about his life all those centuries ago. And there were things Julian himself would just as soon forget, things he didn't need to be reminded of. Besides, Christoff and the others, his fellow vampires, were against sharing too much information with their human helpers, no matter how loyal they proved to be. But that may have to change.

"We've been together a long time, Jules," Thomas said, interrupting his thoughts. "And ... you know I respect your privacy. But something is up, I can tell. You seem agitated. I mean more than usual. You know I can be trusted. Sooner or later, you're going to have to open up and let me into your inner sanctum, despite what the other blood suckers might have to say." He finished quickly as the look in Julian's eyes became more intense.

"Let it go, Thomas. When the time is right, I will fill you in, whether the others like it or not. But not now." Julian began to pull clothing from drawers and cupboards so he could finish dressing. "Are there any messages for me?" he asked.

"Yeah," Thomas said. "Mrs. Ferguson called from the blood bank. The supply is getting low. They need to recruit more help."

"I'll leave that in your capable hands. You seem to handle her better than most." Julian said as he slipped his arms into a shirt made of the finest blue silk.

"I know. She likes my smile," the young man replied, eyes twinkling.

"Indeed?" was Julian's only response. "Increase her *salary* to … five thousand a month. I'm certain that will motivate her to find all the help, as she so eloquently put it, that she needs. Has Christoff risen yet?"

"Yeah, the Bela Legosi wanna-be rose at dusk and was out the door. Probably feeding on some poor farmer's sheep as we speak, unless his smooth-talking convinced some buxom blonde to join him for another rendezvous," Thomas said sarcastically.

"You know, Thomas, this competition between the two of you for the local ladies is becoming a bit tiresome."

"I know, I know, but he refuses to acknowledge my superiority with the fairer sex," Thomas said, ignoring Julian's raised eyebrow. "What's a guy to do? And besides, that Eastern European accent and all his macho crap pisses me off!" Thomas noticed the warning flash in Julian's eyes and decided it would be in his best interest to stop trash-talking his boss's right hand vampire. After all, Christoff had been around a lot longer than he had.

He continued on a lighter note, "Anyway, speaking of ladies, did you know we have new neighbors?" Seeing the startled look on Julian's face, Thomas explained, "The two women that bought the cottage … they're here. They've been doing a lot of work on the place for the past month or so, but it looks like they've finally settled in. Both are real lookers!"

"You've seen them?" Julian asked, trying to seem disinterested.

"Only from a distance as they were moving in. One brunette, one tall redhead. You want me to arrange an introduction?" he asked eagerly, anxious for any opportunity to talk to a beautiful woman. Getting the jump on Christoff would be an added bonus.

Julian stared into the fire, his desire to know more about the newcomers conflicting with his need for secrecy and premonition of impending danger.

"There's plenty of time for that, Thomas," he finally said. "You know I like to keep things quiet around here. Maybe, at some point in the future. Right now I need to speak to Christoff. Let me know as soon as he returns."

"Sure, whatever you say," Thomas said, trying to hide his disappointment. Moving toward the door, he decided it was time to leave Julian alone, for the vampire appeared to be lost in thought. Julian's mind was already back at the cottage and the woman within, making him unaware of the arrival of two figures below him.

The shadowy forms touched down lightly on the front porch of the old mansion, materializing directly in front of the massive front door. Three loud knocks, and the door was immediately opened by a large black man who was almost as wide as he was tall. Simon merely nodded as he strode into the room, but finding no one there, he turned to the big man, "Has Julian risen Samuel?"

"I believe Thomas is with him now."

"Christoff?"

"I am here."

Simon and Adam turned around to greet the dark form following them through the front door. Simon nodded his head slightly in greeting to the approaching figure, whose appearance was in direct contrast to that of the fair vampire. His hair was black as night, and his eyes shone midnight blue. These striking features, combined with his preference for black leather, had earned Christoff the title Dark Vampire. He commanded attention from almost everyone he came into contact with—especially the ladies, much to the annoyance of Thomas.

"We have a problem at the club," Simon said. "Another attack. Two more young people are dead, I'm afraid." Simon filled Christoff in on the events of the evening, watching the midnight blue eyes turn to blood red as anger consumed the dark vampire. When Simon had finished his tale, Christoff could barely control the fury rising within him.

"Shit! Three killings in our own back yard! Once I would call random, but this … this is personal. Someone is deliberately trying to draw attention to us."

The first murder had occurred almost three weeks ago. The victim was a young woman in her early twenties, the strange circumstances of her death completely baffling the local law enforcement. Her body had been found near the club, in the park across the street. One particular road, aptly called Lovers Lane, was a favorite haunt for many of the local couples. The woman was found sitting alone, slumped over a park bench. At first, the boys who stumbled upon her thought she was merely drunk. But upon closer examination, they discovered she was dead. The only injuries that could be found on her person were two small puncture wounds near the base of her neck. An autopsy later found that she had lost a tremendous amount of blood. In fact, she had been nearly drained dry. But not a drop of that blood could be found anywhere—not on her or anywhere around her.

The police could not keep the incident under wraps. After the story was leaked, the media had a field day. The newspaper headlines were calling it the "Vampire Killer," which only fed the public's paranoia. For obvious reasons, Julian had to step in.

On a visit to the police station after the incident, the vampire had to explain things to the officers who had been at the scene, implanting suggestions in their minds as to what should be remembered—and what the vampire population wanted forgotten, thus ensuring no further information would reach the ears of the ever-present press.

The authorities then beefed up their patrols, while the club added more security, and eventually, when there were no other incidents, the public returned to its normal weekend routine. But now it would all begin again.

Christoff knew Julian would not be happy to hear this latest news. "Come," he said. "Julian must be told."

The three figures literally disappeared: one moment they were standing in the entrance hall, and in the next they materialized before a heavy wooden door in the tower high above. Knocking loudly, they waited for a response.

"Speak of the devil, and I do mean that literally," Thomas said, a smirk on his face as he opened the door to Christoff and the others. The irritation was plainly visible on the dark vampire's face as he glared at the smaller man.

"We must talk later, Julian, about your indulgence of this weaker species!" Christoff spat, never taking his eyes off Thomas as he walked past him. "But right now we have more urgent concerns."

"What's happened?" Julian asked, for he knew his friend well, and something was very wrong.

"There's been another attack, patrons of the club yet again. Another young woman and her male companion," Christoff replied.

"When?"

"Just moments ago." Simon then repeated what he had just told Christoff.

"How did you leave things?" Julian asked.

"We left David in charge," Simon said. "He is very capable, and Sonya was there."

"Good. That will buy us some time until we can look into things. Two more innocent victims and more bad publicity the club does not need. Why? Does anyone know if these latest casualties were connected to the first woman killed?" Julian asked.

"Sonya was going to look into that after the police left."

"This is no longer just a random incident, Julian," Christoff pointed out.

Julian walked to the window, his back to the others. "Someone is sending us a message," he said, talking more to himself than anyone else. "They are letting us know that they can kill in our territory, and there's nothing we can do to stop it!" His fist smashed into the wall. "They have succeeded twice now … but no more!" Turning to Christoff, he ordered, "Call everyone together. Tell them to meet us back at the club. Thomas, leave a team of Specials here to watch things while we're gone."

The Specials were humans who had been handpicked by Julian over the years for their skill in combat, armed or otherwise. They had proved invaluable on a number of occasions. He always made sure he was never without their services.

"From this night forward, the house and club are under full guard. Someone is to patrol the grounds at all times," he said.

Thomas nodded, leaving quickly to carry out Julian's orders.

"And Thomas," Julian said, stopping him, "you'd better have someone watch the cottage, too. If someone is targeting us, they may not know, or care, that it no longer belongs to me. We do not need any more innocent victims."

"Sure thing, Julian," Thomas replied as he hurried out the door.

Turning to the others, Julian continued, "Someone wants our attention and will go to extreme lengths to get it. We need to know who that someone is, and soon. If my suspicions are correct, things are about to get much worse. And I can't let that happen, not again." Julian locked eyes with Christoff, for only the dark vampire would understand Julian's concern. "I need to talk to Sonya and make sure everything concerning this latest incident has been handled. Simon, you wait for the others, Christoff and I will go on ahead. We'll meet back at the club. And Simon, be quick."

Simon nodded and disappeared through the window, floating slowly down to land on the ground just as Thomas came running through the front door.

"Does no one use the door anymore?" Thomas said in disgust as Simon stared at him in silence.

Left alone, Christoff approached Julian. "We have been together a long time, my friend. I know that look well. What are you thinking?"

"It's him, Christoff. He's back, but why I am not certain. He destroyed my dreams centuries ago. What more does he want from me?"

"Dra …" But the name would not pass the dark vampire's lips. "Not he. He has been silent for so long, I thought we had seen the last of him. You are certain it is that spawn from hell?"

Taking a deep, tired breath, Julian replied, "It's just a feeling, but my instinct tells me it's true. I hope I am wrong, for our sake, and the sake of this entire town. Come, time is precious."

The two figures stood before the open window, one moment flesh and blood and the next, a heavy mist, thick and swirling, moving through the window into the night air. In seconds, the mist had disappeared only to reappear miles away, back in the elegant office of Julian's club. Sonya was once again seated behind the large desk.

"I was wondering when you would surface," she said. "Nothing like a good murder to summon the troops."

"This is no time to be flippant, Sonya," Julian replied.

"I'm sorry. Forgive me." But it was not sorrow reflected in her ebony eyes as they traveled slowly over the tall form of Christoff, lingering a moment longer than was necessary, her desire burning like a bright flame. "Christoff, always a pleasure," she said, rising to greet him with her hand extended. He gently grasped it, placing a feather-light kiss on her upturned palm as he returned her stare.

A mixture of desire, regret, and resignation flashed in his navy eyes as he held the beautiful woman enthralled. "There was a time," he thought, "when I would have made her mine without a moment's hesitation." But he was a soldier. He had fought alongside Attilla, after all. A warrior's path must come first. There was no time for romance, for real love. A dalliance, yes, there were plenty of woman through the centuries who were more than willing to satisfy his lust—for sex as well as blood. But a woman like Sonya was not to be trifled with. She was to be treasured and worshiped, and this warrior had no room in his life for such a luxury. On a number of occasions, she had tried to convince him otherwise. But years of training and fierce loyalty had given this warrior a will of iron, and her pleas had fallen on deaf ears.

"Simon informed us of the evening's entertainment," Julian said. "Were the police a problem?"

"No," Sonya replied, reluctantly stepping away from Christoff. "I had a quiet conversation with the detective in charge while Charleze and a few others talked to his men. They also managed a little crowd control. The only good thing about the incident was the timing. It happened near closing time, so we had no problem convincing people to leave. Fortunately, the police kept those who wandered outside away from the scene so no one really saw much. You know these humans, so easily manipulated. Still, we can't keep doing this, Julian. Sooner or later we are going to attract unwanted attention."

"My fear exactly. We've worked too hard for the life we lead to have it ruined. What of the bodies?"

"David did some questioning on his own. He found the boy's car. After placing the bodies inside, it was driven to another park across town. The police will have received an anonymous tip to look there by now. What happens beyond that, I'm not certain."

"There was nothing to connect them to us?" Julian said.

"No. There's no need to be concerned on that account. David was very thorough. Julian, this makes three deaths right on our doorstep. Do you have any idea who's behind these attacks?"

"I know as much as you do, Sonya." He knew she hadn't missed the look that passed between him and Christoff. "Did you find any connection to the first murder?"

"No, nothing. Each victim seemed to be chosen at random. For now, it looks like a simple case of being in the wrong place at the wrong time."

"There's nothing simple about it," Julian said. "The police may be unaware of the fact, but this was a precisely planned attack, aimed at drawing attention to us. We have to put a stop to it before some young recruit with an eye on a promotion figures that out, and we find ourselves the center of a full-scale investigation! The others are meeting us here. We're going to have to increase security. There's too much at stake to get careless now."

"The others have arrived," Christoff said, his keen ears having detected movement in the outer rooms.

"Then let's not keep them waiting," Julian said, and he led the way onto the main floor of the club.

The meeting continued for hours, while across town, a meeting of a different sort was taking place. Two figures arrived simultaneously on the grounds of a crumbling stone structure. The two brothers stood staring at each other for a moment, Enoch daring his younger brother to try to beat him through the wooden door that led to their father's meeting room. Hanokh recognized the challenge in those cruel eyes and answered with a challenge of his own. But soon enough, the younger man took a step backward, his head bowed in defeat.

"Good to know you have some sense, brother!" Enoch said as his tall form floated through the front entrance. He came to a standstill before the great staircase. "Not that I really care, but how did the great beast fare in his search?"

"Better than you, I would dare to guess, since I have found the one we seek!"

"You lie!" Enoch screamed, for it was unthinkable that he should be bested by this animal.

"Do I? You be the judge." Hanokh said as he goaded his brother with the discovery he had made during the evening. "You have no real proof this woman is the one, other than the vampire's apparent interest. Let us see what father thinks." Enoch turned to glide up the stairs.

Both brothers stopped before a large door at the end of the hall. Behind it, he waited. For one fleeting moment, the brothers stood on common ground, experiencing the one emotion they truly shared: fear. But it was only for a moment as Hanokh, whose fear of his father was far greater than his fear of his brother, shoved Enoch forward, saying, "Go ahead, brother! Announce your presence."

With a look of disgust at Hanokh, Enoch pounded on the door. "You little …" he said, but his next words were drowned out by one word that reverberated through the room.

"Enter!"

Red eyes followed their every move as the brothers slowly entered. Enoch stood tall as he led the way. He was determined not to allow the figure seated in the stone chair to know it could intimidate him. Hanokh couldn't help but admire his brother in that moment, but he was sure his admiration wouldn't last long.

"Well, what news?" the voice echoed through the cavernous room.

"We think we may have found her, my lord," Enoch replied before his younger brother could speak. Ignoring the angry looks from the smaller man, Enoch continued, "I searched the club as planned, but when I found nothing, I decided to look elsewhere. I proceeded next to the vampire's home, and I saw him leave. As I was following him, Hanokh joined me. The vampire led us right to her fath … I mean, my lord."

"What are you talking about? I … " Hanokh stammered as his brother took the credit for what he had seen. "It was I …" But Hanokh fell silent when Enoch's eyes blazed in warning. He had yet to win a fight with his brother.

"You found the girl. You are sure she is the one?" The room was suddenly plunged into darkness as the figure rose in excitement. Its large wings expanded, the gust of wind they sent forth caused the candles to flicker and die. Enoch knew a moment's hesitation as doubt filled him.

"Julian seemed most interested in her, as if he were drawn to her. He has not shown such interest in a female in centuries. Not since the other one. She must be the one we seek," he said, not knowing if his reasoning would convince the being before him, or cause it to strike out at him.

"Yes, it would seem so. Still, I must be certain." The creature appeared to be deep in thought. "Follow the girl. If Julian's interest in her continues—if he shows a marked preference for her in any way—she must be brought to me immediately, before he can take what he needs from her. If she is the one, and he knows this, he will see that she is well protected. Be cautious, my sons, but thorough. You must bring her here, and destroy anyone who tries to stop you!"

Chapter 3

The ringing phone broke his concentration as Rick Ferrante struggled to straighten the clerical collar under his black shirt.

"Who could possibly be calling at this hour?" he asked no one in particular as he threw on the matching black jacket and flew down the hallway. He nearly tripped reaching for the phone when the tip of his shoe caught on the thick carpet in front of the desk. "That's what I get for jogging in the house," he thought as he answered the shrill instrument.

"Father Ferrante, how may I—"

"Rick? Hey, it's me, Nick."

"Don't reporters ever sleep?" Rick asked as he glanced at his watch, the luminous face flashing a bright 6:30 back at him.

"What? Oh, sorry to bother you so early, but I've got some news. I thought you'd be interested. Rick, there's been another one."

"Another what?"

"Attack. You know, mutilated bodies, lots of blood. What else would have me up at this godforsaken hour? Oops, sorry, no disrespect intended."

"None taken. You mean to tell me there's been another murder?"

"You got it! Same MO as the victim they found a few weeks ago. Just as violent and just as strange, only this time there were two bodies. A couple of dead kids with every ounce of blood drained from their gym-perfected bodies. There was one difference, though." The reporter hesitated, drawing out his story.

"And that difference would be ...? Come on, Nick, you know I have a Mass to say in a few minutes. What was different this time?" Rick demanded.

"Oh, right, sorry. It's the reporter in me, you know build up the suspense and all. Anyway, the first murder was in the park near that new club Nightlife, right?"

"Yes."

"The bodies last night were found in a car parked all the way across town."

"So our killer is on the move," Rick stated.

"Maybe, but I'm not buying it. I was at Nightlife last night and my spidey sense has been tingling ever since. I have a vague memory of some sort of commotion outside the building around closing time, but it's funny, after that my mind's a blank. "

"That's definitely not like you. You have a mind like a steel trap. You never forget anything," Rick pointed out.

"Exactly, so why can't I remember what went on at that club?"

"Too much to drink, perhaps?"

"Always a possibility," Nick replied, "but I don't think that was the case last night. I'm telling you, Rick, those bodies may have been found somewhere else but there's a connection to that club. There's something strange going on in that place. Call it intuition, call it a hunch, but I can feel it in my bones."

"What can you do? You have nothing concrete to go on."

"I know. I'll just have to keep looking, dig a little deeper. You know, you could be a big help, ol' buddy."

"Normally I would just ignore your pleading, but if I can help in any way to catch the monster responsible for these attacks…. What do you want me to do?"

"You know a lot of people, and you hear things. If you come across anything useful, give me a call. I'll keep you updated from my end."

"I'll do what I can, Nick." After a moment's hesitation, he asked, "Do you really think there's something going on at Nightlife? I only ask because I have a couple of friends who've been anxious to go. As a matter of fact, I think they're going this weekend. Maybe I should talk them out of it."

"I would, buddy. I can't put my finger on it, but that place gives off bad vibes. I have to go back and do more poking around. If your friends decide to go, tell them to look for me. I'll keep an eye on them. Gotta go. Catch you later."

"Okay, later." Rick stared at the phone as he replaced the receiver, a troubled frown wrinkling his smooth forehead. Finally, he came to a decision. After this morning's service he had another phone call to make, and this one, he was sure, would end in an argument.

Meanwhile, miles away, the object of his thoughts was awakening to the sound of birds chirping in the branches of the big fir tree right outside her bedroom window. Adrianna lay in bed, the warm sunshine brightening the room , a comfortable laziness enveloping her as she sank further into the soft mattress. "Just a few more minutes," she told herself. Her sleepy thoughts drifted until she found herself thinking about the previous night. Had someone really been outside, in the dark woods? Or was it just an overactive imagination? It had seemed so real. She was certain someone had been there, but she was tired—and there was the wine she drank.

"Oh, for God's sake, stop being so melodramatic," she told herself, rising from the pillows. She really needed to learn how to relax. Her mind was working overtime. She and Kate had been extremely busy at the boutique this week, and they were both looking forward to some downtime. It was the weekend, and they finally had a chance to go to that new club Nightlife, which had opened in town a few months ago.

"That's what I need: some dinner, a little dancing, some drinks. No, lots of drinks. Yes, that's just what I need," she said aloud as she climbed from bed. Moving toward the window, she gazed outside. It was another glorious day. The country was so beautiful. She couldn't figure out why she had been so jittery these past few days. Her life was going well. Busy as it kept her, she loved her job. The house was all she'd hoped for, and she had great friends who cared a lot about her.

"What more could a girl want?" she thought, and forcing herself not to give in to the desire to spend the morning in her cozy little room, she decided to get dressed. The soft tinkling of china told her that someone was busy in the kitchen. Oh well, no chance to lounge around now if Kate was already up.

Kate St. John had been Addie's friend for as long as she could remember. The girls had grown up across the street from each other. Kate was a tall, slender girl with long, red hair that hung almost to her waist. Her looks were a striking contrast to Adrianna's dark brown hair and petite frame. The two friends definitely had no shortage of attention from adolescent boys as they flirted their way through junior and senior high school, much to the dismay of parents and grandparents (who raised Kate).

After graduation, both had gone their separate ways for college, but as luck would have it, they met up again while both were living in New York City. The fashion industry had always interested each of them, so even though Addie's parents had moved west and Kate's grandmother had passed away, both girls realized they were a bit homesick. They decided to return to a much busier town than they had left to open a boutique as partners.

The bustling town was the perfect location for such a venture, since it was situated within easy driving distance of New York City. Both girls had a knack for fashion and, although there were other clothing stores in the area to give them a little healthy competition, none of them carried the kind of merchandise A Touch of the City offered. The girls were pleased to find they were developing a reputation. They also worked well together, so sharing a place to live just seemed logical.

"Bagels and coffee okay for breakfast?" Kate asked as she spied Addie walking down the hallway.

"As long as the coffee is black and hot," Addie replied, sinking into an empty chair. "How long have you been up?"

"Only about an hour. Going to bed early helps. I was exhausted, but I had a good night's sleep, so here you go, breakfast ready and waiting. How about you? What time did you finally go to bed?" Kate sipped a cup of steaming coffee.

"It wasn't much later than you. I just wanted to sit outside for a while, you know, enjoy the night air. It's so quiet, especially after the sun goes down. I thought it would help me relax, which it did, but, you know, just for a minute, I had the strongest sensation that I wasn't alone out there."

"Really, did you see anything?" asked Kate, looking concerned.

"No. I thought I noticed something strange by that big oak near the end of the property line, but it turned out to be just night shadows," Addie said, not sure who she was trying to convince.

"Well, it is pretty isolated out here, Addie. We should probably be careful, at least until we get to know the area better. Maybe we should get a dog."

"Oh, yeah, that's all we need. Us, the workaholics who are never home. The poor thing would go stir crazy. Anyway, that's probably what was staring at me, a dog or some other animal. After all, we are surrounded by woods, and I'm sure it's full of all sorts of things." She shivered. "Anyway, it was probably just my overactive imagination, so I don't think we need Fido yet."

"Good," Kate said. "For a moment, I thought you were going to agree with me, and that would be just one more thing to clean up after." As Kate carried dishes to the sink, the phone began to ring loudly. Reaching up to answer it, she gave a cheerful, "Hello?"

"Hi, Kate, it's Rick. How are you?" announced the deep voice.

"Hey, Rick. I'm fine, and you?"

"Very well, thank you. Is Addie up?"

"Yeah, she finally decided to pull it out of the rack. Hold on, she's right here." Kate handed the phone to Addie and walked away, smiling from ear to ear. Placing the phone to her ear, Addie gave her friend a look that would have struck terror into the heart of a lesser person. Kate only laughed harder.

"Hi, Rick," Addie said. Addie had been friends with the priest at St. Mary's Catholic Church since high school, even going to his ordination. He had been transferred out of town his first year as a priest, but he had returned after the sudden death of his parents in a car accident. He had been at St. Mary's ever since, which suited Addie just fine. Standing about five feet, eleven inches tall, he was ruggedly handsome with overly long black hair for a priest and large, soulful brown eyes that reflected a rare kindness and compassion. Yes, he was something special, which Kate habitually pointed out to her. If it wasn't for the priest part, he would be a great catch for some lucky girl. But as it was, Addie was content to just be his friend and leave it at that—even if Kate had other ideas.

"Are we still on for dinner tonight, before Kate and I hit the club? Or are you calling to cancel yet again, and if so, your excuse better be good!" she said jokingly. They tried to get together at least once or twice a month, but he often cancelled because of parish business.

"Actually, no, I'm not calling to cancel. I'm calling to make sure you're still coming because I was hoping to talk you both out of going to Nightlife tonight, or any other night for a while. Have you seen the news this morning?"

"No. We haven't had the TV on or—"

"Addie, there's been another murder."

Her chest tightened as she remembered the feeling of being spied upon last evening.

"Addie, are you still there?" he asked, his voice rising in concern.

"Yes, I'm here. Tell me what happened."

"Well, details are a bit sketchy, probably because our local law enforcement doesn't want an all-out panic on their hands. But a young couple was murdered last night. Their bodies were found in a park across town about 2 A.M. The young man was brutalized, and his girlfriend had the same marks on her throat as the first victim. Both bodies were completely drained of blood. The media is already calling it the vampire killings. Just what a serial killer loves—an angle for his twisted mind to exploit."

"Oh my God, that's awful. Those poor people. But if it happened across town, why don't you want us to go to the club tonight? Is there some sort of connection?"

"Addie, I talked to a friend who works for the paper. He just happened to be at the club last night. His memory was pretty vague, which is odd if you know him, but he remembers some sort of commotion outside, around closing time. His intuition, which is usually right on, is telling him something went down, and it has something to do with this latest attack. He'd stake his reputation on it. He's going to keep digging and see what else he can come up with, but after talking to him, I just don't think that club is the safest place for two women to be right now."

"Rick, we're big girls now. We know how to be careful," Addie said.

"There's something else you probably should know, and Addie, this is the main reason I think you should avoid that club. My friend gave me another quick call a few minutes ago. He dug up something interesting and, to me at least, very disturbing. The public has yet to be given a description of the murdered women, but Nick got the information. Both women had long, dark hair, brown eyes, and were about five feet, three inches tall. Sound like anyone we know?" There was no mistaking the concern in his voice.

The hair on the back of her neck began to tingle. She tried to shake it off, blaming it on nerves.

"What are you getting at? What's so significant about that? A lot of women around here have long, dark hair and brown eyes." She was a little irritated with him for being overprotective, but she knew it was his way of showing he cared.

"You don't think that's a strange coincidence, Addie? We could have a serial killer on our hands who has a personal reason for not liking women with dark hair and eyes. If that's the case, it puts anyone who fits that description in danger, right?"

"Look, I appreciate your concern, Rick, but aren't you being a bit overdramatic? And to answer your question earlier, yes, we're still going out tonight. I'm not going to hide under a rock because I have the same coloring as two murder victims who were obviously attacked by some nutcase! Has your informant heard anything about the club closing because of what happened?"

"Well, no, but—"

"There, you see. Actually, it's probably the safest place to be tonight. It will be crawling with police and club security. What killer in his right mind would show up under those circumstances?" Still, this latest news had made her a little apprehensive. But she wouldn't admit that to Rick.

"Um, Addie, that's the whole point. This person isn't in his right mind, but that's not going to make any difference to you, is it?" he replied.

"Please, Rick, do—"

"Alright, I give up. There's no point in wasting my breath on any further discussion, but both of you be careful tonight and stay alert. Don't go wandering off alone anywhere. My friend will keep me informed of any new developments, and I'll pass on the information."

"Okay, Father," she teased, trying to lighten the mood. "We'll see you later for a nice dinner, and Rick, thanks for being so concerned. I do appreciate it, really."

She could just make out the sound of a deep sigh as he replied, "You know it's only because I care about you both, so don't give me a reason to worry."

As she hung up the phone, she couldn't shake the feeling that the nightmare was just beginning.

"What was that all about?" asked Kate, noticing the look on her friend's face. "It seemed like an awfully intense conversation."

"There's been another murder. Well, actually two this time."

"What? Not again! Where did it happen this time?"

"In some park across town," Addie said. "But a friend of Rick's was at Nightlife last night and thinks something was going on there, too. His friend thinks the two incidents are connected. Rick doesn't think it's a good idea to go there tonight."

"I gathered that much from your conversation. Do they have any leads? Everything was so hush-hush with the first murder it was like it never happened."

"According to Rick, it's the same thing this time. Maybe if the media kept the public informed, people would be more cautious and alert, and things like this wouldn't happen so often!" Addie repeated Rick's description of the murdered women, but she tried to make light of the situation. "Next thing you know, he'll be telling me to dye my hair!"

"You know how he is, Addie. We're the closest thing he has to family around here, so he's being a little overprotective, but maybe he has good reason. What if he's right and there is some sort of pattern? Maybe we shouldn't go there tonight."

"Are we supposed to stop living because some maniac seems to have an issue with women who have dark hair? Come on, Kate, be practical. We have a good police force, and as I told Rick, they'll probably be crawling all over that club tonight. They haven't shut it down, so they must think it's safe enough. We just have to use common sense and be extra cautious." She began to walk from the room, and then turned back to her friend, "Maybe we should buy some mace, though. What do you think?"

Both girls burst out laughing.

"We're not worried, are we?" replied Kate with a smile. "Come on, I've got some things to do in town before I can go anywhere. I'm going to make a quick run to the grocery store. It's my turn to buy. Need anything?"

"No, thanks, I'll clean up a little and do some laundry. You go ahead and go. I thought, since it's such a beautiful day, that I'd take a nice long walk, maybe grab my camera and take some pictures for the wall. The scenery is so beautiful around here, and maybe, if I wander far enough, I just might get a few outside shots of the grand mansion. Possibly even of our mysterious neighbor. What do you think?" she said, smiling mischievously.

"Good idea and good luck. It seems that our mystery man likes his privacy," Kate said. She paused in the hallway. "Just be careful roaming around alone. I don't want to be the one to tell Rick if anything happens to you."

"Nothing's going to happen to me," Addie said, "so leave if you're going, we don't have all day. We have to meet him at six, and if we're late he may call out the cavalry."

Addie went through the house, doing what little cleaning there was to be done. After dropping a load of clothes in the washer, she ran to her room and changed into a pair of old jeans and a T-shirt. Slipping a digital camera around her neck, she went outside and locked the front door behind her. Running down the sidewalk, she reached a gravel road. The narrow roadway wrapped around the side of their small house before continuing up the hill behind it, through the woods, and all the way to the main house on the cliff high above.

She took a few shots of the cottage before starting down the road. Whoever had done the gardening before had a talent for blending formal beds with natural beauty. Dozens of tulips burst forth in a rainbow of color on either side of the front walk. A rose bush, pink buds ready to burst forth, climbed a white trellis on either side of the front steps. Beds of wildflowers surrounded the house, left to grow untamed and bordered only by a neat wall of small rocks. It really was breathtaking and filled her with wonder as she started heading toward the old stone bridge halfway up the large hill.

Reaching the bridge, she leaned over the side of the wall, the stones starting to crumble in a few places. She was surprised to see that the tiny stream flowing underneath was teeming with all sorts of fish. "My own little paradise," she thought, continuing her climb, snapping pictures as she went. Across the bridge, the woods became a little thicker and edged closer to the gravel road.

Apprehension preyed on her mind. Maybe she shouldn't be wandering around alone. What if someone was hiding behind one of the many thick trees on either side of the road? What if …?

"Oh, for heaven's sake, it's broad daylight. There's nothing here to be afraid of, so relax and enjoy the day," she told herself. God, what was wrong with her? She had never been a scaredy cat, but lately, everything seemed to put her nerves on edge. She walked about a mile further before the woods ended abruptly and the road continued into a small clearing. The scene before her nearly took her breath away as the great mansion came into full view.

The house was Gothic in style, made of solid stone, with massive towers on each of its four corners. A large door of solid oak was set back under what looked like a small portico. A lush lawn of emerald green flowed right up to the building itself, but, unlike the cottage, the only color surrounding this house came from rose bushes. There were hundreds of them, in one color only: blood red. She let her breath out slowly, overwhelmed by the beauty of the place as she snapped picture after picture.

Occupied as she was, she failed to notice the dark blur advancing toward her from the corner of the house, until finally she caught movement from the corner of her eye. The large black shadow bounded toward her, its deep growl filling her ears. She turned instantly and ran headlong for the gravel road that led to the safety of her own home. She wasn't sure she would make it in time, but she would try like hell. She imagined she could actually feel the ground shake as the creature came after her, closing the gap inch by inch, until she heard another sound.

"Brutus, heel!"

The running behind her abruptly ceased. Coming to a stop herself, she bent over with her hands on her thighs to catch her breath. After a few minutes, she straightened, and with as much trepidation as curiosity, she turned around. She found herself locking eyes with the largest dog she had ever seen. The huge black animal stood like an iron lawn ornament—a very large lawn ornament—and watched her intently. Its head had to be higher than her waist. The dog fell back on its haunches as a tall man who was built like a professional wrestler came up behind it. He had a rifle in one hand and rested the other on the dog's massive head.

"Stay!" the man commanded. To Addie, he said in a stern voice as if scolding a small child, "You're trespassing on private property, miss. Did you need help with something, or have you just lost your way?"

"No, no, listen, I'm sorry, I really didn't mean to intrude. It's just … it was such a nice day … I live in the cottage," she stammered, turning to point, needlessly, in the direction of her home. Taking a deep breath to calm herself, she continued her explanation. "I was out for a walk and thought I'd take some pictures. The house and grounds are so beautiful. I really am sorry. I meant no harm, and I didn't mean to intrude. I'll just go back now … it won't happen again."

She saw another man along the far side of the house, pistol in hand stop to watch their conversation. "Why would they need such tight security for a manor house," she wondered.

There was a long moment of silence as the first man seemed to be assessing the situation, eyeing her up and down, before he signaled to his companion that all was well. The whole thing was beginning to anger her, and she stared intently back at him, giving him a taste of his own medicine. He was an extremely large man, with bulging muscles and a shaved head. But his size was not the most disturbing thing about him. No, indeed. It was the three guns he carried. Along with the rifle, he wore a shoulder holster with a gun under each arm. "I'll bet he was a marine at some point in his life," she thought.

"Did you say you were from the cottage?" he asked. His voice was not quite as stern. As a matter of fact, he sounded almost friendly.

"Yes, I did."

"Well, then, I have to apologize for frightening you, Brutus and I both," he said, nodding toward the dog that was now half asleep in the cool grass.

"That's alright," she replied with a smile as she looked at the dog. "I think he's lost interest in me now. He is huge, though. What kind of dog is he?"

"Mastiff, and don't let his lazy demeanor fool you. These animals were originally valued as fierce guard dogs as well as strong fighters. I've seen him take down a man twice my size in a matter of seconds. Brutus here has been trained for security, and he does what he's told. We've been having some trouble with ..." he hesitated a moment, giving her a strange look before he continued, "poaching lately. The owner has taken to patrolling the area so the next time you decide to visit, you may want to ask permission first, okay, miss?"

"Well, I guess that was a tactful dismissal if I ever heard one," she thought.

"Thank you, I will, and, again, I apologize for intruding," she said out loud. "But how do I ask permission if I don't know how to reach the owner?" she muttered under her breath as she turned back to the cottage.

"Miss!" the man called after her, "just so you know, the owner has asked us to patrol all the way to the cottage because the properties are so close, so don't be alarmed if you notice us during our rounds."

"How will I know it's your men and not some poacher?" she asked, a little concerned with this new development. "And will they all have dogs? You know he is pretty alarming."

A large grin spread across his stern face, which made her wonder in amazement, "This guy's just a big teddy bear, unless he's pissed off."

"All our men are in uniform," he said, indicating his khaki pants and shirt with a large brown bar on each shoulder. "And there is only one Brutus. He's master of this domain, and just between you and me, he's a sucker for a pretty face. A dog biscuit and a pat on the head and he's yours to command. Come back for a sec and I'll show you."

"Oh, I don't know," she said, a little hesitant, but she let him grab her hand and lead her to the dog. He really was a magnificent animal, although a deep growl escaped him at her approach.

"Now, Brutus, say hello to the pretty lady, and she'll give you a treat," he said, shoving a biscuit into her hand. "Just say 'Heel' and give him this."

Normally, she was very good with dogs, but this one was so large that it was hard to control her nerves, but she did as he told her. To her great surprise, the growling stopped immediately as the dog sniffed the bone, gently taking it from her hand. She stroked the large head, much to the dog's pleasure, and soon the beast was licking her hand.

"Well, that's a relief," she said, smiling. "I kind of like having two hands." At his soft laugh, she realized something, "I'm sorry, I didn't even ask you your name."

"Brian, miss, at your service."

"And I'm Adrianna. Well, it was nice meeting you, Brian, even under these rather odd circumstances. Since I've obviously taken up too much of your time, I'll let you get back to work."

"Enjoy the rest of your day." he said.

"I will. Bye now." Turning, she ran the rest of the way to the cottage, bursting through the front door out of breath and exhausted. Kate had not returned, so she headed upstairs for a long soak in a hot tub while she tried to make sense of the morning—or was it afternoon? Surprised, she realized she'd lost all track of time. It was nearly one in the afternoon! "Boy, time does fly when you're having fun," she thought as she grabbed a change of clothes and headed for the bathroom. An hour later, as she was having a second cup of coffee, Kate entered the kitchen, her arms full of packages.

"Isn't this the very same spot I left you in this morning?" she questioned as she set the groceries on the kitchen table.

Peeking inside the bags, Addie replied, "No, it isn't. I was over there by the sink, if you want to be specific. And, for your information, I actually had a very interesting morning."

"Really? You can fill me in while I put these away," Kate said, starting to shove cans into the cupboards. "Come on let's hear about your great adventure."

"I met our neighbor ... well, one of them, at least," Addie said, enjoying the confused look on Kate's face. "It seems we may have a small army living up there."

"Are you serious?" said Kate, flopping into a nearby chair.

"Extremely."

"Don't stop there. How many people are we talking about, and more importantly, are any of them good-looking and male?" Addie had to laugh. Her friend did have a one-track mind, and it was focused largely on the opposite sex.

"I can't answer your first question as I was a little too preoccupied to give him the third degree, but the answer to the second is a definite yes." Addie proceeded to fill Kate in on her visit with Brian and, of course, Brutus. She enjoyed herself immensely as she watched Kate's eyes grow to twice their normal size.

"Wow! Everything happens when I'm not around. But he did say we could visit, right?" Kate asked, looking hopeful.

"Yes, only there's a catch," Addie said. "We have to call first and let them know we're coming. Now, you tell me how we do that when we don't have a phone number. I can't believe I didn't think to ask him for that at least, or the name of the person we need to notify."

"I think you made great progress. At least now we have a contact in the great house. It's a start," Kate laughingly told her.

On a more serious note, Addie said, "Yes, contact has been made, but … I don't know, Kate. When you think back over everything, doesn't it all seem a bit odd?"

"Odd? How?"

"Well, for one thing, is all that firepower really necessary for a few poachers? I saw a small arsenal, Kate. Are these people really that dangerous? And they're patrolling near our property, too. I don't know if I'm comfortable with that," she said.

"What other reason could there be for armed guards at an old manor house? There hasn't been anything dangerous happening out here we should be concerned abo … oh my God! The murders! That has to be it. The owner doesn't trust the police to keep his family safe so he's taking matters into his own hands. Sounds like a smart man to me," Kate said.

"Don't you think that's a little extreme?" Addie pointed out.

"Well, maybe," Kate said, "but think about it, Addie. It may be a little over the top, but the police haven't had much luck finding the people responsible for these attacks. If our elusive neighbor does have a family to worry about, he might feel safer with his own security, and if he protects us in the process, well, who are we to complain?"

Kate's theory made Addie think of something else. "Kate, remember when I told you I thought someone was watching me last night? What if it was one of these so-called poachers, or whatever it is they're really looking for? What if it is something dangerous and it was near our house?"

"I didn't think of that," Kate replied, but after a second she laughed. "Oh, come on now, Addie let's not jump to any more ridiculous conclusions. I've already come up with enough for one afternoon. Whatever the problem, our neighbor seems to be taking care of it, and he's including us in his plans. We just have to be a little more alert ourselves and take some extra precautions. No more leaving doors and windows unlocked, and we'll leave on some extra lights in the evening, especially outside. That should do for starters. Now, give me another cup of coffee, and let's talk about tonight. We've been working hard for weeks, and we're going to relax and have some fun. Forget about poachers, vampire killers and anything else unpleasant. That's an order." Kate pounded a fist on the table for emphasis.

"The plan is a simple one. We meet Rick for much-needed sustenance then we go dancing to work it off. How's that sound?" Addie laughed as she poured the steaming liquid into a cup.

"Sounds good to me. We have just enough time to get ourselves up to club standard then we can leave."

"Okay, okay. Well, I'm already one step ahead of you. My bath is finished. The bathroom is all yours."

Later that evening, as she was dressing for their night out, Addie sat before the mirror of her newly restored vanity, wondering if she wasn't taking this seriously enough. Strange things were happening—and not only in town, but right in her backyard!

"Both of the murdered women had long brown hair and eyes."

Rick's words echoed in her mind as she stared at herself in the mirror. She began to wonder if it really was a good idea to go to the club tonight. Maybe this particular maniac did have some twisted obsession with dark-haired women. Maybe he would be back to try again. Maybe they hadn't beefed up police patrols, and maybe she should wear her hair up tonight. Maybe, maybe, maybe!

"Oh, for heaven's sake, maybe you're just being silly!" she told herself, pushing away from the vanity and reaching for the outfit on the bed. Taking a deep breath, she tried to get back the feeling of excitement a night out usually gave her. She loved spending time with her friends, something both girls had been neglecting since they'd bought the cottage—but that was going to change starting tonight. "Life shouldn't be all work and no play. It tends to make you cranky," she thought as she dressed in a black and white floral skirt with a matching black lace camisole.

She checked her image once again in the mirror, satisfied with the reflection staring back at her. Both girls had decided it would be a great idea to wear something from their own shop. "Nothing like a little free advertising," she thought, smiling. Yes, her good mood was returning. She was going to have a great time tonight if it killed her!

"Oops, wrong choice of words," she said out loud as she stepped into the hallway in search of Kate.

"Talking to ourselves, are we? Wow, Addie, that outfit looks even better on you than it did on the rack!"

"Umm, thanks, I guess. And I'll return the compliment. That color really suits you," she replied, admiring the way the burnt orange peasant top and matching wide-legged pants complimented her friends flowing, red locks.

"My thoughts exactly. We really did get lucky on that last buying trip. We made some great purchases, but if we don't stop bringing them home, the shop will never make a profit!" Addie laughingly agreed, and they left to meet Rick for dinner, making sure to lock front door behind them.

Driving down the gravel road, the two women failed to notice the vehicle parked along the dirt path leading into the woods a few yards from the cottage. Hidden eyes watched their every move as a lone figure sat still and silent. One moment he appeared almost lifeless, the next his vehicle roared to life and he was off like a shot. He had decided to try the human way tonight. He loved the feel of so much power under his control as the car sped after its quarry. Although they were a few miles ahead, like the zoom lens of an expensive camera, his powerful eyes allowed him to keep the two women easily in sight.

He could play this game of cat and mouse for a little while. He would follow his prey all night long if need be, but in the end, the outcome would be the same. One victim would finally be delivered into the hands—or claws—of his father. The other would fall before him, a fitting reward for doing his lord and master's bidding.

Chapter 4

Winwood was a quaint New England town about 150 miles outside the great city of New York. Though small, it offered a welcome alternative to the noise and chaos of the larger city with its quaint antique shops, coffee shops, boutiques, and, of course, restaurants with award-winning cuisine.

The Chateau was one of those restaurants. Once the home of a silent screen star, the beautiful Victorian mansion had been purchased several years ago by a wealthy businessman. Fulfilling his retirement dream, he'd had the place completely remodeled, turning it into one of the most exclusive dinner establishments in the area. Staying true to the period, its beautiful decor and lovely antiques, as well as its world-famous chef, were favorites with the local patrons. The long lines on most weekends were proof of that. Luckily, Rick had made reservations well in advance, and as the girls entered the restaurant, he waved to them from a table in the far corner of the room. They noticed he was not alone.

"Hmmm, what an interesting looking young man," Kate observed with a twinkle in her eye.

"Behave, Kate, and don't embarrass Rick."

"Who, me?" she replied with an innocent look as Addie shook her head and smiled.

"Here they are," Rick said to his companion, rising to greet the women. "You both look very nice tonight, as usual." He kissed them both on the cheek and held each woman's chair in turn.

"Thank you," they replied in unison.

"I'm starving," Kate announced.

"Again, as usual," Rick replied, smiling. "Adrianna, Kate, this is my friend Nick Anderson, the reporter I was telling you about." He looked meaningfully at Addie. "He works for the *Daily Gazette*." Nick was a very studious looking young man in his early thirties with sun-bleached blond hair and enormous, startled green eyes. Nick flashed them a quick, easy grin as he shook their outstretched hands, and Adrianna decided she liked him immediately.

"It's a pleasure to meet you, Nick," she said, giving him a ready smile.

"Likewise," said Kate when her turn came to shake his hand.

"The pleasure's all mine," he said.

Rick motioned to the waitress, who came to take their drink orders. When she left, Addie couldn't wait any longer to ask the question she'd been dying to ask since her phone conversation with Rick that morning. "Were you able to find out anything more about last night's attack?"

The two men exchanged a look before Nick replied, "Not much, I'm afraid. It's a very strange case, and trying to get any information from the powers that be is like pulling teeth. I did hear that the police have never had an MO quite like this one before. They have very few leads, so they're keeping things on the down low until they have something more concrete to go on. I guess it wouldn't do to let the public know they're stumped, and given the strangeness of the few things we do know, the police are afraid some vigilante will take matters into their own hands. We would have chaos on our hands if a witch hunts gets started."

"Rick said you thought that something happened at Nightlife last night and it may be connected to the latest attack. Were you able to follow up on that at all?" Addie asked.

Looking around to make sure no one was within hearing distance, Nick leaned in closer.

"Actually, I did luck out a bit on that subject," he said. "A friend of mine called this afternoon. He was in a state because he said the police were on the wrong track concerning last night's murder. He wanted my opinion about giving them some information he had, or thought he had. He said he'd stopped by the club about one to pick up a friend. They were just leaving the parking lot when he heard someone scream. He stopped to listen, but everything had gone very quiet. The next thing he knew, a large group of people came out of the club. They seemed in an awful hurry to get to the park across the street. When he looked in the direction of a group of trees, which seemed to be their destination, all he could make out was a dark figure in the distance. And this is where it gets interesting."

"You're kidding, right?" Kate asked.

"Shhh, Kate, let him finish," Addie scolded.

"As I was saying, this is where it gets interesting and a little strange. The group from the club seemed to be talking to this dark figure hidden in the shadows. They talked for only a few seconds when all of a sudden there was this small … whirlwind is the only word he could think of to describe it. Then poof! The figure just disappeared right before my friend's eyes."

"What? But that's impossible," said Addie. "No one just disappears into thin air."

"Exactly what I said, but my friend insisted that's what he saw. Anyway, by then a large crowd of patrons from the club had gathered to see what was happening. When a few men from the first group, my buddy assumed they were club security, noticed the gathering crowd they seemed agitated. A few of them approached the onlookers, and the next thing he knew, everyone just left. Just like that. As if nothing at all had happened. No one questioned the screams they'd heard or the strange little cyclone appearing out of nowhere or the disappearing man. Nothing! It freaked my buddy out. Call it instinct, intuition, whatever you want, but something told him to leave, and fast, before anyone realized what he had seen. This morning, when he heard about the murder across town, he couldn't shake the feeling there was some connection to the incident at the club. I told him to talk to the police and let them decide what to do with the information. Hopefully he took my advice.
"

"Smart move," Rick replied. "Now do you understand why I'm not comfortable with you going to that place tonight?"

Both girls were staring at Nick as if mesmerized, until Kate, snapping out of it, decided to change the subject before an enjoyable evening turned melancholy.

"Yes, Rick, we do understand. Now, enough of this talk. We appreciate your concern, but Addie and I agreed we're not going to live in a plastic bubble just because some nutcase is on the loose. Nick's friend isn't even sure that what he saw at the club last night had anything to do with the murders—the murders we've been told happened in a totally different part of town. Now, I'm beginning to lose my appetite, which is not a good thing. Here come our drinks, so let's order some food before I fade to a mere shadow of my former self."

"Well, we certainly can't have that," Rick said, trying to hide his frustration as they gave their dinner orders to the waitress. "Besides, I've already said my piece on the subject, and Nick has filled you in as best he can, so all I'll ask is that you promise me you'll both be careful tonight."

"We will," Addie said, reaching over to squeeze his hand. "Please try not to worry. We'll stay together, no wandering off alone, and we'll keep our wits about us. Now, change of subject so we can enjoy dinner."

The next two hours flew by. Nick's strange sense of humor had them all laughing so hard they could hardly eat their meals. When they were finished, Rick insisted on walking them to their car. After good-bye hugs, he tried repeating his warning, "Now remember—"

"We know, we know ... be careful," both women said in unison, laughing.

"It's not a joke, Addie," he said. "There's a nutcase out there preying on women. No one is safe until he's caught. Please try to take this a little more seriously, for my sake if not your own." Seeing the look on her friend's face, Addie immediately regretted her flippant remark.

"I'm sorry, Rick, really," she said. "We do take it seriously. I was just trying to add a little levity into a stressful situation. If we let fear control us, we impede our ability to fight back, and I won't let some maniac control my life."

"I know, just be a little more cautious. Anger, as well as fear, can make you careless."

"He's right, you know," Nick said. "Are you off to the club now?"

"No, not just yet. We have to stop at the boutique and check on a few things first. We have a new employee, Kim. It's her first time closing alone, so I'd like to check on her and make sure there are no problems," Addie said.

"I'm going to the club myself tonight," Nick said, looking at Rick. "Think I'll do a little more snooping of my own, so maybe I'll see you both there."

"Great," both girls replied.

"Good night, Rick. I'll call you tomorrow," Addie said, giving him another hug before climbing into the waiting car.

"Bye for now," Kate said, waving.

Rick watched as they climbed into the car, sighing deeply as they drove away, wishing he could rid himself of the nagging fear in the pit of his stomach.

"I'll keep an eye on them from a distance, so they won't think we're spying on them. Try not to worry. If I find out anything more, I'll let you know," Nick told his friend as he climbed into his own car.

"Thanks. I'll talk to you soon." But as the troubled priest turned to walk to his own car, a feeling of unease came over him, as if eyes were boring deep into his back. Turning quickly, he surveyed the parking lot and the surrounding street but saw nothing out of the ordinary. Maybe Addie was right. He was letting fear rule him. "And that has to stop," he told himself as he slid into his car. Heading back to the rectory, he was so preoccupied that he failed to notice the sleek black Porsche that exited the parking lot after him turning to follow Addie's car.

The boutique was five minutes away from the restaurant, in a prime location on the town's main street. Pulling into the parking lot, they noticed that only Kim's car remained. A strange prickling feeling came over Addie as she turned off the engine.

"Is something wrong?" Kate asked when she noticed Addie shivering slightly.

"Huh? Oh no, it's nothing. I think Rick just has me a little freaked out. Wasn't Nancy supposed to also work tonight?"

"I thought so," replied Kate. "Maybe it was slow and Kim felt she didn't need her."

"Yeah, maybe."

Unlocking the front door, they entered the shop and relocked the door behind them.

"Safety first." Addie smiled at Kate.

"And they think we aren't careful," Kate replied. The shop was open between the hours of 10 AM to 9 PM on weekdays, closing at five on Saturday. The business was doing well enough that Kate and Addie had decided Sunday was a permanent day off for everyone. It also gave them a day alone in the shop to set up new displays or fit in a quick buying trip. Addie noticed right away that everything had already been put back in its proper place on display tables or hung neatly on racks. "Kim seems to be very efficient," she thought, pleased with their decision to hire her.

"Kim, are you still here?"

"Hey, Addie, Kate. I was just about to lock the safe," said a petite young girl with short brown curls and large black eyes as she poked her head out of the back office.

"Everything looks great. Did you have any problems on your first night closing?" Addie asked her.

"None worth mentioning. One customer was a little difficult, but Nancy charmed her into buying three beautiful suits, so it all worked out well. Oh, we did have a rather strange incident about an hour before closing."

"There's that prickling sensation," Addie thought as the hair on the back of her neck stood on end.

"What do you mean by strange?" she asked

"Well, you know we don't get very many male customers. About an hour ago, a man walked in, and you know, Addie, I don't usually let people bother me, but this guy ... well, let's just say he sent chills up and down my spine."

"Why? What was wrong with him? Or was he just creepy looking?" Kate asked.

"No, he was handsome enough. In fact, he was almost too handsome ... so perfect it was unnatural, so, of course, he caught our attention, but the minute I saw those eyes ..." she let it trail off, the fear in her own eyes unmistakable.

"Kim ..."

"Addie, his eyes were solid black. No pupils, no whites like everyone else, just deep, soulless black, like midnight with no chance of daylight," she said, and she actually shivered. "I asked if I could help him, and he stared for a moment. Then he said something about 'just looking,' but since there was someone as good-looking as me to talk to, he might just stick around a while.' I told him we were getting ready to close. That was when he became a little … difficult. Nancy knew we were going to have a problem, so she called Ed from the men's shop across the street and he came right over. When our friend took one look at Ed's six-foot-two, 230-pound frame, he just flashed this evil grin and walked slowly out the door. Ed stuck around for a while, but our visitor never returned, so we started to close up shop." Then she tried to lighten the mood. "Other than that incident, we had a really good day. We were very busy in the morning, with a steady flow of customers almost all day. They were very impressed with the merchandise from your last trip to New York."

"I told you that line would sell well," Kate said, trying to get everyone back in good spirits.

"I wrote out an order for a few things we've sold out of, but Nancy and I had everything pretty much under control by 8:30 so I told her to leave, probably not a smart move on my part, but I was just about to do the same," the girl said, looking tired.

"Talk about perfect timing," Addie said. "We'll wait so you don't have to walk to your car alone."

"Thanks, that would be great. I was a little nervous after that guy was in here. Probably should have had Nancy stay. By the way, did you hear there's been another murder?"

"Actually, there were two, and yes, we've heard. We probably should have a meeting with all the employees on Monday. We need to discuss some safety measures. Come up with some scheduling plan so no one is ever here alone, especially at night, at least for a little while," Addie said as they left the store, locking the door behind them. Everyone was silent as they walked across the darkened parking lot to their waiting cars. Addie thought she should look into getting another security light installed.

"Addie, you don't think our strange visitor could be connected in any way to the murders, do you?" Kim asked.

"Anything is possible when you're dealing with someone as unstable as the one responsible for such horrible acts of violence. There's a security agency not far from The Chateau. I'll stop by in the morning and see if we can hire someone to patrol, even if it's only in the evenings. You're opening again in the morning with Nancy, right Kim?"

"Yes, bright and early."

"Well, try not to worry. I'll come by after I've gone to the agency."

"Okay, thanks again," the girl called after them and waved. Waving in return as she climbed into her own vehicle, Addie drove out of the parking lot and headed for the nightclub.

Just as Kim was about to turn the key in the ignition, she exclaimed, "Damn!" She suddenly remembered a package she had left back in the shop. Sighing deeply, she turned off the car and headed back toward the building, muttering as she walked. She couldn't help but notice the silence. It was so quiet … there was not a car around, not a person in sight, not even a cricket chirping. She quickened her pace.

Eyes watched the girl's every movement, the scent of blood and fresh meat filling the creature's nostrils.

She walked a little faster, the hair on the back of her neck standing on end. Something was very wrong. Looking around, but seeing nothing out of the ordinary, she kept going, almost at a run and nearly losing her supper as a baby rabbit scurried across the parking lot directly in front of her.

"Shit! Come on, girl, get a grip! You're being paranoid!" she told herself, laughing nervously as she unlocked the shop door. Running inside, she went straight to the service desk near the rear of the store, not waiting to hear the lock click behind her and not bothering to turn on the lights. Reaching under the counter, she retrieved the small package and turned quickly to dart back toward the door when she thought she heard … no, it couldn't be … a deep growling. She froze, unable to move, unable to run.

"Who's there?" she whispered, barely able to speak as she slowly forced her foot forward. She sensed movement behind her. "Oh, please," she prayed, "someone help me. I'm not ready to die."

She had only a split second to see the huge, black form come leaping toward her before she felt the agonizing pain of something sharp tearing into her throat, trapping the scream she never had a chance to utter.

Outside, a dark figure stood alone, his tall form blending with the shadows. An evil smile split the handsome face as he listened to the sounds of a woman dying. "Since my brother seems to be well occupied, it is time I sought my own entertainment," he spoke aloud to no one in particular.

But first, he knew he must return to the club and finish the task his father had assigned to him. She would be there tonight, the one his father sought. Of that he was certain. He had watched as the two women drove away only minutes before. Yes, he would find her there tonight, and after delivering her to his father, he would have the one with the flaming hair for himself

Chapter 5

By eleven that evening, Addie and Kate found themselves walking toward the front door of the hottest spot in town ... Nightlife. The club owners were something of a mystery, proving to be elusive during the initial construction phase, much to the chagrin of the media. But being resourceful, the press did manage to uncover a few bits of information. The visible partner, if she could be called that considering that very few people had actually seen her, was Sonya Simone. She was supposedly a woman of exceptional beauty, with gold-red hair flowing halfway down her back and eyes as black as ebony.

Her silent partner was even more secretive, managing to totally elude the press, which made reporters work even harder to uncover the slightest bit of information. So far, they'd had little success.

The secretive partners had purchased a historic movie house on the town's main street and, after extensive remodeling, had thrown a gala grand opening celebration about a month before. The renovators had tried to stay true to the original structure, with awe-inspiring results. The elegance of the Victorian decor attracted the wealthy, and even a few celebrities, from the big city.

This was the first chance Addie and Kate had to finally see the place. Having heard so much about it from employees, they were excited and had every intention of thoroughly enjoying themselves as they climbed the elegant, black marble steps to the main entrance.

Both girls tried not to stare as ushers held opened the exquisitely designed stained glass doors. Both ushers were extremely tall. But whereas one was fair, with long blond hair and clear blue eyes, the other was dark, with black hair cut close to his scalp and long lashes framing deep brown eyes. "Beautiful" was not a word Addie would have used to describe any man, but it was the only one that fit the perfect features both men possessed.

Yet, as gorgeous as they were, she couldn't help feeling a little uncomfortable as she walked between them, feeling their eyes on her the whole time. "Is it just me they seem to be watching so closely," she wondered. Stopping for a moment, she turned to look back at the entrance. Swarms of chattering people pushed through the doorway. She noticed the doormen staring intently at everyone who came through the door, as if they were searching for someone—or something. The description of Kim's tormentor from the shop flashed through her mind.

"If even half the men here tonight are as good-looking as those two we're going to have a great time," Kate said, making Addie jump. Still, Addie couldn't help but smile despite the uneasiness she was feeling,

"Somehow I knew that's what you were going to say."

"What, you don't agree? Have you ever seen such hunks in your life?"

"No," Addie replied, laughing softly. "You're absolutely right. We are going to have a great time, so let's get started."

"Damn straight. Let's find a few of the beautiful people for ourselves," Kate said as they moved further into the room.

Sparkling chandeliers made from the finest crystal hung high above their heads, giving the large, crowded room a luxurious atmosphere. Two long bars on either side of the glistening mahogany dance floor were surrounded by booths of various shapes and sizes. The second floor was an exact replica of the first, except for the wrought iron balcony, newly stripped and painted, circling the entire room. It was packed with patrons eating, drinking, and generally having a good time.

Adrianna studied the smiling faces around her. No one seemed concerned; no one seemed worried. In fact, the thought that any of the people drinking and laughing there tonight could be the next victim of a crazed serial killer never seemed to enter anyone's mind. "Life goes on," she thought. There did seem to be a lot of security. Men and women in red shirts and black pants were scattered throughout the club, watching the throngs of people intently, just like the two men at the front door. That must be it. Even though the doormen were dressed in black tuxedos instead of the red and black, they were still employees and, given all that had been happening, it made sense to be on high alert.

Addie felt herself beginning to relax as she watched couples gyrate vigorously to a popular song. She and Kate carefully maneuvered their way through the crowd, looking for an empty table or booth where they could sit and order a drink.

"Oh, excuse me," Addie apologized as she was pushed into the path of a man heading in the opposite direction. He grabbed her gently, strong hands keeping her from stumbling as she lifted her head up and up, for he was at least six feet, four inches tall. She found herself staring into the most amazing blue-grey eyes she had ever seen. A jolt shot through her entire body, rooting her to the spot. "What was that?" she wondered as he stared down at her with those beautiful eyes.

"I'm sorry, have we met before?" he asked, his voice deep and sensual.

It took her a full minute to come to her senses before she could respond. "No, no … I don't think so. I'm sure I would have remembered." She laughed a little nervously.

"I know I would have," he said, a smile appearing on his handsome face that almost took her breath away. He turned and walked away through the crowd.

"Oh my God! Who was that?" Kate said, looking almost as dumbstruck as Addie.

"I have no idea, but I'm making it my goal tonight to find out," Addie replied, turning slightly to glance behind her. He was standing in the midst of the crowd, returning her gaze. She saw him smile again, nodding his head slightly as he turned and continued walking.

"That's my girl," she heard Kate say.

"Addie! Kate!"

They turned to see two friends from the coffee shop down the street from their boutique motioning for them to join their table. Waving, they worked their way through the ever-thickening crowd. Three steps up from the main floor took them to the rounded booth, where they had the best view of everything going on around them.

"You better sit with us," said a girl with short blonde hair named Lisa. "It's really packed tonight."

"Great, thanks. It's a good thing you two were here, or we might have been standing all night," Addie said as they slid into the booth next to the other two girls. "I had no idea this place attracted this kind of crowd, or we would have been here earlier. Is it always like this?"

"On the weekends, most definitely," Lisa said. "We come almost every weekend, and Joyce and I always get here early to get our favorite booth because the place fills up quickly. This booth has the best view."

"You would think, with all that's been happening lately, less people would come. That certainly doesn't seem to be the case," said Joyce, a very pretty girl with long, sandy brown hair, laughing. "Neither rain, nor sleet, nor snow … nor crazy serial killers can keep us away."

"Yes, it will take more than a few murders to stop Joyce in her quest for the perfect male," Lisa said as a waitress came to take their drink order.

She was also very tall, making Addie wonder if "giant" was one of the job requirements at this place. Addie also noticed the girl had what she could only describe as an aura that seemed to draw the attention of everyone, male and female. She had long blonde hair, very pale skin, and ruby lips, but it was her eyes that seemed to hold people. They were a deep, penetrating, dark green. Addie felt mesmerized as those eyes stared into hers; she was unable to pull her gaze away until the girl broke eye contact and walked gracefully away to get their drinks. A little confused, Addie blinked a few times to clear her head, wondering what had just happened.

Focusing her attention on her friends, she noticed Kate was already deep in conversation with a man who had just walked past their booth. As she scanned the crowd, a familiar face passed through the sea of people and she waved in greeting. Nick, their new reporter friend, smiled enthusiastically and waved back as he pointed to something partially hidden in the pocket of his jacket. "Is that a camera?" Addie wondered, but he was too far away for her to be certain.

"I see our friend Nick is hard at work," Kate whispered in her ear.

"Always in search of that Pulitzer prize, I guess."

She continued to scan the crowd until she noticed something odd. Was it just her imagination, or were people stopping to stare at her as they moved past her booth? She would have thought little of it if it had happened only once, but it happened on at least three different occasions, with three different people.

"Where is that waitress with my drink?" she thought. She needed a good strong cocktail to chase away the fantasies filling her overworked mind. Turning to the bar to see if her drink was on its way, her gaze fell upon a man seated in deep shadow in the far corner of the room. This time she was positive it was not her imagination. His eyes were on her alone! He actually leaned forward to get a better look as she met his penetrating gaze. He was a handsome enough man, she noticed, but something about him made her shiver in fear.

"Is everything okay?" Kate asked, noticing the look on her friend's face.

Addie replied with a forced smile, not wanting to concern her friend. "Everything is fine. I've been working too much lately. I guess I'm just a little tired. We really have to make an effort to get out more. Relaxing shouldn't be this hard." Her gaze returned to the back of the room, but the man was gone.

"Here, here," said Kate as she reached for the drink that had just been set before her.

"Do you know her?" Joyce asked, noticing the waitress's preoccupation with Adrianna.

"Never met her before in my life," Addie replied as she sipped her drink.

"Well, she sure was sizing you up."

"Yeah, I noticed."

"Awe, she's probably jealous because you look so great tonight, but there are plenty of good-looking guys to go around. If she seems interested in one in particular, Addie promises not to mesmerize him with her beauty," Lisa said jokingly, as Addie turned quickly toward her friend, wondering at her choice of words.

"Mesmerize. What a strange word to use. What made you say that, Lisa?"

"I don't know. Just popped into my head. Hey, come on, this group is becoming morose. We're here to party, so let's party!" She downed a shot of whiskey. "Get that jealous waitress back here. Never mind. I'm going over to the bar, anyone else need anything? No? Okay, be right back!" She disappeared into the stream of people making their way to the bar.

"Is she like that all the time?" Kate asked Joyce.

"Yes, she's like a shotgun blast. Wears me out sometimes, but we do have fun."

"And that's why we're here." said Addie, downing a large gulp from her mixed drink in an effort to drive thoughts of the waitress, among other things, from her mind.

As she immersed herself in conversation, Addie failed to notice the man in the shadows focusing on her again, this time from across the room. "This has to be the one," he thought. "She's the woman my father is seeking." He, Enoch, had found her. His father had others in his employ, hovering in the shadows of the nightclub, also searching the crowd. They were all hoping to find the prize that would elevate them in the eyes of their master, but only he knew this particular woman had to be the right female for he had witnessed the exchange between her and the vampire.

His attention had been drawn to her immediately as she entered the club and nearly collided with his enemy, Julian. He hadn't missed the way the vampire looked at her, or she at him. He couldn't help but feel the emotion that sparked between the two as they touched. And he was certainly aware of the panic that burst forth inside the vampire, rising like a tidal wave when, a short time later, Julian noticed him sitting in the shadows watching the girl. Yes, glory would be his when he returned with his captive.

The only problem now was how to get the woman away from her friends without drawing to much attention to himself. It had not escaped his notice that there was plenty of extra security in the club tonight. "My antics from the other night must have them all spooked," he thought, a slight sneer twisting his evil face. It was not going to be easy to escape with her, but he did love a challenge, and the danger only made it that much more interesting.

As Enoch made his plans, someone else sitting across the room was wrapped up in his own thoughts. In the largest of the booths usually reserved for people of prominence, Julian sat thinking of the woman he had met, albeit briefly, only moments before. "Who is she?" he wondered. He remembered the jolt that surged through him as his body came in contact with hers. No one had affected him like that for a very long time. There was something special about this particular woman, and he was determined to find out just what, exactly, that was.

"Jules, hey. Earth to Julian."

"Thomas!" the red-haired woman scolded.

"What? He's acting like he's in the twilight zone or something. I called him twice, and he didn't even hear me," Thomas said.

"I was thinking about something, Thomas," Julian explained

"Yes. That is something you might want to try, human!" Christoff glared at Thomas.

"Alright, enough," said the woman. "We have more important things to be concerned about than petty squabbles." Nevertheless, the dark vampire continued to stare menacingly at Thomas.

"Sonya's right. I'm sorry, Thomas, my rudeness was not intentional," Julian apologized.

"It's alright."

"Is everyone in place for tonight, Christoff?"

"Yes. We have people positioned throughout the club where they can observe everything that goes on. They are outside as well, but with the size of the parking lot and the park across the street, it may not be covered as well as we would like. They will try to keep an eye on as much as possible. Our positions in the surrounding woods are limited because we do not own the land."

"Then that's the best we can do, for now. Let's hope it's enough and we have a quiet night for a change," Julian said as the waitress who had just left the girl's table approached him.

"Julian, a word, please?"

"Of course. What is it Charleze?"

"I'm not sure. It may be nothing, but while I waited on those women over there," she nodded toward Addie and her friends, "I noticed something odd. I sensed a presence ... and there was no mistaking the evil radiating from it. It seemed to be directed at the dark-haired woman. And Julian, she has the same coloring as the two murder victims."

His eyes searched the crowd until he found what he was looking for. Even though she was halfway across the room, he could see her perfectly, every line, every curve—from the large brown eyes to the flawless skin of her soft cheek framed by waves of long brown hair.

Addie's head was turned away from him, but he could still sense the tension that filled her as she sat staring at something … or someone. His gaze followed hers, and he could just make out the form of a man sitting in the shadows near the back of the room. Even in the darkness, Julian knew the other man's attention was focused on Addie, and there was no mistaking his sinister intention.

As Julian continued to stare, the eyes of the stranger shifted from the woman to him. The vampire nearly flew from his seat as flashes of something familiar flooded his mind. Cruelty … destruction … an evil so pure it permeated the entire room. Was this person somehow connected to Julian's enemy from the past? Rumor had it that the spawn from hell had somehow procreated. Was this being one of his offspring? Julian's gaze burned into the man, who merely sneered at him, nodding slightly as he mouthed the words meant for the vampire's eyes alone: "Save her if you can."

Then the figure simply disappeared. One second he was there, and the next he was not. Although he was nowhere in sight, Julian was sure that evil presence was still somewhere in the vast club. Turning to Thomas, Julian said, "Get some men and walk the perimeter of the club. Start on the right side and work your way around. The women in that booth seem to have been targeted. For some reason, they are being watched. Keep an eye on them until I can get there. "

"Sure Jules, you'll get no argument out of me, but targeted? What do you mean?"

"There's someone—or something—here."

The blue-grey eyes looked again toward the booth, but Addie was still safely surrounded by her friends.

"Sonya," he ordered, "alert the men outside. Christoff, come with me."

"Julian, who is it? Who are we looking for?" Sonya asked.

"I'm not sure, but I have my suspicions. I saw only one, but it's safe to say he is not alone. If we have unwanted guests in the club, they should be easy enough to find. I could feel the evil that foul thing gave off halfway across the room!" He turned to follow Christoff down the stairs. Sonya did a quick search herself, her black eyes taking in every detail. She had known Julian a long time. There was not much that could spook him, but something most definitely had him in a state. Closing her eyes, she concentrated. Yes, there it was a feeling of menace so strong it sent a shiver down her spine. Her eyes flew open, and turning quickly, she walked toward the main entrance, where she motioned with a beautifully lacquered finger for the two men at the door to follow her outside.

As she sat sipping her drink with her friends, Adrianna felt herself finally beginning to relax. And why shouldn't she? The music was great, the cocktails even better, and she was surrounded by friends. Kate leaned forward to say something when one of Addie's favorite songs came blaring across the dance floor. Before her friend could get the words out, Addie grabbed her hand.

"Let's dance."

She stood to leave the booth when that now-familiar tingling feeling crept along her spine and the hair on her neck rose in warning. She saw him approaching, the man from the shadows, his black eyes boring into hers as she stood frozen. He continued to inch forward, never breaking eye contact as fear squeezed the breath from her lungs. She saw his long, pale hand reaching out to her, but she couldn't move, couldn't scream. Her will was not her own.

She was suddenly released from the hold those awful eyes had on her when his gaze rose to stare at something behind her. His pale hand fell to his side. The next thing that happened caused her to doubt her own sanity, for one minute he was there, a grin of pure evil crossing his abnormally handsome face, and the next he was gone—completely, without a trace. She twisted in the narrow booth, but he was nowhere to be found. "I must really be losing it," she told herself. "Either that, or I've had more to drink than I realize."

"Addie, come on. The song's almost over," Kate said as she pulled Addie by the arm, dragging her from the booth. "What is wrong with you tonight? You've been acting weird ever since we got here. You're supposed to be enjoying yourself, but instead you're a bundle of nerves. Is it the murders? Is that what's bothering you so much?"

"I'm sorry, Kate, really. I think my imagination is running away with me. Maybe it is the murders. I don't know, but there's something about this place that makes me uncomfortable."

"You're just stressed from everything … the move, work, and, yes, the attacks. We all are. But, come on, I have the perfect remedy. We'll dance until you can't stand anymore and work all that stress out of you." Kate pulled Addie down the steps.

The two women lost themselves in the dancers just as Thomas, along with a few others, reached their booth. Had Addie and Kate turned around, they would have noticed the shocked looked on the young man's face as he stood watching them. Now he knew what Julian had meant by pure evil. He had seen it for himself; he had stared right into those eyes from hell. Only seconds before, those eyes had captured the dark haired woman in their sinister gaze. His approach seemed to make the creature think twice about its plans because it released her and simply vanished, just like that.

"What the hell?!" Thomas muttered to himself. It seemed his boss was right to be concerned. "Well, I'll just make myself comfortable until they return and I can introduce myself properly." He blended into the crowd surrounding the booth Addie and Kate had just vacated.

Addie couldn't help but laugh at her friend's enthusiasm as they stepped onto the dance floor, and soon, she forgot herself in the rhythm of the music. She had always loved to dance—in college, she had gone out every weekend to one club or another. Since then, though, other things had taken priority, and she hadn't gone out nearly as often as she would've liked. "That might have to change," she told herself as one song blended into another, and two very attractive guys asked them to dance.

Matching her movements to her those of her partner (he really was very good), she found herself studying the crowd surrounding them. Her eyes were drawn to the large bar on the left side of the room, where two men stood staring out over the crowd. One was possibly the tallest man she had ever seen, well over six feet, seven inches. His raven black hair fell freely down his back. And the other … she gave a small gasp as she realized it was the same man who had bumped into her earlier that evening.

Because of the lighting, his face was partially hidden from view, but she could feel the intensity of his gaze as he picked her out of the crowd. She hadn't had a chance to really study him earlier. All she remembered were those eyes. Now, as she watched him intently, she took in every detail. He was perfect, and she wondered if everyone in the place was genetically gifted. But there was no other word to describe that face. It was perfection, from his beautiful grey-blue eyes, surrounded by lashes so black she wondered if he used mascara (no, he was much to masculine for that) to the straight nose and classically chiseled chin. His waves of dark auburn hair gently fell forward onto his shoulders. Excitement shot through her. "Oh my God is he …?" she thought. "Is he moving toward me?"

He was! He was moving directly toward her!

Julian leaned toward the Dark Vampire beside him. "He may have disappeared from our sight, but it does not mean he's gone. Continue a sweep of the room, then meet up with Sonya."

Christoff nodded in agreement and hesitated only a moment before asking, "Where will you be?"

"There is something I have to do. I will join you as quickly as I can," he said, descending the three steps to the dance floor with fluid grace, working his way toward her.

She couldn't take her eyes off of him as he moved steadily forward. She felt her body growing warm with excitement … and something more. Her eyes travel from the top of his six-foot-plus frame to the tip of his polished shoes. He was dressed in a black shirt, tailored to fit him like a glove and emphasizing the width of his broad shoulders and strong arms. His pants were also black, hugging lean hips and muscular legs as he moved across the dance floor. He walked with a sensual grace, and Addie realized she was holding her breath.

The tempo of the music changed to a slow, steady beat as something in the depths of her mind screamed "*Run!*" But she couldn't move. She noticed Kate leaving the dance floor, but she stood rooted to the spot. The man she'd been dancing with started to approach her, but thought better of it as he noticed the other man approaching. Then he was there, right in front of her, as her head tilted up and brown eyes met blue. He held his hand out to her, hesitating for only a moment.

Then he pulled her close against him, their bodies moving slowly to the rhythm. She was floating in a dream, caught up in those grey-blue eyes as if in a trance, her body molded perfectly to his. After a moment, he lowered his eyes, and her head seemed to clear a little—until he pulled her even closer, if that were possible. Her cheek rested on his chest, her hands were locked together behind his neck. "Ah, silk," she thought as she melted into the soft fabric.

She was burning inside, barely able to breathe as strong fingers stroked her back slowly, sensuously, until those same fingers, sliding gently upward, brushed stray wisps of hair away from her neck, exposing the long column of her throat. His soft breath sent shivers along her throat. No one had ever made her feel like this. No one had even come close except ... who? She couldn't remember; she couldn't even think of anyone except this man. He consumed her senses as he held her pressed tightly against him. Her arms wound even tighter around his neck, her fingers tangled in the long strands of auburn hair. She felt herself shudder with delight as his lips gently pressed against the small curve where neck met shoulder. Then, without warning, he just ... froze. He came to a complete stop even before the music had finished playing.

Confusion filled her as he slowly stepped away from her, his head bowed , his breathing strained. He avoided eye contact. After what seemed like ages but was really mere seconds, he inhaled deeply, raising his head until his eyes met hers. She could have sworn his eyes were somehow different, but when she looked again, they were the same beautiful grey-blue. He seemed to be struggling with some inner demon, fighting for control. Finally regaining his composure, he spoke in a voice deeper than she remembered, "I must apologize to you. I don't even know your name."

"Adrianna, "she whispered.

"Adrianna. I'm not sure this was a good i… Thank you. Thank you for the dance."

"What had he been about to say?" she wondered.

"I'm afraid I …" he started, but before he could finish, the man he'd been standing with earlier came up behind and gently tugged on his arm. Dropping his arm, which was still loosely wrapped around Adrianna's waist, yet still gripping her hand, they moved a short distance away as he bent his head slightly to listen to what his tall friend had to say.

Adrianna studied the newcomer's black hair and eyes. Where those eyes …? Yes, they were midnight blue. It was amazing. She also noticed that almost every female eye in the place was focused on these two men. She didn't know what the dark haired man said, but the hand holding hers suddenly tensed, causing her to bite her lip to prevent herself from crying out. Nodding slightly, her partner stepped away from the taller man and pulled her back toward him. When he finally looked at her, she almost gasped at the intensity in his eyes.

"I'm sorry but I must go," he said. "Our time tonight was much too short, but we will meet again." He raised her hand to his lips and brushed her knuckles with a feather-light kiss. Then he turned and walked away. She felt shaken and more than a little confused. What had just happened?

She watched the two of them move across the dance floor, the crowd parting automatically. They made their way toward the main entrance of the club, where they were met by a woman with long red hair. "Could this be one of the mysterious owners?" Addie wondered. The woman placed a delicate hand on the arm of Addie's dance partner, leaning close in private conversation. Addie was surprised at the spark of jealousy she felt as she watched them. She barely knew this man, but she had to admit that she didn't like the possessive posture of the other woman.

After a few minutes, the woman looked around the club and, with a flick of her wrist, motioned to someone across the room. Turning, Addie watched as men throughout the club began to rise quickly moving toward the door. When they reached the small group waiting there, everyone but the woman went out to the parking lot outside. Just for a brief moment, one man stopped, turning to stare at her with blue-grey eyes before he, too, disappeared through the door.

"What is going on?" she asked herself out loud, searching the room for Kate. She saw her roommate sitting at the booth talking to a young man who looked as if he were about to leave also. "Was he going to join the others?" she wondered. His brown hair didn't quite reach his shoulders, and he had large green eyes.

Vaguely, her mind registered how attractive he was as she moved toward them. She was almost to the stairs when she noticed Nick, a look of purpose on his face, heading for the front door. As their eyes locked, he stopped for a second and raised a finger to his lips. She could almost hear the "shhhh" as his lips formed the sound, but she knew that was impossible. He was too far away. She started to wave to him but thought better of it. She nodded slightly as he continued to head for the very same door the small group had only just gone through.

"Something's happening," she stated as she finally reached their booth.

"Yes, there's some commotion in the parking lot. Thomas, this is Addie. Addie, Thomas," Kate said.

"Great to meet you, Addie," he said, flashing a large grin.

"He was just going to check it out, but he won't let me go with him." There was no mistaking the frustration in Kate's voice.

"Listen, there have been some strange things happening here lately—" Thomas started to say.

"We know," both girls replied.

"Then you also know it's better to stay inside the club until we're sure it's safe."

"Trouble, Thomas?" another man asked, coming alongside him.

"No, no trouble, Dave. The ladies were just curious to know what's going on. I'm trying, with a little difficulty," he said with a slight smile as he looked meaningfully at Kate, "to convince them we can handle things much better if we know they are safe inside the club."

"Thomas is right. We've had some problems here lately, which is why you should stay put while we see what's going on outside," Dave said, smiling to reassure the girls.

"There's strange things going on inside, too." This came from Lisa, who Addie had almost forgotten was still there.

"There's a lot of security in here tonight to keep an eye on things, right?" Thomas said to Dave.

"Right, if you look closely, we have armed guards all around, ever since the first attack. The owners are working with the police." The two men exchanged a glance as Dave continued, "We're doing what we can to keep the patrons safe. Nothing will happen if you just stay inside."

"How do we know who is security? It's not like it says 'Security' on your uniforms or anything," asked Joyce.

"Oh, they're easy to spot," Thomas laughed. "They all look like freakin' wrestlers! Muscles bulging everywhere, as tall as three-story buildings." Everyone laughed. "I have to go now. I wish we had more time to get acquainted," he told them, taking Kate's hand. "I hope we meet again soon,

and remember to stay inside. Jules will kill me if anything happens to you."
He looked at Addie.

"Who's Jules?" she asked, confused. "And why should he be concerned
about me?"

"Jules … I mean Julian. That tall drink of water you were dancing with.
That's Julian Reynolds, and he seems to have developed a great interest in
you." Leaning toward them, as if he had a great secret, he whispered, "By the
way, just a little known tidbit you might be interested in—but don't let him
know where you heard it—he's half owner of the club and the former owner
of the very house you live in!" Smiling at the astonished look on Addie's
face, he and Dave went to join the others. She had finally met her elusive
neighbor, and she didn't even know it.

"Wow! Did he tell you that when you were dancing?" Kate asked.

"No, he forgot to mention that little detail. Actually, we didn't have much
chance to talk, everything happened so fast."

"Do you think there's been another attack?" Kate asked a flash of fear in
her eyes.

"I don't know, but there's one way to find out. Come on! See you guys
later," Addie shouted to Lisa and Joyce as she and Kate began making their
way through the crowd.

"No, Addie, we can't!" Kate protested, but not with much conviction.
"Thomas said no matter what happens to stay inside the club. Something
tells me we should listen to him." Coming to a halt in the middle of the floor,
Addie glanced around and realized people were still dancing as if nothing was
going on.

Staring at her friend, and seeing the concern in her eyes, Adrianna
relented a little. "Alright," she said, "we won't go outside, but we can work
our way up to the door and see if we can figure out what's going on."

Kate thought about that a moment then agreed, "That sounds reasonable.
He can't get mad if we don't actually leave the building, right?"

"Right."

Squeezing their way through the crowd, they finally made it to the large
front door, where two really large men had been left to stand guard. A couple
approached them to leave, but after a whispered conversation with one of the
men, they turned back and re-entered the club.

"I think the decision has been made for us. It doesn't look like they're
letting anyone go anywhere they don't want them to. There must be
something big happening," Addie said, her voice rising as she tried to control
her nerves.

"Rick is going to kill us if it turns out he was right about this place being
dangerous," Kate pointed out.

"Calm down! If something is going on, they seem to have it under control, but I want to see for myself." Glancing around, Addie noticed that the hall leading to the restrooms had a large stained glass window facing the front of the club.

"Come on!" she said, grabbing Kate's arm and dragging her friend behind her. Reaching the window, she checked to make sure the guards weren't watching, and then, turning the small wrought iron latch, she opened it enough for both girls to look outside. They saw a group of men walking away from the club while another, smaller group gathered around the front entrance where something had, evidently, already happened. Searching the strange sea of faces, she realized Julian had been with the group heading for the park and the woods beyond it. "Where on earth are they going?" she wondered, desperately trying to hear what those left near the front of the club were saying, but only a slight mumbling reached her ears. They were too far away. "Well, that's fine," she thought. "If they won't let anyone get close to whatever's going on out there, we'll just stay put at the window. Something is bound to happen soon … we can wait."

Chapter 6

The two women weren't the only ones interested in the evening's mysterious events. Blood red eyes watched from the shadows as Julian's group exited the club and walked with purpose across the parking lot. A hiss of pure hatred escaped the thin lips as he stared at the man in the lead. "Julian!" he spat out the name as if it were poison. His evil mind flashed back to the dark haired woman for one brief moment. She had to be the one his master wanted. Julian's reaction to her confirmed that as nothing else could. He moved to follow Julian's group, but thought better of it. His brother was near, and brute strength was needed for what was to come. That was his brother's area of expertise.

Glancing around, he noticed armed guards everywhere, confirming what he already knew. There would not be another chance this evening to approach the woman. She was inside, under lock and key. But now that he knew who she was, there would be another opportunity … soon. Now he needed to get this information back to his father as quickly as possible. Stepping back into the shadows, he disappeared in a flurry of wings. A swirl of dust and leaves was the only sign he had been there.

Julian proceeded with caution through the darkened parking lot, motioning the others off in all directions as they entered the park. Someone had broken most of the street lamps, making it hard for a normal person to see, but he didn't have that problem. His eyes pierced the darkness where he saw two bodies, bloodied and broken, lying under a park bench. A moment ago, they were locked in a lover's embrace, never thinking it would be their last. The boy couldn't be more than twenty-one and the girl … something about her made him stop in his tracks as he noticed the long, dark hair. A vision came to mind of similar hair lying against his chest so softly that he wanted to bury his face in its richness.

Anger consumed him. Then he noticed movement to his right, where he saw another victim fall to the ground as a creature, black winged and hideous, spun to face him. Blood dripped from sharp fangs as it hissed and flew at him, screaming in rage. With one swift movement, Julian struck as the thing attacked. Kicking out with his right foot, he caught the creature directly in the chest and sent it smashing into a nearby tree. In mere seconds, Julian was on it. He snapped the head from the shoulders as the creature disintegrated in a cloud of dust. Running over to the broken figure lying on the ground, Julian knelt to examine the victim, already knowing he was too late. There was nothing that could be done for the unfortunate soul now.

The dead man was a little older than the young couple lying only a few feet away, and as Julian rose, the glare from the one remaining street lamp illuminated something lying just under the broken body. Bending forward, he gently moved the man aside and looked strangely at the shattered piece of equipment on the ground. Picking it up, he examined the item closely, opening it to pocket something that had been inside. Then, without a moment's hesitation, he smashed the shiny object to bits on the ground. "I hope whatever is on this film was worth dying for, my friend," he said, sparing one final glance for the body. The man's blond hair was streaked with blood , the green eyes stared back at him, dull and lifeless.

Turning quickly back toward the woods as screams of terror came from somewhere deep within, he motioned to the men around him. He knew they must hurry; all his senses screamed a warning of impending danger.

They used the trees as cover as they moved further into the woods, fanning out in a long line to cover as much distance as possible. From somewhere ahead he heard the sound of running feet, but before he could give the order to take cover, two men from his own Specials squad came stumbling toward him, the larger man literally dragging the other.

Horror filled Julian as he realized the injured man literally had no legs! It was obvious he was dead, but his friend would not leave him.

Spurring into action, Julian ran to them. "Lucas, it's me, Julian!" he shouted in an attempt to get the man's attention, but the sound of his voice only served to panic the crazed mind further as the injured soldier veered away in an attempt to hide among the trees. Julian and Christoff quickly followed, tackling him as he screamed and fought against the two men holding him down. Whispering softly, Julian's voice finally began to penetrate, and the trembling body eventually went limp in his arms.

"Lucas, look at me," Julian ordered. "Try to focus, man. You have to tell me what happened."

The man tried hard to do as he was ordered as he recognized the face before him. Eyes wide with fear, he pulled frantically at Julian's clothing.

"Hurry, Julian, we must run, its coming! That thing," his voice began to rise in panic, "that beast is coming!"

"Beast? What are you talking about? Lucas, look at me and try to concentrate," Julian said as he stared into the man's eyes, willing him to be calm, but it only seemed to agitate him further.

"We have to go, Julian. Now! It's going to—"

But before he could finish, an ungodly howl pierced the night. Terror flashed in the man's eyes as he fought to break free of Julian's iron grip, running back toward the club.

Julian stood slowly, his eyes locking with Christoff's as both men turned in the direction of the howl. Thomas and a few others came to stand behind them.

"What the fuck was that?" Thomas asked, trying hard not to show his fear. His hands were gripped tightly on a small automatic bow loaded with razor-sharp arrows.

"Trust me, you don't want to know," Julian muttered almost to himself. "Thomas, take the rest of the humans and fall back to the club."

"No, Julian, we're here to help—"

Before he could finish, Julian grabbed him roughly by the shoulders. "Believe me when I say that none of you can be of any help in this battle. You will only be a hindrance, because even we cannot keep you safe. Please, do as I tell you, and *go back to the club, now!*" he shouted. His friend, confusion clouding his face, gathered the handful of men surrounding him and hurried back toward the club.

The remaining few stood facing the woods tensely. Loud crashing sounds came from within as trees were split and branches flew in all directions. Before any of them realized what was happening, a large black form sprang from the darkness to land with a thunderous sound not ten feet from where they stood staring with horror-filled eyes. It landed on all fours, the ground shaking from the impact as it sniffed the air with its long snout, the scent of fresh blood sending it into a frenzy.

"Werewolf! Shit!" Julian heard Christoff's shout from behind him.

Another ear-splitting howl pierced the night as the beast rose to its full height, a mass of black fur and razor-sharp claws that stood nearly seven feet high! The huge jaws, filled with dagger-like teeth, and the thick black fur were covered in blood, but Julian's attention was riveted on what was in its hand. Dangling from the sharp claws, a piece of blue denim caught his eye. His fury rose to a fever pitch as Julian realized the creature held the missing legs of the man Lucas had tried to drag to safety. Blood was everywhere, and the vampire found himself fighting to keep his own hunger in check while trying to focus on the problem at hand as the monster's bloodshot eyes scanned the group.

Turning to his men, Julian shouted instructions, "We stay together. The only chance we have to bring it down is a group attack. Go for the jugular. We can't kill it without silver, but we can cripple it!"

But before they could take any action, there was a whizzing sound as an object flew from the shelter of the trees. It struck the beast from behind with such force the onlookers saw the shiny silver tip of the spear protruding through the massive chest, missing the heart by mere inches. The creature screamed in pain as it fell to its knees.

They watched in amazement as the sharp claws grabbed at the shiny metal, the silver burning through flesh and bone as the beast, with the strength of ten men, pulled the entire shaft of the spear out through the front of its chest, a mournful howl once again echoing through the night as it tossed the weapon into the group of men gaping before him. Falling down on all fours, the massive head hung in agony. The onlookers watched in amazement as the gaping hole made by the spear started to close, healing itself in seconds.

When the wound had closed completely, the grizzly animal rose to its full height once again, muscles bulging as it eyed the crowd. Coming from deep within the fur-covered chest, the monster issued a deep growl of frustration as it realized it would not taste victory this day. Turning with inhuman speed, it dove into the woods and disappearing in the opposite direction from which it had come. Christoff gathered his fellow vampires to follow the beast, but he was stopped short by a shout from Julian.

"No! Not tonight, Christoff, we do not have the weapons to kill it. We were not prepared for this. There will be another time." Julian grabbed his friend by the arm. The vampire looked around and saw the bedraggled remnants of the wolf's army fleeing after the leader. Even with their limited reasoning, they knew it was useless to fight without the beast to help them. He scanned the night for his own men, seeing many covered in blood and ash walking toward him. There would be time for a head count later.

Vampire senses tingling, Julian turned his head from side to side, sniffing the night air. Everything had suddenly gone very quiet. The stench of rotting flesh filled the air as piles of ash burned around him. Julian focused on the woods in precisely the spot where the silver spear had exited. Alert to some new danger, he poised himself, ready to face any threat that came his way.

After a few minutes, his heightened hearing picked up a sound … a soft shuffling as blades of grass and weeds were crushed. Someone or something was coming through the woods. Raising a hand, he motioned those nearest him to be silent. Within seconds, a figure emerged from the trees. He had a silver dagger in one hand and what appeared to be a long sword in the other.

Drawing steadily nearer, he bent to retrieve the spear from the ground and, while the others watched, he pushed a small switch and the long staff shrank until it was no bigger than the matching dagger he held. Looking Julian in the eye, the stranger neatly dropped the weapon into a leather belt attached to his waist.

"What is this?" Christoff asked, coming to stand alongside Julian.

"I don't know, but I'm sure we're about to find out." Julian replied as the man approached.

Showing no apparent fear, the stranger came to stand directly in front of the small group, eyeing Julian thoughtfully. While everyone else showed signs of a battle hard fought, this man was barely winded. No torn clothing. No blood anywhere. So it was no wonder that his next statement took Julian completely by surprise.

"This battle may have been won, vampire, but you will not win the war without me. We need to talk!" He met Julian's surprised gaze without the slightest confusion or lack of control—something very few could do! Christoff and Simon stepped up to flank Julian. But this did not seem to intimidate the man, who continued to stare with a smile on his extraordinarily handsome face.

"I am not the enemy here, warrior," he said to Christoff. "I only wish to talk." He spoke in a quiet, soothing voice, as if he were trying to tame the savage beast within the warrior. Julian sensed power emanating from this man, but a power unlike any he had ever experienced before. Taking a step forward, Julian's eyes met the strangers'.

"Who are you, and how do you know me?"

"I am called Michael, and you would be surprised at what I know. You are something of a paradox, my friend," he continued.

"Really and why is that?" Julian asked, not letting his guard down for a second.

"A vampire battling your own kind," he nodded toward the woods, "as well as our furry friend. I would say that is not the normal way of it."

"Evil is evil. Men fight other men, why should it not be the same for our race?" Julian replied.

"Point taken. There may be hope yet, my friend."

As a slow smile creased the man's face, Julian wondered who exactly this person was and what he wanted.

"You have not yet earned the right to call me friend." Turning to Christoff, Julian issued his orders, "All traces of what happened here must be disposed of. Let me know when you are finished then you can escort this one back to the house. Watch him carefully until I arrive." Looking around once more he said to the newcomer, "You will get your chance to talk there." As Michael nodded in agreement, Julian turned and, heading back in the direction of the club, shouted orders to his men. "Simon, see that the wounded are taken care of, especially the humans. No one is to be left behind. "

Christoff grabbed his friend's arm. "Where are you going?" he demanded. "You shouldn't be going off alone." The warrior couldn't hide the concern in his voice. "This enemy is ruthless and cunning. They could be waiting in ambush. You may be good, but you cannot fight them alone. Wait but a moment, and I will come with you."

"They are gone, my friend. If you will just take the time, you will sense it yourself." He took a deep breath and closed his eyes. Then he opened them to look at the man who had been at his side through every battle over the centuries. "Without the beast to stand with them, they are cowards. I am in no danger, and I have something I must take care. I'll return to the house as soon as I can, and Christoff," he said as he looked around the surrounding area, "I'm sorry it must fall on you, again, to clear away the evidence of tonight's trouble." The dark vampire gave a nod of understanding as Julian disappeared into the night. He trusted his men to follow his orders without question. He must get back to the club. He had to know if she was alright.

Addie stood on tiptoe, straining her eyes to pierce the darkness outside of the window. A few others had joined her and Kate. It seemed everyone was trying to get some idea what was happening outside. There had been some sort of confrontation right out in the main parking lot near the front entrance, but that seemed to be over now, and she could find no one who could tell her what actually had happened.

"Where is Julian?" she wondered, a sick feeling settling in the pit of her stomach. "And why do I even care?" She barely knew him, but in the brief time she had spent with him, she realized one thing: she wanted to get to know him … very well. But would she get the chance?

A feeling of intense relief washed over her as Kate shouted, "Oh, Addie, there he is!"

She watched his tall frame walking slowly from the park. She was still amazed at his gracefulness, his sensuality causing her to catch her breath. Those amazing eyes scanned the activity at the front of the club.

"He looks fine," Kate said, grabbing her friend and watching Addie's worried expression dissolve. She understood what her friend was feeling. She'd experienced the same intense relief moments earlier when Thomas and a few others came running from the park—but she also noticed that something had them extremely agitated. Julian, on the other hand, seemed calm and in complete control.

They watched him walk across the parking lot. Some sort of ash or cinders covered his once-immaculate clothing, but other than that, he seemed none the worse for wear. He went directly to a man being tended by none other than their sultry little waitress, Charleze. Evidently, he had been injured in whatever altercation had happened in the parking lot. Their heated conversation was growing louder now, and Addie strained to hear at least a little of what they were saying.

"Is he alright?" Julian asked the girl as he reached the injured man.

"He was cut up pretty badly, but he will heal. He's angry more than anything else," she stated. "When he saw that foul thing attacking the girl," she nodded toward a young woman crying hysterically, "he acted instinctively. They fought. The creature did not survive." Julian followed the direction of her gaze and noticed the pile of smoking ash. "He is sorry there is no one to question, but it stands to reason this attack is related to the others, Julian. That bastard was drinking from her! If Adam had not arrived when he did, she would have been the next victim."

Again, a twinge of fear ran through Julian as he stared at the intended victim and noticed the long, dark hair. His keen eyes took in her soft brown ones, now grown large and round from the fright she had received.

"This can't be happening," he thought. Aloud, he said, "It would seem, though I'm sure she will not agree, that she was the lucky one. There are more in the park who we did not reach in time."

"How many this time?"

"We're not sure yet." From the corner of his eye, he could see the young woman still crying while being attended to by Sonya. When she saw Julian, Sonya walked toward him.

"Sonya," he nodded at the woman. "How is she?"

"She will be fine."

"Good. Take her inside, give her anything she needs," he told her. "Also, see that she gets home safely and that she understands what happened to her."

"It will be taken care of." Sonya led the girl back inside the club.

Turning back to the injured man Julian asked, "How do you feel, Adam?"

The man before him was covered in blood, but how much was actually his was hard to determine. He was shorter than Julian but well muscled. There was a deep, bleeding gash across his chest as well as two smaller ones across his back. The wounds were already starting to close and heal—one of the benefits of being a vampire.

"I'm alright. Sorry we won't be able to gain any information. It all happened so fast. I heard the girl screaming and saw her struggling with someone. He was taking her down right in front of the club. It was as though he purposely attacked her on our front doorstep. Someone is going out of their way to draw attention to us, Julian!"

"It would seem so," said Julian thoughtfully. "But it makes no sense. We have coexisted undetected among the humans for a long time. We've had no problems with anyone, and it's obvious these attacks are not from any of our people. Who would want to stir things up now? And why?"

"Are you sure you do not know?" Julian heard the question as the man called Michael approached him from behind, flanked on either side by Christoff and Simon. He looked deep into Julian's eyes as Christoff grabbed him roughly by the arm and pulled him away.

"We have finished our task, Julian," the dark warrior said. "And you will have your chance to talk soon enough, stranger, as he has already told you, which is more than I would do for you."

"Your hostility, although I understand its underlying cause, is really not necessary, my friend. I am only here to lend what assistance it is in my power to give," Michael said.

"I have very few friends," the dark vampire hissed at him. "And last time I checked, you were not among them. But he," Christoff said, nodding his beautiful head in Julian's direction, "is one of the rare few I know I can count on, and nothing and no one will harm him while I live."

"Fair enough, warrior, but believe me when I say I mean no harm to any who fight for his cause. I am only here to help."

Christoff stared at the strange man for a long time before he replied, "That will be for him to decide. Come." He led the stranger away.

Julian stared after them, not wanting to believe the suspicion forming in his mind. He had tried to capture the stranger's gaze for a moment, hoping to read what was locked deep in that complex mind, but he could not penetrate the barrier the man had placed there. His will was strong, which surprised Julian, for very few could hide their thoughts from his power. How did he accomplish it? Julian was positive he was not vampire or anything similar. The man was merely human—or was he? Turning to the vampire standing next to him, he ordered, "Simon, take Andrew and a few others and see what you can find out among our contacts about any strangers in the area. Also, see if any large estates have been purchased in the last few months and by whom. They will be both remote and long deserted. We have to find out who is behind these killings before the backlash starts to point in our direction. It's getting harder with each incident to contain the situation."

Adam came up behind Julian, concern clearly visible on his face, "Julian, the girl. She saw his face, the eyes, his teeth—"

"Sonya will take care of it," Julian reassured him. "All she will remember is trying to unlock her car as someone grabbed her from behind. She will think you hit the man and knocked him out when she screamed. Her thoughts will be confused about any other details. She won't be able to tell the police very much when they question her." As if on cue, the shrill pitch of sirens was heard in the distance.

"If you say so, Julian. Do you need me to do anything?"

"Go back to the house with Christoff," Julian said as he saw Thomas approaching, "and see if you can find out anything more about our guest."

"Julian! You're alright? Is everyone okay?" Thomas looked at the vampire with concern and immense curiosity. But Julian was not fooled. He could see the fear behind that curiosity.

"Everyone is fine. We had help from an unexpected source and a touch of silver."

"Ahhh, well, what do you need from me now?"

"Just do what you can with the evidence so our friends the police don't get the wrong impression." Julian started to walk away, but a thought occurred to him and he stopped. "There is one more thing you can do."

"Just name it."

"There was a girl I was with inside—"

"I noticed. Quite a looker," Thomas interrupted with a roguish smile.

"Yes, I'm well aware of that. Find out all you can about her." Almost to himself, he finished, "I need to know everything."

With the smile still on his face, the young man replied, "Already taken care of, Jules. Sometimes it really hurts just how much you underestimate me. It just so happens I've already introduced myself to her friend, and there's something I've been waiting for the right moment to tell you."

"Hmmm, indeed. Out with it, Thomas, I'm in no mood for games tonight."

"Oh, right, yeah," the younger man said, not bothering to hide his disappointment in the vampire's abrupt response. "Well, imagine my surprise when, after a few minutes of conversation with this gorgeous redhead, I find out that she is none other than my ... our ... next door neighbor." He watched Julian's surprised expression with satisfaction. "That's right, boss. She and her friend are the ones who bought the cottage. Can you beat that! So, you see, your lovely lady has been sitting there right under your nose all this time. When you're ready to send out the neighborhood welcome wagon, just let me know."

Julian stared in amazement at the back of Thomas's head, his brown curls blowing softly in the breeze. Not missing a step, Thomas turned back to impart one last bit of information, "By the way, her name is Adrianna Avani, and you can thank me later."

His neighbor. Was it really possible? "If this is one of Thomas's little jokes …" he thought. But somehow he knew it was the truth. Suddenly, comprehension dawned. It had been her that first night, the presence that had drawn him to the cottage. That would explain why he was so affected when they had touched earlier. Well, this promised to be very interesting.

But then another thought filled his mind as he remembered dancing with her and holding her close, the feel of her body against his, and again, just as it had happened then, he felt the hunger rise. Yes, this would be interesting but also very, very dangerous. Shaking his head, he turned quickly back toward the park to see that all was in order. But before he could travel very far, three police cars skidded to halt before the club entrance.

The door of the nearest vehicle swung open, and Julian watched as a short man in a rumpled suit climbed out slowly. He was no taller than Adrianna, about five foot three with unkempt black hair sticking out in all directions. "Bertram," Julian thought, sighing deeply. Despite the man's disheveled appearance, he was as tenacious as a bulldog. It was going to be a long night.

Still at the window, both girls watched with interest. An uneasy feeling gnawed at Addie's insides. Something big was happening, she could feel it, but would any information actually reach the public this time? Then she remembered Nick sneaking out of the club, his ever-present camera loaded and waiting. "Where is he?" she wondered. She hadn't seen his tall, lanky frame leaving the park with everyone else. "He'd probably snuck off in another direction so no one would realize what he'd been up to. Yes, that has to be it." She relaxed a little. At least she would be able to find out something from him if the police hushed up this incident like they did the others.

They had heard the screams coming from the park, along with what sounded like men fighting—and what was that unearthly howling? It had sounded like something straight out of a horror movie. Her eyes traveled up, but the sky was starless and the only moon that shone at all was a crescent. So no werewolves, right? God, she was letting her imagination run wild!

Being so far away, they could see nothing clearly, and the guards at the front door were still refusing to let anyone leave the club. "How do they manage to keep things under such tight control," she wondered. A few people panic written all over their faces, rushed forward when the screaming started in an attempt to escape to their cars. But as soon as they approached the guards, it took just a few words to calm them, convincing them to return inside where they would be safer. As the crowd of people trying to leave grew larger, so did the number of guards, with the same results every time. It probably was safer inside, but even so, why did she feel like a virtual prisoner?

Kate had been leaning close to her, straining to see out the window, when Addie heard her exclaim, "Oh my God!"

"What is it? What's wrong? Is Julian—"

"That is the most perfect man I have ever seen!"

Adrianna followed her friend's gaze as two men who had been talking to Julian moments before came walking in their direction. She recognized the tall, dark one from inside the club, but it was the other one her awestruck friend stared at, for he was, quite literally, the most perfect man she had ever seen. Even with the dim lighting, she could see that his hair was like spun gold cascading almost to his waist in long, soft curls. He was easily as tall as Julian, strong and powerfully built, which was the only thing that saved him from looking feminine.

As the two men passed in front of the window, the girls quickly pulled back, but not before the man locked ice blue eyes with Addie's deep brown ones. Suddenly, a feeling of intense calm washed over her. She felt peaceful, as if all was right with the world—which she definitely knew was not the case. But it didn't seem to matter. Shaking her head slightly, she turned to Kate, wondering who this man was and what strange power did he possess? She didn't remember seeing him that evening, and someone like him she would not have forgotten easily.

"Did you notice him in the club earlier tonight?"

"Absolutely not." her friend answered, still gaping at the stranger.

"You're sure?"

"Addie, you know me. A face like that I would never forget!"

"You're right. So if he's not working for the club, who is he? Did they just pick him up in the woods?" They stared at each other for a moment until they realized something else was happening. The police seemed to be moving through the crowds of people, questioning and gathering what information they could.

"I think it's time we left. With the police here, they could decide to question everyone. We could be stuck here for hours," Addie said, realizing she'd had enough of the club scene for one night.

"Would that be so bad?" Kate asked a strange smile on her face. "I was hoping to get a chance to talk to Thomas again. And you might be able to see Julian one more time."

"Kate, I think Thomas has already gone. And, besides, he's our neighbor. We can see him … them … whenever we want. Besides, they are occupied with more important things right now then a pair of infatuated women. Look, there's a group of people leaving," she said, surprised. "The car is close to the front door. If we go out with a crowd, we should be able to avoid being questioned by the police. Come on!"

"You're probably right as usual, but it started out to be such a promising evening," Kate said as they ran quickly down the hallway.

"Hopefully there will be plenty more," Addie said as they blended into the crowd gathering at the exit.

The guards at the front door were now allowing people to come and go. Working their way into a large group of women, the girls flowed, unnoticed, through the front door, where Addie saw the red haired woman talking with a young girl. The girl's pretty face was covered in scratches. A shock went through Addie when she noticed the girl's red-rimmed eyes. They were deep brown, and her hair was long and brown. Had the serial killer been here tonight? Did he have something to do with what happened to this poor girl? Addie stared as they moved past the two figures, but the girl seemed unaware of her surroundings.

Addie found she could barely pull her own eyes away from the scene until she felt a cool breeze against her cheek. They were outside. As quickly as possible, they made their way to the car. Somehow, they were able to avoid the police, for she was in no mood to answer a million questions. She noticed a horrible stench in the air, like burning flesh. But that couldn't be possible.

"Oh my God, what is that smell?" she asked Kate as they ran to her red Mustang, which stood out among the row of cars.

"Addie, something happened out here tonight, right?" Kate asked, confused. "We heard the screams and shouts. We heard fighting, didn't we? I know I didn't have that much to drink, and I wasn't imagining things. But there are no physical signs of any kind of trouble, just that awful smell!"

"No, you didn't imagine anything, Kate. We both heard it, but you're right, there are no injured, no signs of a disturbance of any kind."

"Except for one frightened girl," she added silently as she gave one last glance around the parking lot before jumping hurriedly into the car.

"There's definitely something weird going on here. I only hope more people don't have to die before the police find some answers," Addie said, looking into Kate's wide eyes. "Let's get back to the safety of the house. I think we'll put clubbing on the back burner for a while after tonight."

The car whipped out of the parking space, tires squealing as they sped out of the parking lot and headed for home.

Chapter 7

A tall figure with bulging muscles rippling down a broad back walked quickly along the path, growling angrily at the creature stumbling along beside him. Blood flowed freely from an open wound in his chest.

"Hurry! He will be waiting for our return. I should have let them find you and finish you off back there. All you are doing is holding me back. Of course, he may decide to do that anyway!"

"Who are you to be so arrogant, Hanokh!" the stumbling creature spat at his tormentor. "At least the rest of us were carrying out the master's orders to destroy all who might interfere with the plan. Where were you? Off somewhere else, concerned more with fulfilling your own depraved cravings than his wishes. We could have used your help sooner! We wouldn't have lost so many if you had fought with us."

The hulking figure came to an abrupt halt, causing the grumbling creature to nearly collide with its massive form. Looking down on the pitiful creature, Hanokh whispered through clenched teeth, "Who are you to question me?" He grabbed the injured vampire by the throat, lifting him high off the ground in one swift movement. "What I was doing was my own business! If the lot of you were more skilled, you wouldn't need my help. You should have been able to handle them. They were outnumbered two to one. I cannot fight all your battles!"

"We were fine until the stranger came." The pathetic figure struggled to get the words out. Hanokh stared in disgust as he saw the blatant fear in the red eyes. "Then Julian showed up with more men, and we didn't stand a chance. Even you backed down!"

SLAP!

The impact of a massive fist connecting with rotting flesh echoed through the night as the vampire's head snapped to one side.

"I ... did ... *not* ... back ... down!" Hanokh roared. "And yes, the arrival of the Avenger was unexpected. But he was no threat to me. The only reason I chose to leave the battle was because he had silver. Lots of it! I needed time to form a plan." He tossed the whimpering form aside in disgust and continued walking. The injured vampire picked himself up stumbling to keep up with Hanokh's much longer footsteps.

"This news will not be well received. That, on top of your failure, will not make him happy," Hanokh muttered, preparing himself for the meeting ahead of him. They walked a few miles more until they finally arrived at their destination. The woods abruptly came to an end as they entered a place void of any signs of life. Dried ground, cracked and split from lack of moisture, spread out before them. Grass had long since ceased to grow here, and the land was now decorated only with dead wood and scattered rocks.

They stared at the huge mass of decaying stone that had once been a magnificent monastery. All remnants of the beauty it once held were corrupted by the evil now occupying its empty halls. Even Hanokh, with all his strength and power, dreaded what they must face inside. His steps faltered slightly as they walked toward the crumbling edifice. Slowly entering through the front door, they climbed the grand staircase and proceeded down the long, dark hallway until they stood before a large wooden door.

Stopping momentarily, Hanokh worked to summon enough courage to enter. Taking a deep breath, he shoved the door open. The two battle worn figures entered a cavernous room lit only by torches mounted in stone gargoyles on all four walls. Protectors, weren't they? But they could not protect anyone from the horror within these walls!

A blood red carpet ran the entire length of the room, coming to stop in front of a chair made entirely of granite. Sitting in that chair, seemingly as massive as the structure itself was a dark figure whose face was entirely in shadow. As the two smaller figures approached, they fell to their knees and lifted their heads, one more than the other, to gaze into the eyes of the creature before them. Terror filled the injured vampire, causing the pitiful creature to tremble violently. Hanokh held his own.

Here, in this place, there was no need for their master to maintain the facade he presented to the rest of the world. No, here he preferred to show his true colors. The tall, muscular man, his skin almost as dark as the mane of black curls covering his head, was never seen within these walls. No, this was his domain. Anyone entering here would witness his true nature.

He relished the scent of fear rising from the two kneeling figures as they stared into eyes that seemed to glow like fire from deep within sunken sockets. The nearly nonexistent lips curled away from razor-sharp fangs that could rip a man's—or another vampire's—throat out in an instant. These hideous features were positioned inside a massive skull, twice as large as any normal man's, of deformed bone that nearly ripped through the thin veil of skin covering it. Tangled strands of brittle black hair fell across muscular shoulders and onto his upraised arm as he pointed to the larger man kneeling before him.

"Don't keep me in suspense, my son. What news? Tell me!" His voice sounded like a growl. Hanokh stared back at the only thing that could instill terror in him, but before he could answer, the cowering vampire beside him burst out its mumbled response,

"We destroyed a female who fit your description, my lord, along with her companion, but we were interrupted. Devon and the others were destroyed by Julian and his men!" he shouted, gaining courage. "He," the vampire pointed a bony finger at Hanokh, "came too late to help us."

The ponderous head slowly turned, red eyes burning into the figure cowering before him, and said in a low voice, "Was it her? The woman I seek?"

"I ... I do ..." the creature stammered.

"No, my lord, it was not," Hanokh answered. The red eyes shot a glance at the larger man before turning back to the trembling form before him.

"Anything Julian's men may have done is nothing compared to what I will do to you the next time you fail me!" Rising from the chair with speed uncommon for one so large, he grabbed the injured vampire by the back of the neck and heaved the flailing form across the room with such force that the walls shuddered from the impact. Red eyes watched as the broken body slid slowly to the ground, where it lay motionless and silent. Turning swiftly back to the remaining figure who, though trembling slightly, stood his ground, the deep voice questioned, "You are sure these idiots did not destroy the one I seek?"

"Yes, my lord. The dead girl was with another male of her species. Julian was inside the building. If she was the woman you sought, he would not allow her to be with another man."

"That is the truth. If Julian did know of her existence, he would not share her or leave her attended." The anger in the eyes began to disappear, only to be replaced by a questioning look as he stared once more at Hanokh. "But you continued the search, correct? You found no one else who might have been the one we seek in your prowling during the evening? You must have some reason for not being where you were most needed, and it better be good!"

A chill went up Hanokh's long spine at the hint of menace in that question. "He knows where I was, what I did. He must," Hanokh thought.

He knew he'd better come clean before he was the one on the receiving end of his master's extreme anger.

"I followed the woman from the cottage early in the evening, while I awaited your followers rising. She was in town, but she met with friends. I stayed in the vicinity while she had dinner. Afterward, I followed her and another woman to a small clothing shop, but she was never alone, so I waited, thinking it best not to draw attention to myself."

"Indeed."

Swallowing hard, Hanokh continued, "As it happened, a girl at the shop became suspicious of my loitering. I couldn't let her raise the alarm so, after biding my time I went back and took care of the problem."

"And no one saw you remedy this situation?"

"No, my lord, of that I am certain."

"You'd better be!"

Just then, the door burst open and a tall form glided across the floor.

"Good to see that you made it, brother, not that there was ever any doubt," the newcomer said. He matched Hanokh in height and strength if not in bulk. As he placed a welcoming hand on his brother's back, a false smile spread across his evil face. No good would come from letting their lord know how he really felt about his younger sibling. "Has our father told you my news?"

"News? What news?" Hanokh questioned, looking suspiciously at his brother.

"No, I see he hasn't. Well, let me fill you in. It seems I have found the lovely lady we were so diligently searching for," he announced with a sneer.

"You! You're sure? How do you know she's the one?" Hanokh argued, hating to be bested yet again by his older brother.

"I know," Enoch hissed at his brother, "because I know our friend Julian. He seemed more than a little interested in one particular woman at the club tonight. She fits the description, looking a lot like the others we have already met. I had her within my grasp when someone," he looked pointedly at the broken figure across the room, "drew attention to themselves, and the alarm was given. I had no hope, then, of accomplishing my task. She was well guarded, which confirms my suspicions. So, logically, I returned to give father the good news. I knew it would be more prudent to plan another attack later, when she was not so well protected."

"That's what you thought, is it? Since when do you make the decisions?" Hanokh growled. As his two sons glared at each other, the dark figure stood deep in thought, his evil mind processing all he had heard this night.

"Yes," his voice hissed in agreement. "It does make sense. If Julian is that protective of her, he must be aware of who she is. We must work fast before

Julian takes what he needs from her. I will not allow Julian's redemption while I have the power to stop it!" His clawed fist slammed down upon the arm of the stone chair, causing bits of rock to rain onto the floor.

"I am sure you are right, my father. But I do not think the time frame is as urgent as you think," Enoch pointed out. "Julian, the fool, is not like us. Common sense would dictate taking what he needs from the woman as soon as he was sure she was the one he's been waiting for all these centuries. But he will not. Our Julian is a gentleman. He will romance her until she gives up what he wants willingly. No, there will be no taking by force with him, which works to our advantage. We need a proper plan to make everything come together."

"That is true, my lord," Hanokh agreed. "Only Julian is not our only problem. Enoch was not the only one to make a discovery this night." He realized he might yet best his brother at something.

"You speak in riddles, make yourself clear!" his father ordered.

"The Avenger is here. It was he who turned the battle tonight." He watched his father's face take in this news. Was that fear behind those blood red eyes?

"You're sure of this?"

"There is no doubt."

"Did he have the weapon?

"I did not see it. He had one similar, from which I will bear a permanent scar, for it was silver tipped." The red eyes followed Hanokh's hand as he grasped his wounded chest. "As luck would have it, he was a bit preoccupied and his aim was slightly off, which is the only reason I stand before you with this report."

"And I am thankful for that, my son." A hand with nails like daggers was laid upon Hanokh's shoulder. Hanokh nodded, glad for this tiny acknowledgment from his lord and father.

"If you did not see the weapon, he does not have it, for he would not leave it out of his sight. He and he alone knows that its power is the only thing that can destr … give him the upper hand in any battle against me." He eyed his sons warily, but they hadn't seemed to catch his slip. He'd almost told them the one piece of information that could cause them to revolt against him—and succeed. "But, still, this changes things," he said as he began a slow pacing, his black robes seeming to float above the ground as he moved.

"Send my best minions to keep watch on Julian and the girl. Wait for your chance, for he cannot protect her all the time, not if she is unaware of his true nature. But this time, make sure she is brought to me," he finished, appearing back in the large chair as if he had never left it. His red eyes blazed as he stared at the two brothers, one a prince among the vampire nation he ruled, the other a man-beast whose brute strength had no equal. Each one so like their mothers, yet so completely different from each other. Yes, those women had served him well. Now it was time for their offspring to prove their worth ... or pay the consequences.

"She is to remain unharmed. If there is so much as a scratch on her, the one responsible will answer to me personally! My plans have changed. Julian must be witness, once again, to her demise, as well as the Avenger's. They must know once and for all the full extent of my power!" he said in a loud voice. "Enough talk. Enoch, gather all here within the hour. We will explain everything when they are present. We have plans to make, and they must be made quickly. I want that woman before another night passes, or neither of you will see the light of day, and it will be by my hand that you die, sons or not!"

A look of understanding passed between the brothers for they both knew, without a shadow of a doubt, that the dark figure seated in the chair before them—their master, their lord, their father—would do exactly as he had threatened, blood or no blood, if they failed him again.

While they made their plans, another sat deep in thought, miles away, trying to make sense of the events of the evening.

Chapter 8

Adrianna sat on the bed, absentmindedly stroking the brush through the tangled strands of her long hair. The incident at the club kept running through her mind. The whole experience had been peculiar to say the least. From the moment they walked through the doors, she could feel something was not quite right. She remembered the faces floating among the throngs of people. Was she the only one who noticed them?

Then there was the strange man watching her from the shadows. Even now, a shiver went down her spine as she remembered those eyes and the fear that held her frozen in place as he approached her. What would have happened if he'd actually reached her? Touched her? Her body trembled at the thought. Did she really want to know? No, she didn't. She knew instinctively that the man was evil. Yes, evil was the only word that could describe the misery and despair she had felt at his nearness.

Then another thought occurred to her. Could he be the one responsible for the attacks in the area? He certainly seemed capable of something so horrendous. As she thought back, she realized the trouble seemed to start right after he had disappeared from inside the club. That was also right around the time her dance with Julian had ended so abruptly.

As she thought of Julian, a deep frown creased her forehead. Why had he acted so strangely? One minute they were dancing together, both enjoying themselves. The next, he was pulling away. Was it something she had done and, if so, what? Closing her eyes, her thoughts took her back to that moment as she remembered his strong arms wrapped tightly around her, pressing her close to his body. She couldn't put two coherent thoughts together at the time, but she was absolutely sure of one thing: she had affected him as much as he had her. She could feel it in the way he held her and the way his lips brushed softly against her neck, but something had happened to change everything. It was almost as if he were fighting the emotions rising inside of him. What was it he had started to say?

"I'm not sure this was a good …"

She tried to remember his exact words. Not a good what? Not a good idea to dance with her? Or was it something else? "Oh for heaven's sake, I'm going to drive myself crazy trying to figure him out," she thought. Setting down the brush, she stared at herself in the mirror, the sight of her brown hair reminding her of the incident outside the club.

That was another mystery. Just what had gone on out there? The other attacks had been so brutal. If there had, indeed, been another one, and by the same culprit, wouldn't there have been some sort of evidence? There had been nothing except that awful smell. There were no physical signs of any violence or danger. Maybe they had imagined an attack because of all that had happened lately. It was probably just an argument of some sort, easily settled, and Julian, being somewhat responsible for what happened at his club, was needed to diffuse the situation.

She decided that if she ever saw him again, she would just come right out and ask. But then another memory flashed through her mind, and she shivered again. She remembered the howling that sounded like the hounds of hell. She had never heard anything like it. What on earth could have made such an awful noise, and had Julian and the others heard it also? She made up her mind to make another trip to the big house to see if she could find him and get some answers.

"Hey, are you alright?" Kate asked, standing in the doorway. Surprised, Addie gave a little scream.

"I will be when you stop sneaking up on me," she replied. "And if I can get my very vivid imagination under control."

"Tell me about it. I'm sorry. I didn't mean to scare you. I made us both a nice cocktail," Kate said as she handed Addie a glass of brandy. "Hopefully, it will help us sleep, although I don't know if I will ever sleep again after tonight. Could you see anything that was happening in the park? Was there or wasn't there another attack, or are we just assuming that's what it was? And what was that horrible smell and that awful howling?"

"Whoa! Hold on a minute! When did you become a mind reader? I was just wondering the exact same things," Addie said. "Maybe the papers will have some answers tomorrow. If not, we can always ask Rick what Nick found out, or for that matter, we can ask him ourselves. And speaking of the good Father, you might as well prepare yourself, because you know we're going to hear from him for sure after tonight's events hit the papers."

"That's a given. I guess we'll just have to wait until tomorrow." Then, looking at Addie thoughtfully, Kate asked, "Do you think the police will ever catch the people responsible for this mess? That's why we're all so jumpy."

From her friend's tone, Addie realized just how afraid she really was.

"Hey, we're home safe and sound, and everything is locked up tight as a drum," Addie said. "We have a nice brandy to wash our cares away, so let's try to relax and get some rest. I'll see you in the morning." She hugged Kate and sent her off to her own room. Climbing into bed, she fell back against the pillows, hoping for a restful night. After some time, her eyes became heavy, and she began to drift off into a restless sleep.

Then the dream began …

A gentle breeze flowed through the open doors of her balcony (when had she opened them?), ruffling the lace curtains that cascaded to the floor. The warm night air softly caressed her face as she tossed from side to side, struggling to clear her clouded mind. Was she asleep or awake? She couldn't be sure. But one thing was certain … she was not alone. Yet she felt no fear. Someone was in the room with her, hidden in the shadows, watching over her. She fought to come awake, but her eyes were so heavy. She was tired—all she wanted was to rest. Time stood still, and all was quiet until, finally, something soft brushed against her cheek and she fell into a deep sleep just as the dawn began to creep over the horizon. A shadow drifted away from the bed, stopping for a brief moment to watch the sleeping woman.

"Rest, my love, while you can," came the whisper as the shadow disappeared through the open doors, securing them tightly with the flick of a wrist. Reaching toward the sky, the figure rose into the darkness, or what was left of it.

A short distance away, on the hill high above the cottage, Julian ran quickly onto the darkened porch of the old stone mansion as the sun began its slow rise. Inside the front door Thomas anxiously awaited, pacing nervously until he saw his friend approaching.

"You cut that a little too close, ol' buddy. The sun is almost up! What were you thinking? It's not like you to be so careless, Julian," Thomas scolded. Julian gave him a piercing glance as he walked quickly past, heading up the main staircase. Opening the door to the tower room, he took the flight of stairs two at a time and entered the upstairs bedroom. Approaching the far wall, he stopped for a moment, his hand raised to touch the sconce that opened the passage to his hidden chamber. Realizing that Thomas was just concerned for his safety, he sighed deeply, turning to answer the question his friend had asked moments earlier, "I had to know she was safe. I … she reminds me of someone …" He hesitated a moment, then continued,

"Someone I knew a long time ago. Did you notice anything similar about the women who have been attacked, Thomas?"

"I didn't have a chance to get that close, Julian. Why? What are you thinking?"

"At first I thought it was just a coincidence, but not anymore. The resemblance is too striking. They were all about the same height, the same approximate build. But the most important similarity is their long, dark hair and eyes, the same as Adrianna. The same as the woman I used to know. There's a definite pattern, and our killer wanted to be sure I noticed. Adrianna could be a possible target, Thomas. Tomorrow, sorry, today I want you to do some detective work. See what you can find out about her background, her family. I need to know everything. It's very important because I have an idea who might be behind these attacks, although it seems impossible."

"So you've finally put it together, my friend? I was wondering how long it would take you."

Julian turned to see Michael entering the room, Christoff close on his heels. Christoff had the grace to look embarrassed when he saw the look on Julian's face.

"I'm sorry, Julian, he slips away at the blink of an eye, as if he were not real," Christoff said. "One minute he's there, the next gone. Somehow, he knew you were back before the rest of us realized it. He should be locked up until we know more about him!" The midnight blue eyes turned almost black from his anger. Michael stood very serenely in the center of the room, his perfect features composed as he watched Julian.

"Julian knows he has nothing to fear from me, don't you, vampire?"

Julian stared into Michael's crystal blue eyes and he knew this man spoke the truth. Julian's instincts had never failed him. He knew Michael could be trusted, and if he was right about the identity of their killer, they would need all the help they could get to defeat him. Placing his hand on Christoff's shoulder he said, "It's alright, Christoff, he is no threat."

"But—"

"Enough for now," stated Julian firmly. "I am weak and tired. Find him a room so we can all get the rest we need. We will talk tonight. Thomas, I'm thirsty—"

"Already in your room," the other man replied.

"Thanks. Oh, and just as a precaution, Thomas, select a few men to keep our guest company while the rest of us sleep. " Looking again at Michael, he said, "I may trust you, but a few of the others don't. No offence."

"None taken."

A slow smile appeared on Julian's face as he turned to descend the stairs. Entering his sleeping chamber, he walked directly to the fireplace. Leaning his head against the cold marble of the mantle, he tried to make sense of his troubled thoughts. It had occurred to him back at the club, as he watched Sonya administer to the injured girl, just how much she resembled Adrianna with her glorious, dark hair—although Adrianna's was a bit longer.

He sighed deeply as he envisioned her once again in his arms, the scent of her, the softness of her body pressing against him. She felt so damn good! But again, just as before, he felt the hunger rise as other feelings consumed his thoughts and senses. He reached for the goblet just inches away and drained the glass of thick red liquid.

SMASH!

He threw the delicate glass, shattering it into a million pieces against the opposite wall.

Would he ever be able to touch her without the hunger taking control? He remembered the confused look on her face as he made an excuse to leave—no, to run away. God, how he had wanted her! It had been so long—almost a lifetime—since he had felt desire like that for anyone. He wanted to feel her in his arms, kiss her softly, make love to her … not rip her throat out! He ignored the stab of pain as he slammed his fist into the marble mantle.

What was he to do? If she was who he thought she was, he had been given a second chance. A chance at happiness and redemption. He thought he'd lost his chance forever when his love had died all those centuries ago. Did Adrianna have the gift that could save him? He had to know; he had to be sure. Now that he had found her, he must find some way to keep her. He had done it before. He had learned to control the hunger so he could actually have a relationship with the woman he loved. He could do it again, but it would take time they didn't have. There was something out there hunting her. He had to find whoever or whatever it was before they found her. He had lost happiness once. He would die before he lost it again.

Walking over to the bed, he began to undress, his shirt falling to the ground in a flutter of silk. Still lost in thought he undid the button of his pants, sliding them off in one fluid motion. Standing naked in the firelight, his body tensed as he remembered the alarm he felt when, after the attack, he had rushed back into the club to find her already gone. When he finally left that evening, he had gone to the cottage.

On the balcony of his former home, he waited in silence, listening at the glass doors as the two women talked. He had felt her fear as she discussed the events of the evening. God how he wanted to take her in his arms and comfort her! But he dared not move. He waited patiently until all was silent. Then he heard her rhythmic breathing and knew she was asleep.

With a slight wave of his hand, the doors opened to him. Moving inside, he hid among the shadows and watched as she slept. She seemed restless.

Moving closer to the bed, he had leaned forward to whisper softly, calming her immediately. Her scent was intoxicating as he inhaled deeply, his fingers trailing a feather light caress along her cheek. Then he felt his hunger rising like the tide to wash away all in its path. The hunger flowed within him as long-buried emotions took control. He could feel his eyes bleed to black as they traced a trail across the soft shoulder and down to the gently rising mound of breast just visible through the sheer top she was wearing. With a swift intake of breath, he pulled away, forcing himself back into the far corner of the room.

"God!" he stood very still, fists clenched at his side. "Get control of yourself or you will be more dangerous to her than anything she may have encountered tonight."

His deep breaths came in gasps as the cool night air cleared his head. Fighting for composure, his chaotic emotions eventually returned to normal. Leaning back against the wall, he lost track of time. "So beautiful," he thought. "But I've known so many beautiful women. What makes this one so different?" As he moved forward one last time, he became aware of the night sky and realized dawn was slowly approaching. Moving toward the bed, she began to stir as he leaned over her and softly brushed his lips against her cheek.

"Rest my love, while you can," he whispered. Then he was gone, making it home just in time, much to Thomas's chagrin!

Coming back to reality, surrounded by the darkness of his windowless room, he sat on the bed as he prepared for the day to take him. His last thought was of soft brown hair brushing softly against his cheek as he fell into a dead sleep.

Chapter 9

"What is that ringing?" Addie thought as she fought to awaken. It couldn't be her alarm. It wasn't set. This was Sunday, her day off. But something was definitely interrupting the deep, peaceful sleep she had finally fallen into. As she forced her eyes to open, her foggy brain realized it was the loudly ringing phone. Reaching clumsily across the nightstand and knocking a box of tissues to the floor, she managed to grab the offensive object.

"Hello!"

"May I please speak to Adrianna Avani?" said a gruff voice on the other end of the line.

"Speaking. Who is this?" she asked as she came fully awake.

"Miss Avani, this is Detective Bertram. I'm with the city police department."

"Oh, yes, detective?" she replied a little breathlessly, apprehension gripping her as she sat up.

"Miss Avani, I'm sorry to wake you but there's been an accident at your dress shop. We would like you to come to the station as soon as possible and—"

"An accident! What kind of accident? We were just there last night and everything was fine."

"Was Kim Taylor there with you?"

"Yes, that's why my co-worker and I stopped in, to check on her," Addie said.

"So she was fine when you left?" he continued.

"Yes, she was just closing up. We walked her to her car, then left. I think she pulled out right behind us. What's this about, detective? Is Kim alright?" She tried to control the panic rising inside of her.

"No, miss, I'm afraid she's not alright. Some early morning walkers noticed the door to your shop was open. When they looked inside, they found Miss Taylor. I'm afraid she's been murdered. I really don't want to get into details on the phone. Would you and Miss St. John be able to come down to the station this morning?" he continued politely.

"Yes … I … we'll be right there," she said, her voice barely a whisper as the receiver fell from her hands onto the floor.

She was numb and could barely move. "This can't be happening," she told herself. "Kim is fine, the police are mistaken. Yes, that's it." They would go down to the station and find out it was all a mistake. Throwing off the covers, she jumped from bed and replaced the receiver before running to Kate's room.

"Kate, wake up! It's Addie," she said, pounding on the door. Not waiting for the other girl to answer, she flung the door open and ran to the bed, where a mass of red hair was the only thing visible from under the mound of bedcovers.

"Kate, wake up!" Addie ordered as she pulled the covers back and shook her friend roughly.

"Wha? Addie, for Pete's sake, what do you want? It's Sunday. I'm tired." Kate pulled the bedcovers back over her head.

"No, Kate, please, come on, wake up, something's happened." As the words finally penetrated her foggy mind, Kate jumped up and tried to focus.

"Something's happened? What? What's wrong?"

"The police called," Addie began slowly, trying to control her tears.

"The police? Why?"

"It's Kim. They said she's been … murdered." Addie could barely get the word out.

Kate gasped in shock. "Murdered?! That's impossible, she was fine last night. There must be some mistake."

"That's what I thought, too. They want us to come down to the station. It's the only way we'll find out the truth. I told him we would be there as soon as we can." Addie moved as if in slow motion, grabbing the crumpled clothes Kate had discarded last night and absentmindedly setting them on the bed.

"Yes, go down to the station. That's what we'll do. We'll get it all straightened out," Kate agreed, throwing aside her cover and leaping from bed. "We'll go there and find out it was someone else entirely, that they've made a mistake. Come on, we better hurry."

An hour later, as they both sat in Bertram's office, they realized the nightmare was just beginning. Kate sobbed quietly in the chair next to her as Addie, wiping tears from her eyes, took a deep breath before asking, "I don't understand. You're telling us that you're trying to tie this attack to the previous murders, but the pattern was different this time? The other bodies had been drained of blood, but that's not what happened to … Kim?" Addie could barely say the name as memories of the pretty, smiling face flashed across her mind.

"We were hoping this incident was done by the same person. It would make our job a little simpler if we were looking for just one person, but there are distinct differences with this case." Bertram watched both girls carefully, realizing there was no easy way to say what needed to be said. "While the cause of death in the others was massive blood loss, Miss Taylor's body was … well, there's no nice way to put it. She was literally torn to pieces."

"Oh my God," sobbed Kate.

"I'm very sorry," he said with real concern. "I know it's a lot to take in, but if you can try to tell us what happened while you were with her last night, it would be a great help. If we can paint a complete picture of her last evening alive, we may find something that will connect her death to the other murders. If there is no connection, then things are worse than we thought, if that's even possible."

"What do you mean?" asked Addie.

"If we can't connect Miss Taylor's death to the others, then we have two killers and our job will be twice as hard," he replied as the girls stared at each other in disbelief. Walking over to a large coffee pot on a shelf beneath his window, he poured them each a cup of steaming coffee. After taking a sip, Addie filled him in on the events of the night before, including the disturbance at the club and the strange man Kim had encountered earlier at the shop.

"Very interesting," he said. When she mentioned the strange howling, he could not hide his interest. "But you didn't see what made the sound?"

"No, they wouldn't let anyone leave the club, so we didn't see very much at all. And, strangely enough, there was no trace of any kind of disturbance outside when they finally did let us go. Did your men find anything after they arrived?"

"Yes," he replied cautiously, "but I'm afraid that's all restricted information."

"Of course, I'm sorry," Addie said. "I didn't mean to pry, but, well, it was all so very weird. With no outward signs of anything actually happening, we were both questioning our own sanity."

He looked thoughtfully at both of them then seemed to make a decision, "Well, you didn't imagine anything. Something is definitely going on, and it seems to be centered on that club. And getting any information from the owners of the place is like pulling teeth. We leave with more questions than answers. My advice to both of you is to avoid that place for a while. For some reason, people don't have the common sense to stay out of areas that are dangerous, and then it's too late. It bothers me, these two seemingly separate incidents happening on the same night, only miles apart. I'm missing something, some clue. But if it's out there, I'll find it. We're getting close, I can feel it. Well, anyway, thank you both for coming down." He stood as they rose to leave.

"I'm sorry we weren't more help, detective," Addie said as she shook his hand.

"You've been more help than you know," he told them and, almost as an afterthought, added, "I'm afraid the shop will have to remain closed for a while."

"Of course. Do you know approximately how long?" Addie asked. She was actually feeling grateful because neither of them wanted to go anywhere near the boutique for quite some time. How were they ever going to carry on with business as usual after this?

"Just until we get forensics in there to go over everything with a fine-tooth comb. I'm sorry, I know this is your livelihood. I promise we'll be as quick as possible. But to tell you the truth, I wouldn't feel safe about you going back to work until we have a better idea of what went down there. We'll make sure everything is ready for the shop to open when we're through," he said kindly, not wanting them to walk in on a horror scene.

"Thank you," both replied in unison.

Looking over her shoulder as they went out the door, Addie said, "Find the killer, detective. That's the only thing that's important."

"We'll do our best, miss."

As he watched them leave, the detective leaned back and went over their conversation. One thing stood out in his mind: "A horrible howling sound." That would make sense, for Kim had been brutally torn apart, as if by a wild animal.

Addie drove the red sports car slowly through the center of town. Crowds of people on either side of the busy street went about their daily business. Didn't they know something was wrong? Didn't they know a young girl had died horribly? How could they laugh and shop and be happy as if nothing had happened? "Well, it didn't happen to any of them, did it? It happened to my friend," she thought numbly. Now Kim's life was over, ended savagely by some unknown predator. How many more people were going to die before the monster responsible was brought to justice?

She drove on, slowing to a crawl as they came upon the corner where their shop stood. The police were there, probably looking for any evidence, and their building was cordoned off with yellow tape. A sick feeling settled in the pit of her stomach. "This can't be happening," she kept telling herself, but as she glanced into the rearview mirror, the yellow tape offered proof that it was very real.

They drove home in total silence. When they arrived, Kate decided to lie down as she was suddenly not feeling well. She moved slowly down the hallway toward her room, turning back to look at Addie with red and swollen eyes, a fresh teardrop glistening on her cheek.

"I wish someone would shake me really hard and wake me up from this horrible nightmare. When is it going to end, Addie? Who will the next victim be …" She broke off as the tears flowed.

"I don't know, Kate. I wish I had the answers, but they're doing all they can," Addie replied, knowing her words offered little comfort.

"Well it's not enough!" Kate said, walking into her room and slamming the door behind her.

Sitting at the kitchen table, sipping another cup of strong coffee, Addie tried to absorb all they had learned that morning. Coming to a decision, she grabbed the car keys and headed for the front door. She was certain Julian knew something, and she was determined to find out what it was. She owed Kim that much. She decided driving would be better this time, considering the armed security around the house. Remembering Brutus, she ran back to the kitchen to get some dog treats. They would come in handy if she encountered her furry friend again.

Making the short drive to the main house, she kept her eyes alert for any sign of the security team. She thought she saw a figure off in the distance as she drove through the woods, but she couldn't be sure. "Well, they can stop me if they want to. It might be the quickest way to see Julian," she told herself. Five minutes later, she pulled to a stop in front of the old mansion. Getting slowly out of the car, she looked around for any sign of activity. There was no one, only silence. Where was everyone? But the fact that no one accosted her made her relax a little.

As she was about to go up the front steps, Kate's handsome friend from the club, his shoulder-length head of curls tied in a ponytail, came walking around the side of the house. Brutus was right behind him. Trying not to appear nervous as she heard an ominous growl deep in the animal's throat, she held out the hand containing the biscuit.

"Hey boy, remember me? I brought you something," she said. With the promise of a tasty morsel staring it in the face, the dog immediately stopped growling. But he did not approach and eyed her warily. Was it assessing the situation to determine if she was a threat, or waiting for an order from the man standing beside him? She couldn't be sure.

"Sit," the man ordered, and the animal obeyed immediately. "Hello again. Can I help you? Were you looking for someone?" A quick smile spread across his handsome face.

"I'm sorry," said Addie hesitantly. "I didn't mean to intrude." She held her hand out to Thomas. "I don't know if you remember me, I'm Adrianna Avani, your neighbor from the cottage. We met briefly last night at the club, and if I remember correctly, you said Julian lived here. I was out running some errands and thought I'd drop by and properly introduce myself since we met so briefly last night." The grin widened across his face as he listened to her senseless babbling. "Since we met so briefly last night"? What a lame excuse. She felt the blush climb up her throat, covering her face in a lovely shade of pink.

"I seem to be making a habit of showing up unannounced," she said. "I ran into a man named Brian the other day while I was out walking, and he indicated that it would be alright if I stopped by as long as I could persuade our large friend there to let me enter the grounds which," she showed Thomas the biscuit, "is the reason for my tasty bribe."

"I'm Thomas," he said, the smile deepening as he took her outstretched hand and raised it to his lips instead of the handshake she expected. "And yes, Julian lives here, and I do remember you and your friend, very well. You'd better give Brutus the biscuit before he drowns us in drool." He glanced at the dog. A long strand of saliva was hanging from the side of its huge jaw, but the dog remained where he had been ordered to stay. She could tell by the look in its large brown eyes that it wanted nothing more than to snatch the biscuit from her waiting hand.

"Sorry boy, here you go," she said, letting the dog take the treat from her and watching as he gobbled it down in a matter of seconds.

"So you met Brian? Then you must know we've been having some poaching problems around here lately. It could be dangerous roaming the area alone. You might want to think twice before doing it again." His tone of voice was firm, but there was no real anger at her trespassing—as far as she could tell. Given all that had happened lately, she didn't blame him for trying to point out her carelessness.

"Yes, he did warn me about that, and again, I apologize for showing up unannounced, but as I didn't have any other way of contacting anyone here, I thought it would be alright to drop by. Is Julian at home?"

Was it her imagination, or did he seem to hesitate, as if choosing his words carefully, before replying, "Yes, he is home, but he's usually a very late riser due to his late nights at the club. He doesn't see anyone until evening." Then, with a twinkle in his eye, he continued, "But I will be happy to tell him you were asking about him." Finally, as he noticed her reluctance to leave, he added, "Was there something I could help you with?"

"Oh no," Addie replied anxiously. "It's just … oh, never mind, it's nothing. If you would just let him know I stopped by, I would appreciate it." She turned to go then suddenly changed her mind. She had come here for a reason, and she wasn't going to leave until she had some answers. Turning back to him, she said, "You know, Thomas, that's not true. There is something you or Julian … or someone who was at that club last night … can help me with." The shock of the morning's news caused her voice to rise in anger. "Kate and I just found out this morning that we lost a good friend … she was brutally murdered by some maniac … and I have an awful feeling that it's all connected. The events at the club last night, our friend Kim's death, the earlier attacks. I wish someone would tell me what the hell is going on in this town!" Her control snapped, and tears for Kim rolled down her cheeks, her chest heaving from the force of her sobs.

"Addie, Addie, I'm so sorry. I didn't mean to be a heartless brute," he said as he put his arm around her shoulders. "Here, come on, calm down." He handed her a handkerchief. "Please, tell me what happened to your friend."

Between sobs, she told him about their visit to the police station that morning. She watched him grow angrier by the minute as she related everything the detective had told them. When she was finished he said, "I'm really sorry about your friend, Addie, but I'm not sure Julian can tell you anything that will help you. Your friend's attack sounds different than the others, but you did say the police were trying to tie them together?"

"Yes, that's what the detective hopes to do, or it looks like they may have two different killers on their hands."

"Yes … two," he replied, seemingly deep in thought. "Come on, Addie, I'll walk you back to your car. I'll tell Julian you were here and fill him in on what you've told me. Are you going to be home later?"

"I think so. We're not in the mood to do much after this morning."

"I can't speak for Julian, but I'm pretty sure he will want to talk to you, so maybe we can set something up for tonight."

"Okay. Thank you, Thomas."

"I haven't done anything yet, but you're welcome. Ah, will you give my regards to Kate?" Thomas asked.

"Of course. Bye now. Oh, Thomas, do you want the phone number?"

"Ah, I already have it … from Kate," he said with a grin.

"Right" she said, smiling back. "See you later. Maybe." After shutting her car door, she turned in the driveway and headed back down the road. Reaching the cottage, she parked the car and walked inside lost in thought.

"Where have you been?" Kate asked as Addie entered the kitchen and headed straight for the coffee pot.

"You don't want to know," Addie stated firmly.

"Given all that's happened lately, yes, I do." Kate was staring at her so expectantly that, with a deep sigh, Addie told her about the meeting with Thomas.

"You saw Thomas? Did he ask about me?" Kate asked, trying not to sound too eager.

"As a matter of fact, he did. He said to make sure I tell you hello," she said, smiling at her friend's obvious pleasure. Then, remembering the reason she went to the big house in the first place, she sobered a little. "I was really hoping to get some information, but Thomas said Julian was still asleep. I guess it makes sense. If you work that late every night, you wouldn't be an early riser. But there has to be times when you'd like to enjoy a bright sunny day, right? And Thomas didn't seem any the worse for wear from his late night."

"Maybe your handsome friend is a vampire," Kate said, stunning her friend. "Look at this." She threw the morning paper down on the kitchen table. "Vampire Killer Strikes Again" screamed the headline. The article was about the attacks at the club the night before. It said the disturbance was still under investigation. It also stated there were "similarities" to other attacks in the area, but offered no real details. In a statement to the press, the police said they were following every possible lead to get to the bottom of these bizarre murders.

"This is getting weirder by the minute," said Kate.

The phone rang loudly, causing both girls to jump nervously as Addie turned to answer it.

"Hi, Rick," she said, "why am I not surprised to hear from you this morning?" She tensed as she awaited the onslaught she knew she was going to hear from the other end of the line.

"Sarcasm doesn't become you, Addie," he scolded. "I heard about the trouble last night. It seems I had good reason to be worried about you two. I suppose you were right in the thick of it?"

"Yes, we were, but I made sure to throw a few good punches while I had the chance. You know, give them something to think about," she said. "Really, Rick, give us a little credit. We were safe inside the club the whole time. So we don't know much about what actually happened. Most of the trouble was outside, and they weren't letting anyone leave. When it all started, their security locked the place down tight, so you see, you worried for nothing. They seemed to handle everything just fine. We watched for a while from a window, but it was so dark we couldn't make out a thing. We did hear some screaming, but it sounded far away, and then there was this awful howling sound."

"Howling" Rick repeated, surprised. "What kind of howling? From what?"

"That's what no one seems to be able to tell us," she said. "When they finally did let us outside, there were no physical signs that anything had happened ... no bodies, no damage. Nothing. It made no sense! By then, all we wanted to do was go home. Since everything appeared to be under control, and we didn't want to play twenty questions with the police, we left."

"I told you not to go there, Addie. You should have listened to me," he said, but his voice sounded strange, almost distracted.

"Rick, we're fine. The club owners handled the emergency. They have good security, and the threat was contained. I told you, there was no sign of any trouble," she said.

"Oh, they handled it all right, but not well enough to prevent people from dying!" he said, almost shouting at her.

"Dying? What are you talking about? All we heard was that several people had been attacked, but no one said anything about any of them dying."

"They found several bodies, Addie, dead bodies, in the park across the street from the club! Young kids who'd hardly begun their lives. " He was barely able to keep his voice under control. "But that's not the worst of it. Among the phone calls I received this morning about funeral services for some of the victims was one from a friend of mine. I ..." his voice broke as he tried to continue.

"Oh, Rick, no, not someone you knew," Addie said, shocked.

"Not just someone I knew. You knew him, too. It was Nick's father who called me ... Nick is dead, Addie."

"No ... no, that can't be. I saw ... we saw him," she said, looking to Kate for confirmation. But all the other woman could do was mouth the word, "Who?"

"He's dead, Addie, there's no question. He was found in the park along with the others. The only marks found on his body were two small puncture wounds on the side of his neck. All the victims, Nick included, were drained of blood. Completely. They had no chance, Addie, none at all against whatever it was that attacked them. You probably didn't see anything because you were too far away. God, how I wish you, or someone, had seen something, anything, that would help the authorities come up with some answers. Do you understand now why I don't want you near that place?"

"Oh God, Rick, I can't believe it! Not Nick! I saw him sneak outside with his camera ready … the camera! Rick, maybe he got off some shots. Maybe there are pictures of whoever did this. Did they find—"

"They found the camera, Addie," Rick's said, his voice a little quieter now. "It was empty. Someone made sure that film was destroyed. So we have nothing, no evidence. I hope whatever Nick was chasing was worth the cost because it seems to me that he died for no good reason! But one thing is certain. Someone doesn't want anyone to know what's going on at that club."

"Who told you about the bodies, Rick? The paper said nothing."

"I told you I was called for funeral arrangements. When I heard from Nick's family, I felt I had the right to ask a few questions. I went to the police station and demanded some answers. Then I went down to the morgue and saw the bodies. Some of them had more than just two small puncture wounds."

"What do you mean?" she asked, not sure she really wanted him to explain.

"A few of the bodies were … torn to pieces. Literally. Addie, I've never seen anything like it in my entire life, and I've seen some awful things in my years as a priest."

A chill came over her. "Did you say torn to pieces?" she asked, staring at Kate with a shocked expression.

"What? Addie, what's he talking about?" Kate whispered, leaning closer to the phone in an attempt to hear the conversation.

"Rick, there's something I have to tell you. After Nick—"

"Just tell me, Addie. How much worse can it get?"

"You have no idea," she said. As she told him about Kim and their visit with Detective Bertram, she could hear his sharp intake of breath.

"Kim?" he said. "I'm so sorry, honey. Had I known, I would have been a little more sensitive in breaking the news about Nick. You both must have gone through hell this morning. Is there anything I can do?"

"Yes, talk me down off of the ledge. I feel partly responsible."

"You? What are you talking about?"

"We went to the shop, Rick," Addie said. "We walked with her to the car. She must have gone back inside for some reason. If we'd only stayed to make sure she'd actually left, or made her follow us, she'd be alive today."

"Or the police would have found three bodies instead of one. Addie, you can't blame yourself, and the detective was right. I don't think you should go near the boutique for a while, even when they are through with it, until they find some answers. The murderer struck there once. He may be watching for another chance. Think about it, Addie, why your shop? All the other attacks were in the vicinity of the club. Why wasn't this one?"

"What are you getting at, Rick?" But the sick feeling in the pit of her stomach told her the answer before he said the words.

"Addie, all the victims looked similar. The police are already pretty sure they have a serial killer on their hands. And we already know that, well, that you possess the very traits the killer seems drawn to in his victims. Maybe Kim wasn't the target. Maybe she was just in the wrong place at the wrong time. Or maybe—"

"Alright, alright!" she shouted, visibly shaken. "The police are looking into the apparent change in location for this attack. That and the difference in the way the victims were killed. They are hoping to find something that will tie everything together, though. If they can't, things are worse than we thought."

"What do you mean?" Rick asked.

"If they can't make a reasonable connection, then we have not one but two separate killers, maybe more."

"I guess all we can do now is let the police do their job and try to stay alert. There is something happening here that affects all of us. If we keep our eyes and ears open, maybe someone will notice something that will give the police the break they need to solve this mess. We have a good force. They'll find the ones who did this. If I hear anything else, I'll call you right away. You both be careful. Don't take any unnecessary chances. Give my love to Kate. Talk to you later." Addie heard his soft good-bye as she hung up the phone. Kate stared at her, eyes large and questioning.

"Nick?"

"He's dead, Kate."

"Oh my God!"

"I can't believe it either. It seems he was one of several victims at the club last night. I can still see him heading for the exit, going after his big story. He was so excited. I should have tried to stop him. I should—"

"It's not your fault, Addie. We had no idea that something like this would happen."

"It's just so awful. Nick and Kim. I just can't believe it," she said, shaking her head.

"I'm starting to get really scared, Addie. This has always been such a quiet, peaceful little town. Nothing like this has ever happened here. What's going on? And why is it happening now?"

"I don't know, Kate, but I'm as frightened as you are. Rick said he will let us know if he finds out anything else," Addie said as she sat down at the kitchen table. "We just have to stay alert and be careful."

"I wish I could say he worries too much, but I guess he has good reason," Kate said. "Well, I guess we should eat something. It's way past lunch. We should be starving."

Not surprisingly, neither of them had the slightest interest in food.

Originally, they had planned to spend their day off doing some shopping and checking out Carolyn's, a new boutique in town and their nearest competitor, but now none of that seemed important.

"I would like to go somewhere. If I stay in this house a minute longer I think I'll go crazy," Kate said.

"We could go to Mocha Joe's for coffee and get a bagel or something," Addie suggested. "Are you up for that?"

"That sounds good. The coffee shop it is. We'll have an early supper and head back here for a quiet evening, before it gets dark. "

As they prepared to leave, Addie remembered something she'd forgot to mention. "Um Kate, I forgot to tell you—"

"You forgot to tell me what?" Kate waited expectantly. "Not more bad news, I hope."

"No, nothing like that. It's just that this morning, when I was talking to Thomas—"

"Yes?"

"He asked if we'd be home tonight. He mentioned something about him and Julian maybe stopping by later."

"Are you serious? That would be great, right?" Kate asked, trying to read the expression on Addie's face.

"Yes, I think so. It's just … what do we really know about either of them? And with all that's been happening—"

"I know, I know. We should probably be a little more cautious with any new people. But Addie, I don't know, I'm a pretty good judge of character, and I did spend a little time with Thomas. I picked up nothing but good vibes from him. I think he's okay. What about Julian?"

"I really didn't get a chance to spend much time with him, but he made me feel … safe. Does that make sense to you?"

"Yes, it does. And that's a good thing. Then it's agreed. We'll give them both a chance, okay?"

"Okay," Addie agreed. "Maybe we'll get answers to a few of the questions I've been waiting to ask our handsome neighbor."

Chapter 10

Driving toward town with Kate, Addie watched the passing traffic, already bumper to bumper with weekend shoppers. Again she thought, "How out of sync we are with the world around us when a tragedy affects our life." She realized she had to shake this mood she was settling into or she would soon be dealing with severe depression, and Kim would not have wanted that.

Entering the busy town, they were grateful to find a parking space as they pulled into the lot that serviced the tiny coffee shop. After locking the car door, Addie noticed two women standing near their own car a few feet away, deep in conversation. Trying not to intentionally eavesdrop, she couldn't help but pick up a whisper here and there as she and Kate walked by.

"They said all of the women attacked so far resembled each other … long, dark hair … brown eyes … same height and weight," a petite woman with short brown curls was telling her friend, a tall, willowy blonde. "I'm making sure I keep my hair as short as possible until they catch the crazy responsible."

"Yes, I did hear something like that," her friend replied. "Don't most serial killers usually have some sort of pattern …?"

The conversation drifted off as the women got into their car, and Addie could hear no more. A sick feeling settled in the pit of her stomach as their words played over and over in Addie's mind.

"Are you alright, honey?" Kate asked, noticing how pale she had become.

"I'm fine, I just need some food. Let's go get something to eat," she replied.

"I'm ready. There's a great big muffin just dripping in chocolate icing calling my name. Nothing like a great sugar rush to make you forget the problems of the day," Kate said grabbing Addie by the arm and pulling her up the front steps.

"I can already taste it," Addie said, forcing a laugh as they entered the shop famous for homemade pastries and delicious coffee.

After placing their order at the counter, they found an empty table near the front window that afforded a great view of the main street. After a moment's hesitation, Addie decided to mention the conversation she had overheard.

"Do you really think there is a pattern to these murders, Kate? That this monster is singling out only dark haired women? Maybe I should be worried," she said, fingering a strand of her own brown hair. "Oh my God … poor Kim."

"Yes, I know. I still can't believe what happened—"

"No, Kate, that's not what I meant. I mean … well, yes, it's horrible what happened to her but, well, Rick brought up a point I hadn't thought of. He thinks Kim might have been in the wrong place at the wrong time. That the murderer was actually looking for someone else."

"Of course she was in the wrong place! What are you getting at?" Kate said.

"Think about it, Kate, it's our shop and the profile is women with long brown hair. Kim has short, black hair. What if it wasn't some random attack? What if they were looking for someone in particular—like me—but found her instead. They had to dispose of her because she saw who they were. What if she died because of me?"

"Don't be ridiculous, Addie. Why would anyone want to hurt you? The other girls were random targets, same as Kim was. They were spotted while out for the evening, then followed and attacked. Yes, this psycho may have a preference for long brown hair, but that doesn't mean he was looking for you in particular. Besides, they're not even sure Kim's death is connected to the other murders, remember? I think as a matter of safety everyone, regardless of their hair color should be a lot more cautious, and nothing will happen to anyone else." Kate paused. "Look, we won't go to the club for a while. The shop will be closed for at least a week or more, and we'll keep the cottage locked up tight. If we use our heads, we'll be just fine until they catch whoever is responsible. And they will."

"You're probably right, I know, I'm just a little paranoid right now. I guess that conversation really affected me. What is it they say about people who eavesdrop?"

"You never hear anything good about yourself," Kate answered.

"Exactly. We'll be fine if we just keep our wits about us."

As they drank their coffee in silence, Kate tried desperately to think of something to shake their mood. Then, flashing Addie a huge grin, she said, "Do you really think Thomas and Julian will stop by tonight? Since we won't be going to the club for a while, I was wondering when we would have a chance to see them again."

"I think that problem has been resolved."

"Huh?" As Kate followed Addie's gaze, she saw one of the men in question. Thomas was waiting on the corner to cross the street. As the traffic signal changed, he came straight toward the coffee shop. Kate couldn't seem to take her eyes off the handsome young man.

Entering the shop, he noticed the girls and, after ordering a coffee to go, walked over to say hello.

"Well, what a nice surprise. Here are two beautiful women just waiting to give some company to a lonely fellow. Addie, twice in one day. How lucky can one man be?" he said, flashing a mischievous grin. "Kate, how are you?" he asked, lingering a little as he took her hand.

"Fine, thanks. Won't you join us?" she invited, sliding over to an empty chair hoping he would accept her invitation.

"I would love to, but unfortunately, I'm running some errands and people are anxiously awaiting my return." He winked at them. "You know how it is. But I'd love a rain check."

"Anytime," Kate was quick to reply, and Addie bowed her head to hide the grin on her face. Then, remembering their meeting that morning, she turned quickly back to Thomas saying, "I hope Julian wasn't annoyed by my visit earlier?"

He hesitated slightly before replying, "Um, since that night owl still isn't up yet, I can't answer your question, but knowing him as I do, I can honestly say he wouldn't mind a lovely lady stopping by to visit. I'm sure you'll be hearing from him when he rises."

"Thomas, you're coffee's ready," a young girl said, giving him her best smile as she placed two coffees and two really large muffins on the table before Addie and Kate.

"Thanks, hon," he said.

"Well, I'll leave you to your ... lunch?" he said with raised eyebrows as he stared at the muffins dripping with chocolate icing and whipped cream.

"Sugar. It's good for what ails you," Kate explained, a little embarrassed.

"Riiight ... well, I hope to see you again soon, possibly even later this evening."

"That would be great," Kate was quick to answer.

Thomas said good-bye and quickly left the shop.

Staring after him until he was no longer in sight, Kate turned to Addie who was deep in thought.

"Uh oh, now what?" she said. "I know that look, Addie."

"Huh? Oh, it's nothing. It's just ... what a strange thing to say. 'When he rises.' What do you suppose he meant by that?"

"Isn't it obvious?" said Kate. "The man is still sleeping."

"It's four o'clock in the afternoon!" exclaimed the girls in unison.

"Well, he must be tired," said Kate. "After all, he did have a rather stressful night."

"You're probably right, but it seems such an odd choice of words," said Addie thoughtfully.

Kate smiled. "You know, Addie, I think Thomas could possibly be the handsomest man I've ever met."

"Hmmm, really? Didn't you say that about some muscle-bound blond you met last month?"

"Yeah, I guess I did. But this time I mean it!"

"All right, you've made your point. Now, let's eat this heavenly sight before I starve to death. We probably should head back soon," she said, staring at the kaleidoscope of color in the late afternoon sky.

Thirty minutes later as they left the shop heading for the car, Addie's gaze traveled down the length of the main street. "Kate, do you think we should stop by the shop? See if they cleaned—"

"Absolutely not. Look, Addie, that's the last place we need to be. I want to get back to work just as much as you, but I think we need to give ourselves, and the other employees, time to adjust to what's happened. Let the police finish their job and clean the place up so it will at least look like nothing horrendous happened there. I'm really not looking forward to the first time we have to go back there. Let's not rush it."

"I just feel like we should be doing something more, but I have no idea what. Maybe we could pick up on something the police missed. After all, who knows that place better than we do? We could ... no, you're right, let's just get home. We probably shouldn't be roaming around after dark, anyway." As she looked around the town, she noticed the streets were becoming quiet and empty. It was definitely not a typical Sunday. "And it looks like we're not the only ones who feel that way."

"Yeah. It's kind of spooky, really," Kate said. "Come on, let's go."

Chapter 11

As the sun began to set, the sky was filled with a strange mixture of grey, black, and red before the blackness descended. Julian awoke from a sleep filled with disturbing images, the past once again haunting his dreams. A beautiful face, the lifeless brown eyes staring back at him, long, brown hair matted in blood. How long were those images going to haunt him? How long must he suffer this torment? The crystal goblet waiting on the nightstand glistened in the firelight. Reaching for it, he drank deeply. Feeling raw power surge through his body, he responded quickly to the pounding at his bedroom door.

"Julian, its Thomas. Are you awake?"

Julian opened the door to Thomas, Michael, and Christoff, who seemed impatient to enter.

"I think you need to hear what the stranger has to say," Thomas said as Michael moved to stand beside the fireplace, the flames reflecting off his golden locks actually causing the room to brighten.

Raising a hand to protect his eyes as he tried to stare at the man before him, Julian demanded, "What is so important that you had to awaken me from my rest?"

Eyeing the vampire intently, Michael spoke softly, "Do you want to discover those who are responsible for the brutal attacks in your city?"

"What kind of game is this? We are doing all in our power to solve the mystery of these attacks," Julian stated, fighting to control his temper. Looking deeply into Julian's eyes, Michael replied calmly, as if he was unaware of the anger boiling inside the vampire.

"No game, my friend. But you are not using your wits in this matter. Think! Do you really not know the one who is responsible, the one who has returned? Search your heart, vampire, the answer is there."

"Bahh! This one talks in riddles. He knows nothing!" Christoff raged. "We do not need his kind. He only complicates matters in the guise of helping."

"Easy, my friend," Julian said, laying a hand on the dark vampire's shoulder. Michael had begun a slow, easy pacing, back and forth in front of the small group, but his eyes never left Julian's face. "Let's hear what this Michael has to say. He seems to be under the delusion that he has information we want. Let's see if he's right. Speak, and this better be worth my while."

A slow smile spread across the handsome face. "Your posturing, your show of authority is wasted on me, Julian."

"No, Christoff!" Julian shouted as he stopped the vampire from charging at Michael.

"I mean no disrespect to your leader, warrior. I only meant that Julian's strength and leadership are without question. While I am here, I will follow him as you do. I wish you to know that my purpose is the same as yours, to root out the evil that is plaguing this area and destroy it. It has been the sole purpose for my existence for a very long time. This is not the first time I have seen this darkness. Felt its smothering presence. No, my friends, it has risen from time to time throughout the centuries, leaving a trail of blood as its calling card. I have managed to reduce its numbers over the years, for the evil behind the destruction sends his slaves to do his dirty work. I usually prefer to work alone but now, it seems he wishes to involve you, for there is something connected to you," he said, his eyes still locked on Julian, "or perhaps it's you, yourself, that he wants. I have no problem working together for the common good, but know this. If you are the first to find the one we seek, you will need my help to destroy him."

"Arrogant fool!" Christoff shouted in anger. "Who are you, a mere man, to think we need your help to win a battle? We have been fighting and killing for centuries before you were even a seed in your sire's loins!"

"You think so, my dark friend? You know nothing of my lord and sire, at least not for a very long time," Michael said, and something in his blue gaze caused Christoff to swallow the retort that had been ready on his lips.

"Christoff, please," Julian said, raising his hand. Looking back at Michael, he asked, "And why should your presence be so important to us? Christoff is right, we have fought many battles through the centuries, and I don't recall one of them where a man such as yourself was needed for us to claim victory." Yet something told Julian this was no ordinary man.

"You need me this time, vampire, because of the nature of the one we seek," Michael stated simply.

"If you're so sure you know who this monster is, then why are we wasting time? Tell us where he is, and we will destroy him!" Julian shouted, frustration causing him to lose patience.

A smile crossed Michael's beautiful face as he replied calmly, "Temper, my ancient friend, will get you nowhere with me. Direct your anger where it is most useful. Yes, I know who we seek, but I do not know where he has hidden himself. So, you see, I need you as much as you need me. The answer is buried here," he said, placing a hand on Julian's heart, "but you refuse to believe what you know is true. Yet even you do not know his true origins. He's lived for generations before making you. Yes," Michael said as comprehension dawned on Julian's face. "Ah, the light comes on as the mystery reveals itself. He's lived for generations, causing the same havoc through the centuries as he is now until, finally, I was sent to stop him. You know I am speaking the truth, Julian. We must work together, before he reaches the girl, for she is the key to what he is hoping to accomplish."

Julian heard Thomas whisper behind him, "What is he talking about, Julian?"

Julian turned slowly to stare at his friend. Could Michael be right? Could his past finally be catching up to him? And if it was true, how much should he tell those who would fight beside him? Most of the vampires among Julian's hoard knew his origins, having lived almost as long as he, but none of the humans did, including Thomas. The young man had proven his loyalty to Julian a thousand times over since the night fate had thrown them together. Julian knew he owed him an explanation, but it was the last thing he wanted to talk about.

Moving to stand in front of the fire, hoping the warmth would dispel the coldness he felt inside, he looked again at Thomas and, with a deep sigh, began his story.

"It seems my past is about to catch up to me, Thomas. I have a story I should have told you a long time ago, and it's not a pleasant one. I was not born a vampire as some are. I was turned a long … centuries ago," he paused as his mind drifted back through the years. "I had title and wealth where I came from. This appealed to him. Only the strongest would do for the army he was amassing. Only the most powerful would enable him to be in control, so I was taken against my will and turned into an abomination by the most evil creature of our kind. He was known as Dragon."

"In the early stages, I was like a thing gone wild. I did things I will regret for the rest of my unnatural life, but it was all the monster in me knew. The hunger … that awful hunger drove me until, finally, a small spark of humanity buried deep within my lost soul managed to surface. It was then that I realized there were other ways to exist. I did not have to take human life."

Pausing for a moment, he whispered almost to himself, "He was not happy with this turn of events. The destruction of humankind meant little to him. In fact, that seemed to be his main goal. In his arrogance, he sought to control all before him, become the master of all he surveyed. In his army, he chose well. Only the best, the strongest, would he convert, and most served him willingly. The ones not chosen he would harvest for food."

"That was his only purpose? The destruction of the human race?" Thomas asked, horrified.

"His purpose was the same as most of his kind … power," Michael answered before Julian could respond.

"He planned for the vampires to rule, and he would be their god!" Julian added, his voice rising as anger and hatred, took control. "I convinced others to flee and taught them to feed my way, without killing." He turned to look at Christoff, "And those who were once his most loyal subjects were now his strongest enemies. We searched out his minions and destroyed those we could. The more he created, the more we destroyed. It was our way of paying back a little of our debt to society, to those who had been slain by our own hands before we realized we had another choice."

The room fell silent for a moment as the two vampires seemed caught up in memories of a violent past. Taking a deep breath, Julian continued, "Then a rumor surfaced. Against all odds, I dared to hope, to believe in a miracle. It seems I was not the only one of my kin who had lost his mortality to a monster. But because of my long dead ancestor, there was a chance for a cure to my affliction. A certain gene, unknowingly passed to a few of my ancestor's heirs, could cure a vampire of the same bloodline. I needed to find a woman, the right woman, who carried the gene. She was my one chance to regain what I had stolen from me, my humanity. I searched everywhere, and eventually I found her, and so did he. My maker had also heard the rumor and was immediately on the hunt for anyone he thought would help me accomplish my goal. It became his obsession to thwart me, for he would not allow me something he could never have. Redemption. He destroyed anyone he thought had the power to save me. He found and destroyed her, ending my one chance for a normal life, and the only thing I have ever truly loved!" Julian fought for control as the memories flooded his mind. Turning back to Thomas he said, "But I thought he had been destroyed, for there has been no sign of him for many years."

"None that you were aware of," Michael said. "You just refused to read the signs, my friend. Hitler, Manson, Bin Laden … there are many names a face can hide behind. Evil finds a way. It is always present."

"So he has been with us all this time?" Julian asked.

"It would seem so. As long as you were a vampire, he was content to let you be. But now someone has surfaced that could be the means to your salvation ... once again."

"And so," Julian continued, "he is here. I have been having strange dreams, images of the past, but couldn't understand why. Then the murders began, but still my mind rebelled against what I knew was happening again. I refused to believe it could be the same evil, refused to believe he was here to torment me again. Until I met her," he said looking directly at Thomas.

"Adrianna," Thomas said in stunned surprise.

"Yes, Adrianna. From the moment she moved into the cottage, I could sense her, but even then, I fought against the truth. There couldn't possibly be another," his hopeful face turned toward Michael, "could there?"

"Trust your feelings, my friend."

Wondering, against all odds, if he had been granted another chance, he turned again to Thomas. "Did you have a chance to do some looking into her background?"

"I went to town this afternoon and ran into the lady in question, by the way, along with the lovely Kate," he said, a smile making its way across his handsome face.

"We're not interested in the details of your mating rituals, human. Answer Julian's question!" Christoff shouted at Thomas.

"Awe, someone sounds jealous, but you're right, back to business. I went to city hall first but didn't find much there so I spent some time at the local library. Adrianna's last name is rare and, other than her parents, there wasn't much information on her family history. On a hunch, I called a friend who works at the library of The New York Historical Society. Unfortunately he couldn't find much either but he did come across one bit of information he thought was interesting. It seems the name Avani was originally spelled with a 'w'. He thinks it's a possible variation on the name Awan. " Thomas said as his friend stood shaking his head in disbelief. "What ... what's wrong, Julian? What does this mean?"

"It can't be true," muttered Julian, astonishment mixed with excitement flashing across his face.

"It is true, and you know it," stated Michael simply. "To answer your question, Thomas, Julian is a distant descendent of an ancient bloodline ... the Awanian bloodline. And now, it seems Adrianna may also be of that same line. The fact that he and Adrianna may share the same ancient ancestor is very important. Of course, we still have to test the theory, and our lovely lady will certainly need some convincing as to her role in the plan. But if her blood is a match, if she carries the gene—"

"Enough!" Julian commanded. Did he dare even hope for another chance? He couldn't think about that right now. Adrianna's safety must come first. "All that you say may be true, but she is unaware of everything. It will take time to get to know her, time to make her aware of the existence of our kind, and time to convince her we are not all something out of her worst nightmare. Then and only then will I be able to try to convince her to give me the one thing that I desperately need—her blood. If it's even a match and that's a big if. It's a lot for even the strongest person to take in. How can I expect her to accept any of it?"

"You know as well as I do that time is not a luxury we can afford, Julian. If we can find her, then so can he. We must move quickly. Her safety is of the utmost importance," Michael pointed out.

Staring into the other man's eyes, Julian knew he spoke the truth. "You and I know only we have the power to keep her safe, but how do we convince her of that?"

"I was relying on your considerable charm to take care of that problem," Michael replied with a smile. "But you are right. Courting her takes time, which we don't have."

"Well, I already have kind of a plan in the works for this evening," Thomas spoke up.

"We need a serious plan, not your mindless skirt chasing!" Christoff growled at Thomas.

"Me! At least my women don't have to bleed for me you—"

"Stop! Christoff, let him speak." Julian said, stepping between them. "Explain yourself, Thomas, and it better be good."

"Not much chance of that, considering the source," Christoff said, trying to get the last word in.

Thomas shot him a scathing look before turning back to Julian and saying, "We've already made it known that we have poachers in the area. Brian told her we were watching the cottage along with our own property."

"Brian. How does he figure into all of this? When did he see Adrianna?" Julian asked.

"I haven't had the chance to mention it yet, Julian, but the lady appears to be pretty resourceful. She came looking for you this morning to properly introduce herself after meeting you at the club."

"Adrianna was here?"

"Yes, this morning, and it wasn't the first time. She was here once before while out for a stroll. She came across Brian and Brutus who, by the way, is useless as a watchdog, at least when it comes to the ladies. A dog after my own heart. Anyway, I told her you were unavailable but that I would give you her message. So consider it given," Thomas said slyly.

"Thanks," replied Julian. "Now can you get to the point?"

"The point is that she wants to talk to you. You and I are going to drop by tonight so you can acknowledge her visit, and Julian, she has some interesting information for you."

"What sort of information?"

"I'll let her tell you," Thomas said.

"Indeed. You know, Thomas, I can visit her on my own. I'm a big boy now."

"Of course you are, but she knows me a little better than she does you, so she'll be a little more comfortable if I'm around," he said smiling. "You know, Jules, you can be a little intimidating at first."

"Is that so?" Julian replied with a threatening look at the younger man.

"And besides, I'll keep Kate occupied while you tell Adrianna that the poacher thing is really getting out of hand and we have to beef up security. You can also tell her that you would feel much better if she let you post guards on her actual property because you feel responsible for her safety."

Julian stared for a long moment as Thomas continued his speech. "You know, Thomas, as insane as your babbling sometimes is, your idea just might work. If we can convince her there is a real danger in the area—if the murders haven't already—we might actually be able to keep them both safe if I have someone watching them at all times. It will at least buy us some time."

"I hope you are right, Julian," Michael said. "I only hope it's enough time."

"It's the best we can do for now," Julian said. Then turning to Christoff and Thomas he said, "Gather the others. Pick a handful of our best men and prepare them to watch the cottage while Romeo and I pay a visit to two beautiful ladies. Let's just hope this works."

The dark vampire glared at Thomas as he walked out the door, and Julian turned to Michael. "Who are you and how do you know so much about my life?" he asked.

"All in good time, my friend," Michael said. "We have more important issues at the moment." Reaching inside the long coat he still wore, he withdrew one of the small daggers Julian had seen him use before in the woods.

"Take this it will help in your fight."

"I can't use that," Julian replied, taking a step back. "If you know so much about me, you would be aware of that. It's made of silver, which has an adverse effect on a vampire."

With a slight smile, Michael said, "This knife will not harm you for you harbor no evil in your soul. But if you doubt me still, calm your fears. The handle is made of marble so it can be safely wielded in your hand." As Julian reached for the blade, he saw what Michael meant. The handle was beautifully crafted of white marble, smooth and soft to the touch as he wrapped his long fingers around it. Nodding his thanks, he slid the knife through his belt loop.

"Now, if you will all excuse me, Thomas and I have a short errand to run then we will return to join you." Julian watched everybody file from the room. "Thomas, can you bring the car around while I finish dressing?"

"What? No flying? It's such a short distance you could be there in seconds."

"Since you are to accompany me, and you are severely limited in the flying department, we take the car," Julian explained patiently.

"Oh, right," Thomas said as he left the room. Moments later, Julian slid across the car's smooth leather seats trying, without success, to ignore the wide grin on his companion's face.

"Not a word." he ordered Thomas.

"Lips sealed," came the reply, and Thomas drew an imaginary zipper across his lips while he headed down the gravel road.

*****

A slight rumbling interrupted her quiet daydreaming. Excitement, as well as nerves, filled her as she watched the long , sleek black Lincoln approach the house. It had come from the top of the hill, down the long driveway and across the old stone bridge before stopping in front of the cottage. She sat on the front porch sipping wine and trying, without much success, to look sophisticated. Her pulse quickened because she knew even before she saw his tall, lean frame climbing from the car who was inside—and he was not alone. Thomas's smiling face greeted her as he exited from the opposite side, taking the lead to jump the three front steps and stand before her.

"I told you I would give him the message," he said, the smile widening. Bowing slightly, he leaned forward to whisper, "Is Kate around?"

Smiling back at him, for his bubbly personality was infectious, she replied, "Yes she is, and it's a good thing, too. I would hate to see the look of disappointment on your face if I told you she wasn't here. I think she's in the kitchen. Please, go on inside, she probably has some wonderful home-baked treat waiting."

"Even better, thanks." he said eagerly as he turned and quickly disappeared through the front door.

"You read him well for knowing him such a short time," she heard a deep voice say. She turned, her gaze roaming slowly over every inch of him as he leaned against the porch railing. Even though his face was in shadow, she knew those strange blue eyes were watching her.

"He's very genuine, an easy read. Please, won't you sit down?" she said, indicating the chair next to her. "Can I get you something to drink? A glass of wine, perhaps?"

"No, thank you. I'm afraid I'm not much of a drinker … of wine," he said. "We can't stay long, so our love struck friend will still be disappointed, I'm afraid. He said you came to visit this morning, and I wanted to say how sorry I was that I was unable to see you."

"I'm the one who should apologize to you, dropping by unannounced as I did and not just once, but twice."

"Yes, Thomas told me you also met Brian and Brutus. There's no need to apologize, Adrianna. After all, we are neighbors. You are always welcome at my home. But with my line of work, I am not always available, and if you talked to Brian, you are aware that we are having some problems on the property lately, and it might be dangerous for you to roam around alone." He said staring at her intently.

"Yes, he did mention something about that," she replied, laughing a little to herself.

"That strikes you as funny?"

"Oh no! Please don't think that I don't take your warning seriously. It's just that Kate and I moved out here for the sole purpose of enjoying some peace and quiet. We wanted to escape the pressures of our jobs and the chaos of the city. We thought this would be the perfect place to do that. But no sooner do we arrive than the attacks begin, and there are strangers roaming my property. And now Kim is dead and Nick is, too," she finished as a torrent of emotion overwhelmed her.

Rising from the chair, she began to pace, tears filling her eyes as she tried to tell him what had happened to Kim and Nick and ask him if he knew who could have done such an awful thing. She knew she was babbling, but she couldn't seem to stop the words or the tears from flowing, until suddenly, she was enveloped in strong arms, his soothing voice willing her to relax. Yes, relax … she was safe now, safe in his arms as he held her tightly against him.

As the turmoil boiling inside of her began to subside, Julian's emotions were almost beyond his control. When would he learn that he must feed first if he was to be anywhere near her? He whispered soothingly to her, calming her almost immediately, so he could focus on the torrent of desire rising within him. He wanted her so badly. It had been so long since he'd enjoyed the touch of a woman: the softness, the closeness, the raw passion. It had been so long since he had to exercise such extreme control over the bloodlust and allow himself to feel the pure emotion of love. He thought he would never feel this way again, that he would never have another chance at a normal life. He must feed. What would she think if she knew the real monster was the one who held her in his arms?

After a few moments, her sobbing stopped. He moved her gently away from him, stepping back into the shadows and hoping she had not noticed the tension in his body, that she couldn't see the blue-grey of his eyes already changing to blood red. She didn't seem to notice that his voice was a little deeper, almost a growl, as he whispered, "Better now?"

"Yes, thank you," she said as she turned away to hide her embarrassment. "I'm sorry, I—"

"You have nothing to apologize for, Adrianna, not to me. I'm sorry about your friends. I will do all I can to find out what happened to them, but do you understand now the need for caution? You and Kate," he said, turning as Thomas and Kate came outside to join them, "must be very careful. It is a dangerous time, and things will only get worse before all is said and done. Until we can get to the bottom of the strange things that are happening around here, I will have men posted on both properties. We are on our way to a meeting tonight. We'll talk more with you both tomorrow, but for now, go inside, lock the house up tight, and don't hesitate to call if you need anything." He handed her a card with two numbers on it.

"Thank you again, for everything," she said, still embarrassed at the way she had fallen apart in front of him. She could only imagine what he must think of her.

"My pleasure," he said with a smile that took her breath away. "Now, we must go. The others will be waiting. Good night." He took her hand and raised it to his lips. His light touch sent a shockwave through her body. Looking at Thomas, he nodded toward the car.

"Goodnight, ladies," Thomas said, leaning in to place a kiss on Kate's cheek. "Hope to see you both soon." Running down the steps, he joined Julian in the car.

"We need to get the men in place around the cottage as soon as possible," Julian said. "Two people have died who were close to her." Remembering the message in his mind that first evening— *"I know she's here"*—fear gripped him. "He is aware of her. We must work quickly!"

"Simon was organizing a group as we were leaving to come here," Thomas told him. "They should be arriving soon, if they aren't in the area already."

"Good." The black car sped up the hill.

Back at the cottage, Kate was looking strangely at her friend. "Are you okay, honey?"

"You mean after I made a complete fool of myself? Yes, I'm fine. I just need some rest. Let's call it a night."

"That sounds like a good idea," Kate agreed, and they locked the front door and climbed the stairs to their rooms.

Chapter 12

Hidden in the murky darkness of the woods, red eyes watched as the black car pulled away from the cottage. The dark figure remained hidden as the vehicle drove past its hiding spot, allowing the creature a few moments to study the men inside. Its hideous mouth spread into something resembling a smile as the decaying flesh transformed into the figure of a handsome man with wavy brown hair and green eyes. Eyeing the bedroom near the front of the house, his body slowly rose off the ground before settling down on the small balcony of that very same room. He tapped lightly on the glass doors when the lights went out.

Hearing the soft tapping, Kate quickly reached for the switch as light flooded the room. She peered through the glass then opened the double doors wide.

"Thomas! Whatever are you doing out there? I thought you'd gone," she said in confusion. "Well, don't just stand there. Come on in."

In her own bedroom, as she slipped on cotton briefs and a tank top before climbing into bed, Addie thought about her conversation with Julian. It was somewhat comforting to know she was not the only one who thought strange things were going on. It bothered her that Julian seemed, somehow, to be right in the middle of it all, but she couldn't figure out why. Walking past the vanity, she stopped to stare at the image in the mirror,

"I really don't know why you care so much about a perfect stranger." But she did care—and more than just a little. She barely knew him, but there had been such a strong connection from the first moment she'd laid eyes on him walking across that crowded dance floor.

It wasn't as if a handsome face or a great body (oh, that body!) hadn't caught her attention before. There had been numerous times, but nothing like this. This was something completely different. He invaded her thoughts constantly, as if he belonged there. She sank onto the bed, eyes closed, remembering the feel of his body as he held her against him on the porch. She lost herself in the memory of strong arms holding her close, the scent of him driving all rational thought from her mind.

She was so lost in thought that she failed to hear the first shriek. Then the quiet of the evening was shattered by a second ear-piercing scream!

Her eyes flew open in confusion as she jumped from bed, her heart pounding violently. She listened intently, trying to decide if what she heard had been real or just a daydream. The night was deathly still and quiet. Not a breeze blew or a cricket chirped as she moved toward the bedroom door, all her senses alert to some sound, some hint of impending danger. Opening the door slowly to prevent the telltale squeeek! that always accompanied this particular door, she quietly peered outside. The hall seemed to be empty.

Then an ear-splitting scream echoed in the hall. It was definitely coming from Kate's room. Panic galvanized her into action.

But she stopped halfway down the hallway turning to run back into her room. She searched the closet for something that would serve as a weapon. Spotting an old baseball bat, she wrapped her hands around the smooth, hard wood and ran toward Kate's room with her weapon in hand. Hesitating only a moment, she flung the door open staring in shock at the sight before her.

Kate lay motionless on the bed, eyes closed as if still asleep. Something out of a nightmare leaned over her, a horrible sucking sound coming from its mouth. Its hideous face was buried in Kate's neck. Slowly, it raised the skull-like head, and horror filled her as she stared into its lifeless eyes. Lips curled back from black, rotting teeth to reveal two large fangs that dripped with Kate's blood!

Another piercing scream cut through the night. Adrianna didn't even realize the sound was coming from herself until her mouth closed with a snap. Her eyes moved slowly from the creature's face to Kate's pale, almost lifeless, body. She saw the two small puncture wounds on the side of her friend's neck. A slender stream of blood flowed freely from each one. Anger so intense it felt as if her blood was on fire filled her as she charged toward the bed, screaming. She held the bat with both hands and swung with all the strength she could summon. The jolt of the impact jarred her so badly that she lost her grip as the weapon fell to the floor and rolled out of sight.

She turned to see the creature picking itself up off the floor. The blow had caused it to pitch forward, away from Kate and off the bed. But other than looking completely pissed off, she had done no real damage.

It hissed at her in fury.

Suddenly, she was hit from the side with such force that the wind was knocked out of her. A heavy weight bore down on her, crushing the air out of her lungs as she fought to stay conscious. Through blurred vision, she saw two sharp fangs descending for her, and she knew it would only be a matter of seconds before she would end up just like Kate. Instinctively, she brought up her arms in a futile attempt to both cover her eyes and hold off her attacker.

"Don't mark that one, you fool—"

But before the voice could finish its sentence, the weight was lifted, and her attacker was thrown against the far wall with such force that the plaster splintered. She thought she was dreaming as the hideous fangs were replaced by a pair of ruby red lips in a lovely face surrounded by long blond hair. Vaguely, she remembered the beautiful waitress from the club as the girl knelt beside her to help her rise. Was she dreaming again, or did she hear an urgent voice whispering orders?

"Come, Adrianna. We have to go now!" the voice said firmly. She was pulled upward, standing on legs that felt like rubber. It took all of her concentration to force her legs to move as she followed the young vampire toward the open door. She stopped for one moment to glance behind her. It all seemed surreal. Everything was a flurry of movement with almost no sound. She thought she saw Julian, Thomas, and a few others being attacked from all directions by more of those hideous creatures.

What in God's name were those things? Where had they come from?

They had locked the cottage up as tight as a drum, yet as her gaze traveled the length of the room, it seemed the hideous figures were everywhere, crawling down the walls and in from the windows, flying in through the balcony doors. How did this happen? Who had opened the entryways?

She was mesmerized by the gruesome scene. She saw the tall, dark man who had been with Julian at the club walking toward the open balcony doors. Before he had a chance to reach them, a creature with huge black wings came flying through. She wanted to scream a warning, but the man reacted before she could utter a sound. He crouched low to the ground, swinging his arm up so quickly it moved in a blur. He drove a pointed wooden stake directly into the heart of the winged form. It erupted into a ball of fire.

"I must be going insane," Addie thought.

Julian and his men made short work of their attackers. Wooden stakes pierced broken bodies, limbs were torn off with bare hands, and heads were ripped right off the shoulders, leaving only ash behind as body parts burst into flames! What was happening?

This had to be a nightmare. This could not be real. Again, she felt her body being pulled toward the bedroom door.

"Adrianna, we must go!"

She turned to face Charleze, but something nagged at her … something important.

"Kate! We must get to Kate!" she screamed, fighting to free herself from the girl's amazingly strong grip.

On the bed, she saw Simon holding the head of the creature that had attacked Kate, its body burned to ash on the floor at his feet. She could swear she saw the scream of terror still on its lips as Simon smashed the head against the floor before it, too, burst into flames. Tearing her eyes from the sight of the tall vampire, she saw Thomas bent over Kate.

"She's not moving," she whispered. "And she's so pale."

"Thomas will take care of her, Adrianna, we must leave. They must not get to you; now, come away!"

As Adrianna followed Charleze, she thought she could detect the sorrow in the vampire's voice.

Trembling with anger, Simon glanced around to see the remainder of the attacking vampires fleeing through every possible exit. As Thomas knelt beside Kate, his own emotions began to change from anger to fear.

"She's so pale … and barely breathing," he said, echoing Addie's thoughts as he took Kate into his arms. He desperately searched for Julian, only to find him talking to two of his men, who were roughly holding an injured vampire between them.

"Take him to the house," Julian told them. "We need him alive for now to answer some questions." Sensing he was needed, Julian turned slowly, painful memories flooding his mind as he viewed the scene before him. Thomas knelt on the large bed holding Kate in his arms, his eyes pleading for help as he stared at the blood flowing from the wounds on her neck. Moving closer to the bed, Julian looked down at the deathly white face and the unfocused green eyes, and he knew the choice they faced. He laid his hand on the anguished man's shoulder, trying to offer what comfort he could.

"I'm sorry, Thomas."

"I won't let her die!" Thomas said as he stubbornly refused to give up.

Realizing she was close to death, but understanding his friend's despair, Julian hesitated only a moment before saying, "We must get her to the house as quickly as possible. We have no time to spare. We will do all we can to save her, Thomas, but you do understand what that may involve?"

"Whatever the cost, I will not lose her," Thomas whispered.

Comprehension dawned as Julian realized that Thomas had fallen in love with Kate. Turning away, he motioned to Simon as he stared at the gaping doors of the balcony. "They entered through those doors, but why would she open them to them? We just left here, and I thought I made perfectly clear the necessity for caution. Why would they ignore my warning, unless—"

"Someone or something was playing mind tricks," Simon finished.

"These creatures are not powerful enough to cloud anyone's mind. They are but slaves! But someone else could have been outside," he said almost to himself as a chill ran through him. "Help Thomas get her back to the house. Prepare things. We will do what is necessary there." Turning to Andrew, he shouted more orders, "Keep a few men here with you to clean up this mess. Make sure there is no trace of what went on here tonight. It will be traumatic enough for them to return without visible signs of all that has happened."

Christoff approached as Julian finished giving orders. "I will see that all is taken care of," he said. "You'd better hurry. Charleze has already left, and if my instincts are right, not even she can protect the girl alone. Julian, its obvious how you feel about her, and if we know, he knows! She is the real target. " He watched Thomas gently lift Kate from the bed then he continued, "The other one was dispensable. That is why she was attacked. When he finds out his evil spawn have failed to secure what they were sent for, he will come back with a vengeance. We must not have two tragedies tonight."

"Our dark friend is right, Julian, but something troubles me about the attack tonight," Michael said, coming to stand beside them.

"And what have your instincts been telling you now?"

"Think, my friend. These were not the strongest of his army. We were outnumbered, and yet we defeated them easily. If he were truly after Adrianna, why send weaklings? Why not send his strongest warriors? He knows the importance of his quarry, but does he actually know who the quarry is?"

"This was a test!" Julian said as comprehension dawned.

"Yes, to see how we would react! To see who was most important to you."

"And we gave him exactly the information he needed," Julian replied, anger building inside of him. "Everyone, back to the house quickly! Christoff, finish here as soon as you can, and then join us. We must be at full strength tonight. There will be no more mistakes, no more playing right into his hands. We have a captive now, and one way or another, we will find the answers we seek."

Christoff nodded, but before Julian could leave he said, "I will organize things here, then return to you. But leave the questioning of the captive for me. I will get the answers you need."

"As you wish, my friend," Julian said then quickly disappeared through a nearby window.

"Does he have to do that?" Michael asked, not really expecting an answer from the vampire beside him. Christoff merely shrugged.

*****

The night hides terrors the mind can only imagine. A dark shadow, nearly as tall as the tree it hid behind, stood watching the scene inside the cottage. The beast's face could not hide the evil intelligence behind the black eyes.

"Julian!" he spat out the name, barely able to contain his hatred. Black fur fell from rippling muscles to reveal the man beneath, a man who struck as much terror into the cowering figure beside him as the beast. The rustling of the bushes disturbed his train of thought as the weak voice hissed, "Let's go, Hanokh. They're being slaughtered!" A spark of bravery shot through the wretched creature, and he continued, "Why did you not help them? Why did your brother, Enoch, leave? Why—"

"Why, why, why? Better them than us!" Hanokh roared into the face of the helpless creature as his huge hands grabbed it by the neck, raising the flailing figure high into the air as if it weighed next to nothing. "And it is not your place to question me or my brother. Enoch did exactly what he said he would do. He got them access to the house. The others were supposed to take care of everything else. Besides, we learned what we came to find out. We now know the extent of Julian's forces and his attachment to the woman. My father will be pleased with our report." Tossing the helpless figure to the ground, he ordered, "Come!" Turning, he headed into the black forest.

"You mean this massacre was planned?" the creature screamed at the retreating figure, grabbing at him in a useless effort to stop him from leaving. Turning with the speed of light, Hanokh struck the piteous creature with such force that it slammed into a nearby tree, bones cracking as it cried out in pain.

"Touch me again, and it will be the last thing you do. I told you before it is not your place to question anything. Your sole purpose is to follow the orders you have been given, and you may live to see another day. Disobey them and, well, the choice is yours," he said, smiling cruelly before he turned and disappeared into the night.

Chapter 13

Arriving back at the mansion, Julian hesitated before entering the den, deep in thought as he watched Thomas bolt up the stairs with Kate in his arms. He didn't hold much hope that they would be able to save the girl. How would he ever be able to explain to Adrianna what had happened to her friend? She would never understand, but that was not what he feared most. He knew he would not be able to stand the look in her eyes—the horror—when she realized what they … no, what *he* was. Could he really face her? There was no question. He had no choice. The task was his and his alone.

He had failed to protect them once again. How many more would have to die before he could put an end to this nightmare? He had lived for centuries, the leader of strong and powerful men who had fought and won countless battles, yet he could not keep one small woman safe. He had known the truth about her, yet he doubted. Even at the club, he had a suspicion who she was and what that meant to him, but he had refused to let himself believe, to hope, and thus he'd blinded himself to the danger she was in. She sat on the other side of the door, waiting to hear news of her friend's fate. How did he tell her that Kate most certainly would die? Yes, he could save her, but the alternative he offered was worse than death itself. Would she agree to their only option? What human in their right mind would?

With a deep sigh, he pushed the door open. She was sitting quietly in front of the fireplace. Although it was early spring, the fire had been lit, for she was in shock and shaking violently. Sonya, who had been waiting for their return, sat beside her, the vampire's soothing voice working its magic as Adrianna became visibly calmer with each word. At least until she saw him walk into the room.

As she rose from the chair, her beautiful brown eyes, made larger still by the terror she had witnessed, stared into his. He could read the question waiting there, but he prolonged the inevitable by going over to the wet bar to pour two glasses of brandy. He needed all the help he could get for this conversation. And she would need just as much help—probably more—to hear and accept what he had to say. Turning back to her, he held out the crystal goblet, reading the question in her eyes as she took it from him.

"Where is Kate?" she asked. Sonya laid a reassuring hand on the girl's shoulder.

"Thomas is with her upstairs. He will see that she is taken care of," he replied cautiously.

She moved to stand in front of him, placing her hands upon his chest, a pleading look in her eyes, as she said, "Please. She's seriously injured, Julian, we have to call a doctor. That thing bit …" her voice broke as she fought for control. "What were those things that attacked us?"

He hesitated, glancing at Sonya, as he thought how best to reply.

"Thomas thought I might be needed," Sonya explained. "He asked me to be here for your return. It seems he was right. You need to explain a few things to her, Julian." Her lacquered nails stroked his arm gently as she walked gracefully from the room.

Looking down at Addie and covering her hands gently with his own in a weak attempt to protect her from the shock she was about to receive, he began speaking in a soft voice, "A doctor cannot help her, Adrianna. Only we know how to treat the injuries she has sustained. We are taking care of her as best we can."

"Those things acted like … they were vampires, weren't they? But … but they couldn't be. That's impossible. There's no such thing," she stated, hysteria rising in her voice.

"I'm afraid there is, Adrianna, for that's exactly what they were."

"Real vampires, Julian, the things out of horror movies? But then that would mean … your men … they're vampires, too, aren't they?" She looked into those blue-grey eyes and saw the truth, as well as pain, reflected there. Lowering her hands slowly, he turned to walk toward the fireplace as if its heat could dispel the coldness he felt inside.

"You are partially correct. As I've said, they were vampires that attacked you, but not all of my men can be counted among them." He was thankful his back was to her for he couldn't bear to see the look on her face as he continued, "Thomas and a few others are as human as you both. They guard the rest of us through the daylight hours, our resting time …" his voice trailed off.

"They guard the rest of yo … no." It came out in a whisper. "No, Julian, not you! Please not you!" She ran to him, her fists pounding uselessly at his back.

"Not by any choice of mine!" he shouted as he turned, grabbing her hands to stop the pain, more emotional than physical. The look in her eyes hurt him more than her fists ever could. "I am what I am, Adrianna. Please listen to me!" he pleaded as she fought to pull away from him. "Not all of us are like those who attacked you tonight. Most of us have tried for centuries to live a quiet existence, keeping our secret amongst ourselves and not harming anyone. We discovered a long time ago there was no need to feed from humans, unless they were willing." He tried to ignore the tiny gasp that escaped her.

"We have been waging a battle for centuries against those of our kind who care nothing for human life," he continued. "They are monsters who only wish to satisfy the blood lust any way they can, feeling no remorse for the countless lives they destroy. We try to keep things in balance. We thought we had things under control, that we had found most of their hordes in this country. We send people to investigate any act of violence in the areas we inhabit to make sure our kind are not the ones responsible for that act. You know, Adrianna, sometimes you humans are more monstrous than any of us could ever be, but that is not the point here. Things have been quiet for some time now, but it seems that a new force has risen. One more evil than you could ever imagine. I'm afraid we've let our guard down, become careless." He released his hold on her, suddenly so very tired of it all. His blue-grey eyes looked intently into her brown ones, trying to ignore what he saw there. She backed away from him in horror.

"Please, Adrianna, try to understand. I … we … are not as bad as you may think. I have tried to … this was a situation that was not foreseen, and we have paid a heavy price."

She stood staring at the man before her, trying to grasp what he was telling her. How was she supposed to believe the impossible things he was saying? How could they be true? They … he … were things of legend … imaginary. They weren't real. Were they? But she knew in her heart that everything she had seen and heard tonight was not just her imagination. It had all happened. There was no going back, no waking up from a bad dream. And Julian, the man she thought she cared about, was not even human. How was that possible? And what was she to do now?

Her emotions were in turmoil, battling between passion and fear as she stared into Julian's blue-grey eyes. She couldn't deny what he was, nor could she deny the feelings she had for him. Turning away, she tried desperately to think. Images of the attack flashed through her mind. Those vile creatures … the blood and destruction. But she couldn't forget the valiant stand Julian and his men had made to rescue them. What had he said? "We are not all

evil. We have been fighting a battle for our lost humanity for a long time."
How could she turn her back on them after they had saved her life?

If she gave in to fear now and let those things terrorize her, as well as
others, they would have won. She couldn't let that happen. Somehow, she
must find the courage to accept the truth. Taking a deep breath, she turned
to face him. Was that regret she saw in his eyes?

"I'm so sorry, Adrianna, that you and Kate have been drawn into what I
thought was my own private hell. I promise you that I will do all in my power
to find those responsible for tonight, and they will pay for the pain they
have caused you. We have brought one of them here to question. His kind
are mere slaves, pawns easily disposed of, only doing their master's bidding.
We have to find the one controlling them. When we do, we will end this
nightmare once and for all. On this I give you my word."

Suddenly the room was stifling, and she felt dizzy. She was starting to
sway when she felt herself enveloped in strong arms and lifted up. She was
carried the short distance back to her chair. Contrary to everything she was
feeling, she felt safe in his arms and she laid her head against his chest. How
she wished he could take her away somewhere and make it all go away, but
she knew that could never happen now. He was at the center of all of this.
She also knew that she had to ask the one question still burning in her mind,
even though she feared his answer. Taking a deep breath she asked, "What
will happen to Kate?"

As she waited for his reply, she watched him closely. There was such
sadness in his eyes. No matter how hard she tried to fight against it, her
heart went out to him. In that moment, she realized something, and that
realization both shocked and filled her with the strength she needed to pull
herself together. It didn't matter who or even what he was, she cared for him
deeply. God forgive her, she did. She had to know everything. What had
happened to him, what had caused him to become what he was? She had
to listen to him and try to accept and understand. She was certain there was
good beneath the monster. She made up her mind to help him in his fight or
die trying. And if she died, she would damn well make sure she took a few of
them with her!

Courage replaced fear, anger replaced grief, and her newfound strength
gave her the control she needed as she waited for him to answer.

"If we do nothing, she will surely die," he said softly. "But you may
consider that better than the alternative if our first course of action fails. She
has lost a lot of blood—"

Suddenly the door burst open as an anxious Thomas ran into the room.

"We are ready for the transfusion! Julian, come on!" he said, obviously
agitated. "We have to hurry!"

"You are sure you want to do this, my friend?" Julian asked, knowing the strain Thomas was under.

"It's the least I can do for her since I failed to prevent this. I just hope it is enough."

"Thomas, none of this was your fault," Addie tried to console him. "I realize now that you were trying to warn us as best you could of the danger out there, but what are you talking about? What transfusion?"

"She's lost a lot of blood," he said, explaining what Julian had already begun to tell her. "She needs a transfusion if we are to have any hope of saving her. I will be the donor. We're hoping this will be enough to replace the blood she lost. If it's not, the contamination will spread, and she will die unless ..." He looked sorrowfully into her eyes unable to continue.

"You make her a vampire," she finished, her voice barely a whisper as she caught the look between man and vampire.

"If we do nothing, she will die within the hour. The creature did his work well, Adrianna. When they want someone to die, they drain them dry so they will not rise. By giving her the transfusion from a human, there is a slim chance we can save her," Julian said, willing her to understand. He heard a small gasp as she glanced from him back to Thomas. She reached up and gently wiped a stray tear from Thomas's cheek. She knew Thomas would do what was best for Kate.

"I'm trying to understand all that you're telling me, but it's difficult. I need time to—"

"Time is a luxury we do not have," Julian said. "I wish I could give you that and more, but I can't. We must make a decision right now."

She nodded, but then she grabbed Julian by the arm as he turned to leave. "If you need more blood than Thomas can give, you must use me, too," she whispered.

"Somehow, I knew you would feel that way—"

"Before we do this I must know, if the transfusion fails, if you have to change ... What is to prevent her from becoming like those who attacked us tonight? I would rather see her dead then watch her turn into one of those monsters!"

Leaning down, Julian cupped her face in his large hands. Lord! All she wanted to do was rub her face along their warmth and softness. She leaned into them, forgetting everything in the comfort only he could give—but she would not give in to the urge. Gently, he tilted her chin upward, his eyes holding hers. She felt as though she were drowning in their grey-blue depths.

"We will keep her with us and help her adjust to our ways. The way we were in life usually transfers with the change, but it takes proper guidance, and it will take some time. If we must do this, then you will have to trust her to our care for a while before you can see her again. Can you do that, Adrianna?"

"Oh, God," she muttered as she tried to imagine what Kate would endure. Holding back tears, she nodded her agreement.

"Good girl. Simon will do what needs to be done then leave her in Thomas's care," Julian said. "He cares very much for her. He will not let any harm come to her until you can see her." Gently, he released her and stepped back. "But we will do all we can before we follow that path. We try not to purposely condemn anyone to this life!"

She found herself wishing she knew exactly what his story was. "Do what you must ... both of you," she said. "Just keep her with us."

"We'll do all we can," Julian replied. Nodding to Thomas, he said, "Ready?" They started for the door, but as Thomas moved to follow him, Julian stopped suddenly and, with his back still to her said, "I don't think you should go back to the cottage for a while. It's too dangerous. You will stay here tonight. Thomas can take you back in the morning to get whatever you need for an extended visit. You are welcome to stay here for as long as it takes us to find out who is behind—"

"No, Julian," she said firmly.

"What?" Pain slashed through him as he waited for her to continue.

"I said no." she repeated a little more calmly, but no less firm. "We will not stay in this house any longer than it takes you to help Kate. You and Thomas I trust, Julian, but I don't know your people. How can I be sure there isn't a traitor among them? Think about it. How did those things know where to find us?"

"Adrianna," Thomas whispered in shock, the strain of the evening beginning to show on his face.

"How can I trust people I don't know, Thomas?" she continued, her eyes glued to Julian. "I appreciate everything you are doing for her, Julian, I really do, but how do I know there's not someone in this house who's still a threat to Kate or myself? Thomas," she said, grabbing his hand tightly, "if you care anything at all for her, and the transfusion is a success, you must help me get her to a hospital. Somewhere I know we will be safe. The doctors can help me care for her there once we know the danger is passed. Thomas, please!" she cried as she caught the look on Thomas's face as he stared at Julian.

Julian's beautiful grey-blue eyes smoldered with fury

"I will say this one more time only," he spat out, barely controlling his anger. "My people will not harm any human being! Many of them will die trying to protect you and your kind before this is all over because they realize, even if you don't, that we are your only hope. We did not choose to become what we are. The choice was taken from us long ago, and now we fight for the humanity that is lost to us forever. You can trust them because I trust them with my life, as well as yours!" He took a deep breath. "But if you think you will be safer elsewhere then, by all means, go. Thomas, assist her in any way you can when we are finished with our task." He threw her one last piercing glance and stormed out of the room.

"Addie," Thomas said quietly as she stood shaking.

What had she done? He was so angry. Thomas took her gently by the arm and led her back to the chair. He poured her another glass of brandy at the bar. At this rate she would soon be drunk. "Maybe then I will be able to forget this nightmare," she thought, a sob catching in her throat.

"He only wants to help you," Thomas continued. "You have no idea what he's been through."

"You're right, Thomas, I don't have any idea. I know very little about him, or any of you for that matter. I'm really sorry, but how can he expect anything else from me? This is so unreal. I didn't even know such things truly existed until a few hours ago. Vampires are supposed to be creatures of legend. They're not supposed to actually exist! I don't know who can be trusted, even you. I need to think," she said, rising to pace. "I have a friend who's a priest. If all goes well with Kate and the transfusion, I'm sure we could stay with him. After all, he lives behind a church and," she looked questioningly at Thomas," vampires can't go on holy ground can they?"

"That part of the legend is true for the most part, they couldn't harm you there, but then we, Julian, couldn't help you either. There is no distinguishing between good and evil vampires there, Addie. Holy ground affects them both the same. Listen, Julian is your best chance. He will not let any harm come to you while he is alive."

"He wasn't much help to Kate tonight, now was he?" she said, trying not to sound bitter.

"That's not fair, Addie. He wasn't there, and once he was, your attackers fled. That's why he wants you here, where he can control things. It's true, there is no guarantee of safety in this house, but those creatures will surely think twice before attacking Julian in his own home. If you stay with your friend, you will only put him in danger, too." Then a thought suddenly occurred to him. "But he may be able to do something for Kate, if you can get him here in time. Do you think he would come?"

"If I can reach him, I have no doubt he will want to help, but what can he do?" she questioned glad for any reason to get Rick to the house for she was determined to take Kate to the church with his help. She felt sure they would be safer there.

"If he will bring some holy water and the Communion host, we may be able to stop the poison from spreading before it's to late to save Kate. Can he be here by the time we're done with the transfusion?" he asked hopefully.

"If I can reach him now, it's about a thirty minute drive from the church. Will that be enough time?"

"Yes, that's perfect!"

"Okay, where's the phone?" She looked frantically around the room.

But at that moment Sonya re-entered the room overhearing the last part of their conversation. She was holding in her hand the instrument in question, a look of disapproval on her face. "We do not need a holy man here!" she raged.

"Sonya, I really do think he can help the injured woman. Please, let us try this," Thomas begged. "We may not be able to save her on our own."

She stared at the desperate man long and hard, finally making a decision. "Just make sure your priest knows the difference between us and the enemy. His objects can damage us for life!"

"He won't harm you, Sonya. You're trying to help us," Addie tried to reassure her.

"He's a priest, girl. To him, evil is evil, and I'm sure he puts all of us in that category."

"I'll make him understand, please, we need him. Thomas, make her see we need him here," Addie pleaded.

"I'll watch him, Sonya. There will be no mistakes of any kind."

"Just make sure," she repeated as she handed Addie the phone. "Make the call quickly, Julian is ready."

She dialed the number to the church rectory and waited impatiently. "Come on, come on, pick up the phone, Rick," she muttered.

"Hello, this is—"

But her control crumbled when she heard his voice and she screamed hysterically into the phone, "Rick! Oh, Rick, we need you! Please come quickly! They've attacked Kate!"

"Addie? Is that you? Calm down. Tell me what happened and where you are … slowly now," he said, trying not to upset her further. Addie took a deep breath and willed herself to relax. She told him, between the tears, what had happened.

"This cannot be happening. Addie, what you're saying is impossible. I—"

"Don't you think I know how crazy this all sounds, Rick? But you have to believe me. When have I ever lied to you?"

"Never. Alright, honey, listen to me. I'm leaving as we speak. I'll be there as soon as humanly possible. It will be okay, do you hear me? Do you believe me, Addie?"

"I think so."

"That's my girl. I'll see you soon." She heard the click as he replaced the receiver. Turning back to the others she said, "He's on his way, what do we do now?"

"You must be exhausted. You've been through a lot tonight. I'll take you to a room upstairs where you can get some rest—" Thomas started.

"But I want to be with Kate during the transfusion—" Addie tried to interrupt.

"You will be more help to Kate if you take care of yourself. That way, if we should need you after they are through with me, you will be rested enough to do what needs to be done. Do you agree with the logic in that?"

"Yes, that makes sense," she agreed.

"You will be close by. Your room is across the hall from Kate. We were sure you would want to be near her tonight. It has a comfortable bed with its own private bath." He put his arm around her shoulders, offering what comfort he could. Exhausted from the events of the evening, Addie went willingly with him as Sonya stood waiting at the base of the grand staircase.

"Hurry, Thomas, they need you." The urgency in her voice caused him to move quickly up the stairs. Stopping for a moment, he turned to look at the lovely vampire, a silent message passing between them as he said, "Take her to her room, Sonya. Make sure she stays there until someone comes for her."

"I will take care of things. Now go." Turning to Addie, she said, "Come." They climbed the staircase and walked down a long hallway of at least a dozen rooms. They stopped in front of the third door on the left, but Addie's attention was focused on the room across the hall. It was so quiet. "Deathly quiet," she thought. Were they all in there, and what were they doing?

"They are doing all that is needed for your friend," Sonya said as if reading her thoughts. "You must take care of yourself if you are to be of any use to them. They don't need another worry." Sonya's last words were uttered almost under her breath. Addie knew Sonya resented her. She was only helping because Julian had ordered it. "Just how close are they?" she wondered. She knew they were business partners, but were they, or had they ever been, anything more? There was so much she didn't know about him, and she wondered if she ever would.

Sonya turned the crystal doorknob and led Addie into the most beautiful room she had ever seen. Under different circumstances, she would have been excited to stay in such a room, but now she only felt numb. The walls were a pale blue-grey color—like his eyes—with a soft cream-colored trim. Cream lace curtains adorned two floor-to-ceiling windows, which took up much of the far wall. To the right sat a large queen-size bed, its matching blue and cream satin bedspread smothered in pillows of the same material and topped by a lace canopy.

Along the opposite wall stood a dainty cherry vanity, its top covered in ivory-handled combs and brushes. A door to the right of the vanity led to a large bathroom filled with all the modern conveniences, including a huge marble tub with whirlpool jets that she stared at longingly. As she took in her surroundings, one thought ran through her mind: "The nightclub business must be doing very well."

"Is there anything else you need?" she heard Sonya ask.

"No, thank you, this is fine," she said, realizing just how exhausted she was. "I think I just need to get a little sleep, but please wake me if you need me. And please call me when Rick arrives."

"Of course," Sonya replied, not trying to hide her dislike of the idea of a priest being in the house. As she prepared to close the door, Sonya said, "Lock the door behind me and stay inside until you are called, Adrianna. Don't be foolish enough to wander around alone. They would be crazy to try anything here, but we must be cautious. Goodnight." She closed the door firmly, waiting until she heard the key turn in the lock before continuing down the hallway to the large double doors at the very end.

Chapter 14

Across the hall, Thomas and a few others worked feverishly to save a dying woman. But in a room deep beneath the foundations of the ancient mansion, saving lives was the last thing on the minds of those who worked in the darkness. Christoff had not earned the name of dark vampire for his looks alone. The skills he possessed as a soldier in life had been most useful to Julian over the centuries. His loyalty to Julian was unquestionable. Any threat to them, or the life they had fought so hard to build, was his responsibility. Now, standing motionless against the wall, he watched intently, as a hunter watches his prey, the figure before him slowly waken.

The small eyes, no more than slits in a skull-like face, darted from side to side as its animal instinct sought a way to free itself from the heavy chains that bound it to the thick, wooden pole protruding from the ground in the center of the small room. Darkness surrounded the battered figure as it waited for its eyes, swollen shut from the beating, to focus. Suddenly it stiffened as it sensed a presence, a threat to its miserable existence.

"Who's there? I know someone is there!" it hissed. "Show yourself. You may as well kill me now, I will tell you nothing … nothing! Anything you will do to me will be a pleasure compared to what he will do if I tell you anything!"

"That is your first mistake," Christoff whispered softly as he glided forward, coming to a halt behind the creature. His dagger-like claws sliced across the bare back before him, causing its unfortunate owner to scream so loudly that the two vampires standing guard outside the room stared at each other in fear. "You are assuming you have something I want when, quite frankly, my only need is to indulge my pleasure for inflicting pain." Fear gripped the pitiful mess before him. "And you have nothing that will deter me from my fun. But I am intrigued. Do you fear him that much? He must be a man after my own heart." Christoff seemed to float across the floor, coming to stop before the trembling figure.

"Who could such an interesting person be? Ah yes, I'd forgotten, we're not talking. Well, if we're not taking the time for a little small talk, then let's get down to business, shall we?"

He raised his hand to stare at his own long claws. With lightning speed, Christoff lashed out at the creature's neck. Deep slashes welled up with blood. At the same time, he drove a wooden stake deep into the shattered shoulder and the figure in chains screamed in agony.

Blood flowed freely from the wounds covering the broken body. The sight of so much blood, and the obvious pleasure he took in this particular job, was causing the blood lust to rise uncontrollably in the dark vampire. He had fed at some point tonight, but the events of the evening had taken their toll on him. He was not usually this careless. He knew he should have waited for this interrogation. He should have taken the time to replenish himself after the battle, but time was short. He must get the information Julian needed—and soon.

"I can bleed you all night, my foul-smelling friend, but I have suddenly remembered another engagement, so I'm afraid we will have to end this quickly." Reaching inside the pocket of his long coat, he withdrew a small, glass vial. Roughly grabbing the bony face, Christoff held the vial high and asked whimpering figure, "Do you know what this is, you spawn from hell!" He received a look of pure panic for an answer. "It's silver nitrate. Deadly to our kind." The creature fought to break free of the vampire's hold, terror reflected in his red eyes as he realized what Christoff had planned for him.

"It causes great pain when ingested. It tears at you like a thousand shards of glass, ripping and tearing from the inside out. Death will take a little while, I'm afraid. It will be very painful … you will beg for me to kill you … unless you can think of a reason I would want to keep you alive. No? Nothing?" He shook his head. "Ah well, good-bye my friend. It's been fun."

As he brought the vial to the mouth of the blubbering figure, it screamed out in fear, "No, wait! Please, I'll talk. Please, just take it away!"

Moments later, the door to the hallway opened. Christoff appeared before the two standing watch and said in a low voice, "I think he is ready to tell us what we want to know." They followed him back inside the darkened room.

In another room on the floor above, Sonya entered a private library. The cavernous room had shelves of books lining three of the four walls. Julian and Michael were deep in conversation behind a large, ornate desk. Electric lamps (which Julian had installed on all of the main floors for the convenience of the others) cast a dim light on the antiquated wood, giving the room an eerie feel. Looking up as she entered, Julian watched the beautiful vampire walk seductively across the room.

"Well, what was her decision?" a trace of anger still in his voice.

"For now, she is staying," Sonya replied. "I've put her in the Blue Room. Her priest friend is on his way." She was barely able to hide the disgust in her voice. "I don't approve of this, Julian. We don't need his kind here. Thomas seems to feel his objects of faith will help the injured woman, but they are a danger to us. He's knows that!"

"Right now, this is not about us, Sonya. These women were drawn into this whole mess because of their connection to me, so I will do what is necessary to help them."

"There's no need for such anger or fear, from either of you," Michael said, looking from one to the other. "Just think of what she's, what they've both, been through tonight. Really, how did you expect her to react when she's just found out that the creatures from her nightmares are real and one of them may have killed her best friend? She has a lot to adjust to because, let's face it, after tonight, her world will never be the same again. She needs the priest with her, for more than one reason and," seeing the angry look in Julian's eyes, he quickly added, "yes, he might actually be of some help. The transfusion will give the injured girl the blood she needs to replace what was lost, but we all know that will not be enough. Thomas was right. The items he brings may stop, even reverse, the infection in her system. You can't do that for her, Julian. You must not let your own fears and superstitions get in the way of her salvation. She deserves that chance."

Julian, trying to control the bitterness he felt, replied, "It seems the decision has already been made. I hope your magic works, crusader, for her sake. But I have long ago stopped believing in miracles!" Rising from his chair, he turned to the back of the room. "Now, shall we go see what our captive friend has to say?"

Walking toward the shelf on the back wall he reached up and gently tugged on a beautiful leather-bound copy of Bram Stoker's *Dracula*, smiling bitterly to himself at the irony. No sooner had he touched the book than a section of the shelf, about the size and width of a normal door, swung inward to reveal a passage of solid stone descending into inky blackness.

Here, as in his private chambers, candles mounted in sconces lined the rock walls. Reaching deep inside a large hole, he withdrew a long, tapered matchstick. Before continuing, he turned back to Sonya, "You'd better return to the den to await the priest," he said firmly as he saw the look of distaste on her face. "It would be best, if he can be spared, to have Thomas, or one of the other humans, with you when you meet the man. Fear stemming from ignorance can be a dangerous thing, and we don't want any accidents from would-be crusaders happening to one of our own." He glanced meaningfully at Michael, who simply returned his glare with a calm smile. "Take him directly to the injured girl, nowhere else." As Sonya nodded in agreement, the two men descended the stairs.

Julian lit the sconces, the tiny candles sparkling like diamonds casting dancing shadows along the walls. Continuing down a long, narrow hallway, the two men approached three doors, one on the left, two more on the right. Stopping before the door to his left, Julian knocked twice and waited impatiently. The door swung back slowly to reveal Christoff, his midnight eyes locking with blue and a silent message passing between them. But Julian's main focus was the figure chained in the center of the room. Its blood glistened black in the dim candlelight as it flowed from several deep wounds on the emaciated body. The two vampires flanking the figure stepped into the shadows at Julian's approach.

"I see you've been busy, my dark friend," Julian said as he reached forward and lifted the skull-like head slightly, only to drop it carelessly when he realized it was only half conscious. Christoff merely shrugged as Julian continued, "Did you learn anything worthwhile or was all this for amusement only?"

Pushing his tall body away from the wall he was leaning against, Christoff stared at Julian. But before he could answer, Michael asked in a voice filled with disgust, "Was all of this necessary?" He gestured to the open wounds and the blood.

"Who are you to question my methods, stranger? You are only alive because of the grace of Julian! Had it been left up to me—"

"But it wasn't, Christoff," Julian reminded him. Turning to Michael he said, "Our ways are not like yours, Avenger, and since you are a guest here, we owe you no explanations." He turned back to Christoff. "Now get back to the point at hand. Do we know anything yet?"

The dark vampire tore his gaze away from Michael to answer Julian. "It's as we feared. He's back, Julian. It's Dragon, and he knows about the girl!"

Mixed emotions battled for control as Julian absorbed this news. Surprise and anger flashed across his face as he slammed a clenched fist into the pole in front of him. The half dead being chained there screamed again.

"You knew this, in here," he heard Michael say as a hand was placed over Julian's heart. A coldness filled the vampire, numbing him to everything, until a slight sound began to penetrate the barrier. Julian fought to control the urges rising within him. As he strained to listen, he was finally able to hear it distinctly. It was muffled laughter—yes, laughter—coming from somewhere near him. There were words, too, barely a whisper, but he heard them clearly, "He will destroy you all …"

An uncontrollable rage took him as he sprang forward grabbing the face before him in a vice-like grip. His nails dug deeply into what flesh was left on that tortured face, and blood trickled along his fingers as his eyes bore into the slits staring back at him, "That may well be, demon slave, but you will not survive to enjoy his success!" Quickly, he snapped the creature's neck, and the head fell limply forward.

"Julian! Must violence always be the answer with your kind? He would have been dead shortly anyway," Michael stated, anger blazing in his eyes.

"But not by my hand!" Julian replied, matching Michael's gaze. Turning back to the others, he said, "Burn every trace of that foul thing." He stormed from the room, saying to Christoff as he walked by, "Come, we have plans to make. You need to call everyone together as quickly as possible. Have them meet us in the den. Leave a few of the strongest with Thomas and the women. They'll need to be taken to a safe house while we are gone." Looking back at Michael, he said with a bitter smile, "Maybe the priest will come in handy after all."

Michael followed as the two vampires headed back up the darkened steps to the library. He watched them making their plans for the battle to come. He never thought he would fight alongside their kind, but good and evil come in many forms. Early on, he had looked into their hearts and, although Christoff's was still questionable, Julian's motives were pure and simple. He was in love.

The vampire would do what was needed to protect those he loved: man, woman, and vampire. It made no difference to him. He would fight this centuries-old threat, destroying it once and for all or die trying, if that's what it took to keep those who put their faith and trust in him safe. But Michael knew, even with the strength and loyalty of the men who followed him, Julian could not win this battle without the Avenger himself. The vampire did not have what was needed to see the fight through to its conclusion, the one weapon only Michael could wield to finish the monster they would all soon face. Would he be able to contain the threat without it, protecting Julian and the woman while they took the time needed to find the weapon that could end this nightmare forever? He knew he could count on Julian, but what about the woman? Would she be a help or a hindrance? Only time and circumstances would give him the answer he sought.

*****

Oblivious to the plans being made concerning her, Addie slid deeper into the tub, allowing jets of pulsating water to flow over her tense limbs, soothing … relaxing … helping her to forget. She wished she could wash away the memories of the horrors she had seen tonight, but she knew that would never happen. They would be locked in her mind forever.

"Oh, Kate," she thought as tears rolled down her face. But she gave herself up to the luxury of crying for only a short time. Taking a deep breath, she told herself she had to get a grip, for Kate's sake, if she was going to be of any use to her friend at all. Opening her eyes, she let them travel around the room until they came to rest on a long, velvet dressing gown someone had left for her. It obviously belonged to a man for it was at least three sizes too big, but she was grateful for their thoughtfulness.

Looking at it draped across an old-style Queen Anne chair, she wondered, "Does it belong to Julian?" As the soothing water worked its magic, she lay back and closed her eyes as her mind began to drift. She saw him standing in the doorway, the firelight from the bedroom outlining every inch of his muscular body as he reached for the robe, slipping slowly into the luxurious folds. The vision was so real she actually reached up with her hand to touch the body standing invitingly before her, but the only thing her waiting fingertips could caress was the cold air of the room. She snapped out of her daydream. Turning off the jets she rose slowly, stepped from the tub and reached for a towel. As she did so, she stared at her image in the mirror. "What are you doing? You're obsessing about him. You can't let this happen. He's not even human!" she told herself angrily as she walked quickly into the bedroom.

Sonya had left a glass of brandy on the nightstand to help her sleep. Grabbing it quickly, she was about to swallow the entire contents when she stopped herself. She needed her wits about her. She didn't need her brain hampered by alcohol—or anything else they may have put in the drink to help her rest. She just needed to close her eyes for a few minutes. Replacing the untouched glass on the nightstand, she dropped the towel and crawled under the covers. Her body sank into the folds of the soft mattress, and within seconds, she had drifted off to sleep.

After a short time, she awoke with a start and looked around the dark room in confusion. "Where am I?" she asked herself. All too quickly, the memories came flooding back. She sat up on the side of the bed to get her bearings. What time was it? Why had no one come for her? Surely Rick must have arrived by now. Glancing at an old clock on the vanity she saw that a mere half hour only had passed. Such a short time, yet it felt like she'd been sleeping for hours. Remembering Sonya's warning to stay inside the room, she began to pace restlessly. What was happening? What were they all doing?

"I must see Kate!" she said and began searching the room for her clothes. They were nowhere to be found. Someone really didn't want her to leave that room. But they didn't know her very well if they thought a little thing like the lack of clothing was going to keep her prisoner. Walking quickly into the bathroom, she snatched the black robe from the chair and shoved her arms into the oversized sleeves. She unlocked the bedroom door and opened it quietly to peer outside.

Not a soul was around. No guards ... no one. It was all so deathly quiet. She stepped into the hallway. Walking quickly to the door across the hall, she placed an ear next to the cool wood. There was only silence. Trying the handle, she found the door locked. She knocked, but received no response.

Looking around, she noticed a room at the end of the hall with a tiny spot of light coming from beneath the double doors, which stood slightly open. Shadows flickered eerily, cast by tiny lights mounted along the walls. She felt very uncomfortable as she moved along the hallway toward the open doors.

Reaching them, she hesitated. Whose room was this? Should she knock, or just barge in? Opting for the second choice, she slowly pushed the door open just enough to slip inside. The room was dark except for a welcoming light coming from the fireplace along the far wall. She didn't notice the figure behind the desk until he spoke.

"Since you didn't heed Sonya's advice to stay in your room please ... come into the lion's den!" Julian said, turning in his chair to face her, his tone unmistakable. Fear held her rooted to the spot, but it was quickly replaced by anger. He was the last person she wanted to see right then.

"I'm sorry," she said, not sounding at all like she meant it. "I didn't mean to intrude ... I couldn't sleep, and, well, I want to know what's happening with Kate." She was finding it hard to concentrate. Her eyes were drawn to his ice blue stare and her body was growing hot from the emotions wreaking havoc inside of her.

"Understandable," he said quietly. "You've been through quite an ordeal tonight, but I'm afraid I don't have much to tell you." He leaned back in the chair to study the woman glaring at him from within a black robe—his robe—that was entirely too large for her. As he continued to stare, something inside him awakened. A spark of desire flamed to life and threatened to blaze out of control as his eyes traveled down her petite form. He noticed how the belt around her waist had loosened, the gaping folds of cloth exposing a glimpse of her perfectly shaped breast. Desire fought against the hunger that roared to life inside of him. Something in his eyes triggered a similar response in Adrianna as she watched the blue-grey hue change into something more. The anger and frustration that had been so strong a moment ago changed into something decidedly different, and the heat of her gaze filled with an intensity that matched his own.

"My God, he's so beautiful," she thought, closing her eyes in an attempt to wipe his image from her mind. But that was impossible. She was drawn to him by a force beyond her control. Eyes open again she took a step in his direction, the look on his face making her unable to breath. His hair was tousled as if he had run agitated fingers through it. Soft brown waves fell across one eye and down his shoulder. Her fingers ached to reach up and brush the tangled mass back from that perfect face.

"No, it can't be like this," she thought. His face, his body … they made it so easy to forget exactly what she was dealing with. "Get a grip on yourself. Think of Kate, only Kate." Turning her back on him, she forced her shaky legs to move toward the door.

"I can see this conversation is going nowhere. Again, I'm sorry to have bothered—"

"You really haven't given me a chance to answer your question," he said, and she realized, with a shock that he was standing right behind her! When had he moved? And how had he done it so quickly?

"All I am aware of is that Kate is resting," he whispered against her ear, his breath flowing softly across the back of her neck. She closed her eyes tightly, fighting against her rising desire. "They finished the transfusion, but she has yet to wake up."

She fought against the tears threatening to spill down her face as she listened to what he was saying.

"I'm sorry, Addie," he said softly, his hands resting on her shoulders. They began to travel slowly downward as she leaned back against him, wanting nothing more than to be held by him, to forget everything in the comfort only he could give.

His arms encircled her, holding her tightly against him. Her smell, her scent, weakened his control as hunger and passion threatened to consume him.

She felt his lips brush against her cheek and travel down to the pulse in her throat … a pulse beating wildly out of control. The next thing she knew, she was shoved roughly away from him. She stumbled as she regained her balance.

"You have no idea the danger you are putting yourself in by coming here!" His voice sounded strained, deeper, almost a growl. His head bowed as he fought to control the battle raging within him. "My self-control is not what it used to be. For both our sakes, I suggest you go. Now!"

He lifted his head to look directly at her. Shock gripped her as his beautiful eyes changed from smoky blue to blood red! With a gasp, she staggered back toward the door. But even the fear could not make her take her eyes off of him. She saw intense sadness cross his face as he watched her back away, the fear apparent in her eyes, before he turned his back on her.

"What kind of being are you, so human one minute, but something entirely different the next?" she asked.

"You already know, only too well, the answer to that question, don't you, Adrianna? Now, if Kate was the only reason you came in search of me, I believe I've told you all I know, unless there is something else you came for?" he said, trying desperately to sound sarcastic. She had to leave soon. His control was almost at an end. God, he could smell her blood.

She replied hotly, "I was not in search of you, as you so eloquently put it but, since you asked, I do have one question. Find out if Kate is strong enough to leave because I want us both as far away from here as we can get, as soon as possible! I'm sure there are other places we can stay that are just as safe, probably safer, if you will stop holding us prisoner and just let us go!" The tears she'd been fighting so hard to contain began to roll down her cheek.

Her words were like a blade plunging into his heart, but he would not let her see how much she hurt him. "Still want to run to your priest, Adrianna? Where is he?" he taunted her. "He doesn't seem to be in any real hurry to come to your rescue, he—"

Slap!

Her hand stung from the impact, the sound echoing through the room.

"He'll be here! At least he's never let me down!" she screamed through her tears.

"Then run to him. Run to his church. Do you actually believe that holy ground will protect you?" Taking a step forward, he continued, "Under other circumstances you might be right, but not this time. None of the legends and myths will even come close to saving you from the evil that is stalking you ... stalking us both! You cannot even comprehend what you are dealing with, and all the holy water and crucifixes in the Holy Vatican will not keep you safe from him!" He grabbed her arms as if to shake some sense into her. "I am your best chance, your only chance, whether you like it or not. And I don't know that even I can promise you safety. So go. Run back to your room and lock the door. Try to keep the evil out, which, in your mind, seems to include me. Tomorrow, in the daylight, if you still wish to leave, you can go. Then maybe I can find some peace!" He shouted as he pushed her toward the open door.

Addie fled through the doorway and into the hall, stumbling as tears blinded her. Entering the bedroom, she slammed the door behind her and turned the key angrily before falling onto the bed.

"He's a monster!" she shouted. "What is wrong with me that I let him affect me the way he does?" Even now, when she should hate him with every fiber of her being, she remembered the sadness in his eyes, the longing as he stared at her, and she wanted nothing more than to go back to him and give whatever comfort she could. "But he doesn't want me," she told herself bitterly. He made that perfectly clear. "And where is Rick?"' she wondered. All she wanted to do was leave this awful place.

Closing her eyes, she prayed for sleep to come, but she was not that lucky. After tossing and turning, she fell into a troubled sleep filled with disturbing images of black, winged creatures chasing her as she ran aimlessly into the night, branches from nearby trees slashing at her face. But she kept running. She must keep running. But why? Where was she going ... and to whom?

Then, suddenly, the answer was before her. There was safety at the end of her journey, someone who would protect her and keep her safe from the horror that hunted her if she could only reach him in time, for she knew beyond a shadow of a doubt that if she did not find him, she would surely die.

Chapter 15

The car came to a stop just before the entrance to the bridge. His eyes traveled to the waiting mansion at the top of the hill. He tried to control the fear building inside him. "Vampires," he thought. "Impossible. There is no such thing."

But he, of all people, should know that unbelievable things do happen. He was a priest, after all. Didn't he ask people every day at Mass to believe the impossible? But vampires. Weren't they just a myth, a legend for some would-be writer to sink his teeth into? Then again, why not vampires? He knew, for certain, that many kinds of evil existed. If they were real, what other ungodly horrors roamed the earth? Once again, paralyzing fear rose inside him, rooting him to the spot, preventing him from doing what he'd come here to do.

His friends needed him. Addie needed him, and no matter the cost, he had to be there for her. "She's up there," he thought, "going through God knows what." The fear for his friends consumed his own fear as he threw the late model Grand Am into gear and proceeded slowly across the bridge, up the incline, coming to a stop in front of the old house. Turning off the car, he opened the door and climbed out slowly, his eyes searching the darkness for any sign of the terrors that may be hiding there.

Reaching back inside the vehicle, he retrieved the black duffle bag from the front seat. From inside the bag, he removed a wooden stake about eight inches long and two inches thick, the tip filed to a sharp point. Holding the stake firmly in his right hand and the bag in his left, he adjusted the large gold crucifix that hung around his neck so it was in plain sight. Taking a deep breath, he exhaled slowly and proceeded up the steps. He stood before the heavy oak door and crossed himself quickly before knocking loudly , waiting to see who or what would greet him.

After a few minutes, the door opened to reveal a tall young man with a shock of spiky red hair. He was well muscled under his skin-tight T-shirt A long, thorny vine was tattooed all the way down his left arm. Apprehension filled Rick until the young man spoke, a slight smile on his thin lips, "You must be the priest. Please come in. There is nothing for you to fear here."

Rick stepped cautiously inside, eyeing the young man suspiciously. As the door closed, both men's eyes traveled to a woman standing alone on the staircase. Her stunning beauty left Rick speechless as she stared back at him, only to climb a few steps backwards when she noticed the stake he held, as well as the cross, in plain sight around the priest's neck. Her dark eyes flashed to the man beside Rick sending a silent message, anger … plus a hint of fear evident in her expression.

"Your weapons will not be necessary inside this house," the young man said firmly. When Rick hesitated, the young man walked up to him and gripped the cross between two fingers. Rick waited to see what was to come, but nothing happened. Seeing the look of surprise on his face, the young man explained, "I am as human as you, Father. My name is Seth, and I was sent to take you to the injured woman. They are waiting for you upstairs. No one here wishes you harm, unless you strike first. All we are trying to do is help, all of us, human and nonhuman alike. Those in this house are not the enemy, and if you wish to help your friend we must hurry, time is running short."

Something in the boy's tone convinced Rick so, placing the stake inside the bag he indicated he was ready to follow.

"The cross too, please. It doesn't bother us humans, but it will cause severe pain to the others."

Deciding to trust the young man, Rick unbuttoned the top of his shirt and tucked the cross out of sight.

"Thank you." Seth motioned for him to follow as he, with Sonya in the lead, began climbing the stairs to the room where Kate slept.

"Ah, I see our savior has arrived. Father," Julian said, bowing toward Rick irreverently when he met them at the top of the staircase. Rick stared at him silently, his anger beginning to rise as he noticed the slight smile Sonya flashed at the tall man.

"How did they all come to be in this unbelievable situation? And please God, help me get us all out alive!" he thought as Julian turned and walked to one of the bedroom doors, where he tapped lightly. Moments later, a tired Thomas opened the door wide for them to enter.

"Thank God you're here," Thomas said in an exhausted voice as Rick walked slowly into the room.

"It's nice to know someone wants me here. How is she?" Rick asked, dreading the answer as he forced himself to walk to the large canopy bed in the center of the room. He saw a tall man beside the bed, his long, blond hair almost white in the candlelight. Two others moved to the far recesses of the room at his approach. But his attention was drawn to the small figure lying motionless among the bed covers. He heard himself gasp as he caught sight of her lovely face as pale and lifeless as the white blankets surrounding it. His heart sank. She must surely be dead.

"Her breathing is shallow, and she has yet to regain consciousness," Thomas replied. "The transfusion has replaced most of the blood she lost, but the poison is spreading. We must act soon if ..." but the young man was unable to continue. Rick wondered at this stranger's sadness, for he barely knew Kate, but there was no mistaking the grief in his green eyes.

Not even trying to disguise the disdain for all he represented, Sonya said, "It's your turn now, priest. Let's see if your magic works."

Rick stepped up to the bed and put the duffle bag on the floor. Sliding the zipper open he withdrew a small wooden box. Very gently, he sat down next to Kate's still form with the tiny box on his lap. Just as he was about to open it, he remembered something. Looking around the room he asked, "Where is Addie?"

"We didn't want to upset—" Thomas began.

"She was not needed. She is resting," Julian answered curtly. "She will be called when we know what the situation actually is, when we have exhausted all our options. You'd better hurry before the only course left to us is the one she will have the most problem accepting."

"You don't mean you would ..." Rick started to ask, but he couldn't finish. He really didn't want to know the answer.

"You have a quick mind, priest. And, yes, I mean exactly that. I made a promise to keep her alive any way possible. So you'd better hurry before you are forced to condemn her to a fate worse than death," Julian replied bitterly.

"Alright ... but Addie should be here," Rick said firmly before turning his attention back to Kate. Julian continued to watch from a distance, fighting to control the anger boiling inside of him. Who was this man to tell him anything about Adrianna! He and he alone knew what was best for her in this situation. Still, as he continued to fume in silence, he had to admit the priest was probably right. Adrianna should be with her friend no matter what the outcome. He saw Charleze near the doorway. Sending a silent message, she turned toward him. With a nod of the head, she acknowledged his instructions and silently left the room.

Addie tossed restlessly, deep in a nightmare, when a loud pounding startled her awake. Sitting up abruptly, she tried to focus, still locked in the stranglehold of fear.

"Open the door, Addie!" The pounding came again as she stumbled from the bed and ran across the room. She flung the door open and saw Charleze.

"Are you alright?" Charleze asked, pushing Adrianna aside as she charged into the room.

"Of course, why wouldn't I be?"

"Why wouldn't you ... Addie, you were screaming."

"What? Oh, yes, I'm sorry if I alarmed you. It was just a nightmare," she said, running her hand through her hair.

Looking once more around the room, Charleze seemed to accept Addie's explanation.

"As long as you are alright," she said, looking at Addie curiously.

"I'm fine."

"Good. Julian sent me get you. Your friend, the priest, has arrived. If you will change quickly, I will take you to him."

"Thank God!" Addie said, tears of relief threatening to spill forth as she searched the room for her clothes.

"No, thank Julian," the young vampire said a bit sarcastically.

Addie barely heard her as she found her clothing, freshly washed and pressed. "Who brought them back?" she wondered. "Oh who cares." She thought as she dressed quickly , her desire to see Rick all consuming. Buttoning the last button, she was off like a shotgun blast toward the door when a hand gripped her arm in midflight pulling her to a grinding halt.

"Ouch! What are you doing? Let me go!" she shouted at her captor as she whipped around.

But Charleze held her effortlessly, preventing her from going any further. "Addie, you must stop," the vampire warned in a patient voice as Addie struggled to break free. "They are working on your friend. You can't just go bursting in on them. Calm down. Follow me, and we will enter the room quietly. Stay out of the way until they are finished. Adrianna, do you understand?"

Addie realizing the vampire was right, nodded in agreement.

"Good! Let's go."

An attack of nerves held Addie motionless for a few seconds. What was she going to find on the other side of that door? Would she be able to handle it? She had no choice. That was Kate in there. She had to be strong for her friend's sake, and Rick would be there. He would make everything alright. Taking a deep breath, she indicated to the waiting vampire that she was ready, and turning the knob to open the door, they entered the room.

Once inside, she took in the scene. Rick sat on the bed examining Kate. A wooden box lay next to him containing items used for anointing the sick and dying during last rites. Hearing their approach, he turned, his troubled eyes locking with Adrianna's for a brief moment before turning back to the woman lying still in the bed. Kate's breathing was shallow. She was so pale she looked like death. Adrianna could barley control her fear as she stared at the woman who had been her closest friend for as long as she could remember.

"Is she still alive?" she asked in an almost inaudible whisper.

Thomas, standing ready to assist Rick said, "Yes, but we must hurry. The longer we wait the more the poison spreads."

Michael was on the opposite side of the bed, a look of grave concern on his face. Standing alone in the far corner of the room, Adrianna caught sight of Julian. He was staring at her intently, almost as if he were trying to read her mind. He still seemed angry with her, but after a few seconds, he turned his focus to the small group around the bed. After watching Rick's preparations for several minutes, Julian said to the priest, "Thomas and I will hold her."

Moving to the bed, both men placed a hand on each of Kate's shoulders. "Once your objects touch her, the reaction will be violent," Julian said, again glancing at Addie. "I'm sorry, but there is no other way. I only hope we are not too late to help her, and," he looked intently at Rick, "please try not to touch me in the process. My proximity to your objects is painful enough."

"I will hold her, Julian. The objects will not affect me as they do you. As a matter of fact, I rather enjoy being near them," said Michael, standing next to Julian. The vampire looked at him strangely for a moment but did not argue. Addie noticed Sonya and the other vampires backing as far away from Rick as possible. So some of the legends must be true.

Rick hesitated a moment longer before saying, "Tell me what to do."

"You have your blessed water?" Julian asked.

The priest withdrew a large crystal bottle of what Addie assumed was holy water. Lifting it high, he showed it to Julian.

"Good. Pour a small amount on her neck, directly where she was bitten."

Glancing a little apprehensively at Thomas, who had positioned himself opposite Michael, Rick removed the cork stopper and very slowly poured a few drops onto the two swollen puncture wounds on Kate's throat. The reaction was immediate. The wounds began to sizzle as Kate screamed in pain. The woman who was near comatose just a moment before tossed violently from side to side as she tried to break free from the men holding her down.

"Now make her drink as much as you can," Julian ordered.

"But the slightest drop causes her so much pain! This can't be good. What will happen to her if she drinks it?" Rick questioned, fear and uncertainty filling him.

"The pain she will endure is nothing compared to what she will have to face for eternity if we fail to kill the infection, priest. Now do what you are told!" Julian demanded.

Placing his hand gently behind Kate's head, Rick poured the bottle's contents down her throat as he massaged the side of her neck, forcing her to swallow before she could spit the precious liquid back into his face.

She shrieked in pain her body bucking wildly. Rick was thrown backward, but it gave the others the room they needed to work with the half-crazed woman as Thomas charged forward to grab her.

The vampire bite had given her enhanced strength, and she tossed Thomas aside like a cloth doll. He landed hard on the floor beside the bed. Michael, whose strength matched that of any vampire, held her tightly, but he could not control her alone.

"Let me have her!" Julian commanded, climbing quickly onto the bed. Michael passed the thrashing figure into his lap. Julian held Kate tightly, settling himself behind her, his strong arms pulling the tortured body against him as she continued to scream, the sound so mournful that tears streamed down Adrianna's cheeks as she listened to her friend. Rick moved forward, placing an arm around Adrianna's shoulder trying to offer what comfort he could . Julian watched as she buried her head in Rick's shoulder before he focused all his concentration on the woman in his arms.

He whispered soothingly to calm her. Drops of blood stained the sheets crimson as she clawed at Julian's arms. Kicking and thrashing, she tried to break his hold, but she was no match for the vampire. Ignoring his own pain, Julian held his grip as the battle raged on for what seemed like hours but was actually no more than twenty minutes, until the exhausted woman collapsed against the body behind her. Julian gently brushed the hair back from the tear-stained face, listening as the labored breathing began to slow to a more normal pace.

"I think the worst is over now," he said as he laid her gently onto the bed. Thomas ran to the now sleeping form.

"Come, friend. We must attend to your wounds—" Michael started to approach Julian.

"They are nothing," Julian replied, but he was weak. The strain of the evening had taken its toll on him. He needed to feed to get his strength back and heal. He needed to get away from this room, to escape them all. He was tired and wanted peace.

Turning to find Adrianna still in Rick's arms he said, a sharp edge to his voice, "Take the wafer. Place it to the wounds on her neck. See what happens."

Rick stepped forward and placed the sacred Host on Kate's neck. Again, a soft hissing sound was heard. Removing the wafer, the wounds looked red and raw, but before everyone's amazed eyes, they began to disappear until no trace of them could be seen. Michael stared at Julian with a slight smile on his face. "I think it worked."

"It would seem so," Julian replied. Already, color was returning to her face. "She needs rest," he said. "Thomas, stay with her. Keep her calm if she awakens, and keep me informed of her progress. Dawn's approaching. I have to leave."

Addie noticed he looked tired and drawn as he walked directly in front of her without so much as a glance.

"I'm staying with her, too," she whispered as he passed her.

"As you wish," he replied, too tired to argue. He stopped but refused to look at her as he said, "At this moment, I don't have the will or the inclination to argue with you. When she's strong enough, if you still wish to leave, you can go with the priest." He walked quickly from the room.

Michael studied Kate and Rick with a strange look on his face. As if coming to an important decision, he approached them, "Despite what you know of his kind, he is different. There is good in him, though even he may not realize it. I would not be here if that were not true."

"I'm trying to understand what's going," Rick said. "Everything that I've witnessed is … unbelievable. But the thing I question the most is why there are so many humans here with him? Aren't they afraid of these creatures? Of what they can do?"

Michael studied him long and hard before answering, "It is a long, ugly tale that I don't have time to go into just now, but believe me when I say there is a battle coming, good priest. The humans are with Julian because, despite what he is, he has earned their trust, and he is the only one with any chance of fighting the evil descending upon us. It seeks him out because of something in his past, but it hunts us all. It will require all of us to pull together our resources and do what we can to help him if there is to be any chance of survival. If he fails, the world as we know it will plunge into a darkness so black, a despair so hopeless, there will be no returning to the light. That is all I can say at this point. Any more details must come from him. My advice to you," Michael said, looking intently at Adrianna, "is to talk to him. It appears this whole unbelievable situation may have something to do with you." He walked from the room and left them in stunned silence.

"What did he mean?" Addie asked Thomas. "What would any of this horror have to do with me? I was blissfully unaware of any of this—of any of you—until this evening."

After checking to see that Kate was sleeping peacefully, Thomas came to stand beside them, "Addie, I wish I could tell you." His eyes darted back to the woman lying in the bed, "Especially now, but you really need to get the explanation from Julian himself. I only know bits and pieces. But one thing I do know. Julian was in love once, a long time ago, and the woman, from what I am told, had some connection to you."

"Me!" she said, stunned.

"Yeah, that's the story. Talk to Julian, but you'll have to wait till tonight. Why don't you both try to get some rest? It's been a long, hard night for everyone. I'll stay with Kate. If she wakes up, I want her to see a friendly face." He looked a little sheepish.

"But, Thomas, you're exhausted. At least I've had some rest. Let me stay with her so you can get a little sleep."

"Thanks, but no, Addie. I want to be here when she wakes up. I'll rest my eyes for a while. I think there's an empty room right next door to the one you are in. I'm sure no one will care if you use it, Father."

"Thank you. Thomas is right, Addie. I'm sure he'll let us know when she can see us. Come on, I'll walk you to your room." Taking her arm gently, Rick led her through the door and to the bedroom across the hall.

"I'm right next door, Addie. Call me if you need me," Rick said. Lifting her chin he tried a slight smile. "Everything will be alright, really it will. Try to have a little faith."

She gave a weak nod as she opened her bedroom door and went in. Sitting on the bed, Addie noticed dawn's hazy approach through the bedroom window. She was drained and exhausted. Without undressing, she lay across the pillows falling into a restless sleep that was troubled by strange dreams. A huge, winged creature chased her through a forest black as night. She kept looking behind her, watching the shadows, unaware of the dark form directly in front of her until it was too late. Tripping on a large root, she fell forward landing directly in front of a living nightmare. Slowly lifting her eyes, the scream stuck in her throat as terror filled her. She struggled to free herself, twisting and turning, pulling until the sleeve of her dress tore completely away from the bodice. "No!" she screamed as the hideous face descended toward her. "*No!*"

Almost falling from the bed in a tangle of blankets, she awoke dazed and confused. She saw the sun shining brightly in the afternoon sky and realized she had been asleep for hours. "What is happening to me?" she asked herself, holding her head in her hands. "These awful dreams … what do they mean?"

Rising from the bed, she walked toward the bathroom, hoping a hot shower would warm the chill seeping through her body. As the water enveloped her in its warmth, she began to relax a little, and her thoughts turned once again to Julian,

"I need to talk to him," she said aloud. She turned off the water, dressed, brushed her hair into some kind of order, and went in search of her host.

It was mid-afternoon, and a thick silence hung throughout the house. Everyone was probably still sleeping after last night, but there had to be human guards somewhere on the grounds. She wondered if she should wake Rick, but even as her fist was poised to tap on his door, she thought better of it. "I need to talk to Julian alone," she told herself.

Descending the stairs, she entered the den, hoping to find someone who could tell her where Julian's room was. Even if she found him, she didn't know if she would be able to talk to him. "Are they able to wake during the day, or are they literally dead to the world until night?" she wondered.

The room was deathly still, and it didn't seem that anyone was around. Then she noticed someone sitting in the large chair, facing yet another fireplace. He turned toward her.

"I'm glad to see you were able to get some rest, Adrianna," Michael said, giving her a smile that took her breath away. His features were flawless; his shining blue eyes were so clear they were almost transparent. The oddest thought crossed her mind as she returned his gaze, "It's like he's looking right into my soul, aware of my deepest secrets." She shook her head slightly to clear her senses.

"I slept a little, Michael, but I couldn't stop the nightmares, so I thought it better to be awake. I also thought … is it possible to talk to Julian at this hour of the day? I need some answers, and it seems that he's the only one who can give them to me. That is, of course, if he'll even talk to me."

A slight smile appeared on his face. "Yes, we may have to twist his arm a bit to get him to be civil, but I think we could persuade him to give you a few minutes of his time." Then, becoming more serious, he continued, "Hopefully he is resting, we'll need him at full strength for what is ahead, but it is possible to talk to him. He can go without sleep during the day, but not for long. It weakens him, and he must stay in darkness, so he stays below in his private chambers." He rose from the chair and took her by the arm. "Come with me."

She followed his elegant form back up the staircase to one of the many doors lining the long hallway. As he opened it, she saw nothing but a staircase leading up.

"Where are we going?" she asked.

"This leads to Julian's bedroom at the top of one of the four towers. It's one of the rooms he uses. It also contains the passage to his underground chamber." At the top, they entered a large, very masculine room. No one needed to tell her this was Julian's room. Old world. Elegant. Those were the words that came to mind as her eyes traveled around the room with its large, antique furniture and beautiful, rich colors.

"Are you sure this is a good idea, Michael? He may not have a problem with you or his own people waking him, but do you really think he wants me, of all people, intruding on his private quarters?"

"We aren't giving him a choice," he said simply as he walked to the far wall. He reached beneath the sconce hanging there and touched a switch. A hidden door opened with a grating sound.

"This place is full of secrets, just like its owner," she said as she peered over his shoulder into the darkness. He just smiled.

"Secrecy is the key to his surviving as long as he has, Adrianna."

Michael led her into the darkness, stopping for a moment to retrieve a large, tapered match that he used to light small candles as they descended. They continued deeper and deeper into the bowels of the old house until they reached the bottom of the stone staircase and found a solid, wooden door. Knocking three times, he called out, "Julian, it is Michael. Are you awake?"

The cold silence was unnerving as she waited breathlessly for a reply. She jumped at least three feet in the air as the door suddenly swung open.

"What's wrong? Has something happened?"

And suddenly, he was there, his long mane of hair tangled around his face as if he had just awakened from a restless sleep. He was wearing nothing but a pair of tight fitting black jeans, and she found herself unable to look away. Her eyes traveled from the hollow in his throat down to the patch of dark hair running thickly across his muscular chest all the way down to the waistband of the jeans that wrapped tightly around his narrow hips. She felt a flame erupt deep inside her, and as blue eyes caught brown, she saw the spark of desire reflected back at her. With a shock, she realized that no matter what he was, she couldn't deny the attraction. She couldn't fight the desire. She wanted him more than anyone she had ever known.

"What is she doing down here?" His words struck her like ice water.

"You two need to talk, Julian. I know now is not the ideal time but the opportunity presented itself so—"

"So you thought you would bring her here to the only sanctuary available to me in this hell I live in!"

"Julian you need—"

"It's not Michael's fault, Julian. I asked him to bring me. I'm sorry to intrude on your private time, but I need some answers, and I couldn't wait until tonight. I won't be here then." Hesitating a moment longer, Julian looked from Adrianna to Michael then backed away from the door so she could enter the room. As she walked past Michael, he gently touched her arm, "Keep an open mind, Adrianna, and don't stay too long. He needs to rest." She nodded as he turned and climbed back up the long staircase.

Chapter 16

Julian watched her for a moment before moving forward to light two candles on the mantle above the stone fireplace. With a wave of his hand, the hearth burst into flames. She appreciated the warmth greatly for the room was cold and damp. He caught the stunned surprise on her face as she realized what he had done, but he did not say a word. Grabbing a discarded shirt from a nearby chair, he pulled it over his body but left the front unbuttoned, making it hard for her to concentrate. Turning his back to her, he stood staring at the flames, deep in thought.

Watching him standing there, something in her softened a little, "I'm sorry Julian, I didn't mean to intrude, but I need to know what's happening and how I'm involved in all of this. Thomas said the attack may have something to do with me, so I need you to explain what he meant."

Sighing deeply, he slowly turned to face her. "I will tell you my story, and I hope you will try to understand," he said with a plea in his eyes. "I became what I am a long time ago, Adrianna. Four and a half centuries, to be exact. After my rebirth, I was despondent to the point of self-destruction. You don't know how many times I've waited to greet the morning sun," he said, looking at her intently, "in the hopes of bringing about my own demise, only to be thwarted in my attempts by someone or something."

"Oh, Julian."

"Please, Adrianna, believe me when I tell you I deserved no one's sympathy in those early days. I was every bit the monster my kind is made out to be. The blood lust is all-consuming, and my maker reveled in the terror and destruction we caused. But as time went on, I learned that I did not have to take an innocent life to save my own. There were other ways to survive, to find the sustenance that I required. So I adapted and taught others to do the same. Our lord was furious! He would not rest until I was brought back into his fold, and he would stop at nothing to bring that about. We, on the other hand, defied him at every turn. We made it our mission to destroy those who took innocent lives. As the centuries passed, I was able to live with what I had become and at least give the appearance of a human existence. I was content."

He tried to read her face and her thoughts, to gauge in some way how she was taking this in. He read sadness—and was that pity? Neither was the emotion he longed to see there, but what did he expect? Turning back toward the flames, he continued, "Things were quiet for a while. The evil hordes diminished, and their leader disappeared. Or so it seemed. Then something happened. A rumor surfaced, a story involving my family and our bloodline, and I dared to hope for a normal existence once again, only to have that hope shattered before my very eyes! The story told of a wealthy and powerful man, a leader of many, in what is known today as Iraq. He had a beautiful wife whom he loved deeply, but like so many men of power, he also had a mistress. Awan was her name, and unknown to him, she was more than just a beautiful woman. She was a vampire. This mistress loved him in her own way, and fearful he would leave her or worse, she kept the secret of what she was from him. Her love did not stop her from taking his blood, but only small amounts as he slept after their lovemaking. Though he was weak afterward, he never knew the reason or suspected what she really was, until one fateful night when he awoke as she was feeding on a poor servant girl.

"Filled with horror, he reached for the knife he always kept tucked discreetly beneath his pillow. In a moment of fear and panic, he plunged the silver blade directly through her heart! There was so much blood flowing from the wound. It was everywhere, on the bed, the floor, himself. His arms and hands were covered in it. Climbing from the bed, he tried desperately to rid himself of the red stain, wiping his hands against his robes. That's when he realized he was injured. He had a small cut across his thumb where he'd grasped the blade of the knife. He stared in horror as he watched her blood mingle with his own, and he knew his fate was sealed. He knew the monster he would become. He also knew what he must do to end his curse, but he wished to see his wife one last time.

"She was asleep when he arrived at their home, but she awoke as he kissed her gently. They made love one final time. When she had fallen back to sleep, he went to the cliff behind the house, and driving the silver blade deep into his heart, he fell to the water below. He was found days later and buried. His wife was gravely ill for a long time afterward from what everyone thought was grief. Later, it was found she was pregnant with twins. In her weakened condition, she died in childbirth, which was a blessing, for she never knew the horror she had given birth to. One child was completely normal, a strong son to carry on the line. He was taken away to be raised by the family. The other child was an abomination, born a pure-blooded vampire and craving blood directly from the womb!

"The thing was ordered destroyed, but some misguided soul sought to be merciful and escaped with the creature. Thus the Awanian bloodline began, or should I say bloodlines, for there were two distinct lines: one human and one vampire." He saw her staring at him in horror as she listened to his tale. He knew he must continue, for he had yet to reveal the most important part of the story. Watching her closely, he continued, "This is my family, Adrianna, my bloodline, for that wealthy aristocrat was my ancestor. It was thought his human offspring had mercifully escaped the family curse. But a discovery many years later proved them wrong. For all intents and purposes, his firstborn was human, but as the generations passed, an anomaly appeared in the line of this twin's descendants: a human gave birth to a pure-blooded vampire."

"No," she whispered.

"Yes, I'm afraid it's true. After some research, a recessive gene was discovered, a vampire gene, which lay dormant in the first twin's bloodline. Someone decided further study was needed, and vampires of the line were captured and tested, only to find that a select few carried a dormant human gene. No one realized until years later just how important this recessive gene would become. As time went on, more vampires were created, and more humans were born to carry on our heritage. Then, years later, another discovery was made. A vampire attempted to convert a human ... and failed."

"Is that possible?" she asked quietly.

"I've never witnessed it. When a vampire sets out to turn a human, they are either turned or die during the process," he said.

"Oh," was all she could manage to say.

"It's not a process most of us take lightly, Adrianna, but I'm getting off track. With the knowledge that he could not turn the one he loved, the vampire in question was in for an even bigger surprise. After ingesting a large quantity of her blood, he began to notice a change in himself. He still had speed and most of his strength, but he was not the same. His power was somehow diminished. But more importantly, the blood lust was gone completely. For all intents and purposes, he was human again!" He stopped, not daring to breath.

"Human? Completely human?"

"Yes, Adrianna."

"But how can that be?"

"Another anomaly, a freak accident of nature, who knows. But it happened. Although it appeared there was a certain formula to this miracle cure. A human with the recessive vampire gene must meet a vampire with the recessive human gene. If the vampire bites the human, the human is immune to the vampire virus. The vampire, on the other hand, is cured of the virus and becomes human once more. I witnessed it myself twice. "

"But that's wonderful, Julian. It means there's hope."

Julian was staring at her so intently she couldn't think clearly. Tearing his gaze away, he leaned heavily against the mantle. A great sorrow seemed to overcome him, but he continued, "There's more to the story, Adrianna. I've told you I was once in love."

"Yes," she said softly.

"She was so beautiful," he said almost to himself. "Hair like ebony, soft and flowing, skin like porcelain, and her eyes—you could drown in those eyes so deeply brown ..." He caught himself, then continued, "Anyway, after some time I revealed to her my true nature, and to my surprise and joy, she loved me despite what I was. And I loved her more than life itself. She was my sanity in the nightmare that I was living. She taught me, at great risk to herself, how to control the monster within me, and I began to actually believe I might have some sort of happiness again in my life."

Addie could almost feel the pain inside him as he bowed his head. After a few minutes, he went on, "But it was not to be, for she was taken from me." Clenching his hands into fists, he said with barely controlled fury, "And though I nearly died trying, I could not save her. She was killed in front of me by the one who made me, the monster we hunt today called Dragon. It was my punishment for turning against him, for thwarting his plans for power! He also knew the story of the bloodline and knew that the key to the cure, the gene needed to make me human again, ran through my veins as well as hers. He took away my last chance at humanity, and he enjoyed doing it!"

The anguish in his voice was more than she could bear as she rose from the chair and started toward him.

"No! Let me finish," he said, raising a hand to stop her approach. "I vowed then that if I survived I would not rest until she was avenged and I had completely destroyed him. I would not be alive today if it weren't for Christoff and a few others who managed to get to me in time. After accomplishing what he had set out to do, the monster disappeared into hiding for centuries, or so I thought until I had a conversation with Michael."

"Michael? What does he know of all this?"

"Apparently more than any of us. He thinks Dragon is back. The monster thinks something has happened that is important enough to bring him into my path again."

"What happened?" she asked in a voice barely above a whisper.

"You have happened, Adrianna. You are the threat he feels he must destroy."

"Me! But why, Julian? How can I possibly threaten a creature like him? I don't understand."

Turning away from her, he continued in a low voice, "Have you ever traced your family's ancestry, Adrianna?"

"No, there was never any reason, and I'm afraid I just wasn't curious enough. Why? Is it important?" Fear clutched at her heart—she was almost certain she could predict what he was about to tell her.

"I don't know if you realize the importance of what I'm going to tell you, but please hear me out. I've had Michael and Thomas research your family—"

"What! Why would—"

"Please, hear me out, because, so far, what they have found is astounding," he said, turning slightly to look at her.

Running fingers through his hair, he seemed unsure how to continue. "You are the mirror image of her, Adrianna," he said, and she heard the longing in his voice. "I saw it the moment I laid eyes on you at the club." Tearing his eyes from her face, he walked to the bed and gripped the bedpost for support. "What we have found so far indicates you are of the bloodline— her bloodline, and mine."

"What?" Only his sensitive hearing could make out that single word from her lips.

"It seems Avani is just one of the variations on the name Awan." He watched her closely as she shook her head in denial. "Dragon must have found this out somehow. He fears my reaching you before he does. He cannot take the chance that you carry the gene which can make me human again."

"There must be some mistake. This can't be happening," she said in a quiet voice, shaking with emotion. "You are telling me I have an ancestor who was a ... vampire!"

"An ancient ancestor, yes," he replied softly.

"And you, as a vampire, are of the bloodline also? That makes us related in some way?"

"We are very distant relations, Adrianna, centuries down the line. I was of the bloodline before he made me what I am today. And since I was human first, another human of the line who carries the gene can change me back again—if I also carry the recessive gene," he said. He watched the play of emotion cross her face.

One thought played over and over in her head. He could be human again! She realized that he was still talking, but almost to himself, "There would have to be tests done, but I could sense you as soon as you entered the club that night. I knew then that someone of our line was present, but you cannot imagine my shock when your face came into view on that dance floor. I thought I would never see that beautiful face again, no matter how many generations I was cursed to live." His anguish shone in his burning blue eyes.

Her feet seemed to move of their own volition as she moved toward him. The desire to comfort him overwhelmed all the other emotions running rampant inside of her: the fear, the denial, the disbelief. She stood before him and raised her hand to gently stroke his cheek. He seemed to stop breathing as her fingers followed the contours of his face, traveling seductively to the strong jaw and over the soft, sensuous lips. She couldn't take her eyes off those lips as she stroked her thumb across them.

"Stop now, Adrianna, while I still have some semblance of control," he said in a tight voice, grabbing her wrists. "I told you she taught me control, but it's been too long that I have deprived myself of the touch of a woman, and believe me when I say that you don't want to test my restraint tonight."

"You won't hurt me, Julian, you're stronger than that," she whispered as she leaned into him, gently kissing first one side of his mouth, then the other.

With a sharp intake of breath, he pulled her tightly against him, pinning her hands behind her back. They seemed suspended in time as blue eyes gazed into brown, and then suddenly, with a deep moan, he kissed her hungrily, thrusting his tongue deep into her mouth. Releasing her hands, he encircled her waist, molding her to the contours of his body as her hands found their way inside his open shirt, gently pulling it back from his shoulders sending it fluttering to the ground.

"Adrianna, please," he spoke in a tormented whisper as he grabbed her hands again.

"Shhh," she replied softly, freeing her hands to travel over the coarse, dark hair across his chest. She could feel his heart beating furiously as her arms encircled his neck and she buried her face in the waves of long, soft curls falling across his shoulders.

She couldn't seem to get enough of him as she kissed the side of his neck, slowly brushing her soft lips across the hollow of his throat. She heard him moan deeply, felt herself lifted in his arms as he kissed her so deeply that she could barely breathe. Laying her gently onto the bed he followed, his body suspended above her, bracing himself with strong arms on either side of her. His hair fell forward in a glorious silken veil, and as she reached up to brush a loose strand from his face, he turned to place a soft kiss along her wrist.

Thrusting her hands into his hair, she cupped his head and brought him down, kissing him hungrily. Her body felt as though it were on fire as she felt the hardness of him pressing against her. God, she didn't think she could get enough of him. Her breath came in ragged gasps as she held him tightly, feeling his lips pressed against the vein in her neck—the vein pounding furiously with her life's blood, the vein that his lips were poised directly above.

Suddenly, with a cry of anguish, he pulled away from her stumbling awkwardly to the bottom of the bed.

"Adrianna, please, you must leave." His voice was filled with such pain that she could feel his anguish.

She reached over to gently stroke his bare shoulder, "Julian, let me help you. You can control the beast. You've done it before. You said—"

"I said go, Adrianna! What I am feeling now is long past any control. It takes time to … take my word for it, you must go … now!"

The voice that only moments ago had whispered softly to her now came out as a growl, sending shivers of fear down her spine. What had she done to him? She'd driven him past his limit. How could she have been so stupid! She tripped as her feet touched the floor in her haste to climb from the bed. She hesitated at the door, turning one last time to look at him. He had hidden himself in the shadows near the foot of the bed, but she could feel his eyes upon her.

"Julian, please let me try to help you. You did it before, we can do it—"

"You cannot help me!. You need to leave quickly." His deep voice was strained. "I told you I did not have the control I once had, and if you don't leave soon you will be the unfortunate witness to the truth of this! I will not take from you what is not offered willingly."

"But I am willing!" she screamed at him in frustration.

"You have no idea—*at all*—of what you are saying! Do you think I can stop myself at a little lovemaking? God, I wish it was that simple. I told you, the monster within me will not be denied. Adrianna, please! A few kisses will not satisfy me. I need blood! And yours drives me to distraction so I cannot stop when I need to. I could kill you with my lack of control. Do you understand? Now go, before that very lack of control makes the decision for us. Hurry!"

As fear gripped her, she ran up the stone steps to pound on the massive door at the top. Michael, hearing her cries, pulled it open, the fear in his eyes matching her own.

"Adrianna, are you alright?"

"No, Michael, I'm not!" she said as a sob escaped her. "I want Kate and I to leave here as soon as it can be arranged. You cannot convince me that we are safer here than with Rick at the church, not now. How soon can we leave?"

"Adrianna let me look at you. Did he harm you?" Michael asked, reaching for her and smoothing the hair back from her neck.

"It's not what you think, Michael, he did not hurt me … but he can't promise that he won't, so I think it's best that we leave here tonight." Looking into his handsome face, she asked, "Why do you and the others stay? Aren't you afraid? He could kill you! They all can!" She strained to hold back the tears.

"I am in control of what happens to me, as are the others. Julian and his kind are no threat to us." Gently grasping her shoulders, he looked at her and said, "But you are different. If what I suspect is true, he is in love with you, and that requires a special kind of control that he has not had to master for a very long time. Maybe you are right, and the best place for you right now is with the priest. If Kate is strong enough, we can move her to the church. I will leave some people to watch over things until Julian and the others find this evil and destroy it. Go, check on your friend." He reached inside his cloak and brought out his second small dagger. Looking at it he continued, "I gave its twin to Julian. Now I think you should take this one." He extended the beautiful, marble handle toward her. He saw the look of resolve and determination in her eyes as she took the weapon.

"Thank you," she said.

Sadness weighed on his heart as she slowly left the room. Turning quickly, he ran through the open door and down the steps until he came to Julian's room. The door was still open wide from the force of Addie's thrust. As he stepped inside, he saw Julian, head down, leaning against the bedpost barely breathing.

"Come to destroy the monster, Avenger?" came the deep growl.

"What happened, vampire?" Michael asked, barely controlling his anger.

Slowly, Julian raised his head to look at Michael through a mass of tangled hair. He seemed more like a wild animal than a man. His eyes, blood-red a moment ago, had already began to bleed back to a soft, grey-blue, but the torment in them had not changed. Michael's anger began to melt away as he stared at the creature in front of him.

"Fetch your spear and end my torment now. I will not fight you," Julian said, and walking to the fireplace, he turned his back on Michael. He felt chilled to the bone; even the heat of the fire failed to warm him. Killing him now would be a blessing he would welcome. Michael watched him intently, weighing his options, finally coming to a decision.

"Despite what you are, or I should say because of it, I need you to win this fight, Julian, whether you like it or not. So I'm afraid I must let you continue to live."

Looking over his shoulder, Julian stared at the other man, "Did you ever think that if I were dead there would be no need for a fight? The whole reason he is here, the reason he is looking for Adrianna, is so she will not reach me. If I am gone, he will go into hiding again. She, and everyone, will be safe."

"Will they?" Michael replied. "Or will it just prolong the inevitable? It is no longer just about you, Julian. He now knows I am here. He and I go back a long way, even farther than you and he. Yes, my friend, it's true. He will not stop until everyone is destroyed. I need your help to end this. His ranks are weakened now, so he is vulnerable. The girl is all right. In time she will understand everything."

Julian cast him a look full of doubt and pain. "Will she? And even if she does, it will not change her feelings toward me, not after tonight."

Michael could hear the hopelessness in his voice.

"I will not pretend to understand what you are going through, my friend, but you have to pull yourself together," Michael said. "Something is going to happen, I can feel it, and it will be soon."

"I could have killed her, Michael," Julian said in an anguished whisper.

"But you stopped yourself, which proves you have more control than you think. You would not have harmed her, Julian. Get some rest now. Something tells me we are going to need your strength before too long." Michael walked from the room.

Julian followed him to the door and quietly closed it. Returning to the bed, he laid down and closed his eyes—but he kept seeing her shocked face, and rest would not come.

"I can't lose her again," he whispered and, after staring at the ceiling for some time, finally let the day take him.

Adrianna stood for a moment outside the door of the tower bedroom to compose herself. "You've got to calm down," she told herself aloud. "You can't let Kate see you like this." After a few minutes, she descended the stairs and went to the room where Kate slept. Opening the door slowly, she stepped inside. Her friend lay peacefully. Thomas was asleep in a chair by her bedside. Touching his shoulder, she shook him gently.

"Thomas, wake up."

Before she knew what was happening, he jumped up, grabbed her wrist and spun her around in front of him, locking her arm behind her.

"Thomas, it's me! Adrianna!"

He released her immediately. "My God, Addie, I'm so sorry. I didn't mean … You can't sneak up on a guy like that! I didn't hurt you, did I?" He searched her arms for any sign of bruising.

"I didn't realize I was sneaking. Please calm down, I'm fine. You were just doing your job … protecting Kate," she said, rubbing her arm gingerly.

"Doing my job. I fell asleep! What kind of protection is that? Anything could have happened to her."

"It's alright Thomas. You're ... we're all exhausted. Please don't worry. She's fine. As a matter of fact, that's why I'm here. Do you think we can move her to the church today?" Addie turned away from him so she didn't have to look into his questioning eyes. He sat down on the bed beside the sleeping woman.

"She's still weak, but she's doing much better. I suppose, if we have to, we could move her, but why the hurry? Has something else happened?"

"No, nothing," she said, turning to face him. "I just think we would be better off at the church. I'm going to get Rick. Do you think we could get some help getting Kate to the car?"

Giving her a strange look, he said, "I'm sure Julian was going to send someone back with you when he felt the time was right for you to leave." He stood up and walked toward the door. "Let's go ask him what he planned on doing and we can decide—"

"No! Um, I've already talked to him, and anyway, we don't need his permission to leave. He knows we're going, and take my word for it, he doesn't care." She moved toward the bed. Their raised voices had disturbed Kate. She lay buried in the covers looking pale and tired.

"Addie? Is that you?" Kate asked, her voice barely a whisper.

"Yes, honey, it's me. How do you feel?" Addie asked.

"I have a whopper of a headache and I'm so tired ... and thirsty." A look of alarm passed between Addie and Thomas, but at Kate's next words, they relaxed a little. "Do you think I could get a glass of nice cold water? Other than that, I'm fine. What happened to me?"

Pushing the hair gently from the tired girl's eyes, Addie replied, "First things first." Thomas poured a fresh glass of water from a pitcher on the nightstand. "One glass of ice water coming up." She passed the glass to Kate. "No more questions right now." Kate took a long, refreshing drink, and Addie continued, "It's a long story, so we'll wait until you're a little stronger before we bore you with the details. Do you feel up to taking a little ride with Rick and me?"

"Rick's here?" asked Kate. "Yes, I think I would like to get out of this bed. I'm so stiff. I feel like I've fought a battle or something."

"Or something ..."Addie whispered as she shot a worried glance at Thomas. Rising from the bed, she said, "Great! We'll step outside so you can dress while I hunt for our friend. I'll send someone to help you, okay?"

"Okay."

As she and Thomas walked to the door, he turned back to look at the woman in the bed.

"I'll be right outside if you need anything. Wait for help before you try to stand on your own. You've been lying for a while. You might be a little dizzy. Okay?

"Okay."

Following Addie out into the hallway, he said, "I still think I'd better check with Julian, or at least let him know your plans, Adrianna. He'll literally have my neck if anything happens to any of you."

"He already knows our plans, Thomas. I wasn't lying. I've just left him. I will take full responsibility for Julian's anger, if there is any."

Still hesitant, the young man finally agreed, but said firmly, "Alright, but I'm sending some of our people with you. There are only a few to spare right now, humans from our Specials squad, but there will be more tonight. We'll join you as soon as we can."

"Human is good, Thomas. I think I've had my fill of vampires for the moment."

He gave her a curious look. "Whether you believe it or not, Addie, the vampires are your best hope for coming out of this situation intact. I'm sorry, but that's the truth," he said.

She wanted to argue, but an argument would only delay their chances of getting out of there. Instead, smiling up at him, she said, "I know you believe that, Thomas, and I do trust your judgment. You were there when Kate needed you, and I thank you for all you've done. But I think it's time we made some of our own decisions." Gently leaning forward, she brushed a kiss across his cheek.

"Okay, but Addie, I want you to know, I wish I could have done more. Last night should never have happened."

Thomas, it wasn't anyone's—"

"We were unprepared, Addie, and Kate paid the price. That won't happen again if Julian has anything to do with it, which is why I wish you would both stay here where he can control—"

"My mind is made up, Thomas," she interrupted. "Now, you'd better go find someone to help Kate before our invalid gets tired of waiting and decides to take things into her own hands."

"Right." He knew she was wrong in wanting to leave so soon, but what could he do about it? "I'll be right back." He walked away shaking his head in frustration.

Adrianna knew he was not happy with her decision but she was determined to get them all to the church today. Walking across the hall, she tapped on Rick's door, hoping he was already awake and they could finally leave. Within seconds it swung open. His dark hair was mussed and his eyes a little bloodshot, but he was up—although she was pretty sure that had just happened.

"Oh, Rick, I'm so glad you're up. We can leave now. Kate is awake and seems strong enough to come with us. Are you ready to go?"

"I thought you'd never ask. I've been sleeping with one eye open since I left you. Were you able to get some rest?"

"No, not really," she answered, avoiding his eyes. "I just want to get out of here and back to a little normalcy."

"Amen to that. Let's get Kate and get moving."

Thirty minutes later, they were walking out the front door. After helping Kate into Rick's car, Thomas approached the priest. Leaning inside the window, he whispered, "Despite her wishes, there is no returning to anything you consider normal, not after last night. You have to watch over them, Father. Don't let them out of your sight, especially Adrianna. They will be looking for her. She really shouldn't be leaving here, but I couldn't convince her to stay. Don't let anyone in until the rest of us get there tonight. This is probably a stupid question to be asking a priest, but do you have any type of weapons at that church?"

"No," Rick replied. "But I intend to rectify that once we get home."

"Smart thinking. There may be hope for you yet," Thomas said with a smile. "I've sent plenty of guns with silver ammo along with the guards coming with you. They'll give you a quick lesson in how to use them, and I'm assuming you still have the stakes you came armed with?"

Rick nodded toward the duffle bag on the front seat between him and Addie.

"I didn't want it too far from my sight," he told Thomas.

"Good. Don't hesitate to use them and anything silver, holy water, etcetera. They all make good weapons." Stepping back from the car he finished, "Take care, and stay alert. We'll see you in a little while."

With a wave of his hand, he motioned for Julian's men to head out, and an hour after she formed the plan, Addie, Kate, and Rick were driving back toward town with an escort of seven armed men, three in front and four behind. It reminded Adrianna of a police escort, and for a moment, she doubted her decision. But then the memory of Julian in his underground chamber came flooding back to her. No, they had made the right choice, and everyone would agree when they had time to get used to the three of them being gone. But why did she suddenly feel so nervous?

Chapter 17

The small caravan of cars traveled down the hillside and stopped in front of the tiny cottage. Rick had decided to make a quick visit so the girls to get fresh clothing and a few other things they would need for an extended stay at the church. While two men from the first car stepped out for a quick sweep of the house, Addie stared at the place she had hoped would become her peaceful refuge but had instead become something entirely different. "Will things ever be the same again?" she wondered as she forced herself to climb from the car, moving slowly down the flower-lined walkway toward the front porch as Julian's soldier gave the all-clear sign.

Rick came up quietly behind her. Placing a comforting hand on her shoulder he asked, "Are you alright, Addie?"

"Yes, I'm fine. It's just—"

"You don't have to explain anything to me. After all that I've witnessed in the past few hours, I can understand your not wanting to go back inside. I can only imagine what you both must have gone through last night. And I definitely don't think Kate should enter the house again until she's stronger so just tell me what you need and I'll—"

"No, thank you, Rick," Addie said, looking at him through her tears. "I have to do this. If I let the fear take hold then they win, and I refuse to let that happen." With renewed purpose, she moved up the front steps.

"I'm right behind you," he said following closely.

Entering the house, the quiet calming her a little, she hesitated only briefly before ascending the stairs to the bedrooms. Reaching the top, she stopped again and looked around in confusion. She was surprised by the tidiness of the place. Where was the mess? The destruction? Some kind of sign that last night had actually happened? There was nothing—not a torn curtain or a broken table or a smashed door. Someone had worked very hard to ensure that nothing remained of the chaos from the night before. Even the shattered door to Kate's bedroom had been replaced. Had it really been just a few short hours? It seemed like a lifetime had passed since she had last been here. Could it all have been a dream? A horrible nightmare? But she knew better than that.

"Julian," she whispered. Only he could have accomplished so much in such a short time.

"Is this where it happened, Addie?" Rick asked, confused. "There's no sign of anything. No blood, no ash, no broken furniture. Nothing like I was expecting after what I'd been told."

"I know," she replied. "It was the same that night at the club. After the attack, there was no outward sign that anything had happened. It must be Julian. His men are trained well."

After grabbing a suitcase from the hall closet, she went quickly between the two bedrooms gathering what items they needed then did the same in the bathroom. When she had everything she thought they might need, she stopped on the stairs for one last look around. The hair on the back of her neck prickled as she remembered the attack.

"Let's get out of here," she said, and they headed quickly for the front door. Car doors slammed and gravel spat from beneath spinning tires as the caravan made a hasty retreat down the road for the center of town.

They pulled up in front of the church twenty minutes later. It was a beautiful old building of red brick. Myriad colors splashed across the manicured lawn as the afternoon sun came in contact with half a dozen stained glass windows. Kate was exhausted when they finally arrived, so Rick quickly ushered them through the church to a room near the back. On the advice of Thomas, he chose not to go to the rectory but opted instead to stay as close to the actual church itself. That was the only place that actually had consecrated ground. The room in the rear of the building was used for storage of miscellaneous items and just happened to contain two small cots, which Rick opened up for the women to use.

"I'll find some linens and blankets for you to use as well. There's a bathroom down the hallway that should suit your needs perfectly," he told them.

After making sure Kate was comfortable, Rick and Addie left, with two guards in tow, to go in search of food. The other men also took up their positions, one outside the door of the small room to stay near Kate and the others in various positions around the building.

Descending a staircase near the rear of the building, Rick and Addie entered a large basement. The basement was used as a hall for wedding receptions and other functions. It boasted a full kitchen. Searching the refrigerator, Addie turned triumphantly. She was holding a large, round container.

"Oh, Rick. Is this what I think it is?" Her mouth already watering.

"If you're thinking its homemade wedding soup, then yes. I have a lot of parishioners who feel it's their duty to keep me well fed so, occasionally, they bring me a treat. I hate to disappoint them, so I don't let on that I'm actually a pretty fair cook. We can warm that with a few sandwiches. How would that be?"

"I can't think of anything better," she said, not realizing how hungry she actually was. When had she last eaten? She tried to remember as she lined the counter with everything she could find in the refrigerator. As they worked preparing a light supper, Addie paused to look at the man across from her. What sort of hell had she gotten him involved in? Would any of them survive it?

"Rick, do you think we'll be safe here?" she asked.

Placing the knife he was using on an unusually large tomato down on the table, he sighed deeply. "I have to tell you Addie, I just don't know," he said. "I don't know that much about these things we're dealing with. Vampires. They're supposed to be a myth. Something that came to life in a Bram Stoker novel. I've never believed they actually existed. Devils and demons, yes, that's something I know about. I suppose if they can actually exist, why not vampires? But I've never had to deal with anything like this. I'm out of my element here, Addie. I have to be honest with you." Watching her face, he could see the fear she was trying desperately to hide. With a smile of encouragement, he continued, "But I'm hoping that if the monsters of legend are real, then so are the weapons used against them. We have plenty of holy water and Communion wafers, and after supper, we can get started making more wooden stakes that I will bless." Then another idea struck him, and he reached for the knife he had just set down. "Silver. Addie, we have an abundance of silver. All the eating utensils are pure silver. Grab as many forks and knives as you can and pass them around to everyone. The next time we have to face these rejects from hell, they won't catch us unprepared. We should be fine until Julian and the others get here tonight."

"So you believe there will be a next time?"

He tried to choose his words carefully. He did not want to add to her fears, but coddling her was not going to help her.

"I'm a little out of the loop, Addie. I'm not sure why all of this is happening and why now. I'm the last person any of our vampire friends what to take into their confidence."

"I know," she smiled.

"But from what I can gather from Thomas and a few others, this isn't over. Another battle is coming, and we need to be prepared. We need to do what we can to help them fight this evil. What we do with Julian and his people after this is all over, well, we can think about that afterward."

Julian! How could she have forgotten? He would be coming here this evening. She would have to see him whether she liked it or not. There was no way to avoid it—this place wasn't that big, there was nowhere to hide. Could she face him again after what had happened between them?

"Rick, do you trust Julian knowing what he is?" she asked, avoiding his eyes.

After a moment's hesitation, he replied, "Yes, strangely enough, I do. We've known each other a long time, Addie, and I can read you like a book. Something happened between you two at the mansion, which is why we made a hasty retreat. I didn't question you then. You'll talk to me when you're ready. But I think I'm a pretty fair judge of people, or vampires in this case." He smiled. "I've also seen my share of evil. Human nature is riddled with it. Julian, I feel certain, is not an evil being, or to be more specific, he's fighting to control the evil that took him against his will. He will do all in his power to help us or die trying, and deep down, you know this is true. I think we have no choice but to trust him."

"How does he do that?" she thought. "How does he always find a way to make me feel guilty? He has no idea what I've been through, what Julian did. Of course he doesn't, because I haven't told him anything, and he's probably right about all of this. After all, didn't I make the first move with Julian each time? He tried to warn me, but I refused to listen. I have no one to blame for what happened except myself."

"I know you're right," she said. "I'm just so confused right now."

Taking her hand, he said, "Faith and prayer. They are strong weapons if you choose to use them. That's what we need right now. That and food." A grin lit up his handsome face as he lifted the tray of sandwiches. "Let's feed the masses. Starving people make poor soldiers."

As he started to walk, she placed a hand gently on his arm, "I don't know what I'd do without you in my life, Rick."

"Hopefully you won't ever have to find out. Now ladle some soup in that bowl, and let's go before we all starve."

Outside the church, the sun had disappeared from the night sky only to be replaced by the full moon. All was deathly quiet. If anyone had been foolish enough to take a late night walk on this particular evening, they would have noticed the shadows moving to avoid any contact with the soft light streaming down from the street lamps. They would also have noticed those same shadows creeping ever closer to the church. They soon had the entire perimeter surrounded.

One of the shadows began to take on the form of a ragged, filthy woman looking near death from lack of food. She slowly climbed the steps to the back door and began a steady pounding. After some time, one of the guards opened the door cautiously.

"What do you want, old woman?" he asked in disgust, trusting no one.

"It's alright. I'll take care of her." The church caretaker had come up behind the guard as he talked to the woman. Noticing more shadowy figures standing outside, he told the guard, "They are just hungry, they're the poor of this community. They come for the leftover food from the kitchen. They have nowhere else to go." He motioned the woman inside.

"I can't let you do that, old man. No one gets in here unless I have specific orders. Tonight they'll have to go to bed hungry."

"I don't know who you get your orders from, young man, but they have nothing to do with me. I take my orders from Father Ferrante, and we have always fed the poor," he said, nodding at the pathetic old woman.

"Well, you're a feisty one, I'll give you that," the guard replied. "But it's obvious you haven't spoken to the good priest today. So I will say this one more time," he spoke firmly and slammed the heavy door shut just as the old woman was about to enter. "No one gets in here tonight until I get the okay. Your priest is well aware of this. As a matter of fact, I'll go get him for you. Then you can hear from his own lips why no strange visitors are allowed in here." The guard's face was only inches from the scowling caretaker. Turning quickly, he went in search of Rick.

"Hmmph! Mister high and mighty thinks he can give orders here. Well, he's got another think comin'!" the caretaker mumbled as he proceeded to open the door one more time. "Come on then, all of you, to the kitchen. You've always been welcome in God's house, and that ain't gonna change now. I'll give you some broth then you can be on your way before our uptight friend has a coron—"

The words died in his throat before his scream of terror had a chance to escape as he was attacked from behind, sharp teeth sinking into the shriveled neck.

Watching the color return to Kate's cheeks as she ate, Addie had the feeling they just might make it through this ordeal. Her friend looked so much better, had even smiled at some silly joke Rick had told. Yes, the old Kate was back … almost. There was still the circular scar on her neck where the communion wafer had seared the two puncture wounds. That would probably be a permanent reminder. But she was definitely improving.

Rick and Addie had chosen their words carefully as they explained to Kate all that had happened, especially to her. Thus the haunted look in her eyes. But that would disappear in time. Kate was a fighter. She'd be back to normal in no time.

Addie had to admit that she felt almost human again after a hot shower and change of clothes. She slid the small dagger Michael had given her inside the soft leather of the calf -high boots she'd pulled on over her jeans. A silver kitchen knife lay hidden in the other boot. Kate and Rick also had silver accessories adorning their clothing.

"You look so much better, Kate, and your appetite has definitely returned." She laughed as she removed the tray of empty dishes from the bed and set it on the nightstand.

"I feel a lot stronger, and I was a little hungry. It's just the nightmares. Every time I shut my eyes. I wish they would stop."

"That will come in time," Addie told her, but fell silent when the phone in the hall began to ring. She took a deep breath to ease the nervous feeling that had suddenly risen in the pit of her stomach when she heard Rick answer it.

The door opened and, smiling, he entered. He gave Kate a quick hug.

"Feeling better after that gourmet meal?"

"Most certainly. My compliments to the chef," she said, returning the hug with genuine feeling.

"Whoa!" he said, a little surprised by the strength of her embrace. "Have you been working out?"

"What do you mean?"

Reaching forward he told her, "Take my hand, Kate, and give it a good squeeze. Don't worry about hurting me. Squeeze as hard as you can."

"But why—"

"Just humor me, okay?" he said with a smile. Addie was just as confused as her friend. Taking Rick's hand, Kate grasped it in what she thought was a firm handshake but, after a few seconds Rick said, "Okay, okay, that's quite enough." He shook his hand to get the circulation going again. There was no mistaking the look of pain on his face—and the look of horror on Kate's.

"Oh my God, Rick, I'm so sorry. Are you alright? I didn't mean to hurt you. I'm so—"

"Kate, Kate," he said, gently grabbing her by the shoulders. "It's okay, I'm fine. But that was very interesting. How do you feel, after everything you've been through? "

"I feel fine. Great actually. I'm wide awake after my rest, and I feel almost energized, like I could take on the world."

"Yes, very interesting. No, strange is a better word. I would have expected anyone who had gone through what you did, and survived, to spend at least a few days, if not more, in the hospital. But you actually seem to be in better health than you were before you were attacked."

"Oh my God. It's the bite, the vampire bite," Addie spoke softly, almost to herself, as both of them turned to stare at her. "That creature must have passed some of its power on to Kate. She must have retained some of the characteristics they possess, like their strength."

"You don't mean.... What else have I inherited from those things? Am I going to start craving blood next? I thought Julian said they killed all the infection. Am I going to be normal?" Kate's voice started to rise in panic as Rick took her in his arms.

"Shhh. It's alright, honey. I'm thinking you've just retained some of their abilities, the one's you actually had as a human being, only now, they're enhanced. We'll discuss it with Julian when he arrives."

"But Rick, he can't come in here, and neither can most of his men. They're vampires. They can't enter hallowed ground any more than our enemies." Addie couldn't disguise the concern in her voice. If Julian and his men couldn't enter the church, how were they supposed to protect them from anything?

"Exactly the question I asked Michael, but he said it would not be a problem. As long as they are with him, and invited by me, they could enter. He also said all would be made clear in time. He's a strange one, loves to talk in riddles," Rick felt he had to add. "Actually, that was him on the phone. He and the others are on their way. They'll stay here tonight. These back rooms should be perfect for them. They aren't actually part of the church. Anyway, he seems to—"

Suddenly, a loud commotion was heard in the hallway directly outside their room. Terrified screams echoed in the night. They sounded as if they were right outside the door! Addie could hear shouting and scuffling as the guard posted outside tried to keep someone or something from entering the room. Kate's face went white with terror as another blood curdling scream pierced the air. The three of them stared at each other, for it was now obvious the guard had failed. It was only a matter of time before whomever or whatever was out there came crashing into the room!

"Kate! Kate!" Addie screamed as she saw the panic on her friend's face. "It's just us three now, honey."

She grabbed Kate by the shoulders and shook her gently. "Help is coming, Kate! Julian will be here, but we have to hold them off until then. Do you understand what I'm saying? We have to fight!"

She could see Rick out of the corner of her eye opening a closet door at the far end of the room. He emerged with a large silver crucifix.

"Addie, take this," he shouted, tossing it across to her. "Use it anyway you can!"

"Don't give in to the fear, Kate, we're all in this together," Addie said. "We will not make it easy for them!" She caught the cross and shoved into Kate's hands.

"Hold this close. If the sight of it doesn't stop them, use it as a weapon. I'm sure it's blessed so it should do some damage. Can you do that, Kate? Can you do that for all of us?"

The glazed look slowly disappeared as a look of fierce determination came over Kate's face, and Addie saw the fear change to anger as Kate took the cross from her outstretched hands.

"Oh, I'll use it alright. I'll never let one of those things touch me again!" Kate said.

"That's my girl," Addie said, fighting hard not to let Kate see how terrified she actually was. She looked around for anything she could use as a weapon. There was shouting and gunshots outside the church. It sounded as if they were surrounded. Where was Julian?

"Addie, catch," Rick shouted as he threw a large plastic bottle at her. At first she was confused until she realized it contained holy water. "Throw it directly at them. It should at least slow them down a little."

An old wooden chair sat in the far corner of the room, but before she could reach it, Rick grabbed it and smashed it against the floor, creating four wooden stakes from its legs. Scooping up a stake in each hand while Rick grabbed the remaining two, the three friends looked intently at each other, a silent message passing between them as they all turned to face the door.

Just then, the wood splintered into a thousand pieces.

Addie vaguely remembered the two weapons hidden inside her boots, but she decided to leave them as a last defense.

Her eyes were riveted to the opening where the door used to be. She saw the two guards, or what was left of them, lying in a pool of blood. Pieces of their bodies were strewn everywhere, but that was not the sight that made her stand frozen in fear, unable to move, unable to even breathe. Two huge creatures, one towering at least a foot above the other, which itself was at least seven feet tall, stood in the shattered doorway. And she had thought vampires were the only things they had to worry about.

Blood dripped from mouths full of razor sharp teeth, pieces of skin and human gore plastered to their long, matted black fur. They looked like wolves standing on two legs. These monsters had left a path of destruction in the hallway as they looked for more victims.

They entered the room as three smaller vampires emerged from behind them, the bulk of the beasts having hidden them completely. Then she heard something strange. What was that noise? As the vampires fanned out, her eyes were drawn to the source of that awful sound. She saw a vampire leaning over the still form of the church caretaker. Memories of the attack at the cottage came flooding back as she realized the creature was sucking the blood from the body, just like Kate.

Nausea threatened to overtake her as she fought for control. Sensing movement, her eyes were drawn back to the wolves as they entered the room, sniffing the air as they caught the scent of fresh prey. One of the vampires turned, hissing loudly, saliva dripping from its mouth as it approached Kate.

It came to an abrupt halt as it caught sight of the cross in her hand. She held her ground as the hideous form before her hesitated, screaming in fury as it hid its eyes from the sacred image engraved upon the shining silver. Cowering, the creature turned to face Adrianna instead.

"Finish her, you fool. We'll handle this one. This is the one he wants!" the wolf in the lead shouted in a voice that sounded almost human except for the rolling growl deep in its throat. His long clawed fingers were pointing at Addie as both man-beasts began moving toward her.

The sight of the hideously exaggerated features on the wolf's face was enough to freeze the blood in her veins. But that was not what filled her with terror. No, it was the eyes. The creature's eyes should have been totally black, or brown, or even blood-red, considering the other monsters they were dealing with.

"But these are not the eyes of an animal. These are human," she thought as she stared into eyes almost identical to her own. They were soft brown surrounded by white, and that could mean only one thing: werewolf! She bent slowly, setting one of the stakes she held onto the ground. She knew that particular weapon would be next to useless against a creature like this. Her hand slowly slid deep inside her right boot. She cupped the kitchen knife in the palm of her hand and pulled it carefully out into the open.

"Kate, we need silver! Toss me the cross!" Rick screamed as he threw a wooden stake onto the bed beside the terrified woman before running toward Addie.

Realizing what they were up against, Kate jumped from the bed screaming, "No!"

Running at the vampire in her path with speed born of terror, she swung the cross with all her might, hitting it with such force she could hear the bones splinter as its head exploded. She continued to beat what was left of the creature's mutilated body until it lay, a mass of bloody pulp, on the floor. Seconds later, it was enveloped in flames. A shattering of glass caused her to pivot wildly as she faced another winged creature entering through the large window across the room.

"Kate, the cross!" Rick shouted again as he retrieved the stake from the bed, running toward her. They switched weapons in midair. As Kate prepared to face the winged threat, Rick positioned himself behind the two wolves.

Catching his scent, the smaller beast turned to face the priest. At the sight of the cross, the wolf slowed. It understood the danger as it slowly took a step backward and weighed its options. That was all the edge Rick needed. With renewed courage, he ran forward and drove the shaft directly into the werewolf's chest with all the force he could summon. The howl of pain was ear-splitting as the massive form began to hiss and burn, a stream of blood flowing down the black fur. Clutching wildly at the silver shaft, the wounded creature fell to the ground, twitched a moment longer then went still.

"No!" The larger wolf roared as it spun around in amazement. "You will die for this, priest!" The muscles in its powerful legs corded and bunched as it prepared to spring.

"Rick, run!" Addie screamed as she charged the beast from behind, the silver knife held high in the air.

"Addie, don't!" But Rick's warning was too late. She flung herself at the animal's back just as it turned to face her, catching her in midair. One clawed hand grabbed her by the shirt, pulling her against the solid wall of its massive chest while the other knocked the knife from her hand.

"Addie!" Rick screamed just as a vampire flew at his back.

"I guess I will have to forego the pleasure of ending your friend's life," the wolf growled. "My followers need all the practice they can get. He was lucky once. We'll see if he can survive a second attack." The foul breath nearly smothered her. The last thing she remembered was seeing Rick burning his attacker with holy water just as Julian entered the hall screaming her name. Then the blackness took her.

"Save her if you can, vampire!" the man-beast screamed as he turned to face the enraged figure running toward him. Addie's limp form slumped against his matted fur. The wolf's minions fell upon Julian from every direction. He ripped and tore his way through them, one unlucky vampire making the fatal mistake of charging him head on. His hand snapped forward, grabbing the creature by the throat as it flew at him. Twisting his wrist sharply to the left, he snapped the neck with the sheer force of his grip. Reaching forward with his free hand, he severed the head from the pitiful creature's broken neck, leaving nothing but blood and burning ash in his wake.

The beast felt a twinge of fear as he watched the destruction brought about as Julian continued to fight his way down the hallway. Then a loud swooshing caused the beast to quickly turn in the opposite direction.

"Give her to me!" came the command as the largest of the vampires appeared just outside the window, hovering and waiting.

"And let you take the credit for her capture? I don't think so, brother."

"Now is not the time for petty squabbles. He is almost upon you. We must get her to father at all costs!"

The wolf turned slightly to see Julian fighting his way to him, getting closer with every second. He hated to admit it, but that blasted brother of his was right. He tossed Addie's limp form into the arms of the waiting vampire, his bloodshot eyes burning with hatred.

"This was my doing, Enoch. If you don't tell our father, I will when I return."

"If you return, my brother," the vampire hissed as it turned, disappearing in the night sky.

Hatred burned deep in the heart of the beast, causing it to feel no pain as one of Julian's vampires drove sharp fangs into the tendons of its thick neck. But a mere vampire was no match for the monster's strength as the wolf picked it off like a small insect, biting the head in two and dropping what remained of the body to the floor, where it quickly disintegrated.

Then, it turned to stare at Julian.

The vampire was almost to the beast, but the demon's hordes were everywhere. Julian's men were making short work of them as he saw Thomas fighting alongside Kate, both their bodies covered in ash and blood. But they were not quick enough for him to reach Adrianna. The wolf's followers were slowing him down. He was going to be too late … again. He saw the beast toss Addie's limp form through the window and then turn to look at him. He could swear the beast sneered at him just before it, too, disappeared through the opening.

In horror, Julian watched as the three figures disappeared into the night.

"Adrianna!" came his agonized scream.

Another werewolf, much smaller than the others, rushed him from behind in a frenzy, blood and saliva dripping from its mouth. Fury and frustration filled Julian as he turned to face the charging creature. But before it could reach the waiting vampire, Michael drove the silver-tipped spear into its back from behind. The creature screamed in pain and fell to the floor in a mass of blood.

Spinning around, Julian's eyes scoured the room. Blood, smoke, and ash were everywhere as his men fought feverishly to destroy the remaining creatures that had not fled. Amazed, he watched the priest. Rick was holding a screeching vampire at bay with his cross while swinging his other arm out from behind, stabbing it deep in the heart, reducing it to a pile of dust.

"Remind me never to get on your bad side, priest," Julian said as he stared at Rick, admiration for what the priest had done evident on the vampire's face. Rick just stared back in stunned silence.

The few who managed to escape Julian's men fled through the night, following the vampire who had taken Adrianna. Christoff and a few others were still battling the vampires outside the church. He was not worried about them. They could handle themselves. He took one last look around, assuring himself the others were all right. He saw Kate standing on the bed, a stake in her hand covered in ash. Thomas ran to her, his eyes searching every inch of her body for teeth marks. Her eyes seemed glazed as she started to swing the stake toward the man's chest, but he grabbed her wrists easily.

"Kate, honey. It's me, Thomas. You're alright now," he said soothingly as he took the weapon from her hand.

As she stared at him, reality came flooding back to her.

"I didn't let them touch me, Thomas. I won't let them touch me again," she said through sobs as she struggled against his hold for a few seconds before throwing herself into his arms.

Holding her close he said, "You did great, my girl. It's over now."

Julian watched them as if paralyzed, the pain in his chest making it impossible to breath. The image of Adrianna being taken from him was almost more than he could bear. After a few moments, he forced his body to move, approaching the couple before him.

"Make sure she's alright," he said, placing a hand on Thomas's shoulder. A look of understanding passed between them. Glancing around, Julian noticed Michael standing down the hallway, and as the man turned to look at the vampire, Julian mouthed the words Michael knew were coming but did not want to hear.

"I have to go. They have her."

Before Michael could scream his warning, "No, Julian. Wait!" Julian was gone through the open window, soaring high into the night sky as the transformation took him, the sharp eyes of the eagle searching for any sign of the trail that would lead him to her.

Chapter 18

Slowly, she began to awaken. The wind lashed across her face as they flew high above the rough terrain. A quick glance down revealed bits of rock along with broken branches that had fallen from hundreds of dead trees scattered about in all directions. Disoriented, she could not remember where she was but she thought she heard … was that the flapping of wings? Yes, it was—extremely large wings. But how could that be? Where was she? Suddenly, everything came flooding back to her, memories filled with fighting and screaming and blood. So much blood! Heaving herself forward, she tried to throw herself from the grasp of the creature that held her, but huge claws grabbed at her, pulling her back against its foul smelling carcass.

"No, you don't. I won't have my life ended because you want to destroy yours. That will come in due time," it hissed at her, that horrible face brought close to hers as she stared into red eyes. "Believe me, you will beg for death when my lord is through with you, but for now, he wants you in one piece. We need to be sure our old friend comes calling, and he will surely come for you." Enoch's long tongue darted forward to lick the blood and sweat from her face. "Yes, he will come. Such a tasty thing. Shame to waste you on the likes of him. I must convince my father to let you be my reward after I kill your lover—"

"Never!" she screamed as she spat into his red eyes. "I will kill myself first before I let the likes of you touch me!" She struggled desperately to break free, the stench of decaying flesh causing the nausea to rise inside of her.

Shaking the spittle from its eyes, Enoch's thin, almost nonexistent lips pulled back to show his razor sharp teeth. "Try that again, and I will save you the trouble!" The claws holding her squeezed a little tighter, digging into her arms and stomach. But she would not scream, she wouldn't give this foul thing the satisfaction. Just when she thought she could stand no more, the creature pitched downwards and began their descent. With a thump, he landed in a small clearing. A dark form loomed before her as she shook her head to clear her vision.

Old stone walls, once strong and beautiful, stood crumbling before her as she gazed at the remnants of an old church of some kind, probably a monastery.

"Come on! We don't have time to waste," said her captor as he grabbed her roughly by the arm dragging her toward the ruin. They moved so quickly that she barely noticed her surroundings as she was pulled inside an opening that once had been the front entrance. Once inside, she was aware of climbing many steps until they came to stand before a massive door at the end of a dark hallway. The fear she felt nearly choked her. She could feel the blackness threatening to overtake her as she fought desperately to stay conscious. Something told her she must have all her wits about her for what lay ahead. It also told her that whatever lay behind those doors was more terrifying than anything she would ever experience in her life—if she survived at all!

*****

Julian walked slowly up the steep incline, gnarled tree branches grabbing at his hair and clothing. Deja vu overwhelmed him as the dream came flooding back. "This can't be happening, not again," he thought as he pushed onward. If this was the hand fate had dealt him, he was determined to end it differently this time. The darkness was suffocating, but he remained alert to every sound, every slight movement. He would not be caught off guard again. There was too much at stake.

Cautiously moving around an old oak tree, his vampire senses screamed a warning as they were assailed by the stench of a rotting corpse. His keen eyes searched the area until he could just make out a figure crouched behind the trees ahead, awaiting his approach. He knew from experience that where there was one, there was sure to be more. Scanning the scene in front of him, he saw another figure hiding behind a large boulder directly across from the first creature.

Vampires waiting in ambush, just like before.

"You really need to come up with a new game plan, you son of a bitch!" he said to himself.

Turning sharply to the right, he cut a path through the decaying woods and came up silently behind the figure crouching beside the boulder. With inhuman speed, he grabbed the skull-like head, his desperation to reach Adrianna the only thought in his mind as his arms flexed, ripping and tearing. Bones cracked and blood spurted in all directions as the head came off with the sheer force of the twist. The body disintegrating into a pile of ash. Hearing a sound behind him, Julian fell to his knees as the remaining vampire rushed at him. Pulling a wooden stake from inside his coat, he drove it all the way through the oncoming chest, his hand protruding through the back of the mutilated body before, with a scream of pain this vampire also disappeared in a cloud of dust.

Quickly jumping to his feet, Julian searched the surrounding area but could get no sense of anyone, or anything else. Cautiously, he continued to move deeper into the woods, blackness surrounding him as his senses remained alert to any movement in the shadows, but nothing else approached him. The evening air brought faint whispers to his ears as he inhaled the stench of years of decay. They knew he was coming. It was what they wanted. He was sure there was some sort of trap awaiting him up ahead, but he would not be caught unprepared this time. Reaching inside his long, leather duster, he pulled out another stake, and then, feeling a small bulge in the same pocket, pulled out the silver dagger Michael had given him. The woods came to an abrupt end as he entered a small clearing.

The moon illuminated the decaying building that rose into the night sky. The massive front door lay on the ground some distance from the opening. With weapons in hand, he stepped forward, eyes peering into the darkness, but he saw nothing out of the ordinary.

One second he stood staring at the old building, the next he'd disappeared, only to reappear inside what had once been the grand foyer. A long, winding staircase in different stages of disrepair beckoned him to the rooms above. To his left was a set of beautifully ornate double doors, which he assumed led to a dining hall or something of that sort.

As he started to move forward, he noticed movement to his right as three figures rushed him, dagger-like claws ready to strike, saliva dripping from sharp fangs. Crouching low, he slashed the silver blade across the midsection of the vampire closest to him, slicing the decaying body in half as it exploded in a cloud of ash. Another one attacked him from behind, snapping as it tried to tear at his neck.

Swinging the blade up hard over his left shoulder, he struck the creature directly in the eye. Brown liquid spurted down his back. Screaming in pain, the vampire fell backward, giving Julian the opening he needed to plunge the stake into its chest. It became another pile of foul smelling ash.

Spinning around, he saw the third vampire running up the huge staircase. He quickly followed.

Taking the steps two at a time, he reached the top in a matter of seconds, but the creature had already disappeared. Turning to the left, he stared down a darkened hallway. There were at least six doors on either side, hidden deep in shadow, but he knew the rooms were not empty. He could feel them lurking in the darkness. He stood in silence, planning his next move. His mind screamed a warning to leave. But that was no longer an option. No, Adrianna needed him, and this was the way he must go, regardless of the danger. Waiting at the very end of the hallway was the largest door of all, and behind it, he was certain to find what he was seeking.

For the first time, he felt doubt. He should have waited for Michael and the others. She would have a better chance of surviving if he had, but he also knew that every second he waited brought her closer to a fate he was determined to prevent. He would rather die himself than let that happen again! He began to move cautiously forward, slowly and silently. Suddenly two of the doors splintered open as they fell upon him. There were at least six vampires flying at him, claws extended, fangs ready to strike! But as quickly as they reached him, he took them down, the silver knife gleaming red as blood flowed freely before flames and ash covered the floor.

But they kept coming. It seemed as if he fought forever. Exhaustion overtook him. He could feel his strength waning when, without warning, a dark shadow, at least twice his size, bore down upon him, its claws ramming into his chest. The room began spinning as he grew weak from loss of blood. The last thing he remembered was Michael's face staring in horror, and he thought, "I should have waited." Then everything went black.

*****

Michael had watched in horror and frustration as Julian disappeared through the window into the night sky.

"Fool!" He shouted to no one in particular. "He knows what will happen if he goes alone. Thinking with his heart instead of his head will not save her or himself!"

Turning quickly, he saw Christoff, his clothing splattered with blood and something more, gliding down the hallway toward the room. A shadow entered the vampire's line of vision as he spun quickly, his clawed fist slamming into the rotting chest now directly in front of him. The creature didn't even have the time to realize the mistake it had made in confronting the warrior as Christoff pulled back his arm, the other vampire's lifeless heart clutched in his hand. The figure before him burst into flames. When the smoke cleared, he stood brushing the ash from the front of his black leather vest.

"Christoff," the Avenger called to him. The dark vampire immediately appeared in front of him. "Gather everyone and hurry. There is no time to waste. Julian and the woman are gone. We must get to them before it is too late."

"Shit!" The midnight eyes bled to red as anger consumed him.

No one needed to tell him what was at stake. He had been there before and seen the destruction that spawn from hell had brought about. He had seen what happened to his friend when he failed to save the woman he loved the first time. He knew Julian better than anyone. He knew Julian would do whatever it took this time to save Adrianna, including sacrificing himself. To the dark warrior, that was not acceptable. Nothing but the safe return of them both, and the utter destruction of their enemy, would satisfy him.

Searching the room with his glowing red eyes, Christoff signaled to Simon and Andrew. They gathered the others around them, and soon there was a small army ready to leave with Michael.

"I don't have to tell any of you what we are facing. If Julian and Adrianna are to have any chance of survival we must get there with all speed."

Michael's eyes scanned the room as he took in the blood and destruction. They had destroyed most of Dragon's hordes, but the two creatures most important to that evil demon had escaped. His sons—one werewolf, one vampire—had fled. They were almost as vile and demented as the creature that sired them. If they had only managed to destroy those two, blood of his blood, Dragon would have been severely crippled. But they had failed. Still, his army was weakened. But at what cost to them?

"Christoff," he said as the vampire came up soundlessly behind him. "How many of our men were lost?"

"We lost Brian and James. The priest is … doing what priests do for the dead. I suppose that is a good thing in his eyes, and probably theirs, since they were only human. But they fought bravely. Adam is torn up pretty badly. He needs to feed and rest, but he will heal. Some of the others are injured, but nothing that will keep them from the fight."

As he talked, Christoff was unaware of movement on the floor, unaware of the four-legged beast, presumed dead only moments earlier, now rising to its full height behind him, talons of steel ready to bury themselves deep into the warrior's back.

WHIZZZZ!

A flash of silver flew through the air, missing the dark vampire's stunned face by a fraction of an inch only to bury itself deep within the skull of the attacking beast. Screaming in agony, the man-wolf fell to the ground, motionless. This time there would be no recovery, no chance of rising again.

Michael stared at Christoff for a moment before reaching forward to retrieve the silver knife from the head of the dead beast. It was the knife that, only moments ago, had been knocked from Addie's hand to slide across the floor stopping before the bed where Thomas stood with Kate. The look of surprise on Michael's face was matched only by the astonishment on

Christoff's as he spun around to stare at the lifeless form on the floor behind him.

"Well, done, Thomas," Michael said in admiration.

"Thanks," the young man replied, but his eyes were on Christoff as the vampire slowly turned back to face the man who had saved his life. No words were needed as the two stared at each other. Then, in one fluid motion, the dark vampire bent forward into a deep bow. Rising slowly, a slight smile appearing on his handsome face, Christoff spoke in a quiet voice, "It pains me to admit this, human, but I may have been wrong about you. You actually do have a set of balls, and they are obviously made of steel! I am in your debt."

"It would seem so, my inhuman friend. Who would have thought? Anyway, I couldn't let anything happen to you, now could I? Someone has to ease the pain of the lovely ladies in this community now that I'm no longer on the market," he said as he wrapped an arm around Kate's waist. "I guess they'll have to make do with you. Do you think you're up to the task, my night-stalking friend?"

"Don't push your luck, hum—"

"Enough, we have more important things to worry about," Michael ordered. "Thomas, can you handle things at this end?" Thomas was holding Kate in an attempt to calm her. She had fought as bravely as anyone, but now realty was setting in. Her friend was gone, and she was shaking violently. Thomas nodded as Michael continued, "We will leave a few to guard the area, but I feel certain they will not be returning here. They have what they came for. We seem to have made a mess here, and we can't leave the priest alone to cover our tracks."

Rick approached from the back of the room, looking as battle worn as the rest of them. "Don't worry about things here. We have it covered, right?" he said, looking at Kate.

Taking a deep breath, she nodded in agreement. "Just give me a minute. I'll be fine." Turning to Michael, she continued, "Just bring them back. Nothing else matters. Do you understand, Michael? Bring her back to me—" Her voice broke as a sob caught in her throat.

Thomas whispered, "It will be fine, Kate. It will all be fine. Michael and Christoff will see to it." He stared into the eyes of the vampire who had been his nemesis for so long. "They couldn't be in better hands."

"Thank you for your trust," Christoff said. "Coming from you, human, it has great meaning."

"And don't think I'll let you forget it anytime soon," Thomas said with a slight smile. "Come on, Kate. We have work to do."

"Humans," Christoff muttered under his breath, a slight smile appearing on his otherwise dark countenance as he watched them walk away. He would never let the man know how much that little speech had affected him, because Thomas was right—he would never let Christoff forget.

"Alright," Michael shouted. "Let's go!"

"Wait, I'm coming with you, Michael!" He heard the words as Rick came up behind him.

"Rick, no!" Kate screamed, grabbing his arm in a futile attempt to hold him back.

"You can't go with them. Don't leave me! We need you here. Please, Rick, don't. Please! I can't lose you, too." Tears streamed down her face.

Wiping the tears gently from her cheek, he said softly, "I have to do this, Kate, I love her, too. I can't stay here and wait, not knowing if she's alive or dead." Turning to Michael, he repeated, "I'm going with you."

"Priest, you do not know who you are dealing with. I cannot let a human, however brave, walk straight into hell!" Michael replied vehemently.

Calmly, Rick replied, "Save your breath, Michael, I've already been there, so I'm going with you. It's not for Adrianna alone that I have to do this. This is my fight, too. I have to do what I can to fight this evil. After all, isn't that what my profession is supposed to be about? I would never forgive myself if I didn't do all in my power to help you and her, so I'm going with you. It's not your choice. I know the odds, and I accept them. Besides, we have you," he said, leaning closer to the man in front of him so he could whisper the next words: "And I know who you are."

Brown eyes met ice blue as the two stared at each other in a battle of wills. Michael seemed to look deep into the soul of the priest. He saw terror there, for the man had seen things in the past few hours that no human being should ever have to face, but there was also a fierce determination, and he knew this man would do all he could to save his friend despite the risk to himself. But did he want the priest's death on his conscience?

"If you know who I am, priest, then you must also know that it is not in my power to save you if it's not meant to be," he said quietly, staring long and hard at Rick. "That being said, have it your way. As you say, it is your choice." Looking deeply into Rick's eyes, he continued, "May God protect you."

Looking around at the others, he said, "Do what you can to destroy what's left of his army, but leave Dragon to me."

"No! The creature is mine to destroy," Christoff shouted in protest as the men behind him shouted in agreement.

"You are brave, warrior, and I understand your need. But only I have the means to destroy him, and I'm not certain that even I can finish it at this point in time. You will need to concentrate on his sons. The bloodline must end, here and now. They are nearly as dangerous as he. All must be destroyed if we are to succeed this night."

Christoff nodded his acceptance of the plan, as Michael continued, "Find Julian and the girl, free them if you can, then get as far away as possible. Listen to me when I say do not look for me." His glance singled out the dark vampire as he said, "This monster cannot harm me, but he will destroy you all if given half the chance, understood?"

They all nodded in agreement as Christoff said, "Let's do this, Michael, we are wasting time that Julian does not have. I'll take the priest." Lifting Rick in his arms as if he were a small child, the warrior leaped through the window as wings black as night replaced the leather on his back. Rick's eyes grew large with surprise, but he knew better than to say a word.

Michael watched them all leave before he approached the window. He would let them get a good lead—he knew he would still beat them to their destination. He had only to think about the place, and he would be there. But would they be in time?

Chapter 19

Silence.

Eyes closed, he concentrated on his surroundings. The room was deathly quiet, yet he knew he was not alone. He could sense eyes watching him as consciousness came flooding back. He was weak from loss of blood and his body ached from the many wounds he had sustained, slow to heal because of his weakened condition. He must feed to regain full strength, or he was useless to both of them.

"What have they done to her?" he thought as he fought to control the panic rising within him. He knew she was near he could feel her, hear her soft breathing. She was so still ... so very quiet, but she was alive. Of this he was certain. Slowly he opened his eyes, but he kept his head bowed so as not to alert the two vampires that stood watch on either side of him. Then the sound of laughter reached his ears. It was a slow, maniacal laughter. He watched a long, dark shadow flow across the floor to stop directly in front of him.

"Our friend is awake, father. Can I play with him a little more?" the hissing voice asked as sharp claws scratched a bloody trail down the side of Julian's face. The clawed finger rose slowly to thin lips as a pointed tongue darted forward to taste the blood dripping from its tip.

"Ahh, he is tasty," the voice hissed again. Slowly, Julian raised his head, his eyes blazing with hatred as he stared at the figure before him.

"Enoch," he spat out. "I should have known. The room reeks of your foul stench—"

Addie heard the crack as she watched his head snap back from the force of the blow as Enoch slammed his fist into the side of Julian's face.

"Julian!" he heard her scream.

"Enough! We are not here for games, Enoch," the voice boomed across the room as Julian, head hanging, tired to focus on the direction of the sound.

"Lift your head if you have the strength my friend," the voice continued. "I know you have it in you that will to survive, that last ounce of strength to draw on. I know you. My bloodline made you."

"No," came a soft whisper as Julian slowly raised his head again, this time to look directly at Adrianna. "No," she said again as her eyes traveled from the man she loved to the monster beside her.

She was slumped in a chair, bruised and battered, her clothing torn to shreds, but she was alive. Relief flooded through him, but still his eyes searched the slender column of her throat for the signs. No marks. No blood. They had not tainted her. He exhaled the breath he had been holding. Anything else she could recover from. Sitting next to her, in a massive chair made of solid stone, was the one being he hoped never to see again in his long lifetime. The massive skull, the limp, dangling hair, and those red, blazing eyes. Hatred rose in Julian like a tidal wave as he pulled at his bonds in a desperate effort to break free.

"Dragon!" he cried in frustration.

"No! No!" The creature mimicked Adrianna's anguished cry of disbelief. "Julian is it possible you haven't told the lovely lady what you really are and who was responsible for your transformation?" Dragon reached over to grab her arm, jerking her closer as she stared into his red eyes. "Has he not told you about your part in our little family tale, how important you are to our handsome friend? And how I cannot allow you two to, how shall we say, form an attachment? Ah, I see by the look on your face he has told you, thus depriving me of the joy of telling you myself."

Adrianna turned her head, fighting desperately to break free from his grasp.

He jerked her arm roughly, bringing her even closer. His foul breath left her gasping for air as he stroked her hair, running sharp claws down the length of her cheek to the vein pulsing at the side of her neck.

"This life's blood running inside of you, you are aware of what it means to him? Other than the obvious?" he smirked.

"He's not like you!" she cried. "He's not the monster you are. He has a conscience!"

The clawed hand of the monster lashed out, grabbing her by the throat. "Silence !" the creature screamed.

"Adrianna! Let her go, you foul piece of filth!"

Slappp!

Another fist connected with his cheek. He absorbed the blow, and then, with slow deliberation, turned back to stare directly into the eyes of his attacker.

"I ... will ... kill ... you!" came his slow, strained words. Was that a flash of fear he saw in Enoch's eyes?

"Brave words coming from someone in your present position," Enoch sneered.

"Enoch!" Dragon shouted at his eldest son. Turning back to Adrianna with a look of pure hatred, he went on, "He is exactly the monster I am. As a matter of fact, my dear, you have a little of that monster inside of you." He laughed at her gasp of shock.

"You're insane!"

"You're probably right about that, but it doesn't change things. It was my ... a special relative of mine, you see, that turned your ancestor all those years ago. It was she who was responsible for the special traits of the twins he sired afterward. And since you both share this ancestor although generations apart, you are both, in all actuality, exactly like, well, me. Our friend over there just has different priorities, that is all. My wish is the preservation of a superior vampire race, made in my own image, of course, through the destruction of all that is human. He was once a part of that dream. Only the strongest and the best did I call to join me, and he was magnificent in his day. A true leader of men and vampires. But he decided he didn't like my methods. Instead, he wanted to play savior to this weaker race, thus hoping to regain the humanity I took from him." He finished in disgust.

She nearly fell from the chair as he shoved her aside. He glided over to Julian leaning close to whisper, "If I am condemned to an eternity of living hell then, so, my friend, shall you be. No, Julian, there will be no regaining of anyone's humanity this day, or any other. I will destroy you both before I allow that to happen." Iron claws clasping his chin, Julian was forced to look deep into Dragon's red eyes as the force of his grasp drew blood.

"You can try," Julian said through clenched teeth.

"Julian, Julian," Dragon went on, sounding almost contrite. "Where did I go wrong?"

Julian tried to draw his head back as long, clawed fingers wiped the blood away and gently caressed his cheek. "We worked so well together at one time. You were an obedient child at first. Every father's dream. Why did you leave me?"

"A lot of us disappoint our makers, Dragon. You should know."

"Is that a look of pain in those evil eyes?" Julian wondered, but it was gone in a second as he continued, "And this world has no room for your kind of evil. You and your kind will die. If not by my hand, then by another!"

The red eyes burned with anger, but Dragon quickly regained his composure as he held up his hand, stopping Enoch in midflight as he charged the shackled man.

"Patience, my son. All in good time." Turning quickly back to Adrianna, he said, "Well, since your beloved seems to think our doom is imminent, my dear, I guess I will have to hurry and dispose of you before he can accomplish his threat." He walked slowly back to where Adrianna sat huddled in her chair. "Although I'm not quite sure how he proposes to do that seeing as he's a bit tied up at the moment. Unless, of course, he thinks his Avenger will arrive in time to save the day. Oh yes, my dear friend," he said as he noticed the expression on Julian's face at the mention of Michael. "I know he's here, and we will deal with him just as we will deal with the rest of you."

Panic filled Julian as Dragon approached Adrianna while his monstrous son watched with eager anticipation. Twisting and turning, Julian struggled to loosen his bonds, trying to muster what strength he had left.

"Yes, my dear, it seems I must now put an end to your miserable existence," Dragon said. "Unless …" he pulled Adrianna close. She fought desperately as his horrid face came closer, the clawed fingers running through her hair. "You are immune to the kiss of a vampire of our line but …" His younger son, Hanokh, entered the room in all his human glory. "There are other options. My younger son does have a weakness for the appearance of the human body. He parades around much too often in that disgusting form, much to my irritation, when he can be so much more. Now, my son, show her what true beauty really is."

"Yes, my lord," Hanokh bowed, coming to stand before them, his smile filling her with sheer terror.

As she watched in horror, the room went totally still. Some of the lesser vampires who had recently entered the room began to inch slowly backward toward the door. "Is that fear? What could they possibly be afraid of here, among their own kind?" she wondered. Terror filled her as she looked at the man before her.

His beautiful brown eyes stared at her then he began to crouch and bend as if in great pain. That perfect body, so handsome in human form, started to change before her startled eyes. The smooth skin of the muscular back was suddenly split in two, mounds of coarse black hair bursting through the gaping wound. The legs began to extend, sending the rippling body sprouting upward until it seemed it would touch the ceiling. Bits of shredded human flesh flew out in all directions. She watched the transformation speechless with terror until the silence was broken by a howl so savage it shattered the soul.

Her eyes traveled upwards to stare in horror at the seven feet of raging fury that now stood before her, a deep growl coming from its throat, saliva dripping from the razor-sharp teeth. She fought to stay conscious as Dragon inched closer to the beast, turning to look at Julian as he did so.

"How would you feel about your lady, my friend, if she turned into this once a month?" Dragon asked, looking at his son as the beast caught the scent of fear and blood in the air. The red eyes scanned the room for prey.

"No! You will not give her to him!" Enoch shouted, flying across the room. "If anyone deserves her, it is I. I am your firstborn!" He flew at the beast, driving his own sharp talons deep into his brother's chest. The beast screamed in pain as, knocked off balance, it slammed, headlong, into the wall.

"Enoch!" The room reverberated with the sound of Dragon's cry as his sons turned to face him. "Enough of this petty bickering. I do apologize," he said to no one in particular. "It seems we are a little short on brotherly love in this family, but we have more important concerns at the moment. We will just kill them both and end this all now. Come here, both of you, and do the job I made you for, or I will destroy you along with them!"

"Dragon!" came a cry of pure hatred as Julian tore one hand free of its bonds.

Behind them, a splintering crash shattered the huge wooden door barricading the room. Enoch, wings extended, soared high into the air and landed among the horde of creatures staring at the gaping hole. Anticipation grew to a fever pitch as he watched the scene unfold before him. This was better than he ever imagined. The fools! They actually thought they could free the vampire and his whore from Dragon! Well, such arrogance must be taught a painful lesson.

"Destroy them all! Leave no one alive!" Enoch shouted to the crouching figures surrounding him as his brother's howl of fury pierced the night. The creatures' fear was replaced by their own blood lust. They charged the broken door in an attempt to head off the attackers.

Julian seemed oblivious to what was happening behind him. His focus was on the two figures before him. "If you touch her, I will kill you!" he screamed at Dragon. "One way or another, I will destroy you and your spawn from hell!" Julian stumbled forward, still weak from lack of blood. Chaos erupted behind him, but he was only aware of the slow laughter issuing from Dragon.

"You will never cease to amaze me, my friend," Dragon said, looking at Julian with something like admiration before turning back to Adrianna. Julian watched in panic as the clawed hand grabbed Adrianna around the throat, pulling her forward as she kicked and scratched, fighting desperately to break away. Shaking his head to clear his vision, Julian thought he was imagining things as he saw her small hand slide down her leg to reach inside her boot. Seconds later, a tiny silver dagger glistened in the candlelight as she swung her arm upward and, with all the strength she could muster, drove the shiny blade deep into the neck of the creature holding her captive.

Screaming in pain, Dragon threw her across the floor struggling to grasp the weapon. Blood flowed from the open wound as he tore the blade free, tossing it across the floor. Spinning around, he hissed in fury, "It ends now!"

Stretching his long arms skyward, the grotesque body began to grow until it towered above them, a monstrous being, black as night with skin like leather and wings extending half the width of the room. Dragon's cracked lips curled away from sharp teeth as he noticed the gleaming red liquid streaming from the open wound, down his massive chest. Tiny droplets pooled into a pocket near the tip of one large wing. With a rush of wind, he raised the appendage high into the air dripping the blood into his waiting mouth. When the flow of blood ceased, the red eyes of the monstrous creature surveyed the room before him. Chaos reigned everywhere as Julian's men, with Christoff in the lead, tore their way through broken bodies and burning ash.

"Oh my God!" Addie gasped in horror as she tried to rise from the floor, her head spinning from the force of the blow she'd received. She actually thought she was hallucinating when she heard … "Rick!" she screamed.

"Abomination!" came Rick's shout from across the room. The bony skull of the giant creature turned slowly toward the sound of the voice, it's cruel laughter filling the room, half in triumph, half in pain.

"You are a fool, priest! What do you think you can do? Your kind have no power over me." The powerful voice reverberated through the room, and Addie could have sworn she felt the floor shake. Dragon saw Rick standing alone in the doorway with a large silver cross in one hand and a long, glistening sword in the other. "Your toys will not harm me!"

With a flurry of wings, Dragon took to the air in a spray of saliva and blood as he flew toward the priest. But before Dragon could reach the waiting figure, someone else appeared in the doorway. Someone who had the power to strike fear into the black heart of the charging creature: Michael. He stood perfectly still, his long coat trailing to the floor, his arms crossed over his chest. His hands were hidden beneath his coat's lapels as he watched and waited.

Dragon literally stopped midair as he saw Michael, the lights glistening like sunlight off his golden hair. Turning sharply, the black form climbed up and landed on a windowsill high above the room. He shouted to his two sons below, "Kill them all!"

Hideous creatures of all shapes and sizes stormed into the room from hidden panels in the walls, slashing and tearing in their attempt to stop the intruders. Rick ran to where Julian had fallen to his knees and, with one swipe of the sword, slashed his remaining bonds.

"Hurry, priest, or we will be too late," Julian said in a voice barely above a whisper as Rick turned to see a vampire charge Addie from behind. Crawling forward on all fours, she reached the tiny dagger she had dropped earlier and, flipping onto her back, drove the blade into the creature's chest as it fell upon her. Julian made a mad attempt to reach her, but he stumbled and fell to one knee.

"You're too weak. You've lost too much blood," Rick said. After a moment's hesitation, he added, "What can I do to help you?"

"Blood," whispered Julian. "I need blood. Find ... Christoff ... someone."

Rick glance back at Addie, then turned to face the fallen vampire. "You are her only hope," he said as he slowly extended his arm and, rolling up the sleeve, raised his wrist to Julian's lips.

"No! Not from you. I cannot let you do this. Find someone—"

"There's no time, Julian. Addie needs you now."

"You love her that much?" Julian asked as he stared at the man before him.

"Just do what you must to save her," the priest told him. As Rick turned his head, he felt a sharp pain as the vampire took his arm and bit down, swallowing the life-giving elixir.

Julian could feel his strength returning as the blood surged through him. Power coursed through every vein, every artery, as the precious liquid healed the wounds covering his body. Reaching the danger level, he prepared to release the priest when he felt a sudden jarring. Rick stared at him, a surprised look on his face as a thin trail of blood began to trickle from his mouth and down his chin. Julian saw the brown eyes suddenly glaze over as he heard a scream of terror from somewhere in the room.

"Rick! No!" The screams continued as the voice registered in Julian's subconscious mind.

"Adrianna," he thought, but before he could search for her, the priest staggered and fell to his knees. Everything moved in slow motion as Julian's eyes focused on a spot directly above the priest's head. Cruel laughter echoed through the room as Julian gazed up at the hideous face of the vampire Enoch, then back down to the clawed fist at the monster's side. Large drops of the priest's precious life's blood spread in an ever-growing pool on the floor.

"Oh, dear, did I interrupt your dinner?" the voice hissed, barely able to disguise his pleasure at such an act of cruelty.

"No, not this, please," came the barely audible words from Julian's lips as the body of the priest pitched forward into his arms. Julian feared he might have taken too much blood from the priest's wrist, but it was nothing compared to the large red stain covering Rick's neck and back. Julian knew the wounds were mortal. They were too deep. The blood flowed too quickly.

Addie scrambled forward on her hands and knees, her vision blurred through the veil of tears. Anger surged through Julian as he gently passed Rick's broken body to the woman kneeling before him. The beast took over the man, destroying all rational thought, as blue eyes bled to black then to blood red. He sprang forward, grabbing the sword Rick had used to cut his bonds. Charging forward, he met the winged figure halfway as it flew at him, the scent of blood driving both to madness with blood lust.

Nearly upon the creature, Julian hit the ground and rolled as a clawed hand grabbed for him. It missed him by mere inches. Julian came up behind the giant form and swung with inhuman strength, severing its winged arm at the shoulder. The wounded vampire screamed in pain as it fell into a crumbled heap on the stone floor. Jumping to his feet, Julian ran toward his enemy, hatred numbing his mind to everything except the task at hand as he raised the sword to strike the killing blow.

"Look at me!" Julian shouted as the monstrous face twisted sideways, eyes burning red with hatred. "I told you earlier I would kill you," Julian said as he drove the sword deep into the creature's back. Enoch's heart beat its last on the tip of the silver weapon.

"Enoch!" Dragon screamed as Enoch's black form burst into flames, as black smoke filled the room. "Hanokh! Avenge your brother!"

An agonized howl split the air as the monstrous beast roared with anger. Dropping down on all fours, it sniffed the air as Julian turned to face the man-wolf. Muscles tensed as the beast prepared to strike, but before it could move ...

Zip! Zip! Zip!

Three silver-tipped arrows found their mark, striking Dragon's second born in the head, heart, and neck, felling the beast where it stood. The massive form jerked and convulsed before going completely still.

"I don't think so," the dark warrior muttered as he lowered his crossbow.

"Hanokh! My son!" came the enraged cry as Dragon soared into the air to circle the room.

"It is your turn now, accursed one. Prepare to meet your fate," Michael spoke the words softly but with purpose, advancing slowly into the room. As he did, he pulled his hands free from his coat to reveal a shimmering silver sword in one hand and a smaller weapon that Julian recognized as the shortened spear in the other hand.

"I know who you are, Avenger," Dragon taunted as he flew high above the floor. "Does he always send you to do his dirty work?" he said, diving at Michael with his claws lashing out to destroy his enemy. But Michael was too fast, hitting the ground at a roll and coming up behind Dragon. He swung his sword in a wide arc.

"Ahrrrg!" the man-bat screamed as the silver burned through the membrane of his left wing, causing him to crash into the far wall and slide to the ground. With lightning speed, Dragon launched himself back into the air just as Michael reached the spot where he had fallen. Dragon was forced to land on the window ledge, the tear in his wing throwing him off balance. His evil laughter filled the room as he spread the wing wide. In seconds it began to heal.

"We can keep this up all night, Avenger. We both know you are missing the one weapon that can destroy me," he spat at Michael.

"I may not be able to destroy you but, I can make sure you are unable to inflict harm on anyone else until the weapon is found. Julian," Michael shouted, turning to the vampire, who was kneeling at Addie's side, "get your men away from this room now! But let no one else leave."

Looking at the two people beside Julian, anger and sorrow filled Michael, but the Avenger's focus had to be elsewhere. "Take them with you. The priest's last breath should not be in this place of evil," Michael said. Julian nodded, reaching forward to take Rick from Addie.

"Be careful, Julian, we must be careful with him until we can get him to a doctor," Addie said as she placed a gentle kiss on Rick's forehead.

"I will care for him, Adrianna, but we must go," he said as he lifted Rick's body effortlessly. "Come, we must leave quickly."

As they turned toward the door, Christoff came from behind to grab his arm. "Julian, we cannot leave until that demon and all his horde of vipers are destroyed!"

Looking back at Michael, Julian replied, "I think that's the plan, but it is not by our hand that his destruction will come about. Do what the Avenger says, my friend. See that our men get out quickly."

"Damn it, Julian—"

"Christoff, trust me. I don't know how or why, but I know Michael has something planned. We have to let him handle Dragon. He was sent here for that purpose, of that I am sure."

Nodding, Christoff look around the room. "Simon!" he called.

The vampire, his blond hair covered in soot and ash, turned to stare at the dark vampire.

"Get Andrew and the others and follow us."

The small group fought their way to where the other three stood. Forming a protective circle around Julian, Rick, and Adrianna, they fought their way to the jagged opening where the large door had once sealed off Dragon's sanctuary. Now, only splintered bits of wood lay scattered across a floor running wet with blood and bits of torn flesh.

Dragon's hordes pressed on as Christoff and the others fought off a fresh surge, thus allowing Julian and Addie a clear path to get the wounded priest to safety. The misguided fools attacked with renewed vigor, mistakenly thinking that Julian and his men were fleeing. The faces of the enemy had no time to even register surprise as Julian's men, under Christoff's lead, slashed and tore at everything that came at them, the stench of fresh blood and burnt flesh filling the room. Their eyes flashed red fire from their own blood lust as they finally backed through the opening spilling out into the hallway.

"Andrew! Your help, please!" Christoff shouted as he ran toward the open door of another room midway down the hall.

He grabbed the door with both hands and ripped it from its hinges, then ran back to block the opening into Dragon's lair. Following the dark vampire's lead, Andrew did the same, until three doors covered the gaping hole, wedged in place by various pieces of furniture also taken from the rooms. As Michael had instructed, Dragon's hordes could not follow.

"Christoff!" Julian shouted, "Leave a small opening! I will be returning." He looked at Addie as he laid Rick's unconscious form onto the floor.

Addie fell to her knees, cradling Rick's head in her lap. Leaning forward she grabbed Julian's arm urgently, her hand looking pale and small against the dark material of his shirt. "Julian, no! Please don't go back in there. I need you … we need you. Rick needs to get to a doctor. We can't make it without you. Please, Julian! You are his only hope …" the words caught in her throat as the tears flowed down her cheeks.

"Adrianna, it's not over back there. This is my fight, not Michael's. I can't leave him to do this alone." Looking at the priest, he continued, "We've lost too many already, and I will not let them die in vain. I must go back. Please try to understand," he said as he stared into her tear-filled eyes.

"But we must help Rick. You must help him," she said, looking directly into Julian's grey-blue eyes.

"Adrianna, I cannot," he began, looking at the man in her arms. Rick's face was a pale mask of death. Julian leaned close and was just able to make out a faint heartbeat, but the quiet pounding was getting slower by the second.

"Please, Julian. You have the power to save him. Turn him. Please."

"You know what you are asking? What you are condemning him to?"

"Yes."

"Christoff," he called, coming to a decision. The dark vampire approached, kneeling beside him. Once again Julian looked at Addie. Taking her hand in his he said, "There is a faint heartbeat. The priest is a fighter, or there is something he does not want to leave. The choice is the same as with Kate, but Adrianna, his humanity will be lost forever. I, myself, am sure the priest would have a issue with that, but if you want him here, I will do what you ask."

"Julian," Christoff said quietly, "he was mortally wounded by that demon. If we are going to do this, we must hurry. "

"Yes, I know," he said, then turning back to Addie, he continued, "If we succeed in saving him, you know what sort of life we will condemn him to. We can turn him. As a vampire, we have some control over what he becomes, but it's against all that he ever stood for. He may not forgive us."

"I don't care. I can't lose him—"

"No," came Rick's faint whisper. "No, do … don't—"

"Shhh, Rick, don't talk. Just rest. Save your strength." Addie tried to comfort him, but he became more agitated the more she talked. A fit of coughing overtook him, blood flowing freely from his mouth as well as the gaping wound, making it hard for Julian's men to concentrate as the blood lust pulled them toward the flowing liquid. Julian ordered the others back as Rick fought for breath, "Please … let me … go, Addie. It's … what I … want. Addie … I love … you …" But the words died on his lips as he fell back into her arms.

"Rick! Please don't leave me! Rick!" But she knew it was already too late. "I love you, too," she whispered as her tears flowed freely. She touched her lips to the cold forehead. She felt Julian lay a hand on her shoulder, offering what comfort he could. Anger replaced grief, and she turned to Julian, saying, "Go to Michael. Destroy that son of a bitch, Julian, for Rick and me!" With one last look, he turned to go.

"Julian!" she called, causing him to pause in midstride, "Come back to me. I can't lose you both."

He walked back to her. Leaning forward, he gently took her hand and raised it to his lips.

"Wait for me."

The next moment he was gone.

Chapter 20

Michael watched the creature above him. It was quiet now behind him, so he knew Julian and the others were safe. But the danger to him had only increased for, after losing their prey, the horde was after a new prize: him. They began their approach, the scent of fresh blood strong as they sniffed the air.

"Take him you fools! He is but one man, and his blood is rich and surging with power. It is yours for the taking. It will fill the one who drinks of it with a power beyond their wildest imaginings. They will be nearly as strong as I. And I will share the rule of this world with the one who kills him, if you ... will ... just ... destroy him! What are you waiting for? Attack!"

Spurred on by their master's voice, the throng of creatures closed the circle around Michael, saliva dripping from jaws hungry for the taste of his blood.

Michael closed his eyes, his senses taking in every breath, every heartbeat in the pathetic creatures surrounding him. Instead of the fear they expected, even craved, from their victims, he stood calmly, his body going very still, his head bowed behind a veil of golden locks. The advancing hordes stood still, filled with doubt. Their animal instinct warned of danger, but they were not sure from what source.

Then, as suddenly as the quiet had come, chaos erupted. Michael dropped to one knee, the small weapon in his left hand growing to five feet of gleaming silver as he pressed a small button buried inside the handle. Flames erupted from the silver tip as the blood-crazed horde charged him. He smote the creatures surrounding him, the shimmering staff reducing everything in its path to smoke and ash.

A grey man-wolf, his hair matted with blood and gore, came charging at Michael through the flames, his claws extended to strike a killing blow. Swinging wide with his other arm, the silver sword slashed through the air and connected with its target. The grey head rolled to a stop at Michael's feet as the furry body crashed to the ground. Then silence. Michael rose to his feet. All that remained of the frenzied horde was smoke, ash, and fur.

"That was for the priest," Michael whispered.

"No!" came the enraged scream from the open window. Dragon's eyes burned liquid fire as he stared at Michael. With a great effort, he breathed deeply to calm himself, for this was no ordinary foe. He must have his wits about him if he was to win this fight. "Impressive, but your efforts are wasted. I have thousands more where those came from." Hatred dripped like honey from Dragon's lips as he hissed, "Again I ask you, Avenger, does he always send you to fight his battles? Can he not face me himself?"

"I serve willingly when the cause is just and one such as you is not worthy to be in his presence—"

"Worthy? He created me!" Dragon screamed in fury, spittle dripping from his twisted mouth. So focused were the two figures on each other that they failed to notice Julian crawling through the small opening Christoff had left in the doorway. He darted to the far wall, keeping to the shadows. Dragon continued, "I served him my entire life, but I was never good enough. Then I make one mistake, and I am condemned for all eternity. And for what? Spilling the blood of one worthless man. Where was his omnipotent mercy then?"

"Worthless! The man you murdered was your own brother! A brother who had only love for you and all he kne—"

"Yes, yes, I already know all about my good brother's virtues. It's all I've ever heard about, so much, in fact, that it drove me mad. So I spilled a little blood, and as my punishment, he banished me from the light, my only sustenance the very blood I had spilt. That was his mercy! That was his justice! "

"No, Dragon, I am justice! You committed murder, the first murder. You deserved whatever punishment you were dealt. But even after what you had done, he would have taken you back into his fold, had you but asked and proven you could change. But the evil in your soul was embedded too deep. It rotted you from the inside, blinded you to any chance of redemption, twisted you into the monster you have become. He is not to blame. You did this to yourself!"

Julian began inching forward, trying to get close to Michael without calling attention to himself. As he moved into the shadows, a twinkling of light caught his eye. The silver dagger lay inches away, still on the floor where Adrianna had dropped it earlier. He made his way slowly toward the weapon as Dragon launched himself from the ledge and dove for Michael.

"Enough of this useless prattle, warrior. If it's a fight you want, then I will certainly oblige you. We will see who will be victorious although I'm sure he will not allow me to destroy you." The winged figure dove at the man with such blinding speed that Michael could not raise his weapons. Dragon's razor sharp claws cut deep into his flesh, leaving Michael's arm cut and bleeding as the spear went skidding across the floor. "Or will he?" Dragon hissed, his cruel laughter echoing in the room.

Michael clutched his injured arm, pressing tightly to stem the flow of blood as he fell to one knee, the sword in his right hand nearly falling from his grasp as he did so. The wound was deep, but he'd had worse. Taking a deep breath, he rose to his full height, standing tall in the middle of the room as Dragon hovered above him.

"Let's finish this!" he challenged.

"You know, I can hover above you forever, warrior, or simply fly through the open window and let you scream your frustration as I make my escape, and there is not a thing you can do to prevent it," Dragon sneered at him.

"No?" came the reply as a slow smile spread across the beautiful face of the man they called the Avenger.

Julian, still retrieving the dagger, was transfixed by the sight unfolding before him. Michael lifted his arms and extended them behind him. His coat fell to the floor. He was dressed in blue slacks of some strange material that seemed to shimmer. His chest and back were covered in ancient armor the color of gold that resembled the scales of a dragon. But that was not the strangest part.

A pair of large, feathered wings, so white they dazzled the eyes, sprouted from Michael's back as he began to rise from the floor. Julian couldn't help a small smile as he thought, "Talk about shape-shifting."

Dragon stared, speechless for a brief moment before screaming in rage, "So be it, Avenger! The battle is on!" He charged the figure rising to meet him.

The two bodies came together with a resounding crash, darkness tangling with light, good with evil. Dragon's deadly claws slashed across the flawless skin of Michael's cheek, downward along his neck. The force of the blow snapped the blond head to one side, leaving Michael's neck exposed to razor sharp teeth. The blood lust caused Dragon to forget all reason. All he could sense—all he could smell and taste—was Michael fresh, warm blood pulsating through the vein in front of him.

Tossing his massive head back as he prepared to savage the tender flesh, Dragon was unprepared for Michael's quick reflexes as the Avenger whipped his head forward and butted the creature full in the face. The force of the blow propelled Dragon backward. The creature shook his head violently to clear his vision as he climbed into the air again, ready to dive at the injured warrior. But this time Michael was ready for him.

When Dragon turned his leathery back for the climb upwards, the silver sword flashed brightly in Michael's hand as he launched it skyward. Dragon screamed in pain as the sword buried itself deep into the winged shoulder, nothing but the glistening hilt visible. Michael dove at the injured figure and grabbed the hilt with both hands, forcing the blade downward nearly severing the wing at the joint. Spinning out of control, his wing dangling loosely, Dragon hit the floor as Michael landed a few feet away. Michael watched the mass of black membrane, muscle, and bone slowly rise as Dragon stood before him, head bent, his undamaged wing enfolding his injured body.

Then the sound of laughter—deep, guttural, as evil as that horrible face—echoed through the room. Dragon lifted his red eyes to meet the warrior's blue ones. In the silence of the empty room, Michael's gasp of surprise could be heard, but he was not the only one staring in amazement. Julian, still hidden in the shadows, watched in shock. "What does it take to destroy him? Is there any hope of winning this battle?" he wondered as he watched the creature flex the thick muscles of its back and lift the severed wing. Dragon spread the appendage wide; the wing was now whole and unmarked. Dragon turned in a slow circle, the candlelight from dozens of sconces reflecting off the bulging muscles of his back. There was not a cut or scratch to be seen anywhere on that grotesque body.

"I told you before, warrior, you do not have the weapon needed to destroy me so your efforts are futile, all you—"

The words froze on Dragon's thin, black lips. He stared in shock and surprise as a gleaming silver point penetrated his black, evil heart. Blood streamed from the wound as Dragon fell to his knees, a questioning look replacing his shock.

"Maybe it's not the weapon at all, you bastard. Maybe it's just his aim," Julian said to Dragon. Then he turned to Michael, "You were a little off your mark. I, on the other hand, don't have that problem."

Michael raised his eyes from the creature kneeling before him to the one standing at its back. A look of understanding flashed in his blue eyes as he stared at Julian, but to be sure, he waited to see if the monster would once again heal itself. But Dragon remained motionless, sinking lower onto the floor as the blood continued to flow.

"The bloodline. That's it. It was foolish of me to have forgotten—"

"You're talking in riddles, Avenger, and just for the record, who or what are you?" Julian asked.

"Think about it , Julian. The killing blow can only come from someone of the bloodline. That is why your weapon has taken him down when mine have failed," Michael answered.

"Or maybe the fact that the blade is directly through the heart might have something to do with it." Julian pointed out.

"That would make no difference if you were not of the bloodline. It would have slowed him only until he pulled the blade from his body. Then he would have healed himself again. He is ancient, perhaps the first, but that is not all. He is cursed by God, and only by God's means can we destroy him. The bloodline, in conjunction with one very special weapon, will most certainly bring about his destruction."

"You're talking in riddles again. What is this weapon you are both obsessed with?"

"A spear, but not that one," Michael said as Julian's gaze went to the shaft lying a few feet away on the stone floor. "The spear we seek is special, with a tip made of stone, worked to a fine point, sharp as the dagger in your hand. The stone, too, is not an ordinary stone. This stone was the weapon this monster used to kill his own brother, and it will be the weapon that destroys him as well."

"And this mystery weapon, where is it? It seems a little, shall we say, careless of you not to have it with you," Julian pointed out.

Michael had the grace to look a little sheepish. "It's was misplaced many years ago. I have been searching for it ever since, which is what I was doing when I came across you and your little band at that nightclub of yours," Michael explained.

"Well, that presents a problem for both of us. What do we do with him in the meantime?" Julian asked.

"I will take him," Michael said as he untied a corded belt from around his waist. "Help me bind him. I will see that he is kept where none of his minions can get to him until we find the weapon." Michael reached for the body now lying on the cold floor. Julian helped him bind the creature's hands and feet. "After I see that he is secured, I will return. If you are willing to help me, we will begin our quest for the weapon. Oh, there is one important detail I forgot to mention. We will need the woman, too, Julian."

"No. I will not put her in any more danger than she has already been subjected to. She has seen and done enough."

"She is of the bloodline also, Julian. You are not the only one who needs her. Which reminds me, what will you do now that you have found her, the one who can change you back?"

"I don't know. I haven't had time to think about it. With all that has happened, all that she has lost, how can I ask anything more of her?"

"She is stronger than you think, my friend. You will make the right decision when the time comes. Of that I am sure." Michael began to rise with Dragon's seemingly lifeless body in his arms.

Julian called after him, "You still have one more question to answer, my friend. Who are you?"

"All in due time. For now, I must get him to a secure place. You must hurry also. Dawn approaches, and you must take the priest from this evil place. Get him to sacred ground. He deserves that much."

"You know I can't take him there. It's forbidden to me, and you are not with me to change that."

Stepping forward, Michael rested a hand gently on Julian's head. Closing his eyes, the Avenger seemed to be in a deep trance for a few seconds before his eyes snapped open.

"Sacred ground will no longer be a problem for you, vampire. Go in peace."

Julian nodded in agreement just as a shaft of bright light flowed down from the ceiling. Julian threw himself back into the shadows, shielding his eyes and protecting his body from the light he thought would surely destroy him. In the next instant, the room was plunged into darkness. Julian opened his eyes to find Michael and his evil cargo gone.

"Yes, he definitely has some explaining to do," Julian said out loud. Taking a deep breath, he headed back to the opening, before he noticed something. Hanokh's mangled body lay where it had fallen after receiving the killing stroke. But the red eyes of the savage beast were gone. Instead, the lifeless gaze Julian looked upon was soft brown. In death, the beast returned to his human form.

"You have one more trip to make, you evil bastard! Only in death may you actually be of use to me."

Dragging the body toward the opening, he left it in the room and climbed through alone. Christoff was waiting for him on the other side.

"I had Andrew take the priest and the woman outside, away from this place. A few minutes longer and I was coming in after you," Christoff said.

"I'm glad you stayed, my friend. We have an unpleasant chore I don't want Adrianna to know about," he said, leading Christoff back inside. The dark vampire hissed angrily at the sight of Hanokh's body.

"Easy, my friend, we have need of this vile mass of flesh and bone. Meet our serial killer, drinker of blood and mutilator of women. I need you to take him back to the church, where he can also be blamed for the death of the caretaker, as well as the good priest." Julian was surprised how much it pained him to talk of Rick's death. "That should keep Detective Bertram from digging any deeper into what actually happened. The women need to find some peace, and the priest needs to be laid to rest. I'll send a few of the others to help you."

Christoff nodded and bent to retrieve the disgusting mound. Then he suddenly straightened and looked around the room. Smoke drifted up from the many piles of ash that mingled with blood and pieces of flesh and fur. His handsome face a mask of confusion, he asked, "Dragon?"

"Immobilized for the moment. The Avenger took him to a secure place. I know, I know," Julian replied as Christoff's black eyebrows rose. "It's a long and very strange story that is far from over. Michael will explain all when he returns, but for now at least, Dragon is not a threat to anyone. It is up to us, with the Avenger's help, to see that it stays that way. Come Christoff, let's go, time is growing short."

Outside, Adrianna surrendered Rick's body to the vampire, Andrew. She now stood, numb with exhaustion and sorrow, watching the night sky slowly changing from black to charcoal then light grey as the dawn approached. Her tired eyes kept glancing back to the broken doorway of the crumbling building, but nothing came forward. Where was he? The sun would be up soon, and he would be trapped in this awful place.

Finally, as her anxiety reached fever pitch, she saw a figure emerge from the ruined shell. She watched with bated breath. Suddenly, her hands flew to her mouth to stifle the cry of joy and relief. She broke into a run.

Catching her in his arms, Julian rained kisses on her face and held the sobbing girl tightly as her tears flowed freely.

"Shhh," he whispered. "It's alright, Adrianna. It's over for now. He can't harm you anymore." He breathed in her scent, his face buried in the silken hair.

"I thought I would never see you again," she cried.

"I'm not going anywhere. I'll be here as long as you want me."

"Oh, Julian ..."

He stroked her hair gently. "Just a moment longer," he thought as he held her, but time was running short. He must get to shelter ... and soon. Gently he moved her from him, feeling cold and empty inside as she backed away.

"Come," he said. "Dawn approaches. I must get my men to a safe place and the priest to his home. I promise we will talk later." He kissed her gently on the forehead. "But now we must hurry." They walked back to the small party awaiting them.

"Give the priest to me, Andrew. Take two men with you back to the ruin. Christoff awaits you inside. There is one more task to be done. We'll meet you back at the church. Simon, can you take Adrianna?"

"Of course."

With Rick's body securely in his arms, he watched the blond vampire settle Addie safely in his grasp. As Andrew disappeared into the crumbling mansion, the others were off into the night sky. The slowly approaching dawn was hard on their heels as they made their way back to the church.

Thomas had proven himself invaluable on a number of occasions but never more so than in the early morning hours on that fateful day. He had kept an anxious vigil near the main entrance of the church. He was worried, not knowing what fate his friends would meet at the hands of their enemy. Relief flooded him when he saw Simon walking quickly down the street with Addie by his side. But his joy was cut short as Julian came into view and the realization of what he carried in his arms hit Thomas full force.

"Oh my God, no." He could barely utter the words as he ran to offer his assistance, taking Addie in his arms. "Julian, what can I do to help?"

"There is nothing more to be done for the priest. It's the women who will need you now. You will have to tell Kate," Julian told him.

"No, I'll tell her," Addie said.

"Adrianna, you shouldn't have to do this alone. I'll come with you," Thomas offered.

"She will need you after I've told her, Thomas, but, please, I would like to give her this news alone."

Thomas nodded in understanding, but said he would be right outside the door. His own sadness at the loss of the priest was overwhelming. He could not even begin to imagine what Adrianna was feeling. He made up his mind that he would not let these women deal with their grief alone.

Adrianna walked slowly to where Julian stood alone. "What will you do with him?" she asked.

"I will place him in the church for now. The police must be called. Christoff and I have formulated a plan, an explanation that should spare you and Kate from having to deal with any more of this nightmare. I will fill Thomas in on the details before I leave."

Nodding slightly, she leaned forward to place a kiss on his cold cheek. Then, taking a deep breath, she turned to Thomas and said, "I need to see Kate."

"And she needs you. Come on," he replied as he grasped her cold hand and tucked it in the crook of his arm.

The grief the two women shared at the loss of their friend was devastating. Julian had never felt more useless in his entire life. There was nothing he could do to ease their pain. Even vampiric powers could offer them no comfort as he listened to their tears. "She really loved him," Julian thought as he backed away from the door and walked slowly down the hallway. He would not intrude on her grief. Thomas was there. She was in good hands.

Thomas took charge of everything. Rick and the caretaker were taken inside the church, where they were watched over by Addie and Kate until the police arrived. Hanokh's body was found lying in the back room, where Christoff had carefully arranged it. There was a twinge of doubt on Bertram's face as Thomas related the story of how Hanokh entered the church to attack Adrianna. He told how Father Rick and the caretaker had tried to stop him, sustaining mortal wounds in the ensuing fight. The attacker was finally stopped when Thomas and the others arrived. With Christoff's help, the detective seemed, for the most part, to believe their story.

Julian had lingered a little longer than was safe, hidden in the shadows near the back of the church as the bodies were taken away. He felt as if his heart was being ripped from his chest as he listened to Adrianna's sobs of grief while Thomas took the women to the cottage. Alone now, he entered the church and stood in amazement as the realization came to him that he was, indeed, standing on holy ground. He could not actually remember the last time he had been in such a place. Maybe all was not lost, maybe there was still a chance for him.

As he prepared to leave, he couldn't help but notice the stained glass windows, the light from dozens of candles reflecting their rich colors along the backs of the polished pews. One window in particular caught his eye. It was at least six feet high and featured a large picture of an angel—but this was no ordinary angel.

Recognition dawned as he gazed in amazement at the hair of spun gold. The chest of the figure was covered in some strange armor, like the scales of a dragon, the muscular legs partially covered by a skirt-like garment made of shimmering blue material. He held a silver sword in one hand, the other was thrusting a long spear toward the head of a winged serpent. As Julian stared in wonder, his eyes were drawn to the black script beneath the picture. In large, bold print were the words "St. Michael the Archangel, Warrior of God." A slow smile spread across Julian's face.

"You are full of surprises, my friend," he said out loud. Then he burst through the door in a flurry of wings. He made it to his own door just as the morning sun rose in the sky, much to Thomas's chagrin … again.

Chapter 21

The following week found Adrianna once again seated in her favorite rocker on the front porch of the tiny cottage. Thomas had been the one constant in their lives since that awful night, watching Kate with a keen eye for any ill effects from the vampire attack and the loss of her friend. But other than feeling tired during the daytime—and having the strength to match any man—she didn't seem to pose a threat to herself or anyone else.

Adrianna breathed deeply, inhaling the fragrance of the myriad blossoms. "Will I ever again feel the calm and peace that once attracted me to this lovely place?" she wondered. She missed Rick terribly, the memory of his death haunting her dreams. But she knew they had done the right thing by letting him go. Still, he had been such an important part of her life ... and Kate's. His death left a huge void that would never be filled. How could things ever be normal again after all they had been through, all they had witnessed?

Her thoughts turned to Julian and her heart ached. She had not seen him since that awful night. According to Thomas, he needed the rest to heal properly from the injuries he had sustained in battle. But she didn't buy it, not completely. He was a vampire. She had seen how quickly he could heal. She was certain he was avoiding her. What she wasn't certain of was why. He probably thought she needed time to grieve and heal. But what she really needed—wanted—was him.

She loved him fiercely. That was the one thing she had learned for certain through this whole nightmare. And if he would just give her the chance, she would tell him exactly that. She also knew that he loved her in his own way, but he was holding back. He would say it was for her own protection, that he couldn't love her the way she needed to be loved. But the memory of being in his arms caused a burning heat to rise deep within her.

She continued to rock gently, eyes closed to the soothing sounds of the night, as an idea began to form in her mind. She was aware of him before he actually entered her line of sight, her mind was so filled with thoughts of him. Breathing deeply, she slowly opened her eyes to stare at the millions of stars sparkling like tiny diamonds in the clear night sky.

"How long have you been standing there?" she said to the shadows.

"Only a moment. I did not want to frighten you." Julian moved out of the darkness.

"You could never frighten me."

He stood with his back to her as he, too, pondered the evening sky. Her heart skipped a beat as her eyes hungrily traveled over his body. He was dressed in his usual black attire, the fitted shirt hugging his muscular arms and back, the black silk pants leaving nothing to the imagination. His hair flowed in soft waves across his shoulders, falling forward as he placed strong hands on the banister, his head bowed slightly. She had the overwhelming urge to go to him, to wrap her arms around him, feel the muscles of his back against her cheek. But, instead, she sat and waited for him to speak.

"I'm sorry I haven't been here sooner—"

"Julian, please. There's no need to apologize for anything. Nothing that happened was your fault. If it hadn't been for you and your men, well, who knows how things would have turned out?"

"I'm sorry about Rick, Adrianna, I really am. I only knew him a short time, but in that time he earned my respect. He didn't deserve to die like that. Christoff said they tried to stop him from coming with them, but he refused." He turned his head as if straining to see her, but Adrianna knew he could see every line, every curve, perfectly with those piercing eyes. "He must have loved you very much," he continued. "Even the threat of death couldn't stop him from coming for you." She could almost feel the longing deep inside him. "We should have tried—"

"No," she interrupted. "We did the right thing. It was selfish of me to want to keep him here by any means possible. He would never have forgiven me if we had turned him into something unnatural."

The word was out before she realized what she'd said. She saw his tall form stiffen. Rising from the chair, she covered the short distance between them, coming to stand directly behind him.

"Julian, I'm sorry. I didn't mean ..." She reached out to him.

"No," came the reply. "You're right, Adrianna. What I am is unnatural ... an abomination ... no better than Dragon himself." He spat out the words as frustration and despair overwhelmed him, and his body trembled with the force of his emotions.

"Don't say that! You're nothing like that monster," she said angrily. She stepped forward and wrapped her arms tightly around him, feeling his warmth as she pressed against him. Softly she whispered, "There is goodness in you,

Julian Reynolds, that Dragon could never begin to understand. Michael saw it. You would not have been able to enter the church unharmed otherwise. No more talking this nonsense." She thought she felt him relax a little in her arms. "Besides, if you're not happy with what you are, we can change that, you and I." She waited with baited breath for his reply as she felt him stiffen once again. "You said I may have what you need, that my blood could make you human … oh!" she gasped in surprise as her hands were locked in a grip of steel. He broke her hold and spun to face her.

"Adrianna, you don't know what you're saying—"

"Yes, Julian, I do." She smoothed a strand of hair across his shoulders and brought her hand up to cup his handsome face. She could feel the hunger rise between them like a hot flame as she stared at him. She brushed one finger, ever so lightly, across his soft lips. Leaning forward, she placed a feather light kiss where her finger had been. She heard his sharp intake of breath as she spoke, "I'm am very well aware of what I'm saying and what it entails, and I've never been more sure about anything in my life." She willed him to understand what she was trying to say. "The nightmare of the past few days has taught me one thing for certain. I love you, Julian, in spite of, or maybe it's because of, what you are. But being a vampire, in your mind, is the reason we can't be together."

"Adrianna, listen to—"

"No, Julian, you listen. I will not lose you, too. I am willing to do whatever it takes to keep you with me, including doing what must be done to help you become human again, if it's really possible. But I won't lie to you. I'm willing, but I'm frightened. I need your patience to guide me through this. You need to tell me exactly what needs to be done and how it will affect you and me afterward. If this is the only way to have you with me, day and night, then let's do this."

Blue eyes stared into brown eyes moist with unshed tears. He could see the love and desire burning there, feel the answering spark rising within him. He dragged her to him in a crushing kiss, passion pushing him beyond reason. His lips blazed a trail of soft kisses across her cheek, along her jawline. He could hear her blood pounding hear the soft moan of pleasure as she clung to him. It nearly drove him mad as he continued to rain kisses down the side of her neck to the hollow at her throat. But with desire came the hunger—always the hunger—as he fought to stay in control.

Suddenly he stood very still, breathing deeply as she held him tightly, her hands tangled in his hair and her face buried in its soft waves.

"Adrianna," he said hoarsely, pushing her slightly away from him, resting his forehead against hers, "we'd better stop now." He waited while his breathing slowed, and then, lifting his head, he told her, "I love you for what you are offering. How much, you cannot even imagine, but I can't accept your gift."

"Julian, please," she pleaded, taking his face in both hands and fighting back tears. "It's what I want. I thought it was what you wanted, too."

"I know," he said, pulling her close. He kissed the top of her head gently as if comforting a distraught child. "And believe me, my love it's what I want most in the world. To be human again, to have a normal life with you, but—"

"Julian—"

"Shhh, let me finish. I know you mean every word, but you must hear me out." He led her back to the rocker and knelt before her, taking her shaking hands in his. "We still have a job to do, Adrianna, whether we want to admit it or not. Dragon, technically, is still alive, and the world will never be safe as long as he is. Michael is returning, and when he does we will begin our search for the one weapon that will destroy that evil beast once and for all. But while he lives, my love, I need to be at full strength to help Michael and protect you." He looked at her meaningfully. "And full strength means I must remain what I am, at least for a little while longer. It will take a monster to catch a monster. So I must refuse your generous offer, which means all the more to me because it was offered out of love." He placed a finger under her chin and gently lifted her head. "But I will ask something of you, if you are still willing."

"Anything," she said, and he knew, without a shadow of a doubt, she meant it.

"Help me control the beast within because I cannot live without you," he said as his lips met hers in a kiss so full of hunger that it took her breath away. Tearing himself away, he whispered against her lips, "I must have you near me always, but it's that very nearness that causes my demon to rise." Placing another kiss, gentler this time, on her lips, he continued, "It can be controlled, but it will take practice and discipline. I'm afraid I've grown lax over the years because there was no need for me to exhibit such extreme control. No one has affected me like you for a very long time. Will you help me, Adrianna? Can you be patient enough?"

"Yes," she said, hearing the desperation in his voice. She stroked his cheek. "I want you in my life anyway I can have you. We will work this out together, and we will hunt for the weapon together, with Michael. I have paid heavily for the right to join you in this fight, and I want to stand beside you when it's finished. I'll help you control the demon inside of you, but you must do something for me."

"Whatever you want."

"Teach me how to fight. I'm tired of being afraid and helpless. I want to be able to defend myself, and you, against the ones we must face. I want you to train me in combat. Show me how to properly use the weapons that will destroy them. Show me the physical moves that will keep me alive when I face them again, because I will not let them hurt me, or take someone that I love away from me, ever again. Will you do that for me?"

"If I had my way, Adrianna, I would place you as far away from this nightmare as possible, but I know you will not have that. So yes, if you must face danger, I will make sure you are prepared to face it properly, and heaven help the monster that comes up against you!"

He laughed as he pulled her into his arms—the one place she felt safe. Somehow, she knew as long as they were together they would be all right.

THE END

Epilogue

He walked for another mile, or maybe it was two, before coming to a stop. It was difficult for any human being to see clearly in the murky grey light of dawn, but then again, he was not human. He was Michael, archangel, warrior of God. Turning slowly, his crystal blue gaze settled on a place he had left moments ago. The mound of dirt and rock rising before him was called Skull Place. It was aptly named, for two caves in the sheer face of the formation looked like empty eye sockets.

A slow smile spread across his face. "Now the name is even more fitting," he thought as his mind focused on the skull-like countenance of the creature now buried deep beneath the rock formation. Early Christian tradition had named this place as a possible burial site for the skull of Adam, the first man and father of humanity. The irony caused him to shake his head in wonder, his waist-long golden curls moving slightly with each twist of his head.

Now the father must watch over the son. The image of a silver coffin, a life-size crucifix welded to its lid, filled the traveler's mind. Would it be enough to contain the evil within? Enough to keep that foul presence buried safely away from humankind while he and his friends searched for what they needed? It had to be. He must begin the hunt for the one weapon he knew would destroy that evil forever, and he must find it before the demon's minions had a chance to locate their master. They were everywhere, and they would not rest until their lord was free again. Free to bring misery, pain, and death to anyone who crossed his path.

Closing his eyes, he concentrated on his destination. Who would have thought that a small New England town like Winwood would harbor the means for the salvation of the entire world?

"Well, they say good things come in small packages," he said as he slowly ascended into the sky, propelled by pure white wings. "Time to find out if my partners are ready for their next adventure."

BOOK TWO coming in 2010
The saga continues as Julian, Adrianna and Michael search for the one weapon in existence that will finally destroy their enemy. Will Julian be vampire or human for the final confrontation with Dragon in The Spear of Redemption coming in 2010.

Made in the USA
Lexington, KY
10 December 2009